Lucky Star

also by susannah nix

STARSTRUCK SERIES

Star Bright

Fallen Star

Rising Star

Lucky Star

CHEMISTRY LESSONS SERIES

Remedial Rocket Science

Intermediate Thermodynamics

Advanced Physical Chemistry

Applied Electromagnetism

Experimental Marine Biology

Elementary Romantic Calculus

KING FAMILY SERIES

My Cone and Only

Cream and Punishment

Pint of Contention

A Starstruck Romance

Lucky Star

USA TODAY BESTSELLING AUTHOR

SUSANNAH NIX

Haver Street Press

FIRST EDITION: May 2022

ISBN: 978-1-950087-17-4

Haver Street Press | 448 W. 19th St., Suite 407 | Houston, TX 77008

Edited by Julia Ganis, www.juliaedits.com

Cover Design by Cover Ever After

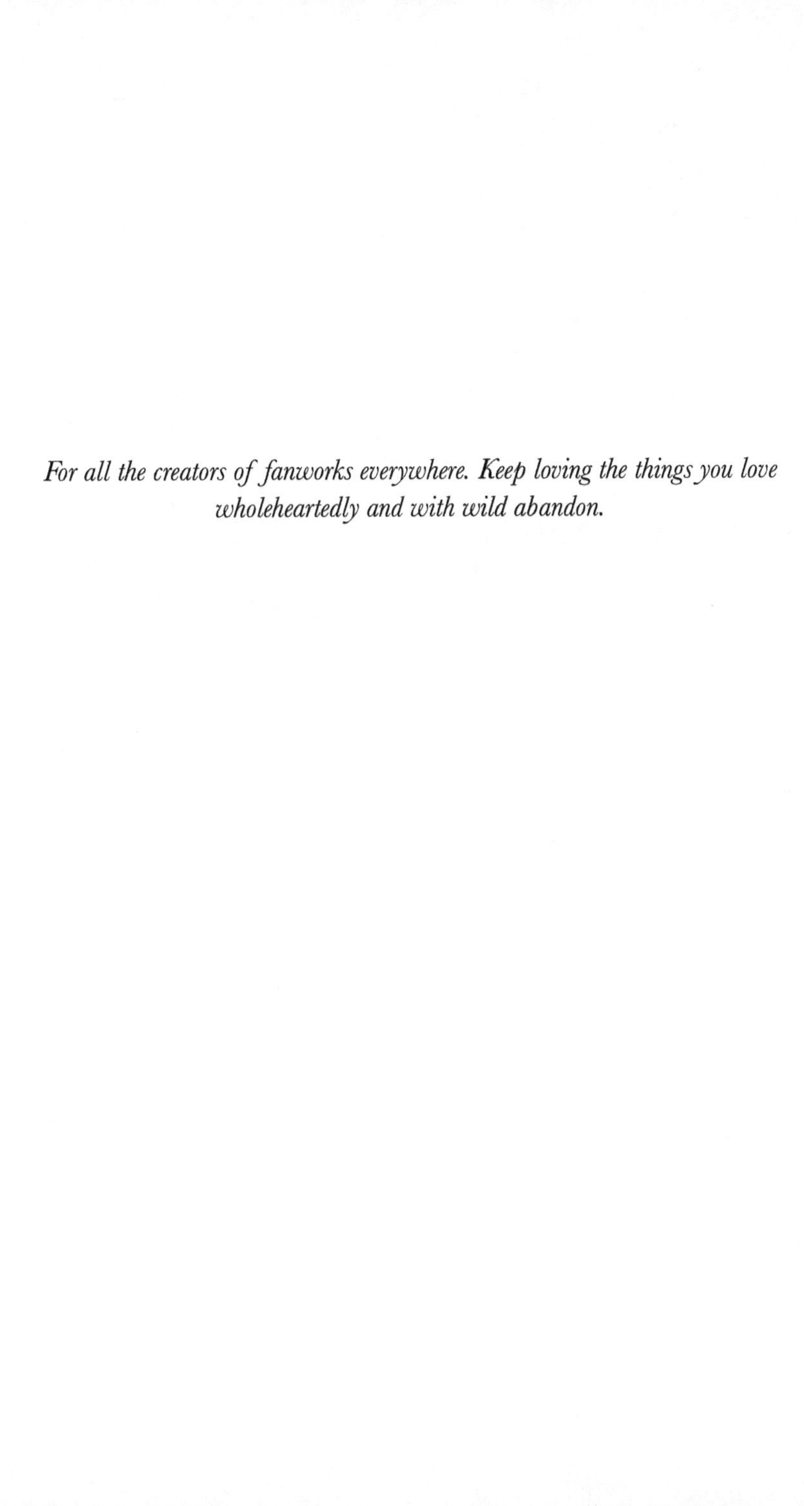

For all the creators of fanworks everywhere. Keep loving the things you love wholeheartedly and with wild abandon.

one

"ISN'T he that dude from that show?"

Eve Tracey didn't need to look up to know who the customer in line was talking about. It was after ten a.m., which meant Boone Sheridan had just walked into Antidote Coffee like he did every morning around this time.

Not that Eve would have looked even if she hadn't known who it was. Gawking at celebrity customers wasn't how she rolled. The Studio City coffee shop where she worked got their fair share of recognizable actors stopping in for a caffeine fix. She'd long since gotten used to being blessed by their superhumanly symmetrical visages on the reg. Most of them just wanted to be left alone to consume their rejuvenating beverages in peace, and they tipped better when she helped make that happen for them.

Sure, the first few times a celebrity had walked in during one of her shifts, she'd startled at the shock of recognition. There was always that weird disorientation of seeing a familiar face out of context. It took the brain a second to place it and realize it wasn't someone you knew, but a stranger you'd seen so many times they instinctively felt like an acquaintance.

Yes, maybe Eve had stared a little when it was all still shiny and new to her. She remembered her very first celebrity customer four years ago when she was working at a different coffee shop in Santa Monica. It was a B-list movie star who'd later turned out to be involved in a sex cult running a human trafficking ring—which was horrifying in retrospect. Not that she'd known about that part at the time.

She'd stammered a little taking his order, distracted by his unnaturally tanned face, blindingly white veneers, and unexpectedly small stature. But she'd still known better than to try and talk to him or get overly friendly. Thank god, given the whole sex cult thing. *Yikes.*

These days, Eve was much better at playing it cool. Even with Boone Sheridan, who was her biggest celebrity crush. Or had been, back when she still watched his show. She'd been so obsessed with *Abnormal Investigations* when she was in college that she'd even run a fansite for it.

But that was all ancient history now. She didn't want anyone to know about her youthful fangirl past—least of all Boone Sheridan, who'd been a regular at the coffee shop for nearly a month, and who she treated no differently than any other customer who walked in the door.

"What show?" the guy in line asked in response to his girlfriend's question. He craned his neck, peering at the other customers behind them. "What dude?"

"Don't stare," his girlfriend admonished him. "Be more obvious, why don't you?"

"I think I know who you're talking about," the boyfriend said, glancing over his shoulder at Boone with marginally more subtlety. "He's on that show with all the monsters. The one with that hot blonde. I can't remember the name of it."

Eve finished ringing up the customer in front of the gawking couple and greeted them with a plastic smile as they stepped up to the counter. "What can I get you?"

"Do you know who that is at the back of the line?" the girl-friend asked Eve in a loud whisper. "He's someone famous, right?"

They had to be from out of town. Only out-of-towners got this excited about celebrity sightings in LA. Other dead give-aways: their comfortable shoes and the anti-theft travel purse the woman was carrying. Definitely tourists. Most likely headed to Hollywood Boulevard or one of the studio tours. Eve empathized with their enthusiasm, because she'd felt the same way when she'd first moved here for college. That didn't mean she was willing to enable it, however.

"No idea," she said, smiling wider. "Do you know what you want? We've got a brand-new lavender latte on the menu that's good."

Looking disappointed, the couple finally got down to the business of ordering their to-go coffees.

"You really don't recognize him?" the woman asked as her boyfriend paid with a twenty-dollar bill.

"Nope, sorry," Eve replied. "Your coffees will be right up at the other end of the counter."

The man dropped the coins from his change into the tip jar as they moved along. All twenty-seven cents of it. *Gee, thanks.*

"Tourists," the next guy in line muttered under his breath as he approached the register.

A small twitch at the corner of Eve's mouth was her only acknowledgement as she offered him the same plastic smile she'd given the last customers. "What can I get you?"

He was a semi-regular, a businessman who worked in an office nearby, and he recited his order and paid for it with the kind of efficiency Eve deeply appreciated. He also tipped well. Always a pleasure.

Next up was a youngish girl, high school age by the look of her, with thick black eyeliner and chipped nail polish. Behind her stood Boone Sheridan, attempting to fly under the radar in mirrored aviator sunglasses and a beard he'd been gradually growing out since he started frequenting the coffee shop four weeks ago.

Eve knew from her former obsession with *Abnormal Investigations* that the Vancouver-based production was currently in its between-season shooting hiatus, which explained Boone's presence in Los Angeles and apparent excess of free time. Next month, he would head back to Canada to start filming season ten, and his regular visits to Antidote Coffee would come to a sad end.

The high school girl ordered a bottomless coffee and one of the giant chocolate chip cookies in the bakery case. While Eve plated the cookie, the girl dug into the pocket of her scuffed backpack, extracting rumpled dollar bills that she set on the counter.

Her search became increasingly frantic when she came up a dollar short. "I thought I had a five in here," she mumbled in embarrassment, her face bright red as she tore through every pocket in her bag a second and third time hoping to find the cash she needed. "I'm really sorry. I have to put the cookie back."

"Don't worry about it." Eve pushed the cookie and plain drip coffee across the counter. "You're covered."

"Thank you." The girl's eyes were wide and shiny as she gave Eve a wobbly smile. "I'm *so* sorry."

"It's no biggie. Really. Enjoy the rest of your day."

As the girl gathered up her purchases and fled to a table, Eve retrieved a dollar bill from her pocket to add to the till with the rest of the girl's money.

"I'll cover it," Boone Sheridan said as he stepped up to the register. He flipped open his wallet and pulled out the Platinum Amex he always used to pay for his coffee. "Can you put her whole order on this and give her back her money?"

Eve looked up in surprise. Boone didn't usually talk to her

this much. Or at all, really. He always ordered the same thing, so he didn't even have to say his order anymore. She'd ask if he wanted his usual, and he'd tip his chin in silent confirmation while holding out his credit card.

"Sure." Eve shoved the bill back in her pocket and swept the girl's money off to the side for safekeeping. "That's really nice of you."

Boone replied with his trademark silent chin tip.

"What can I get you?" she asked, feeling slightly flustered by the deviation from their normal routine.

"The usual would be great, thanks." His tone was clipped —not unfriendly, exactly, but not inviting extraneous conversation.

She didn't blame him, considering how much unwanted attention he must deal with in his daily life. The curious couple this morning weren't the first people to have noticed him here. The regulars ignored his presence like typical jaded Angelenos, but now and again he'd get approached with requests for autographs or selfies, which he always granted with forced good humor, flashing a dazzling actor-smile that dropped away as soon as the fans' backs were turned.

Eve added Boone's double wet whole milk cappuccino to the teenage girl's order and pushed the card reader toward him. "Is it safe to assume you don't want me to tell her who her Good Samaritan was?"

"It is," he replied without looking at her. "Thanks."

Eve allowed herself to watch him as he retreated to an empty table in the corner to wait for his coffee order. He was dressed in his usual casual attire, which today consisted of charcoal jeans that hugged his thighs, a tight blue T-shirt that left very little of his muscular physique to the imagination, and a pair of dingy green low-top Chuck Taylors.

He was even better looking in person than she'd imagined when she used to lust after him on TV. Especially with the slightly shaggy hair and scrumptious hiatus beard, which made an intriguing change of pace from the clean-cut look of his character.

When Boone sat down, Eve dragged her attention back to the register. He normally added a generous fifty percent tip, but today he'd tipped twice that on top of paying for the girl's order. An inconsequential amount of money to someone who made a hundred thousand dollars per episode, but enough to matter to an hourly barista.

It was a shame his job kept him in Vancouver most of the year. Eve was going to miss his regular visits to the coffee shop when his hiatus ended.

ONE OF THE FIRST LESSONS BOONE HAD LEARNED WHEN HE became famous enough to get recognized on the street was the importance of keeping his emotions off his face. When you were out in public or interacting with fans, you couldn't let people see that you were tired, or having a bad day, or annoyed by their intrusion into your private life. Because sure as shit, if he had an unfriendly look on his face, someone would snap a photo of him and post it online with a story about what a self-important dick he was. Or worse, he'd end up in another goddamn meme.

Therefore, Boone was careful to keep a neutral expression on his face as he skimmed through his Twitter mentions. No one sitting around him in the coffee shop would have been able to guess he was screaming inside his heart.

The internet was a mistake.

Sure, it had seemed like a pretty awesome idea at first. Sports scores, IMDb, Wikipedia, easy access to porn—who could complain about any of that? But then social media had to go and ruin everything. The fact that every bored yahoo with a smartphone could blast their ignorant opinions and shitty jokes out to millions of disciples jonesing for a dopamine rush had twisted something fun and useful into something nasty and dangerous that was currently trying to ruin Boone's life.

He ought to stop vanity-searching his own name. His confidence had taken enough hits lately without injecting more poison directly into his veins. But he couldn't help himself. Besides, he needed to know what people were saying so he knew how bad the situation was, and if he needed to do something about it.

His assistant Priya would tell him that was what he paid her for and to quit self-flagellating. But since Priya had gone to visit family in India over the hiatus, she couldn't confiscate his phone like she usually did when he got like this.

Movement in Boone's peripheral vision caught his attention, and he watched through his mirrored sunglasses as the cute barista took the high school student's money back to her. Discreetly laying the crumpled dollar bills on the table, the barista tucked her short dark hair behind her ear as she bent down to speak to the younger girl. Boone studied the barista's bright red lips, trying to decipher what she was saying—not that he didn't trust her to keep him out of it. He was just curious.

According to the tag she wore on her apron, her name was Eve. Boone liked looking at her. It was part of the reason he came here for coffee every day even though he had a three-thousand-dollar Italian espresso machine at home. Eve was short and curvy with glossy cupid's bow lips she always painted different bright colors, a heart-shaped face accentuated by high cheekbones, and bold eyebrows over wide, dark eyes that looked almost as black as her sleek, chin-length hair. He'd spent a lot of time observing her on his daily visits, secure in the knowledge she wouldn't be able to tell with his eyes hidden behind his reflective sunglasses.

She'd already finished talking to the student, who was putting her money away in her backpack. As she straightened, Eve's gaze flicked in Boone's direction for a fraction of a second before she went behind the counter again.

He sipped his coffee as he watched her stop to chat with the other employee working this morning and felt a small, irrational twinge of jealousy when the male barista with the tattoo sleeve and eyebrow piercing said something that made her laugh.

Watching was all Boone ever planned to do with the cute barista. It was the only thing he trusted himself to do anymore. In his younger days, he might have asked for her number and spent a night with her. But the novelty of casual hookups had worn off for him years ago, and anything more than casual was out of the question. His last relationship had fucked with his head too much. It wasn't an experience he was ready to jump back into anytime soon. Maybe ever.

So here he sat. Watching. Because watching was safe.

Boone's phone's screen lit up with an incoming call from his manager. This time he did scowl faintly before he managed to school himself. Standing up, he chugged the last of his coffee before heading out the back door of the café.

Only after the heavy metal door had slammed shut behind him and he'd confirmed the alley was empty did he answer the call. "Hey, Kurt."

"Hey," his manager drawled in the preemptively sympathetic voice he only used when he had bad news to deliver. "You got a minute?"

"Sure." Boone currently had all the time in the fucking world, as Kurt knew damn well.

"Nintendo canceled the meeting next week."

Well, shit. It had taken months of back-and-forth to get that meeting on the calendar. It would have been a lucrative, high-profile endorsement for him, but he wasn't as concerned about the money as what it meant that they'd canceled.

Boone squeezed the back of his neck in frustration. "Why?"

"A scheduling issue, they claim. But you and I both know the real reason. I doubt they'll be rescheduling."

"I can't believe they give that much of a shit about baseless gossip."

"It's not exactly baseless, is it?" Kurt's tone held a faint note of reproach.

"That picture didn't prove a goddamn thing," Boone growled in response. He wasn't allowed to defend himself publicly, but he'd be damned if he'd roll over and accept Kurt's censure for something he hadn't done.

"The court of public opinion has different rules than a court of law. It doesn't matter what the photo proves, it only matters what it makes people believe."

Boone sighed and rubbed his hand over his face. They'd had some version of this same conversation too many times over the last six weeks, and he was pretty fucking sick of it.

"It all comes down to bad timing," Kurt said. "The fans have always wanted to believe you two were more than costars. If a photo like that had surfaced four years ago, the publicity would have been golden. But now that Simone's married, it's a whole other story. Especially with a kid in the picture."

"Yeah, I get it," Boone gritted out. "The whole world thinks I'm a sleazy, adulterous destroyer of happy families."

"Don't give yourself too much credit. You're not that famous. Only about forty percent of the American public knows who you are."

"Great."

"Anyway," Kurt said, getting serious once more, "it's a

family-friendly campaign. They're going to want a family-friendly name to go with it. Them's the breaks."

It was the exact same reason Boone had been dropped at the eleventh hour from the movie he'd been set to shoot over the hiatus. Thanks to one privacy-invading asshole with a camera and a whole lot of wild speculation, Boone was no longer considered "the right fit for a family film."

"I thought this shit would have blown over by now. That people would get bored and move on to a more interesting imaginary scandal."

"They might have if Simone's husband had been anyone else. But he's a beloved sports figure and a bigger household name than you are, and he's out there keeping the story going by milking his victim status for all it's worth. Meanwhile, you and Simone have gone radio silent, so the only narrative the public's getting is the one he's telling." Kurt paused for dramatic effect. "I think you should reconsider Reagan's suggestion."

"The girlfriend thing? Hell no. I'm not so desperate I need my publicist to hire a girlfriend for me."

She'd been pushing to stage an arranged public romance between Boone and some wholesome, up-and-coming actress to distract from the current PR shitstorm. He could imagine how the whole thing would play out with Reagan running the show, and it was too distasteful to contemplate.

"Then I recommend you get your own girlfriend," Kurt said. "It's not like it would be hard for a guy like you. Go get yourself photographed a few times cozying up to a new steady squeeze. Give people something to talk about besides the fact that you broke up your costar's perfect marriage."

"You think it would make that much difference?"

"It sure as hell couldn't hurt. At least then people wouldn't assume you were sitting around pining for someone else's wife."

"Jesus." Boone couldn't believe it had come to this.

Or that he was actually considering it. But it wasn't just his image that was being dragged through the dirt. The ugly gossip was hurting Simone even more than it was hurting him. Especially with her asshole husband stirring the pot to build a case in his favor for the divorce settlement.

Kurt cleared his throat. "You know what people have started saying now, right? That her kid is really yours?"

"That's a fucking lie," Boone snarled.

"Take it easy, man. I'm not the one spreading it around. But the idea is in people's heads now, and it's not going away on its own."

"Then maybe it's time to make a statement. Issue a denial."

"Reagan and I discussed it, but we still think it'll do more harm than good. No one's going to have their mind changed by a press release, and the act of issuing the statement will lend legitimacy to the rumors and fan the flames even more." Kurt paused to let that sink in. "We need to change the narrative by giving them something else to talk about. Something positive that works in your favor, but is intriguing enough to pull focus."

"And you think a girlfriend's going to accomplish that?" Boone asked doubtfully. It seemed like a tall order.

"If everyone thinks you've settled down with a steady girlfriend, they might not be so quick to jump to other conclusions. It needs to be the right kind of girl though. Sweet. Wholesome. Clean as a whistle. No one with even a whiff of artifice or scandal clinging to them."

A sweet, wholesome, nice girl. Where the hell was Boone supposed to find one of those in LA?

two

THE PEACEFUL LULL after the morning rush was Eve's favorite part of her shift at Antidote. By the time things started to get busy again at lunchtime, she'd be out the door with two whole hours to herself before she had to be at her second job at two. Today she was thinking about running back to her apartment to grab a quick nap before she headed to the Montessori school where she worked in the afternoons supervising the pre-K aftercare kids.

Between her two jobs, Eve averaged fifty hours a week and just barely made enough money to cover her living expenses. But at least she liked both of her jobs, which was more than most people could say. She'd floated around a lot of different employment situations since she'd dropped out of college five years ago, and the two she had right now were the best so far.

Sure, it'd be nice to make more money, but she was getting by okay. Anyway, she liked the variety. It kept things from getting boring.

After casting her eye around the café to check there was nothing that needed doing, Eve leaned back against the counter and pulled out her phone. Her roommate, Becca, had sent her a text an hour ago that she was only now seeing.

I'm sorry, but you needed to know, Becca had written and attached a video.

Uh oh. That meant it was something weird or appalling. Becca could have a weird sense of humor sometimes. She was always trying to shock Eve.

Checking to make sure her volume was turned most of the way down, Eve cast another glance around to make sure there was no one nearby before clicking on the video. It took a few seconds to download on the coffee shop's Wi-Fi. While she waited, she squinted at the thumbnail, attempting to guess what horrors awaited her, but it was too dark and blurry to make anything out from the one frame.

When the vid had finished downloading, the image moved jerkily for a second before stabilizing and coming into focus on a naked man on a bed.

No, Eve realized with a sense of horror. Not just *a* man.

It was her boyfriend, Vince.

A sick feeling unfurled in the pit of her stomach as she watched Vince lie back on the bed with a full erection. Not his bed either. Vince had Batman sheets on his bed, but this one had a plain white comforter and sheets.

Where the fuck had Becca found a sex video of Eve's boyfriend?

"Come on, baby," Vince said in the video. "Quit messing with the camera and get over here. I'm waiting." So clearly he'd been a willing participant.

A woman appeared in frame with a curtain of long blonde hair hiding her face as she crawled up the bed, hovering over him on all fours. Unlike Vince, she was clothed in a white tank top and black leggings. The unknown woman on the bed with Eve's naked boyfriend sat back, straddling his hairy thighs, and pulled her hair up into a ponytail.

Eve felt like she was going to be sick.

It wasn't an unknown woman.

It was Becca.

Eve's fucking best friend and roommate.

STILL CHAFING AT THE CONVERSATION WITH HIS MANAGER, Boone shoved his phone into his pocket and yanked open the back door of Antidote. As he headed down the hall to the restroom, a dark-haired whirlwind came barreling around the corner and crashed face first into his chest.

He jerked back in surprise as the cute barista ricocheted off him with a yelp of pain. The impact sent her staggering backward and knocked her phone out of her hand. Reflexively, Boone grabbed her arms before she could fall over.

"Whoa. Sorry," he said as he steadied her. "Are you okay?" That had to have hurt like hell, as hard as she'd hit him. He searched her face for signs of injury. She looked more surprised than concussed. Her nose wasn't bleeding and her pupils seemed normal, but there were tears in her eyes.

Shit. She was crying. *Fuck.*

"I'm fine," the barista mumbled, ducking her head as she pulled out of his grasp.

"I'm really sorry if I hurt you."

"You didn't." Her gaze remained fixed on the floor as she swiped the tears off her cheeks. "It was my fault. I'm the one who should be sorry."

Boone rubbed his chest and found a damp spot on his shirt where she'd face-planted. That meant there'd been tears on her face *before* she crashed into him. He studied her more carefully. "Were you crying?"

"No." She hugged her arms across her chest, clearly lying.

Her phone had landed on the floor behind him, and he

scooped it up to hand it to her. But as he checked the screen for damage, he noticed the video playing on it.

"Is that porn?" he asked in surprise as he squinted at the image of two people very clearly getting it on. Faint sex noises came out of the phone's speaker. "Were you crying and watching porn?"

"It's not porn." The barista snatched the phone out of his hand and mashed the screen to stop the vid.

"Sure looked like porn." Amateur, sure, but definitely porn. Not that he was judging.

Backing up against the wall, she sank to the floor and pulled her knees to her chest. "It's a video of my boyfriend cheating on me with my roommate."

"Whoa," was all Boone could think to say.

The barista let out a dark laugh that turned into a strangled-sounding sob. "Aren't you glad you asked?"

Something shifted inside him at the sight of her hunched on the floor, looking so small and heartbroken. It drove his own petty problems right out of his head. All he could think about was how he could keep her from looking like this ever again, and how much he wanted to dick-punch the assholes who'd done this to her.

"Your name's Eve, right?"

She nodded as she scrubbed at her eyes.

Boone lowered himself to the floor beside her.

"What are you doing?" she asked in alarm.

"I'm sitting down. This seat's not taken, is it?"

"This floor's not clean. You shouldn't sit here."

"You're sitting here."

"Yeah, but those jeans you're wearing look like they cost more than my rent."

"They're jeans. They can be washed." He tapped his green Chucks against her purple one. "Nice shoes."

Eve cut him a sideways look. "I know who you are, you

know."

"I know you know. I use my credit card here every day."

"No, I mean, I know what you do. I used to watch the show."

He nodded. "I figured."

"Was it that obvious?" She looked disappointed.

"No, you played it cooler than most people. But I can always tell when people recognize me."

She turned her face forward, giving him her profile. "Sorry."

"You don't have to apologize for it." Boone pushed his sunglasses up on top of his head and regarded her silently. "Sounds like you're having a pretty bad day, Eve."

A muscle tightened in her jaw. "You could say that."

"I'm sorry your boyfriend is a dickslit."

"*You* definitely don't have to apologize for anything." She dropped her forehead to her arms with a sigh. "He has Batman sheets on his bed. That probably should have been a red flag."

Boone had to agree, but he kept it to himself. "How'd you get the video?"

"My roommate sent it to me. Can you believe that? She said I needed to know. Whatever that's supposed to mean."

"Did she know you were at work when she sent it to you?" Not that there was a good time to send someone a video like that. But sending it while Eve was at work seemed particularly cold, as if her roommate had wanted to do as much damage as possible.

Eve's head lifted as she thought about it, and her face fell even more. "Yeah, she did. She knew I had a shift this morning."

"You need better friends."

Another dark laugh. "No shit."

"I hope you're gonna kick both of them to the curb."

"Oh, don't worry." She drew in a deep breath, blew it out

again, and wiped under both her eyes. "I have to get back to work."

Boone stood and held his hand out to help her off the floor. After a brief hesitation, she put her hand in his and let him pull her to her feet.

"How much longer is your shift?" he asked.

"I get off at noon."

He nodded, chewing on the inside of his cheek as an idea started to form in his head. Boone couldn't decide if it was a brilliant idea or a terrible one. It was definitely one or the other. "You gonna be okay?"

"I'll be fine. Thanks for, uh…caring, I guess." Backing toward the bathroom, Eve hooked a thumb over her shoulder. "I'm gonna go wash my hands."

Without waiting for him to respond, she turned and fled.

———

Once she was safely hidden in the bathroom, Eve washed her face and tried to pull herself together.

The weird thing was, she wasn't that upset about Vince. Sure, she was super pissed he'd cheated on her, but it wasn't like she was falling apart over it.

They'd only met three months ago through a dating app. Eve had been flattered by his interest at first, but the better she'd gotten to know Vince after the initial shine had worn off, the less enamored she'd become. She couldn't say she'd miss him all that much.

But Becca didn't know that. Eve hadn't told her that her feelings for Vince had cooled. As far as Becca knew, Eve was still crazy about him.

Becca's betrayal was the one that hurt. They'd been room-mates for over six months and friends for two years before that.

Becca was Eve's closest friend. Her *only* close friend, for that matter.

Eve had drifted away from her college friends after she'd dropped out. She'd changed jobs so often since then that she hadn't had a chance to get close to many people. Becca was the only friend who'd stuck.

She couldn't believe Becca had done this to her. And then sent her the video as if she was doing Eve some kind of favor. What kind of psychopath did that? Who the fuck had Eve been friends with all this time?

There was no way she could keep living with Becca after this. But that meant Eve would have to move out, and before she could do that she'd have to find somewhere else to live. That was going to take time. And cost money Eve didn't exactly have to spare.

She couldn't think about that right now. One problem at a time. First she needed to get through the rest of her shift. Later, she'd figure out what to do about Becca.

When Eve ventured out of the bathroom, she was relieved not to see Boone in the café. Of course it had been him who witnessed her meltdown. He'd even seen the video. God almighty, she'd never be able to face him again.

Austin was at the register taking a customer's order, and Eve got to work making their mocha latte. Too bad it wasn't a busier time of day. All the downtime between customers made the last excruciating hour of her shift pass more slowly. She couldn't even look at her phone to distract herself. She'd powered it off so she wouldn't have to deal with any communication from Becca or Vince until she was ready.

Eve did her best to keep herself occupied by wiping down tables and tidying up the condiment bar. The sugar shakers had never been this clean before. Someone should give her a goddamn medal.

She'd nearly made it through the last of her shift and was

so close to escape she could practically taste it when Boone Sheridan walked in the front door of Antidote for the second time that day.

This was unprecedented. He never came in twice in one day—not once in the entire time he'd been a regular customer. The fact that he'd come back today of all days couldn't possibly be a coincidence. Although Eve dearly hoped it was.

For a moment, she considered making Austin help him. But Austin was zoned out on his phone so she'd have to make an obvious point of asking him to take Boone's order, which would be even more awkward.

It was fine. She could do this. Boone had been perfectly nice to her, after all. Far nicer than he'd needed to be after she'd basically blitzed him. Her massive embarrassment wasn't his fault.

"Hey," he said when Eve met him at the register.

Already he was treating her differently. He'd never greeted her before, and his tone was softer and more hesitant than his usual businesslike clip. He must think she was really pitiful.

As she returned his greeting with a stiff nod, she avoided looking directly at his stupidly handsome face. "You want your usual again or—"

"Just this." He set a bottle of water on the counter.

"Right. Okay." Eve rang up his water, praying he'd take it and leave.

"Can we talk when your shift is over?" he asked as he inserted his card in the machine.

Eve froze like a deer in headlights. She tried to swallow, but her mouth had forgotten how to make saliva. "Um…I guess. If you want."

"I want."

The way he said it, all low and rumbly with a hint of flirtatious suggestion, made her stomach flip upside down. It was the same playful, sexy voice she'd heard him use on TV a thousand times before, and nothing at all like the brusque, impersonal tone she was accustomed to getting from him in real life.

"You said you get off at noon, right?"

"Yes," she croaked in reply.

He cocked his head toward an empty table in the corner. "I'll be over there."

As soon as he walked off with his bottle of water, Eve turned her back and drew in a panicked breath.

What? The hell?

Boone Sheridan wanted to talk? To *her*?

three

EVE HAD NOT the faintest idea what Boone Sheridan could possibly want to talk to her about. She was dying of curiosity—but also a bit afraid to find out. Whatever it was, there was no way it could live up to her fanciful hopes.

Boone Sheridan was not going to ask her out on a date. She might as well give up that starry-eyed idea right now. Things like that didn't happen outside of fairy tales and her own personal fantasies.

As a rule, good things didn't happen to Eve. Therefore she braced herself for something bad.

The next ten minutes dragged on for a thousand years. Eve tried not to look in Boone's direction, but every so often her eyes flicked that way on their own. He was just sitting there calmly sipping his water while staring at his phone like he did every day.

Only this time he was waiting for Eve to come join him. *Wild.*

When her shift finally ended, she went into the back to clock out, take off her apron, and collect her purse. Boone was still patiently waiting when she came back, his attention so glued to his phone that he didn't seem to notice her approach.

Dropping into the chair across from him, Eve clutched her purse in her lap so he wouldn't see how her hands were shaking. "What's up?"

Boone slid his mirrored sunglasses off and set them on the table next to his phone before giving Eve his full, undivided attention.

Wow, those eyes of his were something else—a pale ice-blue so striking they almost looked otherworldly. It was the first time she had ever looked directly into them in person. She had to clench her teeth to repress the goofy, besotted expression her face wanted to make in response.

Jesus god, the amount of time Eve had spent fantasizing about this man and imagining him in all kinds of unseemly scenarios. She'd written fanfic about him, for cripes' sake! Seriously smutty, *explicit* fanfic. And now she was supposed to sit here and look him in the eyes while having a normal conversation?

He was even more attractive this close up. He actually had freckles—faint ones she'd never noticed before, and found unbelievably endearing. All that time Eve had spent gazing at pictures of him, and none of them came close to doing him justice. The real thing was infinitely better than the fantasy.

A slight frown creased his forehead as his gaze swept over her face. "You doing okay?"

"I'm fine." She cast a tense glance around, but no one in the café seemed to be paying them any attention. "You didn't come back here just to ask me that, did you?" Whatever he wanted, she really needed him to spit it out and put her out of her misery before she lost her cool completely.

"Maybe I did," Boone countered.

Arching a dubious eyebrow, she tried to stare him down, but his blank expression didn't change even a microfraction.

Why had she thought she could win a staring contest with an actor?

"Is that all you wanted or…?" She shifted in her seat, ready to jump up and make her escape.

He shook his head as he rubbed a hand through his beard. "You really aren't making this easy."

"Making what easy?"

"Can you maybe relax a little? I'm not going to bite you."

"I'm relaxed." Leaning back in her seat, Eve attempted to mimic his loose, easy posture. With unsatisfactory results, since her chair overbalanced and tried to tip her over.

"Yeah, I can see that." His lips twitched with amusement as she sat upright again.

She glared at him. Or tried to. Honestly, her brain was barely functioning, and she really had no idea what her face was doing at this point. She was just lucky she was still breathing. Yay for the autonomic nervous system.

With a small sigh, he leaned forward to rest his forearms on the table. "I'm just trying to ask if I can take you to lunch."

Eve's mouth fell open. Then closed. Then opened again. "What?"

"You heard me."

"Why would you want to do that? We don't even know each other."

His mouth twisted into a smirk. By rights, it should have made him less appealing, but unfairly it had the opposite effect. "You know who I am, right?"

"We already established that."

"What's your last name?"

"Tracey."

"Nice to meet you, Eve Tracey. I'm Boone Sheridan. So now we know each other. Or do I need to submit some sort of formal application before we can hang out?"

"*You* want to hang out with *me*?" Eve's bullshit detectors were on high alert now. He had to be fucking with her. Was he seriously so bored that he had nothing better to do than mess with her for entertainment?

"Why not?" he asked, fiddling with his sunglasses.

"For starters, until this morning you'd never said a word to me other than your coffee order. Not a single hello or goodbye, not how are you, not even a thank-you. And now I'm supposed to believe you want to *hang out?*"

"Maybe I just thought you could use cheering up." When Boone's unnervingly blue eyes locked onto hers, it felt like he was staring directly into her soul. "I'm offering to take you to lunch, Eve. That's all. Yes or no?"

Jesus, take the wheel. Eve's stomach could have earned a spot on her high school cheerleading squad, it was doing so many somersaults. She swallowed. "Yes, okay. Sure."

Like she was going to say no to lunch with Boone Sheridan. This was basically a fantasy come true. She didn't even care if he was doing it to recruit her into his cult or bitcoin scheme or whatever. If it meant she got to stare at his face a while longer, she'd gladly sit and listen to his pitch. Whatever had inspired him to make the offer—whether he was acting out of self-interest, pity, bored curiosity, or was genuinely being kind—Eve couldn't let a chance like this go by.

But after lunch was over, she would say thank you very much and goodbye, they'd go their separate ways, and that would be the end of it. Because she wasn't foolish enough to believe she could be anything more to him than a momentary diversion.

Except for the stupid, hopeful voice whispering in the back of her head.

But what if...

What if it could turn into something more?

And then there was the way Boone's eyes lit up when she

said yes. That inexplicable flash of what looked like genuine warmth made Eve want to believe all sorts of foolish things.

Absurd, impossible, *dangerous* things that would surely end in disappointment.

"I don't have that much time," she added, staring down at her lap because it was easier to think straight when she wasn't looking at his face. "I have to be at my other job by two."

"I won't let you be late," Boone said. "Trust me."

"You like tacos?" Boone asked as he opened the passenger door of his steel gray Chevy Camaro. It was a new, top-of-the-line model, but not especially clean. Not that it was filthy or anything, but there was a layer of dust coating the exterior and dash like it hadn't seen a car wash in a while. Maybe that shouldn't have surprised her, but before today Eve had assumed that celebrities' cars were always pristine.

"Doesn't everyone like tacos?" she answered, ducking into the car and settling back in the leather bucket seat.

"You'd be surprised." Boone shut her door for her, then walked around and slid behind the wheel.

When the engine rumbled to life, a Rage Against the Machine song blasted out of the speakers. He cranked the volume down before pulling out onto Ventura Boulevard.

Some old receipts lay on the floor at Eve's feet. She tried not to look at them, feeling it would be an invasion of his privacy. Even though she was wildly curious to know what he'd bought at Rite Aid.

"What's your second job?" Boone asked as he navigated the lunchtime traffic.

"I work at a Montessori preschool on weekday afternoons."

"You're a teacher?" He shot a sideways glance at her. He'd put his sunglasses back on, which made it difficult to read his expression, but Eve had the sense she was being assessed and evaluated. For what, she had no idea.

"Technically, I'm just a teacher's assistant. I supervise the aftercare kids who stay until their parents get off work."

"You must like kids a lot."

"They're okay. No worse behaved than some of the customers we get at the coffee shop, but at least I'm allowed to put the kids in time out."

Boone's husky chuckle made her stomach flip. "Fair enough."

A few minutes later, they pulled into the parking lot of a small taqueria off Moorpark that Eve had never been to before. They ordered their food at the window outside, and Boone shook his head at her when she started to take out her wallet.

Once they'd collected their drinks, they sat down at one of the tables out front along the sidewalk. The morning's June Gloom had burned off to reveal gorgeous blue skies and a bright, sunny afternoon. Boone settled back in his chair, looking effortlessly cool and relaxed with his legs splayed wide and one arm resting on the table.

Eve wished she could say the same as she shifted her butt on the metal slats of her chair. Everything about this felt weird. It would have been weird enough going to lunch with any customer from the coffee shop, but the fact that it was *Boone Sheridan* sitting across from her rocketed the situation into the weird stratosphere.

She knew way too much about him, for one thing—while at the same time she didn't *know* him at all. She'd seen and read countless interviews with him and watched hours of videos of his convention appearances over the years. She knew where he'd grown up (Colorado), what had inspired him to become an actor (getting the lead in *Grease* in high school), and that he was allegedly having an affair with his longtime costar that had recently broken up her marriage. Awkward.

There was also the fact that people walking past on the sidewalk kept doing double takes as they recognized Boone. A teenage girl over by the order window was not so subtly taking a picture with her phone. For his part, Boone didn't seem to notice any of it—either that or he didn't care.

He cracked the seal on the bottle of water he'd bought himself and took a sip before looking at Eve. "Have you talked to your boyfriend since your roommate texted you that video?"

Wishing she had sunglasses of her own to hide behind, she shook her head and sucked on the straw of her fountain Coke. "I turned my phone off. I didn't want to deal with it while I was at work."

Boone's mouth turned down. "And now I'm keeping you from dealing with it when you're off work. Sorry."

"Don't be. I'd just as soon put it off for as long as possible. Avoidance is my preferred strategy for dealing with things that suck." Eve offered him a small smile. "I'm glad to have an excuse to put it off."

He smiled back. "I'm glad I can be your excuse."

Her cheeks grew hot, and she took another drink of Coke. Although she couldn't see his eyes, she could feel them watching her closely.

Leaning forward, he folded his arms on the table. "What *are* you going to do, if you don't mind my asking?" He appeared genuinely concerned about her situation, which was flattering but also odd, considering they were total strangers.

"Find a new roommate, I guess." She didn't bother explaining about it being Becca's apartment and therefore Eve would have to be the one to move out and until she could find someplace else she could afford she'd be stuck sleeping under the same roof as her backstabbing former best friend. No way was Eve unloading all her problems on Boone just because he was nice enough to buy her lunch.

"And a new boyfriend too, I hope."

She grimaced at the surface of the table. "Yeah, I think I might leave that position vacant for a while."

"As long as you don't take the prick back." When she looked at him, Boone held his hands up. "I know it's none of my business, so feel free to tell me to shut the fuck up if you want, but you deserve better than that loser."

"How do you know what I deserve? Maybe I cheated on him first. You ever think of that?"

"Nope." He shook his head. "I don't buy it."

"Why not?"

"Because I pay attention to people. And I've been coming into that coffee shop long enough to notice things about you."

Her eyes narrowed. "What kind of things?"

Boone leaned back in his chair again, spinning the lid of his water bottle on the laminate surface of the table. "Like how patient you are with elderly customers and that new employee you were training last week. How you always protect my privacy—you even kicked out that one woman who was taking a video of me on her phone. And this morning, you were going to give your own money to that teenager so she could have a cookie. You're a good person."

Eve didn't know what to do with that or the fact that he'd been watching her all this time. She'd assumed he'd been ignoring her the way he seemed to ignore everyone else around him. It had been easier to think that than to allow herself to imagine he might be paying attention to her.

The woman shouted out their number at the window, and Boone went to get their order, leaving Eve to process what he'd said. By the time he returned with their food, she'd mostly recovered from the revelation that her celebrity crush had been paying attention to her for the last month. As much as a person could recover from something that had blown their mind.

He passed Eve her torta before unwrapping his burrito. She watched him methodically apply two different kinds of salsa before biting into it with the enthusiasm of a man who seriously enjoyed eating.

"You've been spying on me, huh?" she said, picking up her torta.

He finished swallowing before he answered. "I wouldn't exactly call it spying. It's something I got in the habit of doing as an acting exercise. When I'm out in public, I study people's expressions, gestures, and mannerisms for details to incorporate into my performances." He shrugged as he added more salsa to his burrito. "People watch me all the time when I'm in public. Shouldn't I be able to do the same?"

Eve had to concede he had a point about that. Still, it freaked her out to know she wasn't as invisible to him as she'd assumed. But it was also kind of a rush? He'd not only noticed her, but had apparently grown to respect her? How wild was that?

"How's your torta?" he asked between bites of burrito.

"It's good. Thank you."

"I love this place. I eat here at least once a week when I'm in town."

"You must live nearby. Or am I not allowed to ask you that?"

"You can ask me whatever you want."

She raised her eyebrows. "And you'll answer?"

Boone shrugged. "Depends on the question. Maybe."

If only she had a great, insightful question ready to spring on him. Too bad nothing came to mind. Then something did, although it was more of a request than a question. "Will you take off your sunglasses?"

"Why?" he asked, looking up from his burrito mid-bite.

"It's hard having a conversation with someone when you can't see their eyes."

He tugged his aviators off and hooked them on the collar of his T-shirt. "Better?"

"Yes." Only no. Because now she was staring into his freakishly blue eyes again. But at least she could tell when he was looking at her.

"You want to ask me stuff? Ask away." He pointed a finger at her. "But I get to ask you questions too."

Eve thought about it, considering and discarding potential lines of inquiry until she realized what she most wanted to know. "Why am I here?"

"You mean existentially? Because I've got some deep thoughts on that if you really want to hear them."

"Why did you invite me to lunch?" she clarified, suppressing a smile.

He shrugged again. "I wanted to cheer you up."

"Why?"

His gaze lifted to meet hers briefly before dropping back to his burrito. "Because I didn't like seeing you sad."

She had no idea how to respond to that. None at all.

"My turn," Boone said, wiping his mouth with a napkin. "How old are you?"

"Twenty-six."

"Where'd you grow up?"

"San Antonio."

"What brought you to LA?"

"College."

"Which one?"

She reached for her Coke and took a sip. "Loyola Marymount." After a hesitation she added, "I thought I wanted to be an animator."

"You don't?"

"It turned out not to be for me."

"Did you finish school?"

"That turned out not to be for me either."

As Boone regarded her in silence, she squared her shoulders, bracing herself for a question about why she'd dropped out. If he asked, she'd tell him. Learning to talk openly about her struggles with anxiety had been one of the keys to overcoming them. All the same, Eve wasn't eager to revisit that particular chapter of her past today of all days.

"Did you love the guy in the sex tape?" he asked instead.

She flinched at the abrupt subject change and personal nature of the question. "No."

Boone's eyebrows inched upward as he searched her face. "You sure about that?"

"Do I hope he contracts a wasting disease that makes his testicles rot off? Hell yes. But I'm more pissed off than broken-hearted. I'd already decided Vince wasn't someone I could see myself staying with long-term."

"If that's true, why do you still look so sad?"

Eve swallowed and looked down, picking at the bread on her torta. "Because of Becca. She wasn't just my roommate, she was my best friend. Or I thought she was. Guess not so much after all."

"And you haven't responded to her since she sent you that video?"

"Nope." An all too familiar stir of anxiety twisted in Eve's stomach at the thought of the confrontation ahead of her.

"I'll bet that's driving her crazy." Boone sat back, scratching his beard. "She must have sent that video because she wanted to get a rise out of you, and you're denying her the reaction she was hoping for."

"Good. Then I'll keep on denying her that satisfaction as long as I can."

"You'll have to go home and face her eventually though."

"True," Eve agreed, attempting to sound light. "It is where I keep all my stuff."

Pity creases sprouted across his brow. So much for sounding light.

"Enough about me," she went on before Boone could say anything else. "Pretty sure it's my turn to ask you questions again."

"Fair enough." He picked up his burrito and gestured for her to go ahead.

"Have you ever been in love?" she blurted off the top of her head.

He froze mid-chew, his expression growing wary.

"You don't have to answer. This whole question thing was your idea, not mine."

His gaze lingered on her as he swallowed and took a drink of water. "Have you?" he asked finally.

"No." Other than parasocial infatuations with unattainable TV stars, which obviously didn't count.

"You're lucky," he said darkly.

Eve's eyebrows lifted. "I take it you have been in love, then."

His lips pulled into a sneer. "I thought I was."

Wow. Okay. Sensitive subject, apparently.

Was she dying to know if the person Boone thought he'd been in love with was his costar, Simone Alexander? Absolutely. But the look on his face made it pretty clear that a question like that would bring their friendly little lunch to an abrupt end.

Eve shifted to what she hoped was a more benign subject. "When do you go back to Vancouver?"

Boone seemed to relax again. "Second week of July."

So next month, as she'd suspected. Too bad. "Do you like it there?"

"I do, yeah. Although I don't love freezing my balls off when we have to shoot outside in the rain."

She laughed. "I'll bet."

"You've got a gorgeous smile, you know that?"

Eve looked down as she felt her face go bright red. *It's only empty flattery. No need to get overexcited.*

Boone's shoe nudged hers under the table. "Hey, come on. Don't hide your smile away just because I complimented it."

"I'm not very good at taking compliments."

"That's not right. You should have someone following you around, complimenting you all the time until you get used to it."

Eve snorted, because she was all dainty and ladylike that way. "Sure. I'll just put an ad on Craigslist."

The corners of Boone's eyes crinkled as he smiled. "Maybe I'll apply for the job. I'm free for the next month."

Whoa. That definitely sounded like flirting. Except the man was supposedly in a relationship, wasn't he? Maybe not. Maybe they'd split up. Either way, it didn't matter. He was just teasing her, that was all.

"You're not working on anything over the hiatus?" Eve asked, changing the subject.

Boone's expression tightened. "Nope. Taking some time off for once."

She seemed to have accidentally hit another sore spot. *Oops.*

"Is it my turn again?" he asked, leaning forward.

"If you want."

His eyes narrowed as he considered her. "Why'd you quit watching the show?"

"Oh. Um…" Eve flailed at being put on the spot. "No reason in particular. You know how it is. Life gets busy and you don't have as much time for TV."

In fact, she had a long list of very particular reasons she'd quit watching his show, all of which she'd explicated on Tumblr in obsessive detail at the time. But no way was she letting him know how much of a crazed fan she used to be. Nuh uh.

Not to mention that it would be plain old rude to take a huge dump on his hard work right to his face. It was one thing to dissect and critique with other fans, but she would never inflict her negative opinions on one of the creatives directly.

"You can tell me the truth. It won't hurt my feelings."

"I'm not so sure about that."

"Ouch. Must be pretty bad. Now I really want to know." He looked for all the world like he was serious. "Please."

The please was her undoing. Apparently she was powerless to resist when Boone said the magic word. She'd most likely hand over her virtue, first-born child, and the PIN to her ATM card as long as he said please like that.

Eve chewed on her lip as she tried to condense her extensive list of gripes into a diplomatic answer. "Well…I suppose I got frustrated after a few seasons because the main characters never seemed to grow. They kept going through all these traumatic, life-altering experiences together, but it never had a lasting effect on them or changed how they related to each other."

"You're a shipper," Boone said, leaning back with a smirk. The way he said it made it feel like a put-down. "You lost interest because they didn't bang."

"That's a crude oversimplification."

He raised his hands in a conciliatory gesture. "Hey, I've got nothing against shippers. If it wasn't for them, the show never would have made it past the first season."

"That's the whole problem," Eve said. "The writers kept teasing the idea that Deke and Jules were more than just platonic partners to keep the audience invested, but never paid it off. Every time sweeps rolled around there'd be some big cliffhanger with the two of them thrust into yet another tantalizing situation, but they'd always cook up a flimsy reason to drive them apart again. After a while it stopped being fun and started to feel like being jerked around."

Boone nodded, seeming to take this in stride. "You don't think it would get boring if they got them together?"

Eve couldn't help her eyeroll. "Plenty of shows have proven you can put characters in a romantic relationship and keep things interesting. Any TV writer who says it can't be done is admitting they haven't evolved creatively since the nineteen hundreds. What's boring is season after season of ever-rising stakes and plot twists that get bigger and more implausible while the characters remain stagnant. It's ridiculous that after ten years of partnership these two people with insane chemistry who've literally been to hell and back for each other are still dancing around their feelings the same way they were in season one when they first met."

Only when she finally took a breath did Eve notice the look of amusement on Boone's face.

Shit. She'd gotten carried away and gone off on a rant. So much for being diplomatic.

"Sorry," she said as her face flushed hot. "I didn't mean to ramble at you like that."

His eyes lit up with delight. "You didn't just watch the show—you're a *fan*."

"I guess," she mumbled at the table. Why was there never a sinkhole around when you wanted to disappear?

"Hey, don't be embarrassed." His foot nudged hers under the table again. "You're passionate about the show—there's no higher compliment than that."

Eve nodded mutely, refusing to look at him.

"For what it's worth, I happen to agree with you completely."

That had her head jerking up. "You do?"

"This is just between you and me, okay?" Boone leaned in

and waited until she nodded before continuing. "Simone and I have been petitioning the writers room to let our characters take the next step for years. But the showrunner is dead set against it."

"I knew it! I always thought you were playing up the romantic subtext on purpose." It was either that, or the long-rumored attraction between Boone and Simone was so potent it had inadvertently bled into their characters. Eve refrained from mentioning that popular fan theory, however.

Boone's smile was wry as he leaned back in his chair again. "It's possible I take a little artistic license to keep things interesting. Ten years is a long time to play the same character."

"Do you think they'll ever let Deke and Jules be together?"

"No idea. Maybe in the last episode? Or maybe not." He shrugged as he wadded up his burrito wrapper. "You done? We should probably get you back."

Eve deflated at the realization that this unexpected and thrilling experience would soon be over. Boone would drop her off at the coffee shop and that would be that. The end of whatever this was. No more shared confidences or probing questions. Her life would go back to boring old usual.

As they walked to Boone's car, Eve thanked him again for lunch.

"It was nothing," he replied, slipping his sunglasses back on.

To him, maybe. To her, it was a once-in-a-lifetime experience she'd remember for the rest of her life. That one time her celebrity crush randomly took her out to lunch.

The ride back to Antidote passed mostly in silence. They seemed to have run out of conversation. Ah well. It was fun while it lasted. A pleasant distraction from Eve's real-world problems.

"Which car's yours?" Boone asked as he turned into the parking lot next to Antidote.

Eve pointed out her Mazda, and he pulled into a space near it. When he cut the engine, she unbuckled her seat belt.

Boone pushed his sunglasses up and cleared his throat. "Before you go, I need to ask for a favor. A big one."

"O-kay," she said, unsure what to expect.

"Are you free tonight?"

EVE'S BRAIN SHORTED OUT.

"I don't—I mean I—what?"

Nice. Very smooth. Much cool.

Taking a breath, she tried again. "Why?"

There was no way Boone had meant what it sounded like he meant with that question. Lunch was one thing, but asking her on *a date*? Preposterous.

He looked away, rubbing the back of his neck. The way he was fidgeting and avoiding her eyes, he almost seemed embarrassed. It couldn't be a date, then. She didn't believe for a second that a man like him was shy about asking women out.

"There's somewhere I'd like to take you," he said finally.

Oh great. Here it was. The part where he invited her to an orientation session for his multilevel marketing scheme or celebrity religious cult. And he'd seemed so nice up until now too.

"The thing is…" He grimaced like it was causing him actual physical pain to force the words out. "I need someone to pose as my girlfriend for the next few weeks, and I'd like it to be you."

Eve didn't know what she'd expected, but definitely not that. "You're kidding."

"I wish I was."

A million questions tumbled around in her head, most of which boiled down to some variation of *WHY?* or *WHAT??* or *THE FUCK???*

"I don't understand," she said.

Boone's head fell back against his seat with a sigh. "Believe it or not, this sort of thing is fairly common in Hollywood. Publicists set dates up between their clients all the time to boost their visibility or promote a project." His expression tightened as he paused. "Or to counteract negative publicity."

Ahh. Now it was starting to make more sense. One aspect of it, anyway. "Is this about your relationship with Simone Alexander?"

Other than a clench of his jaw, Boone didn't respond.

"Ohh-kay," Eve said slowly. "We'll leave that alone for now. But if publicists typically set this sort of thing up between their famous clients, why are you asking *me* to do it?"

"If it looks too much like a stunt, people won't buy it. I need someone who feels authentic. Someone real."

"Surely your publicist could find you someone who fits the bill."

Boone made a face like he'd smelled something rancid. "I don't want my management team treating my personal life like a reality show they're producing. If I'm going to do this, I'd rather control the situation and do it with someone I trust than a stranger my publicist picked for me."

If possible, Eve was even more dumbfounded. "You trust me? Why?"

He turned his head to look at her finally. "You're compassionate, levelheaded, unimpressed by fame, and willing to protect my privacy. That puts you miles ahead of anyone my publicist is likely to choose."

"But why not date someone for real? Why do you need to fake it?"

The only response was another jaw clench.

Eve took a stab in the dark. "Is it because you're already seeing someone, and you need to keep it a secret?"

"Don't believe everything you read online," he growled.

"Look," she said, losing patience. "You're the one asking me to do you a completely bananapants favor here. Don't you think you owe me some candor about *why* I'd be doing it?"

Cool blue eyes met hers grudgingly. "No, I'm not seeing anyone right now. And yes, this is because of the rumors about me and Simone. The situation has blown up into a major fucking mess, and my team thinks the gossip would die down if people believed I was in a relationship with someone else."

Eve could see how much it cost him to say even that much, so she resisted the urge to ask more questions. Even though she wanted to.

"And you're right," he went on, his face set in grim lines. "I could ask some unsuspecting woman out on a few dates and parade her around for the paparazzi. But it feels like a shitty reason to start a relationship, especially when I don't want to be in a relationship. A girlfriend is the last thing in the world I want right now."

Well, ouch. Good thing Eve hadn't gotten her hopes up about that. But hey, she'd been right. It was preposterous to think that in a million years Boone Sheridan would ever want to date her. That had never been what this was about. Nice to have it confirmed, at least.

"Lunch was an audition," she said as the realization hit her. "That's what this was, wasn't it? A job interview."

"I suppose, in a way," Boone admitted, wincing as his gaze sought hers again. "Mostly I wanted to get to know you better before I sprang this whole thing on you."

"So I guess that means I passed the interview."

"You did, yeah." The corners of his mouth twitched, threatening a smile. "With flying colors."

Well. This was quite the conundrum Eve found herself in.

The smart move would certainly be to say *thanks but no thanks* and get out of the car right now. Considering she was already nursing a major crush on Boone, this whole situation seemed like a surefire recipe for ruin and heartbreak.

But did Eve say no? Did she get out of the car? No, she did not.

Instead she foolishly stayed right where she was and said, "How would this work exactly? What would I have to do?"

In the quiet of the car, she heard Boone release a breath.

He rubbed his palms on his thighs in a gesture that reminded her more of a nervous teenage boy than a famous television sex symbol. "We'd need to go out a few times over the next month to public places where we'll be spotted and photographed. My publicist will make sure there are paparazzi there to document it so we're not wasting our time. All you have to do is show up and play along like we're dating."

"Right," Eve murmured. "That's all."

Acting like she was infatuated with Boone Sheridan? No problem whatsoever.

But being on the receiving end of Boone's attention was bound to mess with a girl's head, no matter how many times she told herself it was fake. Eve had read enough fake dating fanfics to know that much for damn sure. Heck, it was already messing with her head, and she'd only spent an hour and a half with him.

"I'll make it worth your while," he said. "You'll be generously compensated for your time."

"Whoa. Hang on. Are you offering to *pay me* to date you? Like an escort or something?"

His expression pinched. "I'm paying you to *pretend* to date me."

"But we'd actually be going on dates though, right? Whether or not there's a chance of it leading anywhere is beside the point. I'm not accepting money for that." Was she being irrational? Possibly. Impractical? Definitely, considering she was staring down an unplanned move she couldn't afford. But rational or not, it pushed the situation out of her comfort zone. The mere thought of Boone giving her money to go on dates with him made her queasy.

"It's a business arrangement. You're helping me solve a problem, and I'm paying you for your time. Otherwise I'd feel like I was taking advantage."

"No. Sorry." Her head shake was firm. "Getting paid to date someone squicks me out. If I do this, I'm doing it as a favor like you said. End of story."

Boone's tongue worked behind his cheek as he gave her a long, measuring look. "Does that mean you're considering it?"

"I don't know. Maybe." She squeezed her eyes shut and massaged her temples. "I'm still trying to wrap my head around everything. Tell me what's happening tonight."

"There's a party I have to go to." The tightness of his voice said he wasn't excited about it. "Think of it as a sort of trial run."

"What kind of party?" Eve asked warily. Her mom would never forgive her if she let herself get lured into a cult.

"It's just a small get-together. A friend of mine bought a new place with his girlfriend, and they're having a house-warming party. It'll be super chill and casual. No press or anything."

That didn't sound particularly illicit or depraved. Didn't mean it couldn't still be some sort of freaky sex party, but it seemed like an odd theme for a housewarming.

"You want to lie to your friends about us? If there's not going to be any press there, why bother with the ruse?"

A shadow passed over Boone's face. "Let's just say I've got my reasons."

Eve's lips pursed. "Don't suppose you care to share any of those reasons with me?"

"It's nothing you need to worry about." He stared out the windshield. "It'll be easier for me if everyone believes we're a real couple, including my friends and management team."

"I still don't understand why you want me for this."

Those dazzling blue eyes locked onto hers. "I like you."

Her stomach flipped over, but she sternly reminded it that Boone didn't like her enough to ask her on a real date. Only a pretend one.

"You barely know me," she said, struggling to make this make sense.

His mouth twitched into a cheeky half-smirk that was clearly meant to be appealing. And it was. Devastatingly so. "Isn't that the point of dating? To get to know each other better."

"That's the point of *real* dating. Not whatever we'd be doing." If she agreed to go along with this bizarre scheme, she'd need to build up more immunity to his charms.

The beguiling gleam in his eyes softened into something warmer and more earnest that Eve found even tougher to resist. "It's like I told you. I've seen enough to know you're a decent person. Plus you're easy to be around." He shrugged. "Spending time with you won't be an unpleasant chore."

Whoa with the flattery there, buddy. But she supposed it was a compliment of sorts. He didn't want to date her, but he wouldn't mind fake dating her. What an honor.

"Look," Boone said, glancing at the clock on the dash. "You don't have to make up your mind about everything right this second. Come to the party with me tonight and see how it goes. If you hate it, you don't have to do anything else."

"Okay," she said. "As long as your motivations aren't nefarious, I'm game." Of course she was. There was never any real possibility of her turning him down.

He lifted a brow. "Nefarious?"

"Just promise me I'm not going to get trafficked at this party or tricked into joining a cult. And no pyramid schemes either. I'm not buying into any diet plans, I'm telling you that right now."

A smile quirked his lips, but when he spoke his voice was solemn. "I promise I won't let anything happen to you against your will."

"So what should I wear to this party? How fancy is it?"

"Not fancy at all."

"Okay, but what does that mean in real people world? Imagine if you didn't have a closet full of designer clothes custom-tailored to make you look like a sex god. Then what would you tell me to wear?"

The skin around his blue eyes crinkled. "You think I look like a sex god?"

"Stop trying to get me to stroke your ego and answer the question." Eve's face was not turning red. That was someone else.

"Honestly, what you're wearing is fine."

She looked down at her milk-spattered T-shirt and thread-bare jeans, then back up at Boone. "Now I know you're lying. Am I being set up? This isn't some kind of freaky ritual sacri-fice is it? Just so you know, I'm not a virgin, so I'm no good for throwing into volcanos."

"So noted," he said with a laugh. "But seriously, whatever you want to wear is fine. The dragon my satanic cult will be feeding you to isn't picky about fashion."

"Ha ha," she replied dryly, biting back a smile. "What will you be wearing? Like a bespoke Valentino suit or something I assume?"

"I'm flattered you think I own one of those, but I'll be

wearing jeans and a button-down shirt. Does that make you feel better?"

"A little. I still think I'm being punked though."

The smile that broke over his face was so impossibly beautiful it punched her right in the heart. "Guess you'll have to wait until tonight to find out."

My god, this was a terrible idea. Eve was going to be in so much trouble.

She couldn't wait.

five

BOONE WAS FIFTEEN MINUTES LATE. Eve had about decided the whole thing had been a practical joke after all when his Camaro finally pulled into the parking lot at Antidote. She'd told him to pick her up there so she wouldn't have to wait around for him at her apartment and risk seeing Becca.

Eve had been overjoyed to find the apartment empty when she'd stopped off at home after work. She'd only stuck around long enough to take the fastest shower of her life, throw on a change of clothes, and grab her makeup bag before calling an Uber to get her the hell away from there.

"You look gorgeous," Boone said when she slid into the passenger seat.

"Thanks," she replied with a shy smile.

"Hey, did you just take a compliment?" He held his fist out for a bump. "Well done. I'm proud of you."

She scowled as she felt her cheeks heat, but still supplied the requested fist bump rather than leave the man hanging. "Making a big deal about it doesn't make me feel any less self-conscious, just FYI."

"Right. Sorry. Forget I said anything." Flashing an irresistible grin, he made a zipping motion across his lips.

As promised, Boone was wearing a plain black button-down shirt and dark wash jeans that looked even more expensive than the ones he'd been wearing earlier in the day. His Converse had been replaced by a pair of black ankle boots, and his hair was slicked back to tame the shagginess. The overall effect was stupidly hot.

Forcing herself to stop ogling him, Eve turned her face to the window as he pulled out of the parking lot. The setting sun had painted the sky in shades of orange and purple that bathed everything in a rosy glow. As she gazed at the sky, she attempted to find her zen. Tonight was actually happening. Until she'd seen Boone's car pull up, she hadn't quite believed it.

"I'm assuming from the wardrobe change that you've been home," Boone said. "How'd it go with your roommate? You okay?"

"She wasn't there."

"You haven't talked to her at all?"

"Nope." Eve had finally turned her phone back on. Becca had sent a series of increasingly worried-sounding texts throughout the day, apologizing and asking if Eve was okay. As if she possibly could be after what Becca had done.

Eve hadn't texted her back yet. She'd thought about it and had stared at her phone for a good twenty minutes trying to come up with some kind of response. But when it came down to it, she didn't have any idea what to say.

"What about your boyfriend?" Boone asked.

"Also nope."

There'd been nothing at all from Vince yet. He might not have any idea Eve had seen the sex tape unless Becca had told him.

Eve wondered how long it would take him to notice she'd

stopped talking to him. Maybe she could ghost both him and Becca. Slip away like a thief in the night and never have to speak to either of them again. Wouldn't that be nice?

Boone was frowning. "Don't you think you should—"

"If it's all right, I'd rather not talk about it." Two could play the *not wanting to answer personal questions* game. So there.

"Sure," he said, throwing a worried look her way. "Whatever you want."

"Thank you."

His thumbs drummed on the steering wheel as traffic edged forward. "How was your shift at your second job?"

"Not bad. I didn't get peed on or thrown up on today."

"Sounds like a win."

"What about you?" she asked. "What did you do this afternoon?"

He grunted. "Not much."

"You know, it's going to be hard to convince people we're in a relationship if I don't know anything about your day-to-day life."

His mouth tightened as he checked his blind spot before changing lanes. "I read some scripts, worked out, took a shower, then watched a little TV. Nothing groundbreaking to report."

"What kind of scripts?"

"Stuff my agent sends me to consider for future projects."

"Anything good?"

"No," he said tersely and turned up the music.

Conversation over, apparently. So far, this fake date was not going so great.

They passed the next ten minutes in silence. Eve finally spoke as they were wending their way through one of the more exclusive parts of Los Feliz. "Are there going to be a lot of celebrities at this party?"

"A few, maybe."

"But it'll be all rich people, I'm guessing."

Boone glanced over at her. "There's no reason to be nervous."

"I'm not nervous."

He cast a pointed look at her knee, which was bouncing up and down like a jackhammer.

She crossed her legs and clutched her purse. "I had too much caffeine while I was waiting at the coffee shop."

He parallel parked between a Ferrari and a Mercedes G-Wagon on a winding street in the hills below Griffith Park. Somewhere not far to the northwest loomed the Hollywood sign, blocked from view by the trees.

It was nearly full dark by then, and a smattering of stars winked overhead when Eve got out of the car. She could only see tiny glimpses of the lit-up mansions hidden behind the lush greenery lining the quiet street. Très private. Très upscale. Très exclusive.

"Do we need to go over our story?" she asked when Boone came around to her side of the car.

He frowned as he shut her door for her. "What story?"

"How we met. Who I'm supposed to be."

"You're just you. I'm just me. We met how we met. No reason to complicate things unnecessarily." A playful smirk curved the corner of his mouth. "Although I guess we could try role-playing if that's something you're into."

Eve wasn't impressed by his teasing-slash-flirting-slash-whatever the fuck it was that he was doing. "I'm serious."

Back to a frown. "Okay."

"I don't want to be anyone's joke."

His frown got even deeper. "What does that mean?"

"It means I still don't get why you'd want to bring a barista as your date to a swanky party in the hills." They were surrounded by ten-million-dollar houses, and she was wearing a twenty-dollar shirt from Target. It didn't compute.

"Eve." The softness with which he said her name sent goose bumps shivering down her arms. "You're not a joke to me."

She swallowed, flustered by the intensity of his gaze. His eyes were so pretty, even in the half-light of evening, it almost hurt to look at them.

"I'm not going to let anything bad happen to you. You can trust me on that, okay?"

His solemn expression went a long way to putting her anxiety to rest. Not all of her anxiety, because it was always going to be there, lurking in the back of her mind. But at least she could believe he wasn't out to make a fool of her

She gave him a nod. "Okay."

When he smiled, she smiled back. Everything was going to be all right. Better than all right. She was living a dream come true—or at least a simulated version of a dream come true. Which was still way more than she'd ever expected. Time to chill out and enjoy it.

Boone's thumb touched the corner of her mouth. "There's that gorgeous smile."

And just like that, Eve was drowning in self-consciousness. Her head dipped down as she plucked at the hem of her blouse.

He let out a sigh. "How about we both try to relax and have a good time tonight? If at any point you're not having fun, all you have to do is say the word and I'll take you home. Deal?"

"Deal." She tried to smile again so he wouldn't think she was unhappy to be there.

"Come on." He slipped his hand into hers. His skin was warm and slightly callused, and his fingers squeezed hers gently as he led her down the sidewalk.

They turned up a narrow front walk so surrounded by vegetation Eve hadn't realized it was there until they were right on top of it. A half flight of steps led up from the street to a white brick wall with a paneled door set in it.

After pressing a button on the intercom, Boone raised a quizzical eyebrow at her. "You good?"

Eve nodded, too distracted by the fact that he was holding her hand to answer with actual words.

"Who the hell are you?" demanded a tinny male voice through the intercom speaker.

Boone presented his middle finger to the security camera. "Let me in, asshole."

The door latch clicked, and he pushed it open. More front walk bisected a small patch of lawn in front of an enormous European-style house. As they approached the arched front door, it opened to reveal Eve's first celebrity sighting of the night.

Griffin Beach, star of *Las Vegas General*, the last two *Trouble-makers* movies, and the summer's big Jerry Duncan blockbuster, grinned at them from the doorway. "Goddamn, you actually showed up! I owe Alice twenty bucks."

"I told you I would." Boone's hand slipped out of Eve's as he stepped forward to accept a back-pounding hug from the man whose face was currently plastered on billboards all over town.

Eve hung back, absorbing the fact that Boone was not only friends with Griffin Beach, but had brought her to a party at his house. All of which was information he might have shared with her before they got here.

Whatever. She could handle this. All she had to do was put on her customer service face and pretend she wasn't affected by the glamour and fame.

When the two men separated, Griffin Beach turned to Eve with an openly curious and slightly surprised look. "Hi," he said, flashing a dazzling movie star smile. "I'm Griffin."

Boone's arm slipped around Eve's shoulders, pulling her

against him. The shock of making contact with his body just about annihilated her composure. They were close enough that she could smell his skin and feel his body heat radiating off him like sunshine. "This is Eve," he said, showing her off as though they were a real couple. Which was the whole reason she was here, but it still felt weird as heck.

Operating on autopilot, she stuck her hand out at Griffin. "Nice to meet you."

His smile beamed even brighter as they shook. "The pleasure's mine, I promise you." She seriously doubted that, but the man was such a good actor he looked for all the world like he meant it. He kept hold of her hand as he led her into the house, forcing her to leave the comfort of Boone's side. Alas. "Come on in."

A murmur of voices and music beckoned from the room beyond the bright, spacious entry hall. As Griffin shut the front door, a small scruffy dog came skittering across the polished wood floor and launched itself at Boone's legs.

"Hey there, buddy." Boone bent to scratch the dog's head as it pawed at his knees. "Who's a good boy who missed me?"

"This is Taco," Griffin explained when the dog came over to sniff Eve's foot. She squatted down to let Taco nose the back of her hand, and he shoved his head into her palm. "He's real slow to warm up to people, as you can see."

"Boone!" Eve looked up as a cute young blonde woman threw herself into his arms. "I'm so glad you're here."

"Hey, Doc." Boone's face split into a grin as he gave her a warm hug. A *very* warm hug. That was not jealousy burning in Eve's stomach. It was probably hunger.

"Alice, quit hugging that loser and come greet Eve," Griffin said. "Boone's *date.*"

Alice drew back, lifting her eyebrows as she looked at Boone in surprise. "You're dating again?"

"This is Eve," Boone said in lieu of answering her question. "Eve, meet Griffin's girlfriend, Alice."

"Hi!" Alice threw her arms around Eve in a hug nearly as enthusiastic as the one she'd given Boone.

Okay, then. "Nice to meet you," Eve said. "You have a lovely home."

"Oh my gosh, isn't it ridiculous?" Alice stared around like she couldn't believe she lived there. She was strikingly pretty, but without the perfect symmetry Eve had come to associate with celebrity faces. Her simple knit top and denim capris made Eve feel more comfortable about her own wardrobe. "Let's go get you fixed up with a drink." Alice hooked her arm through Eve's and dragged her away, leaving the men behind.

Eve threw a panicked looked over her shoulder, and Boone gave her a thumbs-up. Great. Apparently she was on her own.

When he'd said there'd "maybe" be "a few" celebrities at the party, apparently what he'd meant was famous faces every direction you looked. As Alice swept her past the guests mingling in the stylishly furnished living room, Eve recognized several of Griffin's former TV castmates, as well as a few big-name film stars, including an Oscar nominee. *Holy shit.*

"How long have you and Boone been together?" Alice asked as she led Eve into a gleaming white kitchen stocked with professional-grade stainless steel appliances.

"Oh, we just…" Eve lost her train of thought when she recognized action star Chuck Hammer standing at the kitchen island mixing drinks. Unlike a lot of actors, who were smaller in real life than they appeared on-screen, Chuck was absolutely massive in person, like a six-and-a-half-foot wall built of bulging muscles.

"You what?" Alice prompted, gazing expectantly at Eve.

"Oh, um, this is only our second date," she said, sticking close to the truth like Boone had suggested. If you counted their lunch date today, it almost wasn't a lie. "But we've known each other for a few weeks." Technically sort of the truth.

"Really?" Alice seemed intrigued by this answer. "I can't wait to hear how you met. But first, what can I get you to drink? We've got wine, beer, and sparkling water in a rainbow of flavors. Or we can have Chuck make you one of his martinis." Alice flicked her wrist at the former professional wrestler turned blockbuster movie star. "Eve, this is Chuck. Chuck, Eve."

"Hi," Eve said, trying not to gape. He'd only starred in at least two dozen megahit action flicks. She'd seen some of his movies so many times she could recite them by heart.

"Hey there." Chuck's deep, rumbling voice sounded exactly like it did in his movies, but he looked different out of character. A pair of glasses with cool fashion frames gave him a softer, more intellectual look than the brutes he typically played on-screen, and his trademark shaved head was covered in a short layer of salt-and-pepper stubble that matched the stubble on his unbelievably square jaw. The man had to be in his fifties by now, but he was a stone-cold fox. He knew it too, based on the seductive smile he was giving Eve.

Alice rolled her eyes. "Put your sex-me-up face away, Chuck. She's here with Boone."

Chuck pressed a hand to his heart with an aggrieved expression. "Alice, sweetheart, how many times do I have to tell you this is just my regular face? You know I'm nothing if not a gentleman."

"It's true," Alice said to Eve. "Underneath the swagger he's all teddy bear."

"Don't tell anyone," Chuck murmured, his eyes lit with mischief. "I've got a reputation to maintain in this town."

"Your secret's safe with me," Eve promised giddily.

Chuck beamed a broad, friendly smile at her. "Eve, my new good friend, would you care for a martini?"

"I don't know. I've never had one before."

"Never had a martini?" Clucking his tongue, he filled a cocktail glass and presented it to her. "Taste this. See what you think."

Being this close to Chuck was like standing in the shadow of a skyscraper. Just looking up at his face gave Eve a crick in her neck. She took a sip of the martini and tried not to wince when it burned her throat. "It's strong. But delicious."

"Of course it is." Chuck gifted her with a cheesy wink. "Just like me."

She laughed, and he laughed along with her. Eve couldn't believe she was at Griffin Beach's house right now talking to Chuck freaking Hammer. What a day she was having.

"Quit hitting on my girl, Hammer." Boone strolled into the kitchen with a smile and exchanged a hearty handshake with Chuck.

"Are you really here with this scrub?" Chuck asked Eve as he tried to ruffle Boone's hair.

Ducking away from Chuck's hand, Boone sidled up to Eve and draped an arm around her shoulders. He lifted his eyebrows at her, waiting for her to answer Chuck's question.

"I am," she confirmed before cheerily flashing Chuck her flirtiest smile. "At least for now."

"Ouch!" Boone mimed being shot in the heart. "Clearly I need to up my game."

Chuck clapped him on the shoulder. "Good to see you, little buddy. And Eve, it was a genuine pleasure to make your acquaintance." He gave her another one of his sex-me-up smiles on his way out of the kitchen. "You come and find me when you're ready to trade up to a real man."

"Boone, you want a beer?" Alice asked from the fridge.

"Yes, please, and one for Griff," he called over his shoulder. When his gaze settled on Eve, his smile dimmed a little. "Would you really trade me in for Chuck Hammer?"

She couldn't tell if he was serious or still playing around. "No," she said truthfully. "Muscleheads aren't my type."

The way his smile lit back up made her stomach erupt in flutters.

"Here." Alice thrust two beer bottles at Boone.

His arm dropped away from Eve's shoulders. Too bad yet again. She was seriously enjoying the cuddling part of this whole pretend dating thing. Greatest job perk ever.

"Are you good with the martini?" Alice asked Eve. "You don't have to drink it if you'd rather have something else."

"No, I like it." Eve took another sip. It made her feel like a real adult, which was a nice change from the rest of her life.

When she lowered her glass, she caught Boone watching her with an odd expression she didn't trust herself to think too hard about. Feeling self-conscious, she licked martini off her upper lip.

He swallowed and looked away. "I'm gonna take Griffin his beer," he announced, leaving Eve on her own again to fend for herself in a house full of celebrities.

Sure, fine. No problem. She could handle this without him.

Hopefully.

six

BOONE WATCHED Eve through the open French doors
as he stood by the grill in the outdoor kitchen. She was still
inside chatting with Alice. The two of them seemed to be
hitting it off as well as he'd hoped.

In the twenty minutes since they'd arrived, he'd seen Eve
smile—her real smile, not the fake one she used with customers
—more than all the times before this put together. He was glad
he'd brought her tonight and glad she'd agreed to come,
despite her obvious nervousness. Maybe this whole pretend
relationship thing wouldn't be so bad after all.

"Dude, I asked you a question."

Boone dragged his attention back to Griffin. "Sorry, what?"

"I asked what you've been doing with yourself the last
month." He pulled a smirk as he shot a look inside the house.
"But I think maybe I can guess."

Boone didn't correct Griffin's assumption. Let him think
he'd been distracted by a woman. Maybe it would get him off
Boone's back.

"She seems nice," Griffin said, cocking his head at Eve.

"She is nice," Boone agreed.

"How'd you meet?"

"She's a barista at the coffee shop I've been going to."

Griffin turned a raised eyebrow on him. "Really?"

Boone nodded as he lifted his beer to his lips. "Really."

"Is she the reason we've barely seen you since you've been in town?"

A pang of guilt hit Boone in the pit of the stomach, and he looked down with a wince. "I'm sorry about that."

Things had been strained between him and Griffin lately. Ever since they'd had that temporary falling-out last year. It was entirely Boone's fault. Griffin had been trying to look out for him, and Boone was the one who'd gotten pissed off and refused to speak to his best friend for two months. That was how long it had taken for Boone to realize Griffin had been right. He'd since apologized and they'd allegedly patched things up, but the distance between them still made itself felt— no matter how much they tried to act like things were all good now.

"Are you?" Griffin asked quietly. "Thought you might be avoiding me."

Now Boone really did feel like shit. He *had* been avoiding him, but not for the reason Griff probably thought. Boone had been ducking almost everyone's calls since he'd been back in LA.

Unfortunately, Griffin knew him far too well. The more time Boone spent around him, the harder it would be to pretend he was fine. Griffin would see through his facade eventually, and then he'd want to help, because that was what Griffin did. Only Boone didn't want to be fixed. He just wanted to be left alone.

"It's not that," Boone said. "I've just been—"

"Licking your wounds?"

"Trying to keep my head down and enjoy having time off

for the first time in ten goddamn years. I've had to relearn how to relax."

Griffin gave him a dubious look. "This is supposed to be you relaxed?"

"It's a work in progress," Boone replied.

"Speaking of keeping your head down…how are you handling all the shit in the press?"

A scowl twisted Boone's face. This was exactly why he'd been keeping to himself. People always wanted to *talk* about things. "I'm trying not to think about it."

"Yeah?" Griffin let out a wry snort. "How's that working out?"

"Pretty well until you brought it up just now."

Griffin eyed him as he sipped his beer. "How's Simone holding up?"

"Not great." Boone looked away with a scowl. "That walking hemorrhoid she married is doing his damnedest to make this as ugly as he can and doesn't seem to care how it might be affecting their son."

The irony of the situation only made Boone angrier. Simone's husband had been stepping out on her for most of their marriage, yet she was the one taking heat for having an affair when she'd always been faithful to the sorry asshole. Boone had only been at her house that night to support a friend whose marriage was falling apart. But nobody seemed to give a fuck about the truth. They'd rather demonize a woman over one alleged infraction and let the man with a long history of womanizing off scot-free.

"Some people don't deserve to be fathers." Griffin frowned as he lifted the lid on the grill, eyeballed the kebabs, and closed it again. "I assume you've heard the latest garbage people are spreading now? About her son being yours?"

"Can we please not talk about that shit?" Boone said irritably. "I'm begging you."

Griffin pressed his lips together. "Yeah, okay."

This was the problem with being around Griffin. Boone loved the guy, truly, but he always wanted to talk everything out these days. And he got that wounded look on his face if Boone didn't want to bare his soul.

Was it any wonder Boone hadn't wanted to hang out with anyone when all people seemed to do was bring up subjects he didn't want to talk about and asked him eight million times if he was okay?

Boone sighed and tried to steer the conversation onto a more pleasant subject. "How's the new house working out?"

"It's good." Griffin shrugged. "We both miss the old place, but the extra security is worth the peace of mind."

They'd moved out of Griffin's smaller Studio City house after an overly enthusiastic fan had broken in a few months back. The alarm company had found the guy hiding in their bedroom closet when they showed up to investigate the tripped alarm. Boone was just glad no one had been home at the time. He couldn't even think about what might have happened otherwise. Understandably, Griffin had decided it was time to relocate to a more secure, gated property after that.

Boone's gaze wandered into the dining room, where Alice and Eve were staging a dual assault on the buffet. Alice looked happy and relaxed tonight, but as he knew all too well, you could never tell what was really going on with people beneath the surface.

"Alice still having nightmares?" he asked Griffin.

"No, but I am."

Boone's head jerked toward his friend.

"Kidding," Griffin said with a halfhearted grin.

"*Are* you kidding?"

"Well, no," he admitted. "But it's fine. It's only been a few nightmares." He scratched the back of his head. "I can't stop thinking about what could have happened if the guy hadn't tripped the alarm and Alice had come home with him still in the house. That kind of thing'll give anybody nightmares."

Boone felt yet another stab of guilt. He'd been so wrapped up in his own problems, he hadn't considered that Griff might have needed him. "I really am sorry I haven't been around more, man."

"It's okay." Griffin waved away his apology. "You're here now. That's what matters."

"Yeah."

Griffin gave him a long look. "Are you sure you're doing all right? I know the breakup was rough, and then you lost that part because of all the bad press. I've been worried about you spending so much time alone."

"I'm hanging in there." Boone forced his jaw to unclench as his gaze flicked toward Eve again. "It'll blow over eventually."

Or it wouldn't, and his dreams of extending his career beyond *Abnormal Investigations* would go up in a puff of smoke. Easy come, easy go.

"But maybe you haven't been spending that much time alone after all?" Griffin elbowed him with a grin. "What's the deal with you and this girl? Is it serious?"

"It's new," Boone said vaguely. "We'll have to see how it goes."

He didn't feel as bad as he should about lying to Griffin about Eve. If Griff knew the truth, Boone would never hear the fucking end of it. Not after Griffin had been pressured into a PR romance of his own last year, and it had come close to costing him his relationship with Alice. Understandably, the guy had some strong negative feelings about it now.

Boone shared a lot of those negative feelings, but desperate times and all that. If it had only been a matter of his own image, he never would have agreed to it. He was doing this to help Simone as much as himself. The more he could do to change the conversation away from those damn photos, the easier it would make things for her.

"But you like her," Griffin said, still talking about Eve. "I can tell."

"Yeah, I like her," Boone admitted. That wasn't a lie, at least.

But it didn't matter how much he liked her. Getting involved wasn't an option. He couldn't risk losing himself the way he had with Gemma. The thought of giving anyone that much power over him again made his blood run cold.

This thing with Eve was a business arrangement. Plain and simple. Assuming he could convince her to let him pay her for her trouble. As long as he was paying her, the employer/employee line between them would be clear, and there'd be no question of crossing it.

If it worked, everybody would come out ahead. Eve would improve his image, and she'd earn enough money to change her life. He'd make sure of that. If their ruse had the added bonus of convincing Boone's friends he'd bounced back from his breakup with Gemma, all the better.

Truth be told, he hadn't been a hundred percent sold on the arrangement when he'd first invited Eve to lunch today. But now that he'd spent more time with her and seen her around his friends, he knew she was the right choice.

He really did like her. Hell, if he'd met her a few years ago, then maybe…

No.

There was no point in thinking about that. He was different now. *Everything* was different. It was what it was. He was still too much of a fucking mess, and Eve sure as hell deserved better than that.

But maybe they could get to be friends, at least. He'd like that a lot. He just needed to be careful not to get carried away. No getting unnecessarily attached.

And no letting Eve get attached either. He didn't want her to be hurt when he went back to Vancouver next month.

ALICE WAS COOL, EVE HAD DECIDED. SHE WAS UNDERSTANDABLY curious about Eve and had peppered her with questions while they grazed at the impressive spread laid out on the dining room table. But her interrogation had seemed friendly rather than suspicious or judgmental, and she'd been just as happy to answer questions about herself and Griffin. Eve had found her easy to talk to, although she'd been a bit intimidated to find out Alice was a PhD data scientist—hence why Boone had called her Doc.

No one else at the party seemed to be eating anything, so they had the buffet all to themselves. Mini ham and cheese biscuits, honey fried chicken sliders, tiny empanadas, an assortment of tapenades and bruschettas on toasted crostini, not to mention a giant charcuterie board and huge selection of bite-size desserts—tiny food was the best. Everything tasted better when it was fun-sized.

After they'd finished piling their plates with as much food as they could carry, Eve followed Alice outside to find the guys. The backyard was even more stunning than the inside of their house. Multiple decks and balconies overlooked a stonescaped pool that glowed with color-changing lights, the whole property surrounded by a privacy screen of foliage that made it feel like its own little tropical world. A gentle murmur of conversation and laughter floated above the music playing from hidden speakers. A small group of people had gathered around a fire pit, while others mingled along the edge of the pool sipping drinks.

Griffin and Boone were over at the grill by themselves, and

both of them were frowning. Whatever they were talking about looked intense.

"We come bearing food," Alice announced loudly as she approached.

The two men turned toward them, quickly affixing smiles on their faces. Eve's stomach tightened when Boone's eyes found hers. There was a hollow sort of joylessness about him, despite his smile. It triggered the strongest urge to give him a hug.

"Is that for me?" he asked, tipping his chin at the plate in her hand.

"It's for us to share," she corrected. "Half those desserts are mine, buddy."

"No one's eating the food," Alice complained as she tucked herself under Griffin's arm.

"I'm eating it," Eve said, picking up a bacon-wrapped date. "It's freaking delicious."

Griffin looked pleased. "I like her," he said to Boone. "You should bring her around a lot more."

"You like anyone you can feed," Boone replied as he plucked a piece of cheese off Alice's plate.

"You're wasting your time grilling all that meat," Alice told Griffin.

He looked offended. "Grilling meat is never a waste of time. Chuck will eat it if no one else will."

"How many calories do you think that guy has to consume a day?" Boone mused as he helped himself to a fried chicken slider.

"Between four and six thousand spread over seven meals," Griffin replied. "I've seen him put away a ten-egg omelet in one sitting."

Boone whistled. "Even I can't eat that much."

"These are all done," Griffin announced as he pulled the

skewers off the grill and stacked them on platters. "Can you help me carry them inside, Doc?"

"I can do it," Boone offered, but Griffin shook his head.

"You two sit and chill," he ordered. "We'll be right back."

Boone snagged some of the shish kebabs before Griffin took them away. Balancing them on Eve's plate, he guided her over to a nearby outdoor sofa.

As soon as they sat down, Griffin's dog jumped up next to Eve. "Is he allowed to be up here?" she asked Boone as she ruffled Taco's ears. "I don't want to get him in trouble."

"It's fine." Boone fed the dog a piece of chicken from one of the skewers. "Watch out though. If he sees an opening, he will a thousand percent stick his tongue in your mouth without consent."

"Are you a French kisser?" Eve cooed, scritching Taco's neck with both hands. "I'll bet you're a real Casanova."

"You having an okay time so far?" Boone asked between bites of kebab.

She shot him a smile. "Better than okay."

"I'm glad." He didn't seem all that glad. He seemed down. Whenever he let his smile slip, she could see tension in the lines of his face.

"Are *you* having a good time?"

He looked away as he stuffed more kebab in his mouth. "Sure."

Eve plucked a meringue off the plate. It melted on her tongue like lavender-flavored cotton candy. Exquisite. "It's just I got the feeling you didn't particularly want to come tonight."

"It's complicated," was all Boone said. The man was sealed tight as a safe.

"I thought that might be why you wanted me to come with you tonight. As a buffer or a distraction or something."

"That's not…" Boone's mouth pulled tight. He shook his head, caught out. "…entirely wrong."

"It's okay. I don't mind. We can be each other's distraction today." She was itching to ask him what he needed a distraction from, but everything about his body language begged her not to. Instead, she took pity on him and changed the subject. "Alice and Griffin seem great."

"They are." Boone was putting away the kebabs like he hadn't eaten for days, despite the giant burrito she'd watched him inhale at lunch.

"How'd they'd meet anyway?" A brainy data scientist and a movie star seemed an unlikely pairing. They couldn't possibly run in the same social circles.

"You should ask them when they come back."

Eve pursed her lips in annoyance. "You're not going to tell me?"

Boone offered a cryptic smile as he bit a chunk of meat off the skewer. "It's better when they tell the story."

After Taco jumped down to go beg someone else for affection, Eve rubbed her hands on her jeans. "I didn't realize you knew Griffin Beach. Alice said you're best friends."

Another one of those odd shadows flickered across Boone's expression. "We've known each other since he first moved to LA. Back before either of us were anybody."

"But you didn't want to come to his party."

He turned away from her to set the plate on the table next to him. "Like I said, it's complicated."

Eve sighed and leaned back, swinging her legs in front of her. "I'm afraid to go back to my apartment and face my roommate, so there's not going to be any judgment coming from my direction."

As Boone's pale blue eyes swept over her face, they looked as desolate and unreachable as a pair of distant moons. His gaze flicked down to her arms with a frown. "You're cold."

"I'm okay."

"You're all goose bumpy. Come here." Draping an arm

around her, he hauled her against his side. Eve had no choice but to rest her head on his shoulder and snuggle into his warmth. What a tragedy.

He smelled incredible, like rainwater and evergreen trees with a hint of something spicy she couldn't put her finger on. Whatever it was, she couldn't get enough. It was taking all her willpower not to press her nose into his shirt and huff him like a Sharpie.

His palm smoothed up and down her arm, leaving even more goose bumps in its wake. "Better?"

The best. She'd just discovered her new favorite place on earth: tucked into Boone's arms. "Yes. Thank you."

After a hesitation, she rested her hand on his stomach. She wasn't trying to cop a feel, although she was certainly appreciating the firm muscle she could feel through his shirt. It just happened to be the most comfortable place to put her hand in their current position.

He covered it with his. "Your hand's like ice. You want me to ask Alice to loan you a sweater?"

"No, I'm fine."

Boone was the best sweater in the world. She wouldn't trade him for even the most luxurious cashmere money could buy. If she could have swaddled herself in him like a baby burrito, she would have immediately fallen into happy unconsciousness.

He rubbed her fingers to chafe more warmth into them. "The stuff between me and Griffin isn't anything like what Becca did to you."

"What's it like?"

"Me being a dumbass."

It wasn't exactly an explanation, but at least he hadn't shut the door completely. Yay for progress. "I seriously doubt that," she said.

"You shouldn't. I can be a pretty big dumbass when I want to be."

"Maybe you should consider not being a dumbass, then."

A ghost of a smile tugged at the corner of his mouth. "I'll give it some thought."

He released her hand to reach for his beer. She watched his throat move as he swallowed. She was so close she could hear the *glug glug*. He set the beer back down and slid his fingers between hers again.

Eve attempted to recall the last time she'd felt this happy, and came up with a whole lot of nothing. Pretty sad that she was having more fun on a fake date than she'd had doing anything real in a long time.

"This isn't at all what I expected from a Hollywood party," she commented as her gaze traveled over the other party guests outside.

"What'd you expect?" Boone asked, idly toying with the rings on her fingers.

"Nothing this relaxed and low-key. There's nary a solid gold champagne fountain in sight."

Another near smile tugged at his perfect lips. "I'll tell Griff he needs to get one for the next party."

"What I want to know is, where are all the strippers and blow? The lavish costumes and illegal exotic animals? The wild, drug-fueled antics? And does the orgy start later or…"

Boone snorted in amusement. "It's not that kind of party."

"Have you been to parties like that?" For all she knew, that was more his speed. Although she wasn't entirely sure she wanted to know if it was.

"A few. I wouldn't bring you to one of those though." His fingertips stroked the back of her hand.

"Why not?"

"Because you're too sweet."

Eve couldn't decide if that was a compliment or not. "You don't think I can handle it?"

He tipped his head back as his eyebrows twitched upward. "Would you want to go to a party like that?"

"Not really." That probably made her uncool, but that kind of stuff didn't sound like much fun to her.

"Me neither. I hate that shit." Boone turned his head away to yawn into his other shoulder. Not even ten o'clock and he was getting sleepy.

That was something else they had in common. Thanks to working the opening shift at the coffee shop, most nights Eve was out like a light by now. Both Vince and Becca had accused her of being a party pooper numerous times and complained about her propensity for nodding off while she was watching TV. As if it was Eve's fault she had to be up at five a.m. for work.

Not tonight though. Tonight she felt wide-awake. As alert as if she'd downed a gallon of coffee, but without the accompanying shakes and jitters. It must be the excitement of where she was and who she was with. A natural contact high from being with Boone.

She traced the calluses on his palm as she gazed across the pool. "Is that Kimberleigh Cress over there?"

He craned his neck to look. "Yep."

"Didn't she and Griffin used to date?"

"It's complicated."

Eve huffed in exasperation. "A lot of stuff is complicated, isn't it?"

Boone grunted. "Remember when I told you PR stunt relationships are common?"

Her eyes widened. "Is that what that was?"

Lines furrowed his brow as he nodded. "But that's not for spreading around, right?"

"No, of course not. We're inside the cone of silence. Everything I see and hear stays between us."

"Don't bring it up around Griff or Alice either. It's a pretty sore subject."

"Why?" Eve was excited to have finally gotten something resembling an answer out of Boone. "And why is Kimberleigh here, then?"

"It wasn't because of anything Kimberleigh did. They're all friends now and everything's fine." He shrugged as he fiddled with Eve's rings some more. "Griff and Alice started dating while he was pretending to be in a relationship with Kimberleigh, and I guess the strain of keeping it secret and all the publicity got to be too much. They even broke up over it for a while."

"Oh, wow. Is that why you didn't want to tell them the truth about us?"

"Partially." Boone's gusty sigh sounded dispirited. The flat, stony look on his face didn't tell her much either. It wasn't a happy look, whatever it was about.

"You know, if you want to leave, you could blame it on me. I'm happy to fake excruciating menstrual cramps if it would help you out."

Snorting softly, he gave her hand an appreciative squeeze. "I don't want to leave yet. But I appreciate the offer."

Eve snuggled into the crook of his neck to conceal her smile. Also possibly to inhale some more of his intoxicating scent, but she'd deny it under questioning. "Let me know if you change your mind. I'm here for you, partner."

Boone rested his head against hers and breathed in slowly. She could almost swear he was sniffing her hair, which made her feel better about how badly she wanted to snort him like a truffle-hunting pig. "You make a nice distraction," he murmured as he twined their fingers together.

Eve's chest felt like it was going to burst open and spill

glitter and rainbows everywhere. Possibly a few kittens and an edible bouquet as well.

"Don't you two look cozy," Alice declared. She stuck a martini in front of Eve's face. "Here. Chuck told me to give this to you."

Boone lifted his head and released Eve's hand so she could take the drink. Leaning back, he peered at her from beneath an arched eyebrow. "Sure you don't want to dump me for Chuck Hammer?"

"Positive."

The corners of his mouth turned up. "Good."

While Griffin and Alice curled up on the love seat across from them, Boone snagged his half-empty beer off the table and settled back with a mischievous smile on his lips. "Eve told me she's disappointed by your party."

"Hey!" She elbowed him in the ribs. "That is *not* what I said."

"Right. Sorry." Boone nodded in faux solemnity. "She said it was sadly lacking in orgies."

"Oh my god!" Eve's face burned with embarrassment as Alice and Griffin cracked up. But she didn't mind because Boone was laughing too, and his face was lit up like someone had plugged him into an outlet. It was such a pleasure to see all the tension replaced by laugh lines, she didn't mind being teased. She wished she could make him laugh like that all the time.

Boone got Griffin and Alice to tell Eve how they'd met, which was predictably adorable. But the best part was how warm Boone's smile got as he listened, jumping in to add his own commentary and tease Griffin at every opportunity.

Whatever trouble might lie between the two of them, there was obviously tons of affection too. They completed each other's sentences like an old married couple, especially once they started reminiscing about the old days when they'd roomed together as struggling actors. For the first time that night, Boone looked genuinely happy to be there.

As they were strolling down memory lane, Eve's phone began vibrating in her pocket, puncturing her pleasant mood. Especially when she saw the caller's name on the screen.

Vince.

More than anything, she wanted to turn her phone off and stay cuddled up with Boone. But hiding from her problems wouldn't make them go away. She might not be ready to deal with Becca yet, but Vince would be easier. Might as well rip the Band-Aid off and get it over with.

"Everything all right?" Boone asked.

Eve turned her phone so he could see the incoming call on the screen.

"You gonna take it?"

She nodded. "I need to."

His hand squeezed the back of her neck as he bent his head to whisper in her ear. "You've got this. Give him hell, gorgeous."

seven

A SUDDEN CHILL shivered through Boone when Eve left his side. The cool night air shocked his skin everywhere she'd been touching him, leaving an imprint of her body on his.

"Everything all right with her?" Griffin asked.

Boone nodded as he watched Eve walk to the far side of the pool to take the call from her boyfriend—soon to be ex-boyfriend, hopefully. "It's just an unpleasant conversation she has to have. She'll be fine."

She would be. He knew that. Still, he had the strongest urge to follow her, just to make sure.

Except it wasn't his business. Not really. He shouldn't be this invested in Eve's personal life.

Reluctantly, he forced himself to turn away from her and found Alice watching him with a knowing smile.

"I really like Eve. She's great."

"She likes you too."

Alice's smile grew brighter. "I'm thinking I might check out the coffee shop where she works. Which one is it again?"

"Antidote on Ventura. They make a great cappuccino there."

"Maybe I'll ask her to lunch sometime." She seemed to be daring him to object. "You wouldn't mind, would you? If I made her my friend."

"You should do that," he said, meaning it. "She could use some friends who don't suck."

Alice gave him a curious look, but he didn't elaborate. It wasn't his tale to share.

"You sure she's okay?" Griffin asked, staring past Boone's shoulder. "She looks upset."

Boone swung his head around. Eve was pacing back and forth with her hand clenched in a tight fist at her side. What he could see of her face was twisted in anger as she spoke into the phone. The sound of her raised voice floated across the pool, but not clearly enough to make out the words.

"Maybe I should go check on her," he said, getting to his feet.

As he approached, Eve's voice became clearer. "I don't care if it was just the one time, Vince. You fucking betrayed me! Once is all you get to do that."

She spun around at the sound of Boone's footsteps behind her and gave him a tight smile. Instinctively, he smoothed his palm down her bare arm, frowning at how chilled her skin felt.

"Just *stop*," she snapped into the phone. "I already told you I'm not coming over there. There's nothing more to talk about. We're done."

Vince's angry response was loud enough that Boone could hear it. "You know what? Fine, if that's what you want. You were only ever good for one thing anyway."

Boone stiffened, but Eve fired back without missing a beat. "And you weren't even good for that."

Good for her.

"The truth is, Eve, I feel sorry for you." Vince's tone was as cold and cruel as his words. "No life, no friends. Honestly, it's pathetic. At least Becca has a college degree and a real job. I don't have to be embarrassed to introduce her to my friends."

Eve recoiled like she'd been struck. "Fuck you." Her voice shook as she blinked back tears. "Seriously, fuck both of you."

Boone's protective instincts flared into blood-boiling fury, and he seized the phone from her to snarl at Vince. "Time's up, asswipe. Eve's done talking to you now. She's already moved on to someone who's not a complete waste of oxygen, and you're interrupting our special time together."

"Who the fuck is this?" Vince demanded.

"This is Boone Sheridan. If you don't know who I am, you should Google me. Because I'm the guy who'll be pleasuring your ex-girlfriend tonight in ways you're neither creatively nor physically capable of, and I want you to be able to picture it while you cry yourself to sleep on your jizz-soaked Batman sheets, you miserable dick."

"How do you know about—"

Boone ended the call and held Eve's phone out to her. "We accidentally got disconnected. Oops."

She stared at him in open-mouthed shock.

There was a chance he might have overstepped by jumping to her defense. "Sorry," he muttered, unable to feel too bad about it.

"No, you're not." Eve's hand trembled as she took the phone from him.

"I'm sorry I lost my temper. I recognize it's your life and I should let you handle it yourself, but he seriously fucking pissed me off when he said that shit to you." Boone shoved his hands in his pockets and hung his head. "Are you mad at me?"

"No." Her lips curved in a tremulous smile as she shoved her phone in her pocket. "That was pretty awesome, actually."

He expelled a breath, relieved as fuck. "I really hate that guy. He and that roommate of yours are living, breathing proof that having a college degree doesn't mean you're not a loathsome garbage person."

Eve's chin wobbled, and she turned her back on Boone to wipe her eyes. "I'm not going to cry. I swear."

He only hesitated for a second before pulling her into his arms. She released a long, shaky breath and burrowed into him, pressing her damp cheek against his shirt.

"It's okay if you want to cry," he said as he touched his lips to her temple. Beneath the brighter, floral scents of her shampoo and perfume there was a subtle, delicious scent of coffee he'd detected when they were cuddled up on the couch. God, he hoped she hadn't noticed him shamelessly sniffing her hair.

As her head nestled under his chin, warmth spread through Boone's chest—a sense of rightness that radiated outward from his heart at the feeling of her body next to his. Faint alarm bells sounded in the back of his head, but he ignored them in favor of comforting Eve.

"You know why women cry when they're angry, but men don't?" His fingers gently stroked her hair as he spoke. "It's because men are encouraged to channel their anger into aggression, but women are expected to internalize it. You're taught to swallow your rage until it leaks out as tears."

She lifted her head and blinked up at him. "Is that true?"

"I don't know. I read it somewhere and it stuck with me." He swiped a tear off her cheek with his thumb. "Hey, you know what? Guess who else doesn't have a college degree? Me. Also Griffin, who owns this huge fucking house. And Kimberleigh Cress over there who's been nominated for an Oscar. Not to mention Chuck fucking Hammer, who probably has more money than the rest of us put together. Half the people at this party didn't go to college."

Eve gave him a watery smile. "Thank you for trying to make me feel better."

"I'm sorry that asshole hurt you. You're worth a hundred of him. You know that, right?"

Some of the ache in Boone's chest eased when he saw her smile grow stronger.

"At least that's done and over with," she said. "We're officially broken up now."

"Glad to hear it. So what do you want to do? Go back to the party? Or you want me to take you home? It's your choice."

Eve's smile disappeared. "I definitely don't want to go home."

"Back to the party it is, then." He slipped his hand into hers.

"Do I look like I've been crying?" she asked, swiping beneath her eyes.

"You look beautiful." He tugged her toward the house. "Come on. Let's get you a drink. You've earned it."

* * *

Two hours and several drinks later, Boone was watching Eve cry again, but this time with laughter. He smiled as she clutched her stomach and doubled over, cracking up at Griffin's story about the first acting job he'd ever booked, which had been an extremely ill-conceived commercial for diarrhea medicine.

Boone had heard the story at least a dozen times before, so his smile was about Eve rather than Griffin's impression of himself pretending to shit his pants in his professional acting debut. It was a good story though. Even Kimberleigh Cress was snickering, and Boone wasn't sure he'd ever seen her laugh out of character before.

But it was Eve who'd captured all of Boone's attention. That gorgeous smile of hers turned radiant when she laughed.

He couldn't tear his eyes away. Cheeks glowing with rosy color, a flash of perfect white teeth, two matching dimples winking at either side of her lush lips. Her laugh brought out the sun. It was a crime she didn't have reasons to laugh more often.

They were sitting around in Griffin's living room now, after moving inside when Merit Lebese, one of Griffin's costars from the *Troublemakers* franchise, had organized a game of Celebrity. The man was suave as fuck with his South African accent, roguish smile, and courtly manners. When he'd kissed Eve's hand, she'd looked like she might faint dead away.

Not that Boone was jealous. *Nope.*

The women's team had decimated the men at Celebrity, thanks in large part to Eve's encyclopedic pop culture knowledge. After that, Alice had brought out Telestrations, a party game that was a cross between Pictionary and the telephone game. Eve had wowed everyone with her drawing skills, making Boone wonder again what had happened to her dreams of being an animator.

After a few rounds of gameplay, they'd devolved into simply sitting around talking. Eve was sitting on the floor, leaning against the couch between Alice and Kimberleigh's feet.

It was nice to see Eve relaxed and enjoying herself. Although she'd been hitting the vodka pretty hard, going drink for drink with Kimberleigh, who seemed to have the alcohol tolerance of a rhino. Not that Boone blamed Eve for cutting loose. She'd certainly earned it after the shitty day she'd had. But he worried she might pay for it with a mother of a hangover tomorrow.

He went to fetch a glass of water from the kitchen and handed it to Eve as he sank onto the floor next to her. "Drink this. You don't want to get dehydrated."

"Thanks, Mom." She rolled her eyes, but drank some water anyway.

She'd been doodling on one of the dry-erase sketch pads from the Telestrations box, and he leaned in for a closer look. It was a sketch of an alien wearing a poufy princess dress.

"That's amazing," he said. "You're really good." His own scribbled efforts during the game had been near indecipherable.

Ignoring the compliment, she drew in a couch behind the alien princess and next to that a TV. It was impressive how easy she made it look. The nubby dry-erase marker and laminated card stock weren't exactly high-quality art tools.

She added something to the TV screen next. Some trees and two tiny people holding hands. Recognition dawned when she sketched a cowboy hat onto one of them.

"Is that me?"

Eve shot him a smile as she sat back and reached for her water. "She's a huge *Abnormal Investigations* fan." She drew a crown on the alien's head. "You're her favorite actor."

For some reason, Boone's stomach did something funny at that. "Do you take commissions? I should have you design my next tattoo."

"Okay." She reached for his hand. "What kind of tattoo do you want?"

"I'm thinking of having a picture of my face tattooed on one of my butt cheeks. What do you think? Good idea or great idea?"

Laughing, she turned his hand over to examine the inside of his wrist. "Seriously though."

Kimberleigh was in the middle of telling everyone about a practical joke Griffin had played on her during the international press tour they'd just come back from. Alice was pretending to listen, but Boone could tell at least half her attention was on him and Eve.

"I don't know what I want," he said. "That's the problem. I can't make up my mind."

"Then I guess I'll have to improvise." Eve pushed the rolled cuff of his shirt up higher and rubbed her thumb over the inside of his forearm, studying it like a blank canvas.

Boone's fingers flexed as he suppressed a shiver. She'd rested his arm on her thigh, and he was far too aware that his knuckles were cradled in her hip crease. It was all he could do to keep his breathing steady.

The tip of the marker was cold, in sharp contrast with Eve's warm hands. He liked the tickling sensation as she moved the pen over his skin, and the way it felt to be held in her firm, steadying grip. He liked it so much his dick stirred to life, doing its best to make things awkward. With his free hand, Boone adjusted his shirt to make sure the front hem was hanging in front of his crotch.

"I have done some freelance graphic design," Eve said, her focus intent on her pen strokes.

"I'll bet you're good at it."

"After I dropped out of school, I had this idea that I could freelance full-time." Her creation was already starting to take shape. A stem, leaves, and now petals. She was giving him a rose.

"Why don't you?"

The pen paused for a second. "It's not that easy to find clients." She drew in a few more petals. "Starting up a business takes time, and I'm already working two jobs to pay my rent. It makes it hard to do much of anything else."

"I can imagine." He lifted his gaze to watch her face as she worked. There was a tiny vertical line between her brows, and her lips were pinched together in a frown of concentration. But her eyes were bright, the dark depths sparkling and full of life. She looked happy. Serene. Like she was doing what she was meant to do.

Kimberleigh reached the denouement of her story, and everyone except Eve and Boone erupted into peals of laughter.

She was too busy concentrating on her drawing, and he was too busy concentrating on her.

"Maybe you should be a tattoo artist," he said.

Her nose scrunched up. "I couldn't handle the blood. Or touching strangers that much."

She didn't seem to mind touching him. He didn't mind it either. Quite the opposite.

It wasn't difficult for Boone to imagine what it would be like if he let himself have her. How natural it would feel to cup Eve's cheek, tip her head back, and devour those lush, soft lips. How sweet and citrusy she'd taste as she smiled against his mouth. If he closed his eyes, he could almost feel her hands sliding over his body and down to his hard dick. He could even guess what kind of noises she'd make when he touched her. God, her body would fit his perfectly, just so damn perfect...

His hand and his dick both spasmed, and Eve's fingers tightened on his arm.

"Be still," she admonished. "I'm nearly done."

Boone looked down as he felt the pen tick against his skin. She was adding tiny thorns to the rose stem and hatch marks around the edges of the leaves. The level of detail she'd achieved with that crappy, blunt pen was nothing short of amazing.

She paused to inspect her work, then added a few more touches until she seemed to be satisfied. When she pursed her lips and blew on his arm there was no suppressing his shiver.

"All done," she announced, releasing him. "Don't touch it for a few minutes or it'll smear."

"I love it." He smiled when she did.

"Good." Grabbing his other hand, Eve drew a quick smiley face on the back. She capped the pen and dropped it on the table as she pushed herself to her feet. "I've got to pee. I'll be back."

As soon as Eve was out of the room, Alice's foot nudged Boone's leg. "You really like her, don't you?"

He nodded, swallowing hard as he stared at the rose Eve had drawn on his arm.

Yeah, he did like her. Way too much.

eight

EVE WOKE with her head pounding. Every muscle in her body ached, and her mouth felt like it was coated with dryer lint. Thank god she didn't have to work today. She buried her face in the pillow and tried to will herself back to sleep.

Wait.

These sheets didn't smell like her sheets. They didn't feel right either. Her sheets were not this soft, and this cloud-like thing under her head bore no resemblance to her lumpy pillow.

Oh shit.

Eve's eyes flew open in panic. Sunlight stabbed through her head as she squinted at the unfamiliar surroundings.

Where the fuck was she?

The last thing she remembered was dozing off on Alice and Griffin's couch last night. Was she still at their house? She blinked a few times until the room came into better focus. This didn't feel like the same house she'd been in last night. The windows and doors looked different, and the wood floor was more rustic. The barnwood bedroom set didn't seem to match Alice and Griffin's style either.

Eve relaxed a little when she spotted her purse on the nightstand. She was still wearing all her clothes from last night, but her red ballet flats had been neatly placed beside the bed.

Throwing back the handmade quilt, she staggered over to the window. The bedroom she was in overlooked a pool, but it was completely different from the one last night. Instead of a stonescape waterfall, there was a tiered fountain inlaid with colorful decorative tiles and surrounded by a patio of terra-cotta pavers.

It was all very nice, but how the heck had she gotten here? And where exactly was here?

While she was staring out the window, Boone emerged from the house below wearing a tank top, athletic shorts, and flip-flops. Eve's shoulders sagged with relief at the sight of him. This must be his house, she realized as he uncoiled a hose and began watering potted plants.

Which meant he'd brought her back here with him last night.

Eve's relief turned into mortification. Why couldn't she remember coming here? Had she been that drunk? Oh god, what must Boone think of her after this? He had to be annoyed after lugging her drunk ass back to his house to stow her in his guest room until she'd slept it off.

Some pretend girlfriend she'd turned out to be. She wouldn't blame him if he decided to pick someone else after this. So much for her trial run.

Further exploration of the room Eve had slept in revealed an en suite bathroom supplied with a generous selection of guest toiletries. Once she'd done her best to make herself more presentable, she went in search of Boone to apologize for her inconsiderate behavior.

The hallway outside the bedroom opened onto a staircase with a curved wrought iron railing which she followed down to the next floor. Although the stairs descended for yet another flight, the sound of running water drew her to what appeared to be the main level of a Spanish Mission style house. A quick glance around revealed a street-level front entry, formal dining room, and a living room with beamed ceilings, cozy leather couches, and a bright sunroom beyond.

Eve found Boone in a large, sunny kitchen, standing at the sink with his back to her. The ash-colored cabinets and terra-cotta tile counters and floor reminded her a bit of her parents' kitchen back home, only about four times larger. In fact, the whole house brought to mind the Spanish architecture she'd grown up around in San Antonio.

"Morning," Eve said timidly when Boone shut off the faucet.

"She lives." He turned around to offer her a smile as he dried his hands. "How're you feeling?"

She winced at the floor, too embarrassed to meet his eyes. "My head's not great, but it will probably recover. My dignity, not so much."

There was something about seeing him barefoot in his kitchen that made this whole situation feel even more unreal. She was in Boone Sheridan's house! And he wasn't wearing shoes! Why his bare feet should be such a big deal, Eve couldn't explain. But they were.

"Here." He pulled open his giant Sub-Zero fridge and offered her a bottle of Pedialyte sports drink. "This'll help with the headache, anyway."

The aroma of fresh-brewed coffee filled the kitchen, and Eve cast a longing look at the coffee maker next to the sink. "I'll give you a million dollars for a cup of that coffee instead."

With a disapproving shake of his head, Boone reached for her hand and firmly put the Pedialyte in it. "Get some elec-trolytes in you first. Then you can have all the coffee your heart desires."

Wow, who knew he could be such a mom? It was awfully sweet though.

Eve made a face as she choked down a mouthful of the vile yellow concoction that tasted like lemon-flavored Windex. *Blech.*

"Nasty stuff, isn't it?" As he turned his back to dig through a drawer, she couldn't help noticing how his tank top afforded a truly excellent view of his muscular arms.

She swallowed another mouthful of Pedialyte as punishment for leering at him in his own home and tried not to gag. "I don't want to seem ungrateful, but it's not my favorite thing I've ever tasted."

He laughed as he opened a bottle of painkillers. "I'd be worried if it was."

There was hair on his chest. Eve could see it where his tank top dipped down below his collarbone. He'd never had chest hair on TV or in any of the photos she'd seen. They must make him wax for the show, and he was growing his chest hair out over the hiatus along with his beard.

Annnd now she was ogling his chest. Great. She forced herself to take another drink. "I'm really, really sorry about passing out on you last night. I can't believe I did that."

"Don't sweat it." He shook two pills into his palm and offered them to her.

"Thank you." She knocked them back with more Pedialyte and made a face. "On a scale of one to ten, how much did I embarrass myself last night?"

"You've got nothing at all to worry about." His smile took on a mischievous twist. "Merit thought it was sweet when you got down on one knee and proposed by serenading him with 'My Heart Will Go On.'"

Eve squinted. "You're messing with me. I didn't do that."

"No, but it would have been hilarious." Boone shot her a

grin as he got out a coffee mug. "How do you take your coffee, coffee girl?"

"Black's fine." She glugged down more Pedialyte before capping the bottle. Loathsome as it was, it did seem to be helping with her headache. "This isn't like me, just so you know. I'm not usually the kind of person who gets drunk and passes out in strangers' houses."

"If anyone deserved to cut loose a little last night, it's you. Don't beat yourself up about it."

"No avoiding that. Sorry. The self-flagellation is going to be epic and protracted."

"I would have driven you home, but I couldn't get you to wake up enough to tell me your address."

"How embarrassing," Eve muttered, rubbing her forehead. "I'm sort of a deep sleeper. I can be hard to wake up sometimes."

"No shit."

When he handed her a cup of coffee, her attention snagged on the blurred remains of the rose she'd drawn on him last night.

Following her gaze, he turned his forearm up to show off the black smudges. "Ah yes, the tattoo you gave me. It mostly rubbed off in my sleep, I'm afraid."

"It wasn't meant to last." A pang of wistfulness struck Eve. She didn't want all this to end. She felt like Cinderella, dreading the strike of midnight when she'd have to leave the prince and go home to her ordinary life of drudgery again.

A smile played over his lips as he gazed at his arm. "You remember doing that, huh?"

She took a hasty sip of coffee. *Ow.* Too hot. "I remember everything, right up until I fell asleep on the couch. I just don't remember how I got from there to here."

Boone leaned back against the counter and reached for his own mug of coffee. "I carried you to my car, drove you back here, and carried you upstairs to the guest room. You were out like a light through all of it. Pretty impressive."

"God, I'm so sorry." She dropped her head into her palm. He'd *put her to bed*. She wanted to die.

"It's really not a big deal," he said kindly.

"It kind of is though. I'm lucky you're a good guy. My mom would kill me if she knew I'd been that stupid."

His forehead creased. "I told you I wouldn't let anything bad happen to you, and I meant it."

"And I'm extremely grateful for that. Thank you for taking such good care of me." Eve's gaze fell on his forearm again, and she smiled to herself as she remembered how boldly she'd grabbed his arm last night and started drawing on him. And how willing he'd been to let her. Then she remembered the way he'd held her after she'd gotten off the phone with Vince, and how snuggled up they'd been on the couch outside before that. "I had a good time last night."

"Me too."

She arched a dubious eyebrow. "Even after I passed out at your friend's party and made you bring me home with you? Because I wouldn't blame you if you'd changed your mind about wanting me to do the girlfriend thing after that."

"I haven't changed my mind." He gave her a long look. "Have you had enough time to decide if you want to do it?"

She bit her lip and nodded. "I'm in if you are."

Boone's relieved smile was a beam of pure sunshine. "Now it's my turn to say thank you. I really appreciate you doing this."

Warmth spread through Eve's chest, and she took a sip of coffee to hide her blush. It was delicious—of course he used top-quality coffee beans. He also had an expensive Italian espresso machine sitting next to the drip coffee maker, which made her wonder why he bothered coming to the coffee shop every day. Maybe he just liked getting out of the house.

Although, if Eve had a house like this, she'd never want to leave.

"We probably should talk about how it's supposed to work," she said. "Go over the ground rules or whatever."

He nodded. "And we need to revisit the subject of compensation—"

"Nope." She shook her head, adamant. "I'm still not going to let you pay me. I won't be budging on that."

That had him frowning. "You have to let me reimburse you somehow."

"I really don't. But I will let you foot the bill for the food and drinks when we go out. How about that?"

"I was planning to do that anyway." He looked seriously unhappy.

"Well, I'm assuming it will be more expensive than anything I'd be able to afford on my own, so that will be enough of a treat to make it worth my while." As if getting to hang out with him wasn't reward enough.

"Eve." He was making angry eyebrows now. "I have to insist—"

"Stop." She held her hand up and gave him her serious eyes, so he'd know she wasn't playing around. "This is a deal breaker for me. I'm seriously not comfortable accepting money from you to do this."

After the taste she'd gotten last night of what it would feel like to play at being Boone's girlfriend, payment was even more out of the question. No way Eve could let herself be that cozy with someone who was her employer. She was already fighting against her growing feelings for Boone. She couldn't let herself be financially indebted to him on top of that.

"If you can't accept that, then you'll have to find someone else to be your pretend girlfriend." Which would seriously suck, but this was the hill she'd picked to die on, and die she might.

She held her breath as Boone digested her ultimatum.

When his angry eyebrows turned into dejected eyebrows, she was positive he was about to call the whole thing off.

Instead, he let out the sigh of all sighs and grudgingly muttered, "Fine."

It was all she could do not to sag to the floor with relief. "Thank you," she said, breaking into a smile. "I'm glad we could come to an understanding."

"I wouldn't want you to be uncomfortable." He still didn't look happy, but at least he'd accepted her terms.

"So, what's the next step?" she said now that all the unpleasant money talk was out of the way. "What do you need from me?"

With another sigh, Boone dug his phone out of his pocket. "I'll call my publicist. My guess is she'll want to meet with us to go over the plan. We're under time pressure with me going back to Vancouver next month, so the sooner we can get started the better."

"I'm ready when you are," Eve said cheerily. "Initiate Operation Girlfriend."

nine

"THAT'S it on the right, with the turquoise roof," Eve said as Boone's car approached her North Hollywood apartment building. He was dropping her off at home for the time being, but she'd agreed to come back to his house that evening to meet with his manager and publicist about setting up some appearances for them—starting as soon as tomorrow, potentially.

Eve's stomach plummeted when she spotted her roommate's bright red Jetta in the parking lot. Which meant Becca was home. *Oh, joy.*

After he'd pulled into an empty space, Boone peered through the windshield at the L-shaped nineteen seventies complex. "Which one's you?"

"Second floor, next to last unit on the right."

He directed an appraising look at Eve. "You ready to go in there and face your roommate?"

"Ready or not, it has to be done." She summoned a smile for him. "Thank you for letting me hang out with you last night."

"You make it sound like I was the one doing you a favor."

"You were." Her smile grew less forced. "You have no idea how grateful I am to have had somewhere else to be. It was exactly what I needed."

A wrinkle formed between his brows. "You're going to be okay, right?"

"Yeah, of course." She forced her smile wider. "I'll be fine."

Eve bid him goodbye and hauled herself out of the car, refusing to look back as she trudged up to her apartment for the showdown she'd been putting off.

When Eve let herself into the apartment, she found Becca ensconced on the couch with her laptop. For a second they stared at each other in wary silence. The windows were open to let in the breeze, and the oddly appropriate sound of a Post Malone breakup song drifted in from another apartment.

"You're back," Becca ventured finally, getting to her feet.

"I am," Eve responded in a terse, flat tone.

"So I guess you're pretty upset, huh? Considering you didn't come home last night." The way she said it sounded like an accusation, as if she was trying to position herself as the wronged one instead of Eve. Had she always been this passive-aggressive and self-centered? How had Eve not noticed before?

Remembering what Boone had said about Becca wanting to provoke a reaction, Eve gave her nothing. Not a single word in response. She'd be damned if she'd give Becca the satisfaction of knowing how much she'd succeeded in hurting her.

"Where have you been?" Becca asked, the faint whine in her voice setting Eve's teeth on edge. "I've been crazy worried about you. I almost called the cops."

Still, Eve said nothing. She didn't owe Becca an explanation. It was no longer any of her business where Eve spent her time. Not that she believed for a second that Becca had genuinely been worried. Now that Eve knew how two-faced Becca was, she didn't trust anything that came out of her mouth. The wool had been pulled from her eyes, and for the first time she was seeing the woman she'd thought was her friend for who she really was.

Frustration furrowed Becca's brow at Eve's nonreaction. "I'm so sorry, Eve. It was horrible, what I did."

"Yes, it was," Eve agreed.

"Do you totally hate me?"

Eve didn't see the point of answering that, so she countered with a question of her own. The only thing she really wanted to know. "Why did you do it?"

Becca's gaze skidded away. At least she had the decency to look guilty. "It was a moment of weakness. Vince has been coming on to me for weeks, and I'll have you know I've turned him down every time. But he kept on texting me and coming around when he knew you wouldn't be here. Eventually he wore me down."

"And all these weeks that my boyfriend's been hitting on you, you didn't think to give me a heads-up that I was dating a scumbag?"

Once again, Becca refused to meet Eve's eyes. "I thought about it, but I was afraid you'd blame me."

Eve suspected Becca hadn't been the passive recipient of Vince's advances she claimed to be. It was entirely possible she'd been the one doing the pursuing. Or maybe it had been mutual. Honestly, it didn't matter at this point.

"Right," Eve said. "So instead you decided to sleep with my boyfriend, make a sex tape, and send it to me while I was at work for shits and giggles."

"He wore me down. I was weak and I slipped."

Eve let out a disbelieving laugh. "You slipped? What, like you tripped and your mouth fell onto his penis? Are you for real with this? And how do you explain the video? What on god's earth could have possibly possessed you to record that, much less send it to me?"

Becca started to respond, but Eve cut her off.

"You know what? Don't bother explaining. I just realized I don't care why you think you did it after all." Eve was officially out of fucks. Whatever twisted explanation Becca had to offer, it could never justify her actions. "Wanna hear something funny? I'm almost grateful to you in a weird way, because you helped me realize I've been settling for less than I deserve. You gave me the wake-up call I needed."

Becca blinked, clearly thrown by Eve's calm acceptance. It only took her a second to recover and go with it though. You had to admire her resilience.

"Well, you're welcome, I guess." She offered a syrupy sweet smile. "Does that mean you forgive me and we can still be friends?"

Un-fucking-believable. Eve had to laugh. Talk about delusional. "We're not friends, Becca. A friend would never do something like that to me."

"I said I'm sorry, okay? I feel like shit."

"Good. You should feel like shit, because that's what you are. A giant steaming pile of shit."

Becca actually had the gall to look offended. "Look, I know you're mad right now, but give it some time. Like you said, it all worked out for the best. You and Vince were never right for each other, you have to know that. He and I make a way better couple than you two ever did."

"You're still seeing him?" Eve didn't know why she was surprised.

"You broke up with him. What do you even care at this point?"

So much for remorse. What a swell best friend Eve had chosen for herself. Too bad she hadn't seen Becca's true colors sooner. Like before she'd moved all her worldly possessions into Becca's apartment.

Eve shook her head in disgust. "Congrats. You two deserve each other. Truly."

"It's not like you and Vince ever had anything in common. No offense, but you're not exactly on his level."

"What does that mean?"

"Oh come on." Becca rolled her eyes. "Vince is on the management track. He's working toward his MBA. He's got dental insurance and a 401k."

"And? What does that have to do with anything?"

"And you're not in the same league. You couldn't even hack it as a temp. In five years, Vince will be an executive making six figures, and what'll you be? Still slinging coffee for pennies above minimum wage?"

Something cracked inside Eve, and cold fury pulsed through her veins. "You know, Becca, I really wish I'd realized sooner what a heinous fucking cunt you are."

"Nice, Eve. Real mature, using the C-word. This is exactly what I'm talking about. Maybe you should think about growing up a little instead of blaming everyone else for your shortcomings."

Eve's head was *this close* to popping off like the top of one of those old-timey glass thermometers. "Why would you think I give two shits about the opinion of someone who pretended to be my friend and fucked my boyfriend?"

Becca's face hardened. "If that's how you feel, so be it. We have five months left on the lease, so we only have to put up with each other until then."

"Yeah, no. That's not going to work for me. Not happening."

"You want to move out sooner than that? Fine. Pay me your half of the rent for the remainder of the lease upfront and you're free to get the hell out whenever you want."

"You're deranged," Eve gritted out. "Here's what's

happening instead: I'm moving out today, and you and your rent can both get fucked."

She was so beyond done with Becca and her poisonous bullshit. She'd intended to hold her nose and stick it out here until she found a new place to live, but that wasn't going to work. Not even a little. Living with Becca wasn't a viable option. No way could Eve stay here even one more night. No fucking way.

She had no idea where she was going to go, but she'd figure something out. Even sleeping in her car would be better than spending another night here.

Becca sputtered. "But the lease—"

"Has your name on it, not mine," Eve pointed out with a perverse sense of satisfaction. She might be completely fucked, but at least she could enjoy fucking Becca over too.

"I can't afford the rent on this place by myself!" Becca shrieked.

Eve simply shrugged. "Maybe you should have thought of that before you slept with my boyfriend. Did you seriously think I was going to keep living here and paying you rent after that?"

"We had an agreement!" Becca's face was turning all kinds of interesting colors. Any second she'd be frothing at the mouth. "You made a commitment when you moved in!"

A cold smile twisted Eve's lips as she crossed her arms. "I never signed anything, because you wanted to keep the apartment in your name. Technically, I'm an illegal sublet."

"We had a verbal agreement!"

"Yeah, well, I thought we had a verbal agreement not to stab each other in the back, but you already went and violated that. As far as I'm concerned, any obligations I might have had to you are hereby null and void." Turning on her heel, Eve snatched a box out of the recycling pile and headed into the kitchen.

"What am I supposed to do?" Becca whined. "I can't afford to pay an extra nine hundred dollars a month."

"Don't know. Don't care," Eve said as she started pulling her coffee mugs out of the cabinet. "Ask Vince. Maybe he'll use his 401k to help you out."

As if. Vince was outrageously stingy with his money. He'd insisted on going Dutch for everything. The cheapskate had even tried to get Eve to reimburse him for half the cost of her own birthday dinner.

"You're really packing up and moving out today?" Becca said in disbelief. "Like, right this second?"

Eve had no choice. Now that she'd told Becca to get fucked over the rent, she couldn't trust her not to take vengeance on her belongings. She'd just have to fit as much of her stuff as she could in her car and let the rest go. Anything she left behind, Becca would likely sell or toss in the dumpster. Or spitefully burn in a bonfire in the courtyard if she felt like being really dramatic. Or maybe she'd make a video of herself having sex with it. *Ha!*

"Where are you even going to go?" Becca demanded. "Don't tell me you've found another place to live already?"

If only. Eve had no plan at all. She'd just made herself homeless and had no place to sleep tonight. But hell if she'd tell Becca that.

Eve probably had enough available credit on her cards to pay for a hostel while she looked for a new apartment. Hopefully. Assuming she could find a decent, affordable one with an available bed tonight. If not, she really would be sleeping in her car.

"You're bluffing," Becca said. "There's no way you found a place to live this fast."

"I'm staying with a friend," Eve lied.

"Who? You don't have any friends besides me."

Sad but true. Eve had plenty of friendly acquaintances, but

nobody she knew well enough to ask for a favor this big. She'd let herself depend too much on Becca's friendship and hadn't bothered to develop any other meaningful relationships. Becca had become her entire emotional support system. Without her, Eve had no one.

Except her parents, of course. But they were in San Antonio, and they'd been pressuring her to move back there for years. If she asked them for help, their answer would be a plane ticket home.

"None of your business," Eve said as she continued searching the kitchen cabinets for the few items that belonged to her. At least she didn't have that much to pack. She'd sold a lot of her stuff when she first moved in, because Becca had already filled the apartment with her own things.

"Is it your new boyfriend, Boone Sheridan?" Becca said in a sneering voice.

Eve went still.

"That's right, Vince told me about that. Cute trick. Who was that you put on the phone anyway? How'd you get somebody to impersonate Boone Sheridan for you?"

"I didn't," Eve said, refusing to look at Becca.

"Was it one of those Cameo things where you pay celebrities to record a message for you? How much did that cost you? I didn't realize Boone Sheridan was so hard up for cash. Pretty pathetic, if you ask me."

Eve spun around to say—something. She wasn't sure what. But before she could figure it out, the front door opened and Boone sauntered into the apartment.

Becca's jaw unhinged itself as he strode across the room with all his cool, offhand sex appeal dialed up to eleven and casually affixed himself to Eve's side.

"Hey, babe," he murmured, sliding his arm around her waist. "Miss me yet?"

ten

EAVESDROPPING WAS all kinds of wrong. Boone knew that. In his defense, he hadn't intended to do it.

He'd been on the verge of going home, in fact. Only he hadn't been able to make himself do it for some reason. The more he'd thought about Eve coming up here alone to face her roommate, and how fragile she'd looked when she got out of the car, the more his chest had hurt, and the more impossible it had been to drive away.

When he'd spotted Eve's phone lying on the passenger seat, it had been such a relief. Because it gave him an excuse to check on her and take the measure of her psychopath roommate for himself. He'd had no choice but to follow Eve up to her apartment so he could return her phone. What else could he do?

It wasn't his fault their living room windows had been open. Or that he'd been able to hear both of their voices clear as day when he approached the apartment. The conversation had been so heated, Boone had frozen in place, reluctant to interrupt but unable to leave.

Until he'd heard Becca say his name in that shitty, disbelieving tone. As if it was inconceivable that someone like him would be with someone like Eve.

It had made him see red. Just like last night with Eve's dirtbag boyfriend, Boone had reacted on instinct. The only thing he'd been able to think about was making Becca eat her words by showing her how fucking wrong she was.

Was it satisfying to see Becca's frog-eyed stare when he walked in? Hell yes. So satisfying he hadn't been able to resist giving Eve's cheek an affectionate nuzzle.

Once again, Boone realized he might have gone too far as he watched Eve fight to hide how flustered she was by his unexpected appearance in her apartment.

Staying in character, he gave her his most affectionate smile. "I know you wanted me to wait in the car until you texted, but it's kind of hard for you to text me when you forget this, babe." He lifted his eyebrows pointedly as he held up her phone.

"Oh. Whoops. Silly me." Eve grabbed it from him, returning his smile with a grateful one. "Sorry about that, *babe.*"

"Holy shit!" Becca screeched, finally finding her voice again. "You're him! You're really Boone Sheridan!"

Boone swiveled his head to aim a hostile glare at the so-called friend who'd hurt Eve. His lips pulled back in a snarl as he prepared to tell her exactly what he thought of her.

"Boone." The hesitant touch of Eve's fingers on his jaw snapped his attention back to her—just that small, fleeting contact setting his heart thumping unexpectedly in his chest. "Don't. She's not worth it."

"Hang on," Becca said, still struggling with the reality in front of her. "You two are actually together? Like, for real?"

Boone ignored her, keeping his focus on Eve. "Should I go wait in the car again? Or do you want me to stay and help you pack up your stuff?"

Those big dark eyes of hers were brimming with a constellation of thoughts he wished he could decipher. He could easily spend a whole day staring into their unfathomable depths. At the thought, a dizzying, misguided warmth uncoiled in his chest.

Dangerous.

"Can I talk to you in my room?" Eve asked, worrying her lip.

Remembering he needed to stay in character, Boone flashed another smile. "Sure, whatever you want, gorgeous."

He was seized by the arm and dragged through the apartment before being unceremoniously shoved into a cramped bedroom mostly taken up by a double bed covered with a floral duvet. Eve's scent, which had already become familiar to him, permeated the room. As she shut the door behind them, Boone took a long, slow breath through his nose, drinking it in.

In addition to the bed, there was a cheap particle board nightstand, an even flimsier-looking bookcase, and a crowded closet with some cheap plastic storage drawers stacked on the floor. A collection of drawings, most of them taken from sketchpads, were tacked to the walls all around the room. Boone drifted toward the closest one for a better look. It was a beautiful pencil sketch of an owl. Beside it was an ink drawing of a cat, and next to that another pencil sketch of a houseplant.

"Did you draw all this?" he asked. "These are phenomenal."

"How much did you hear before you walked in just now?" Eve demanded in a whisper, ignoring his question.

He spun around with a contrite wince. "Enough."

"Great," she muttered, lifting her eyes to the popcorn ceiling.

"You didn't tell me it was your roommate's apartment, and you were the one who'd have to move out." He couldn't help feeling a little hurt that Eve hadn't confided in him about her problems more. And yes, he knew exactly how hypocritical that was, considering how little he'd been willing to tell her.

"I guess I forgot." She turned away from him, but not fast enough to conceal the signs of stress in her expression. She'd done a good job of acting tough in front of Becca, but now that the confrontation was over the cracks in Eve's armor were starting to show.

Boone moved closer as she started jerking clothes off the hangers in her closet. "So what's the plan, Evie?"

"The plan is to pack up as much of my stuff as I can fit into my car and get the hell away from that boyfriend-humping succubus."

"And go where?"

A muscle spasmed in her jaw. "A friend's got a couch I can crash on until I find a new place."

"What about the furniture?"

"I'll have to leave it behind."

He surveyed the scant furnishings. "I've got a pickup truck back at the house. If I run home and swap cars, we could bring all the stuff in here, at least."

"There's no point. My friend doesn't have room for it, and I don't have anywhere to put it while I'm couch surfing."

"You can store it at my place. I've got plenty of room."

"You don't have to help me," she said tightly. "Really. It's fine."

"Hey." Boone tugged on her arm to make her face him. "You're already doing me a huge favor. Let me at least do you a small one. If you're supposed to be my girlfriend, helping you move is part of the gig."

He watched her hesitate, so damn reluctant to take anything from him, which only made him more determined to help her. He was used to people wanting things from him—intruding, asking for favors, making demands on him. Treating him like a product they were entitled to a piece of because his face was on TV.

But Eve had never asked for anything from him. From the moment he'd first laid eyes on her, she'd treated him like a person instead of a commodity.

"Evie," he said, squeezing her arm gently. "If you don't let me help, I'm going to get my feelings hurt, and you know how fragile actors' egos are. It won't be pretty, trust me. There might be crying."

The sight of her smile eased something inside him. "Fine," she said with an exasperated eyeroll. "If you're going to be a baby about it, I guess you can help me load my car."

Eve didn't understand why Boone wanted to help her, but she was too tired and stressed out to fight him on it right now. So she swallowed her pride and put him to work cramming her clothes and bedding into garbage bags while she packed her stuff from the bathroom into her only suitcase.

The unpleasant reality of her situation was starting to sink in, bringing on a sickening churn of panic. She had nowhere to go and no idea where she was going to sleep tonight. Or the next night, or any night after that until she could find a new place to live.

But she didn't want Boone to know that, or she'd lose all pretense of being a strong, independent adult capable of looking out for herself. That was why she'd lied to him, even though she felt guilty about it. She was too embarrassed to admit she didn't have a single friend she could stay with in a pinch. It made her seem helpless and pathetic, and she couldn't stand for him to see her that way.

Once again, she'd driven her life off the rails by making bad choices. Instead of taking sensible steps to mitigate problems, Eve had gotten caught in a cycle of reacting to them after they'd blown up in her face.

If only she'd seen Becca more clearly from the start, none of this would be happening right now. If she'd forced herself to make more friends, she'd have somewhere to go tonight. If she'd found a better job instead of drifting from one low-paying gig to another, she'd have more money put aside for emergencies. If she hadn't let Becca get under her skin so much, she could have stuck it out in the apartment for a few weeks and wouldn't be homeless right now.

Eve didn't want Boone to know how much of a train wreck she was. He'd let her passing out on him at the party slide, but this might be enough to change his mind about her. He was the only good thing in her life at the moment, and she didn't want to lose him too. She felt tears sting her eyes and angrily scrubbed them away.

Pull yourself together, girl.

There'd be plenty of time for a self-pity spiral later. Right now she needed to focus. Step one was clearing out of the apartment. After that she'd deal with step two: getting Boone to go home so she could figure out step three, which was finding a place to sleep tonight.

Simple, manageable goals. That was the key. Concentrate on completing the immediate next step instead of stressing about everything else after that. Otherwise the big, bad anxiety monster would rear its ugly head, and she'd end up paralyzed, unable to do anything at all.

After Eve finished emptying her things out of the bathroom —generously leaving Becca a bottle of expired moisturizer that had given her a rash and some deodorant that smelled like musty grandmother—she dragged her suitcase back into the bedroom.

Boone had made himself useful in her absence by pulling all the boxes down from the shelf in her closet. And also apparently snooping, because he was sitting on her now-bare mattress looking through one of her plastic storage containers.

"What are you doing?" she hissed as she shut the bedroom door behind her.

An unsettlingly gleeful expression spread over his face as he looked up at her. "Imagine my surprise when I saw my own face staring back at me through the bottom of this clear plastic bin in your closet."

The blood drained from Eve's face when she realized what it was he'd found.

Oh god. No no no…

"Give me that! It's none of your business." She lunged for the box, but Boone pushed it out of her reach as he banded his other arm around her waist to keep her away from it. Pulling her onto the bed beside him, he held her imprisoned against his side as she flailed in a futile attempt to free herself.

"It's got pictures of me in it," he said in delight as he restrained her with no apparent effort. "Pretty sure that makes it my business."

How had Eve not seen this coming? She never should have left Boone in here unsupervised. Also why did he have to be so freakishly strong? Stupid attractive muscles.

"It's just some old magazines I meant to throw away a long time ago. Give it to me, and I'll take the whole thing down to the dumpster." She made a violent dive for the box and nearly managed to give Boone the slip.

"Now, now, let's not be hasty." Retightening his grip, he hoisted her onto his lap like a squirming puppy. "They're not just any old magazines are they? It's interesting that they all seem to have my face on the cover."

"It's not interesting at all," Eve said miserably, giving up the struggle.

"Sure it is." His mouth pulled into a smug grin as he continued to paw through her stash of fandom memorabilia. "I find it *very* interesting that you have so many of my old maga-zine covers. *Details, Entertainment Weekly, TV Guide*—wow, I didn't think anyone besides my grandparents bought that one anymore. I'd totally forgotten about some of these photo shoots. Like this one." He dragged out a 2013 *Men's Health* and shook his head. "Jesus, look how vascular I was. Probably delirious from dehydration. No wonder I can't remember that shoot."

"Okay, you've had your fun," Eve said. "Let's close the box up now and get back to packing."

"Hello, what do we have here?" It was like he didn't hear her. He was enjoying himself way too much. "I wonder what could be in these notebooks."

Eve broke out in a cold sweat when she saw what he'd unearthed. She couldn't reach to snatch them out of his hand, so she attempted to cover his eyes instead. "Do *not* look at those, Boone! I'm serious!"

"Hey now, settle down. Quit trying to claw my eyes out. Shit." Abandoning the notebooks, he pried her hands off his face and pinned her arms across her stomach in a straight-jacket hold so she couldn't move at all.

"Please don't look at those." Begging was her only recourse at this point. "Please, Boone, I'm asking you not to."

His breath warmed her neck as he spoke into her ear. "I won't look if you tell me what's in them."

"It's private."

"One of them looks like a sketchbook. Are there drawings of me in there?"

Eve had officially lost the will to live. Her brain was going to self-destruct from humiliation in three...two...

"It's drawings of me, isn't it? Are they pornographic? Please tell me they're pornographic." The man was pure evil.

"They're not." She didn't draw that kind of fanart. Hers

was all PG-13, thank god. But she still couldn't bear the thought of Boone seeing it.

"But it is sketches of me though, right?"

"Yes," she admitted in a pained voice. She'd done a lot of character studies, plus a bunch of drawings of his character in various romantic poses with Simone's character. Which felt extra icky now that she knew they'd had an off-screen relationship.

Boone loosened his grip, and Eve slid limply to the floor. Pulling her knees to her chest, she hid her face in her arms. Looking him in the eye was officially a thing of the past. Never going to happen again.

"You've been holding out on me," he said, sounding unbearably pleased with himself. "You're not just a casual viewer. You're a *super*fan."

"I may have drawn some fanart," she mumbled.

He dropped to the floor beside her and bumped his arm against hers. "You don't have to be embarrassed. I'm flattered."

"And also maybe written some fanfic." The majority of those had *not* been PG-13 either. Why hadn't she burned all this stuff years ago?

"It's fine, Evie. I'm not bothered by it."

A zing of pleasure warmed her chest at the nickname he'd started using and the level of intimacy it implied. "I also ran a website for a couple of years."

"Which one?"

"AbnormalAlmanac.com."

"Really? I remember that one. It was pretty cool."

She lifted her head. "You saw it?"

"I did. Back in the first few seasons, I used to check in on the fansites occasionally to see what everyone was talking about. Curiosity, I guess. Or maybe I did it for the ego boost." He stretched his legs out as far as he could in the small room, stopping when his feet hit the baseboard. "That was the site with those cool diagrams of all the monsters and artifacts on the show, right? Did you draw all those?"

"Yes." The way they were sitting, side by side on the floor, reminded Eve of the way he'd sat down next to her in the back hallway of Antidote. God, had that only been yesterday? It felt like her whole life had turned upside down in the last twenty-four hours.

"They were really good drawings," he said. "It must have taken a lot of work."

"It was just a hobby."

"Are those the drawings that are in that sketchbook?"

Sadly, no. It wouldn't be so embarrassing if that was all it was. "Those were digital illustrations."

"So the ones in that sketchbook are…"

"Character sketches."

"Of me."

"Of your character," she corrected and hesitated before adding, "and Simone's."

He seemed to take that in stride. "Can I see them?"

"I don't want you to."

"Can I read your fanfic?"

"Definitely not."

His face up in a grin. "The fanfic's pornographic, isn't it?" He was vibrating with delight. "Is it self-insert? Please tell me it's Mary Sue fic."

"I hate you," Eve said, fighting a smile.

"You don't hate me." He nudged her shoulder again, but this time he left his arm pressed warmly against hers. "You're totally obsessed with me. You're my number one fan."

She attempted to give him a sour look. "I wouldn't go that far, and frankly I'm liking you less and less every second." That was a total lie. She was liking him more and more, to an extent that was quickly becoming unmanageable.

"You wrote erotic Mary Sue fanfic about me."

"It's not Mary Sue, and how do you even know what that is?"

"I told you, I used to poke around on the internet the first few years. I doubt you could shock me. I've seen it all. Body swap, omegaverse, fuck or die, mpreg, you name it."

Her mouth fell open. "You really read fanfiction?"

"Sometimes."

The thought that Boone might have stumbled across some of *her* old fanfic was truly alarming. Yet also a teensy bit thrilling, she had to admit. "Doesn't it weird you out?"

"What? That people write stories about a fictional character I play? I hate to break it to you, babe, but there's a whole staff of writers here in LA who get paid to write about my character. Everything I say and do on the show was written by someone else. And then of course there are the novelizations."

"It's not the same."

"It's not that different either. I've seen fanfic that's better than some of the shit we've put on the air. Just because a lot of the people writing fanfic are amateurs doesn't mean it's all bad."

"Yeah, but so much of it is—"

"Dirty?" he suggested with a smirk.

"I was going to say objectifying."

He appeared unbothered. "People are always going to have fantasies. That's the whole reason stories exist. If someone watches the show and is inspired enough to write their fantasies down or draw them or make fanvids or dress up in cosplay or whatever else they want to do, I take it as a compliment. Sure, some of it can get a little disturbing, but it's not like anyone's forcing me to look at it. People everywhere are into all sorts of freaky stuff—that's not unique to fandom. Who am I to judge them for their kinks if they're not hurting anyone?"

"That's very open-minded of you."

He shrugged again. "It took me some time to get there, but once I became a regular fixture on TV I had to make my peace with the thought of people getting off to images of me." His smile grew wider. "You don't have to be embarrassed that I found your spank bank."

Eve covered her face with her hands. "Oh my god. That's not what it is."

"Sure it is." Boone's arm draped around her shoulders with what was apparently supposed to be a comforting squeeze, except she could feel him shaking with laughter. "It's okay to admit it. There's no shame in a little self-love. Everybody wanks, Evie."

"You're making it worse," she complained, unable to resist laughing along with him.

He dragged her against him and smacked a kiss on her head. "I'm your celebrity crush."

"You're never going to let me live this down, are you?"

"Probably not." His fingertips touched her jaw, gently turning her face to his. He wasn't laughing anymore. His eyes were serious and fond, his face so close to hers she could feel the tantalizing tickle of his breath on her lips. Ever so slightly, his fingers stroked the hollow under her jaw. "I like that I was your fantasy."

The husky tone of his voice shot straight through her, curling low in her stomach. She swallowed as every nerve in her body stood at attention. "Don't let it go to your head."

"Too late," he whispered as his gaze dropped to her lips.

<h1 style="text-align:center">*eleven*</h1>

EVE TENSED INVOLUNTARILY, not because she didn't want Boone to kiss her, but because she wanted it so much it made her nervous.

He pulled back abruptly and dropped his hand from her face, swallowing as his gaze skittered away. For the first time in this entire mortifying conversation, Boone seemed to be embarrassed.

"We should probably get back to work so we can get you out of here," he said, pushing himself to his feet.

As he started gathering up the magazines and notebooks on the bed, Eve wondered if she'd imagined the whole thing. That might be preferable to knowing Boone had thought about kissing her for a moment and changed his mind.

But she couldn't believe she was that fanciful or dense. The hazy, captivated look on his face had been unmistakable. Her stomach tightened again just thinking about it.

"Come on, fangirl. Don't make me do this all by myself." He extended a hand to pull her off the floor.

Right. Priorities, etc. She had more pressing things to worry about than kisses that might or might not have almost happened. She needed to focus on figuring her shit out and finding herself someplace to sleep tonight. *Dammit.*

They got back to work packing up what remained of Eve's stuff. It was sad how little her worldly possessions amounted to. But on the bright side, it only took another few minutes to get the rest of the bedroom packed and ready to be carried downstairs. It might all fit in Eve's car, even.

Everything in the living room was Becca's except the television. "We'll take this down last," Eve told Boone as she knelt to unplug it. "We can set it behind the front seats and stuff the bags of clothes around it for padding."

Becca made a sound of indignation from the couch. Up until now, she'd been quietly typing on her phone—texting with Vince, was Eve's guess—and pretending to ignore them as they stacked things by the door to go downstairs. But as Boone carried the TV away, Becca got to her feet and confronted Eve. "I can't believe you're doing this."

"It's my TV." Eve shrugged and headed into the kitchen to clean her food out of the pantry. Since she didn't have a fridge, she'd have to leave all the perishables behind. Shame, but oh well.

Becca followed her to the kitchen and stood with her hands on her hips and her chin thrust as high in the air as it would go. "This is super low, even for you."

Eve couldn't help laughing. "I'm the one who's low? *Me?*"

"You're totally screwing me over."

That was the only part of this Eve felt good about. It might have been a rash decision, and she might be singing a different tune later tonight, but for now she took a great deal of petty pleasure in making Becca suffer.

Grabbing another grocery bag off the shelf, Eve tossed an icy look over her shoulder. "And what do you call what you did with Vince?"

"You didn't even like him that much!"

Amazing that Eve had never noticed before how selfish Becca was. It was always *me, me, me* with her. Looking back on their relationship with the friendship goggles torn away, she could see now that it had always been that way. Becca wanting things and Eve passively going along with them.

It felt like that was what Eve had been doing her entire adult life—passively going along. The last time she'd actively pursued a goal was when she'd decided to come to LA for college. And look how that had turned out. Ever since she'd dropped out, she'd been dog-paddling through her life, content just to keep her head above water.

"Well he's all yours now," Eve said, turning back to the pantry. "I hope he was worth it. Personally, if I was going to stab a friend in the back for the sake of some dick—not that I would, because that's some messed-up bucket of crabs shit—I sure wouldn't do it for a dude who treats foreplay like he's trying to beat a land speed record and thinks going down on a woman is too much work." Eve plucked the Lucky Charms off the top shelf and spun around to offer Becca a disingenuous smile. "But hey, to each their own. Maybe you're fine settling for a guy like Vince."

Becca's face had turned a satisfying shade of scarlet. While she was stewing, Eve's gaze drifted to Boone, who was standing by the door listening to every word. She couldn't help smiling at the sight of him being all handsome and protective, ready to jump in and defend her honor the second the need arose.

He was looking extra casual and scruffy today in his workout clothes, but without even trying he was still almost too hot to be real. More importantly, he was kind, supportive, trustworthy, and a heck of a lot more fun to be around than Vince had ever been. Even if Boone hadn't been rich, famous, and hotter than the sun, he'd still be a total catch.

"I don't know what you're talking about," Becca sputtered,

finally managing a comeback. "Vince and I have banging sex. Sounds to me like the problem was *you*."

"If you say so," Eve replied, still smiling at Boone. "I just know I deserve better, and now I've got it. I feel like the luckiest girl in the world."

So what if it wasn't true? Becca didn't know that. The whole world was about to believe Boone had chosen Eve.

In a way, he had. Maybe he didn't want her to be his girlfriend, but he thought she was good enough to play the part. That had to be worth something. Eve would take all the confidence boosters she could get.

She met the daggers Becca was glaring at her with a cheery smile. "I can't tell you how great it feels to be with a *real* man who understands how to make a woman feel special. And to think you helped make that happen for me, Becca. Maybe I should thank you for it, but I'm not going to. You know why? Because you're a terrible person, and I can't wait to never see you again."

"I'm glad you're leaving," Becca spat back. "I never liked you and neither did Vince."

"Yeah, you both made that perfectly clear," Eve replied calmly. "I might be broken up about it if you were the kind of person whose good opinion was worth having."

Without another word, Becca stalked off to her bedroom and slammed the door behind her.

"Buh-bye!" Eve called after her. "Have a shitty life, you toxic slag!"

Moving out of here today had been the right decision. Even if she ended up in some shithole hostel or had to spend a few night sleeping in her car until she figured something out, it'd be worth it to have Becca out of her life for good.

"You okay?" Boone's deep, soft voice asked behind her.

"Never better." It was strangely true. Eve couldn't remember when she'd last felt this powerful and free. Maybe it was adrenaline from the confrontation with Becca, but at the moment she felt pretty great.

His hand squeezed the back of her neck. "That was fucking awesome."

Goose bumps shivered down Eve's arms as she turned to face him. "Thank you for being here to help. It means a lot."

"It's my pleasure," he said, gifting her with a dazzling smile. "You ready to start carrying your stuff out to the car?"

"Yep. Let's get this done."

They each grabbed a load and trekked down to the parking lot. While Eve was opening the trunk of her car, Boone took the boxes she'd brought down over to his Camaro.

"Where are you going with those?" she asked.

"It's not the biggest trunk in the world, but these smaller boxes should fit. We can put the bigger ones in your trunk."

Eve followed him. "That's not necessary. I can fit everything in my car just fine." She wasn't sure that was true, but she was going to do her damnedest to make it work.

He ignored her as he put the boxes in his trunk. "I really wish I'd brought the truck. You sure you don't want me to run home real quick and get it so you can take your bed with you? You don't want to have to buy a new one, do you?"

"It's an uncomfortable mattress anyway." She bent to take her boxes out of his trunk. "Let's just put it all in my car."

Wrinkles creased his brow. "Why would we do that when we've got a second car right here? I'll just follow you over to your friend's place."

"There's no reason for you to go all the way over there. I can take everything myself."

He trailed her back to her car, crossing his arms as he watched her put the boxes in her trunk. "Where does your friend live, anyway?"

Eve pretended to be busy rearranging boxes so she didn't have to answer. Lying to him sucked, and she didn't want to make up a whole fake friend story and stack more lies on top of lies. But that didn't mean she was prepared to admit the truth.

"Look, I'm following you over there no matter what," Boone said. "There's no way I'm letting you carry everything inside by yourself."

"That's not necessary. We can manage fine without you."

"What's the deal, Evie? Just let me help you, for chrissake."

She gave his arm a friendly squeeze, attempting to soothe away his frustration. "I appreciate the offer, really I do. But I don't need you to go with me."

"Why does it feel like you don't want me to know where you're staying?" His frown deepened. "What's your friend's name, and where exactly do they live? I want to know where you're sleeping tonight."

She bristled at his tone. "What's with the interrogation?"

Boone gave her a long, hard look. Then he sighed loudly and rubbed his head. "There is no friend, is there? You lied about having a place to stay."

Stubbornly, Eve crossed her arms and kept her mouth shut. What was there to say? Except admit he was right. Saying nothing was absolutely the better bet.

"What were you going to do after you got rid of me? Sleep in your car?"

Again, she said nothing.

Boone's eyes widened. "Holy shit. You weren't, were you?"

"I was going to find a hostel."

"Are you serious? Have you seen some of those places?"

"They're not all bad. It's fine."

"It's not fucking fine! Why didn't you tell me the truth?"

She drew back, startled by the intensity of his reaction. "You're angry."

"Of course I'm angry. You lied to me. Not to mention,

you'd rather sleep in some bedbug-riddled hostel than ask for my help. That doesn't make me feel great."

"I didn't want to be an imposition."

"Goddammit, Eve." He scrubbed his hands over his face and dragged them through his hair. "You understand you're doing me a huge favor, right? You're entitled to ask for something in return."

"I didn't want you to think I only liked you because of your money and fame and big fancy house."

An odd look came over Boone's face. "Come here," he said with a tip of his chin.

Her feet refused to move. "Why?"

"For fuck's sake," he muttered. "So I can hug you, that's why."

"Oh." That sounded pretty great, actually. Eve edged closer, and his arms wrapped around her, pulling her to his chest.

The man gave good hug. There was something truly divine about being surrounded by him. In addition to the muscly bare arm thing he had going on, he smelled amazing, like cedar-scented soap and acres of warm male skin. And his tank top was insanely soft. What was it made out of? Baby skin? The whole experience was sublime.

But there was more to it than his physical perfection. Eve couldn't remember the last time anyone had made her feel this safe and valued and...*cherished*, simply by holding her. It sounded silly, but there was no other way to describe the feeling.

Not so discreetly, she rubbed her face in his ridiculously soft shirt, breathing in a lungful of him. If there was a heaven, she hoped it smelled just like Boone.

"That was a nice thing to say," he mumbled into her hair.

"Was it?" It hadn't seemed like much to her, but she wasn't

inclined to argue from her current, extremely comfortable position.

A soft laugh rumbled through his chest. "You like me, huh?"

"You're pretty hard not to like."

"Really? Because from where I'm standing it feels like you've been making me work my ass off for it."

A stab of anxious guilt had Eve lifting her head to apologize. But then she saw the smile on his face and realized he was only teasing.

"You're staying at my place," he said, growing serious again. "No arguments. I'm not letting you go to some gross fucking hostel where I'll have to worry about you constantly."

She wanted to say yes, but something made her hesitate. This whole pretend relationship scheme was already weird as hell. Now he wanted her to move in with him? Talk about trial by fire. They'd be all up in each other's space all the time. Not to mention the uneven power dynamic because of the massive difference in their incomes.

Part of the reason she'd refused to let Boone pay her was so she'd have more control over the situation. As long as she was the one doing him a favor, she could retain some of the power. He'd be the one dependent on her. If she accepted his offer to move in, she'd be obligated to him. Dependent on his kindness instead of doing this on her terms.

At her silence, Boone gave a small, resigned nod and let go of her. "If you're not comfortable staying at my house, that's fine—but then you have to let me put you up in a decent hotel until we can find you a new apartment."

Eve stiffened. "No way."

His lips pressed together. "Look, I get that the money thing makes you uncomfortable."

She thrust her chin up, meeting his gaze with a challenging glare. "Yeah, it does."

He nodded, his expression softening. "I understand that your autonomy and pride are important to you."

"They are."

"But you know I didn't always live in a big nice house with a pool, right? I've stayed in a few hostels myself, and I know exactly what they can be like. For the first six years I was in LA, I waited tables and rented some stunningly crappy apartments. When I got the pilot of *Abnormal*, I was subletting a shared bedroom in a falling-down house with five other out-of-work actors that smelled like Vienna sausages."

Eve frowned. "The actors smelled like Vienna sausages? Or the house did?"

"Both, actually."

When she smiled, Boone smiled back at her.

"What I'm saying is, I know exactly what it's like to live or die by tips and wonder how you're going to survive to your next paycheck. It's not something I'm ever going to judge you for. But I'm pretty sure the cost of even a sleazy budget motel or hostel is more than you can comfortably afford. Tell me I'm wrong."

Since she couldn't, she said nothing.

"That amount of money is nothing to me. I spend more than that on haircuts every week."

She gave his shaggy hair a raised eyebrow. "You expect me to believe you get your hair cut every week?"

He ignored the quip, his expression somber as he took her by the shoulders. "Please just let me help you, Evie. I couldn't live with myself if I let you go to a fucking hostel. It's either a decent hotel or my guest room—whichever you're least uncomfortable with."

She chewed on the inside of her lip. "Are you positive you don't mind me crashing at your house and invading your privacy? Like *really* positive?"

The hotel might be the safer, more sensible option, but she

liked being around Boone too much to choose a hotel over the possibility of spending more time with him.

"A thousand percent."

"Okay," she relented with a theatrical sigh. "I guess I can stay with you if it'll make you happy."

The smile that broke over Boone's face banished the last of Eve's doubts. Just like that, it felt like a hundred pounds had been lifted from her shoulders.

She was moving in with Boone Sheridan.

What even was her life anymore?

twelve

"FIRST THINGS FIRST, I'd like her to sign an NDA." Boone's manager whipped a piece of paper out of a leather portfolio and set it on the coffee table. His name was Kurt, and he looked like a less handsome Matt Bomer. He'd arrived at the house with Boone's publicist, a Black woman named Reagan with intimidating posture and killer high heels.

"Absolutely not," Boone said through clenched teeth. He was seated close enough to Eve on the couch that she could feel the tension radiating off him in buffeting waves.

They were meeting with his team in the formal living room on the main floor of Boone's beautiful Sherman Oaks home. After he'd finished moving Eve in earlier, he'd given her a full tour of the house she'd be living in for the immediate future. The floor below the main level connected to the garage and featured a home gym, sauna, and spacious, cabana-like rec room with sliding glass doors that opened out onto the tropically landscaped pool and backyard. Eve thought of it as Boone's man cave, because of the rec room's full bar, pool table, and comfy sectional sofa for kicking back and enjoying his high-end home theater system.

Nice as that room was, Eve preferred the more formal great room where they were sitting now, with its plush, dark brown leather furniture, tiled fireplace, and vaulted ceiling with exposed wood beams. Beyond a pair of arched open doorways, a sunroom provided a gorgeous view of the sunset-tinted sky and the Valley spread out below them.

Boone had told her he used the sunroom for yoga, which had of course inspired an image of him in a pair of those teeny tiny men's yoga shorts, his skin glistening with a sheen of sweat and his muscles bulging as his lithe body moved through a series of impressively bendy positions. *Yum.*

He could use a little namaste right about now, because he'd been wound up like a clock spring ever since his manager and publicist had walked in the front door.

"It's just a standard precaution," Reagan explained in a more appeasing tone than Kurt's.

Boone wasn't the least bit appeased. "There's nothing standard about asking my girlfriend to sign an NDA."

"It's not that we don't trust her—"

"Of course we don't trust her," Kurt cut in. "We don't trust anyone. That's the whole reason NDAs and contracts exist."

Reagan gave him a tight smile that said he wasn't helping and should let her handle the temperamental talent. Her expression grew markedly warmer as she turned back to Boone. "What I meant was it's not personal. We don't have anything against her. We're just protecting your interests like you pay us to do. With the increased media scrutiny you've been getting, it's probably time to start asking all your intimate partners to sign a nondisclosure agreement."

"Fuck that," Boone growled, his eyes flashing with anger. "She's not signing anything."

"*She's* capable of speaking for herself," Eve piped up finally. She'd planned to mostly keep quiet and follow Boone's lead, but this was getting too damn annoying. "Maybe everyone could stop talking about me like I'm not here. What do we say?"

Reagan and Boone looked properly chastened, while Kurt merely grunted. The guy was a real charmer.

Boone reached for Eve's hand. "You're right. I'm sorry."

"That's more like it." She smiled at him as his warm fingers twined with hers. Since Boone didn't want his team to know his relationship with Eve was fake, they were back to pretending to be a real, lovey-dovey couple. "I almost had to deduct a few points from your otherwise stellar boyfriend rating."

"You two are way cute," Reagan said, shaking her head. "People are going to eat you up."

"More likely eat us alive," Boone muttered.

"Reagan's right," Kurt said. "A goddamn preschool teacher? And cute as hell to boot? It's fucking perfect. The two of you are like a fairy tale. Nicely done. Reagan couldn't have cast the role better herself."

Kurt's approval might have meant more to Eve if he'd actually bothered to make eye contact with her even once since he'd walked in the door. It wasn't so much that she thought he didn't like her. More that she was beneath his notice—nothing more than a tool to be used to achieve a desired result. Reagan likely felt the same way, but she at least had the manners to pretend otherwise.

Eve leaned forward to read the NDA. It seemed simple enough. Nothing onerous or objectionable in it. She hadn't planned on sharing any private information about Boone with anyone anyway, much less selling her story to a tabloid.

"I'll sign it," she said.

"Evie." Boone's fingers tightened on hers. "You don't have to."

"I know that. No one's making me do anything. But Reagan's right that it's a justified precaution under the circum- stances." It was an easy thing she could do to make Boone's team happy. If she gave them this, maybe they'd be more chill about the next sticking point in the negotiations. Given Boone's attitude, Eve had a feeling there were going to be more than a few.

He looked pained. "I trust you. You know that, right?"

She gave him another smile. "I do know that, but it's nice to hear you say it."

Reagan removed a Montblanc pen from her designer handbag, and Eve signed the NDA. It earned her another grunt from Kurt when she pushed it toward him.

Boone reclaimed Eve's hand, pulling it into his lap so it rested on his thigh.

"Right," Reagan said, swiping across the screen of her iPad. "Now that we've got that done, let's talk about how we're going to reveal your new love to the world. There are already some fan candids of you two floating around from your lunch yesterday, so that gives us a nice little foundation to build on."

"Are there really?" That was news to Eve, but then she hadn't exactly had a lot of free time for surfing the internet in the last twenty-four hours.

Reagan held her iPad out so Eve and Boone could see the screen. There were three photos: one of Boone posing with a teenage girl next to the order window at the taco stand, and two longer shots of him and Eve in profile as they were eating their lunch. Those two were blurry and mostly focused on Boone. Half of Eve's face was blocked in one of them, and in the other she was biting into her torta.

"Flattering," she said with a grimace. "Of course they'd catch me stuffing my face with food."

"Get used to it." Reagan arched a warning eyebrow as she settled her iPad back on her lap.

Boone released Eve's hand in order to put his arm around her. "No one's ever looked sexier eating a sandwich," he murmured, tugging her against him.

Well. This was certainly nice.

"It's important to keep things low-key at first," Reagan said. "We don't want this to feel like a stunt, so we'll start off with a simple coffee date tomorrow. I'm picturing you two sitting at a table outside a high-traffic café, enjoying each other's company for an hour."

That didn't sound so bad. Eve had been expecting something more involved and high-profile.

Boone gave her a questioning look, and she nodded her assent. "Fine," he said with a nod at Reagan. "That's no problem."

"Excellent." She tapped the screen of her tablet. "We'll ramp you up into the more hard-core couple-y activities over the coming weeks, starting with a dinner date next weekend. After that I'm thinking brunch, an afternoon at the Farmers Market, and finally some very domestic grocery shopping."

"Celebrities, they're just like regular people," Eve muttered.

Reagan acknowledged her with a wry smile. "I'll of course make sure there are paps there tomorrow to capture the totally spontaneous and casual moment between two beautiful people in the throes of new love. And I'll plant a hot tip about Boone's recent change in relationship status."

"We're keeping Eve's name out of it," Boone said.

"For now," Reagan agreed. "Before you two make your red carpet debut as a couple, we'll need to release her name. And at some point we'll want to book you some interviews so you can tell everyone how happy you are with your new girlfriend."

"No." Boone sat up stiffly, withdrawing the arm that had been around Eve as he flashed his angry Hulk eyes again. "Her identity stays protected. No red carpets and no interviews."

"You know people are going to figure out who she is," Kurt broke in impatiently. "It's only a matter of time. One of her old high school friends or coworkers will recognize her and the cat will be out of the bag."

"If that happens, it happens." Boone directed an intimidating glare at Reagan. "But I want you doing everything you can to guard her privacy."

"I understand your protective instincts," Reagan replied, not the slightest bit intimidated. "It's sweet, really. But the reality is, Eve's identity will get out, and it's better for us if we control the narrative. We're working on a tight timeline here, and there's a lot of damage to unwind. If you want this to work, you two need to be photographed on a red carpet together." She pointed a flawlessly manicured fingernail at Boone. "And you're going to have to give an interview where you talk candidly about your relationship."

"The hell I am," he shot back. "I've never done that before, and I'm not starting now."

"You've never been in this much hot water before," Kurt pointed out, earning a scowl from Boone.

"Listen," Reagan said, her pleasant expression concealing a spine of solid steel. "If you're not willing to go the distance, then we're all wasting our time here, and I might as well go home and get back to bingeing *The Witcher*. Either you're committed to doing this or you're not."

Boone pinned Kurt with an accusatory glare. "You told me it would only have to be a few photos!"

Kurt offered a casual shrug in response. "I'm not the PR expert, am I? That's what you pay Reagan for."

"That's right," she said. "And I'm telling you this is what it's going to take to even have a chance of making this problem go away. Don't forget—in a few weeks you're going to be back in Vancouver, getting papped alongside Simone almost every day. What do you think's going to happen then? You think people will remember a couple of photos of you with some unnamed woman you were never officially linked with? No. They'll be right back on their bullshit, talking about you and Simone hooking up off camera. You want to change the narrative? You're going to need to step outside your comfort zone and put in some work."

"Fuck," Boone muttered, rubbing his face. "You're asking me to drag her name through the mud to clear my own."

"You're doing it again," Eve said quietly. Apparently she hadn't just signed on to play girlfriend, but also handler and mediator. Still, she'd had far worse jobs.

Boone's gaze met hers, and he swore under his breath as conflicting emotions warred on his face. He needed this. She could see how much. But he didn't want to put her through it. Well, too bad. She was part of this now, and that meant she got a say.

She reached for his hand. "No one's asked me what I want."

"Good point," Reagan said. "What do *you* want, Eve?"

Eve kept her attention on Boone. He looked like he wanted to say something more, but wisely kept his mouth shut when she arched an eyebrow at him. He didn't look happy about it though.

"Reagan's right," she said. "What's the point of going public at all if we're only half-assing it? I don't care if my name gets out there. Let them release it when the time's right. I think we should do the red carpet if it will help, and you should suck it up and do the interview." The prospect of being photographed on a red carpet scared the pee out of her, but she'd agreed to help Boone and that meant doing whatever it took. He was worth it. "I'm willing to take the fallout if it helps you out of this mess."

Boone's forehead was lined with furrows, his lips pressed together so tightly they'd lost all color. But Eve knew she'd won him over. She could read it in his eyes even before he gave her a short, reluctant nod of assent.

"That settles it," Reagan cut in before Boone could say

anything further. "Now, when I plant the story about you two tomorrow, I'd like to leak that Eve's a preschool teacher."

Eve felt Boone tense up, and she gave his hand a warning squeeze.

Reagan ignored him, addressing Eve directly. "The fact that you're a plain Jane nobody with a wholesome job working with children is too good to sit on. It'll go a long way to cleaning up Boone's image as a homewrecking manwhore."

"How flattering," Eve grumbled.

"At least you're not a homewrecking manwhore," Boone grumbled back.

"For our purposes, plain Jane nobody is a good thing," Reagan said as she tapped her iPad. "It makes Boone look less shallow and lends credence to the possibility that this is a true love match."

"Oh, so I'm shallow now too?" Boone said. "Great."

Reagan's eyebrows twitched up as she shot a look at him. "Not with Eve by your side, you're not."

"Still not all that flattering to me though," Eve pointed out.

"Flattery is your boyfriend's job. Mine is to direct public perception. Which is why I'd like to make the most of the preschool teacher thing. How do you feel about that, Eve?"

"I'm fine with it, if you think it will help."

"Good. So we're all set for tomorrow. I'll have my assistant send Boone the when and where. People will be coming in the morning to get Eve ready for her date, so expect to be up bright and early."

"Wait," Eve said. "What kind of people?"

"I've hired a stylist to work with you. He'll be bringing some clothing options and a team of aestheticians to do your hair and makeup. For tomorrow, we're going très casual and au naturel—think messy bun and minimalist makeup. I want that lazy, *just rolled out of bed with my man on the weekend* look."

"Is all that really necessary?" Eve turned a pleading look on

Boone, who knew very well she wasn't comfortable with him footing the bill for that kind of stuff—and that was before he'd given her a place to stay rent-free. All of this had to be costing him thousands of dollars.

There was no help to be had from him. "You should let them do it."

And the hits to her self-esteem just kept coming. "Are you saying I need a makeover?"

He squeezed her hand. "No, not at all. I think you're perfect exactly as you are."

"If I'm supposed to be so casual and au naturel, I don't see why I can't just *be* casual and au naturel."

"You're adorable," Reagan said as if Eve was a five-year-old who still believed in Santa Claus. "Do you know how much makeup it takes to achieve the perfect no-makeup look? You'll be kissing my feet in gratitude when you see the photos, trust me."

"Evie," Boone said, calling her attention back to him. "I need you to be as prepared as possible for the attention you're about to receive. It might seem frivolous to you, but when you're in the public eye, the hair, the makeup, the clothes, all that stuff that we put on, it acts like armor. Because then it's not *you* people are seeing and tearing apart. It's only the false outer shell someone else created for you."

Eve had never thought of it that way. "Does that actually work?"

"It's not a magic bullet, but helps blunt some of it. Not all though. It's still going to be plenty painful."

"Speaking of the internet…" Reagan pulled a packet of papers out of her bag and tossed it onto the coffee table. "That's a preliminary snapshot my people pulled together of Eve's internet footprint. It's not comprehensive. There may be more lurking out there waiting to be unearthed, but it's the things that are easiest to find and likely to come out first when your name is linked to Boone."

"You did a background check on me?" Eve scooted forward and reached for the packet, curious to see what it contained.

"Everything in there is easily accessible through the data brokers used by reporters and private investigators. Scary, huh?"

"Little bit." They had Eve's birthdate, phone number, all her previous addresses—including her parents' current and former addresses—the schools she'd attended, some of her previous employers, and the names of most of her closest relatives.

Holy crap.

"We've engaged a digital privacy protection service to scrub as much of your personal information as possible, but that only goes so far. You should comb through all your social media and delete anything you wouldn't want made public. Even if your accounts are private, assume that people close to you—old friends, relatives, former coworkers, et cetera—might repost it or sell it to a tabloid. Anything potentially embarrassing needs to be gone well before your name comes out."

"That shouldn't be a problem." Eve had deleted her Facebook account years ago, and most of her other social media profiles were pseudonymous fandom accounts that had never contained any personally identifying information. "The only social media connected to my real name is an Instagram I hardly ever use."

"We know," Reagan said. Because of course her people had snooped through Eve's socials too. "And that's perfect for our purposes. It gives you an authentic social media footprint dating back years, but one that doesn't reveal much about you. I'd like you to let us take it over, starting tonight."

"Take over my Instagram? You mean you'd be posting as me?"

"That's right, like we do for Boone already. We're going to plant a trail of carefully curated bread crumbs on both of your Instagrams. When we're ready to make your identity public, Boone's account will tag yours. At that point, people will be able to go back and see the evidence of your courtship that's been subtly playing out in plain sight all along."

Eve shook her head in wonder. "This sounds like a spy op."

"It essentially has to be. You wouldn't believe the way fans will tear apart every detail of their fave celeb's social media to ferret out clues about their private lives. The FBI should recruit these people and put them to work doing something useful like hunting down serial killers."

Eve did believe it because she'd seen it for herself. That was how the rumors about Boone and Simone had started in the first place. Tinhats—aka fans who believed the people they shipped were secretly a real couple—had been scrutinizing Boone and Simone's every move for years, reading into their interactions and constructing elaborate theories to prove there was something going on between their favorite actors off-screen.

Reagan stood up, phone in hand. "Let's get a few pics now to get us started."

"Now?" Eve asked in alarm. She hadn't exactly primped for a photo shoot.

"Don't worry, your faces won't be showing. We don't want to give the game away yet." Reagan considered the two of them with her hand on her hip, then gestured for them to move together. "Get cozy, you two."

Boone lifted his arm and Eve scooched toward him. Once she was settled against him, he draped his arm around her shoulders.

"I know," Reagan said as she moved behind them. "Feet up on the table, kids. Right next to each other."

Eve and Boone did as directed while Reagan leaned over the back of the couch between them. They were both wearing their Chucks tonight, and she zoomed in on Boone's green sneakers as he tapped one of them against Eve's purple one, just like he'd done in the back hallway of the coffee shop.

Reagan snapped several shots, framing them so it looked like Eve had taken them herself. "Good. Now let's get one zoomed in on you holding hands."

She continued to direct them through various poses, all of them disconnected shots of body parts so you couldn't tell who either of them was—but always looking cozy enough to make it clear Eve was hanging out with an anonymous boyfriend. The final picture Reagan took was a longer shot from behind of Eve's head resting on Boone's shoulder.

"That should be enough to work with for now," she said.

"Can I see?" Eve asked, and Reagan leaned down between them as she swiped through the photos on the screen.

"Will you send me copies of those?" When all this was over, it'd be nice to have some keepsakes to remember the brief time she'd been Boone Sheridan's pretend girlfriend.

"Me too," Boone said.

Eve's gaze met his. "We look pretty cute together."

The corner of his mouth twitched. "Damn right we do."

thirteen

AFTER REAGAN and Kurt had left, Boone ordered Chinese food which he and Eve ate on the terrace outside the dining room. They didn't talk about the meeting. Instead, Eve asked him questions about the house and his usual routines, trying to orient herself to her new living situation so she could avoid stepping on his toes too much.

When they'd finished eating, she helped him carry the dishes into the kitchen and clean up. Eve was still learning her way around, so Boone had to show her which of the many kitchen cabinets hid the trash can and recycling bin.

"You sure you don't want more wine?" he asked, holding up the bottle they'd shared over dinner.

She shook her head as she rinsed her glass. The last thing she wanted was a hangover during their first official public appearance in the morning.

"We can have a grocery order delivered after we get back tomorrow." Boone leaned against the counter as he finished his wine. "You can add whatever you want to the cart so you'll have food to eat."

Eve nodded absently, preoccupied by thoughts of everything else that would be happening tomorrow. The stylists that were coming first thing in the morning to give her image an overhaul, all the people who'd be staring at her when she was out with Boone on their fake coffee date, and the photos of them that would be posted on the gossip sites. Not to mention all the fan speculation and judgment that was about to rain down on her.

Until now, pretending to be Boone's girlfriend had been a small-scale operation and not that big a deal. Eve knew the whole point of doing this was to generate a public reaction, but that aspect of it had only been theoretical so far. After tomorrow it would be very fucking real.

She'd been so busy reassuring Boone that she could handle everything that she hadn't stopped to ask herself if it was true. Was she ready for this? Could she handle it?

"You're not going to argue and insist on paying for your own groceries?"

"What?" Eve spun around to find Boone arching an eyebrow at her. "Oh, um, I can pay for my own groceries if you want."

"I don't want you to pay for your groceries, Evie." Frowning, he set his empty wineglass on the counter. "You okay?"

"Fine." She flashed a bright smile as she whisked his glass away to wash it. "Just tired. It's been a long day. A lot on my mind, I guess."

"Anything you care to talk about?" He moved to her side and picked up the dish towel, ready for drying duty.

She handed him the clean wineglass and shut off the water. "Well…originally you said this would just be for the next month while you're here. But Reagan made it sound like it might take more than that."

Boone let out a sigh. "I didn't plan to need you any longer than that, but I guess she might have a point. Even if I agree to the interview and red carpet appearance she wants, it might not be enough once I'm back in Vancouver."

"I don't mind maintaining the ruse longer if you need me to."

"You sure?"

"It's no skin off my nose. They could post stuff on our Instagram accounts to make it look like we're happily doing the long-distance thing."

His expression grew thoughtful. "You know, I could always fly you up for a weekend if it turns out to be necessary. We could get ourselves photographed together around Vancouver."

"Really?" Eve broke into a grin at the prospect. "Is it wrong that I kind of hope it'll be necessary?"

"I'll tell you what, how about if I promise to do it anyway, just to say thank you. You can come hang out on the set for a day, and then I'll take you around town and show you all the sights. How's that sound?"

Like a fangirl's dream come true, that's how. "It sounds amazing. But you don't have to do all that."

"It would be my genuine pleasure." Boone's eyes crinkled with a heart-melting smile that made her stomach dip with giddiness. When he reached up to put the wineglasses away, his T-shirt rode up, exposing a shadowy band of firm stomach to Eve's covetous gaze.

She looked away and swallowed, her mouth suddenly dry. "We should probably discuss physical contact too."

Boone closed the cabinet and turned back to her with a frown. "What do you mean?"

"Public displays of affection. How much are we talking about? What are the boundaries?"

"You mean on our date tomorrow?" He shrugged. "I'm used to doing all kinds of physical stuff on camera, so I'm okay with pretty much anything short of junk touching."

Wow. Okay. She wished he hadn't put it like that because she was definitely blushing now, which was not helping her seem relaxed and nonchalant about all this.

"What about you?" he asked, watching her closely. "How much PDA are you comfortable with?"

"I don't know." Great, now her voice had gone squeaky. She cleared her throat. "I don't have any experience with faking this sort of thing."

Boone nodded, his tongue working behind his cheek. He probably thought she was some kind of prude, which was totally not the case. Eve's problem was that she'd devoted entirely too much brain space to imagining what it'd be like to kiss him—and a lot more than just kiss him, for that matter. The thought of actually doing it with a real live Boone Sheridan instead of the imaginary one who lived in her head made her a little panicky and a lot intimidated.

"Do you want us to kiss tomorrow?" She tried to sound breezy and unconcerned as if it didn't matter one way or the other. Kiss or no kiss, it was all the same to her.

"Are you uncomfortable with that?"

"Nope. No, it's fine. I'm cool with it."

His eyes narrowed and he cocked his head. "You sure? Because you seem pretty uncomfortable talking about it right now."

"It's just weird, that's all."

"What is? Kissing me or talking about kissing me?"

"Both, actually." Eve crossed her arms, feeling more self-conscious by the second.

"We don't have to kiss if it makes you uncomfortable." Boone's expression had gone oddly flat, giving her the impression she'd managed to make him uncomfortable as well. Terrific.

"I told you it's fine. I can handle this."

His lips pressed together. "I'm just trying to figure out your boundaries here. I want you to feel like you can say no to anything that's outside your comfort zone."

"It'll sell the story better if we kiss, right? I don't have a problem with it. I just have to get used to the idea."

"Your enthusiasm is doing amazing things for my self-esteem right now." A wry smile twitched at the corner of his mouth. "Believe it or not, I don't usually have to convince women to kiss me."

She let out a laugh. "I'll bet."

"If it helps, I have extensive experience kissing—both on- and off-screen—as well as five-star reviews from satisfied past customers."

"Good for you, I guess." Funnily, being reminded how many women Boone had kissed did nothing to allay Eve's nervousness.

He considered her for a moment, his expression growing thoughtful. "You didn't seem to mind it when we held hands. Or when I put my arm around you."

"That's because I didn't. That was all totally fine." Massive understatement. If he knew exactly how much she'd liked it, he'd for sure be uncomfortable doing this. To preserve her dignity and his peace of mind, she couldn't let him know what his fake affection did to her.

Boone lifted his hand like he was about to touch her face, and she fought the urge to tense up as every nerve in her body went into high alert. His fingers grazed her cheek as he pushed her hair back and tucked it behind her ear. "You didn't seem to mind when I kissed your cheek in front of your roommate earlier today."

Eve swallowed, feeling faint. "That was different."

"Why?" His eyes swept over her face as he toyed with the ends of her hair, apparently testing her reaction.

"Because it was spontaneous," she managed to say despite the tingling shivers running down her spine. "I didn't have any idea you were going to do it, so I couldn't get nervous ahead of time."

His brow creased with a frown. "I make you nervous?"

"A little bit."

He dropped his hand to his side. "Are you afraid of me?"

"No." Concerned she might have upset him, she slid her fingers around his wrist to prove she meant it. "I'm not afraid of you. I promise."

He relaxed slightly, but still seemed unsettled.

"I'm not used to kissing that doesn't mean anything. And it's even more intimidating because you're, you know…" She gestured at his face.

"What?"

"All famous and handsome. But I can handle it. I will be able to handle it. You don't have to worry about me."

His frown came back. Slipping his hand out of her grasp, he shoved it into his pocket. "Reagan said we should start low-key, so I don't see any reason for us to kiss tomorrow."

Great. Now she'd made him worry she was going to fall in love with him and make things all messy. It was a definite possibility, but Eve didn't want him knowing that.

"That makes sense," she said, attempting to sound indifferent. "Probably better to save the kissing for later. Build up to it, right?"

He nodded. "No reason to worry about it yet."

"Cool. Yeah. We'll cross that bridge when we come to it."

His eyebrows twitched up. "Try not to sound so excited."

"Sorry. I'll do my best to be less weird."

"Don't worry about it." Boone gave her an encouraging smile. "You don't need to stress about tomorrow. I'm sure you'll do fine."

"Sure," Eve said, hoping he was right. "It'll be a piece of cake. Easy as breathing."

fourteen

EVE FELT like she was going to puke.

She probably wouldn't. Hopefully. Her anxiety had never caused actual vomiting before, but there was always a first time for everything. Boy, wouldn't that make for a great debut? *Boone Sheridan's Mystery Date Pukes on West Hollywood Sidewalk!* The gossip blogs would have a field day.

Boone shot her a worried glance as he cut the car's engine. "You okay over there?"

Eve nodded. "I shouldn't have eaten that protein bar you pushed on me. It's not sitting well."

"I didn't want you going into this hangry."

It was a fair point. She'd been at the mercy of Reagan's team of aestheticians for the last four hours and hadn't had a chance to eat anything. Eve had been exfoliated, masked, deep conditioned, trimmed, painted, moisturized, curled, teased, primed, contoured, and sealed with thick clouds of setting spray and hairspray. Her "messy" bun alone had taken half an hour and a clip-in extension to achieve the ideal not-really-trying casual look.

She pulled down the visor to check her reflection in the

mirror and make sure her bun was still in place. Loath as she was to admit it, Reagan had been dead-on about the no-makeup makeup look. Never in her life had Eve looked this good, but from more than a few feet away, you'd never know she was wearing any makeup at all.

"You look great," Boone assured her as he unfastened his seat belt. He'd been left in charge of his own look this morning, aside from a brief consultation about his wardrobe.

Miguel, the stylist in charge of Eve's transformation, had coordinated her clothing with Boone's. They both wore simple outfits of jeans, Converse, and T-shirts in contrasting colors. Except the jeans Eve was wearing had been constructed of some magical, otherworldly material that rendered them a thousand times more flattering than any other jeans she'd ever had on her body. And her slouchy pink T-shirt had a perfect, soft drape that looked even better after Miguel had added a few darts to tailor it to Eve's shape and tied a knot at the hem.

She'd expected to be forced into a pair of painful high heels, but had been pleasantly surprised when Miguel let her wear her own slightly grubby purple Chucks. Apparently Reagan had posted the shoe photo to Eve's Instagram late last night and instructed Miguel to use it as the basis for today's aesthetic.

The caption Reagan had posted with it had read: *Matchy-matchy #hotdate*

Not super subtle, but not too over-the-top either. None of Eve's forty followers would ever guess those were Boone Sheridan's feet they were looking at.

"Ready to do this?" he asked.

"Sure," Eve muttered through gritted teeth as she unfastened her seat belt.

Boone lifted his mirrored sunglasses and gazed at her in concern.

She forced a smile for him. "I'm fine."

He didn't smile back. "Stay there. I'll come around and open your door."

Things had felt weird between them since their PDA conversation last night. Boone had been acting vaguely distant all morning. Not unfriendly, just more reserved. Cautious almost. It seemed to have left him wary of touching her or getting too close. Which was not at all what Eve had intended and kind of sucked.

She started a little when her door opened and Boone held his hand out for her. Taking a deep breath, she slid her fingers into his palm and let him help her out of the car.

They ended up standing face-to-face staring into each other's eyes for what felt like a weirdly long moment. For a second Eve nearly thought Boone might be about to kiss her, despite what he'd said last night. But then he backed up, allowing her to step away from the car so he could close the door.

Maybe that had been part of the act? She couldn't always tell what was real with him and what wasn't.

Reagan had chosen a trendy café on Melrose for their soft launch coffee date. Boone had parked on a side street two blocks away, and he kept hold of Eve's hand as they walked down the sidewalk together.

Now that they were out in the open where people could see them, Eve's performance anxiety kicked into high gear. Her body seemed to have forgotten how to perform basic functions. Like walking. Her movements felt stiff and clumsy. She was desperately afraid of tripping and falling. And what did she normally do with her face? She had no clue what a natural expression felt like anymore.

As her stomach churned with panic, she found herself wishing Boone would put his arm around her. But he didn't. Instead he kept a safe distance between them, holding her hand loosely in his.

Eve's gaze darted around, looking for cameras. "Are the photographers here already?"

"Probably." Boone appeared unconcerned as he tugged her down the sidewalk.

"Where do you think they are? Will we be able to see them?"

"Try not to look for them. We're not supposed to know they're here."

"Right." She jerked her gaze down to the sidewalk in front of her feet. "Sorry."

"They're probably across the street from the patio. I doubt they'll get closer than that today."

"Okay." She tried not to look that direction as Boone led her inside the café.

Unlike when he visited Antidote, he immediately took his sunglasses off and hooked them on the collar of his T-shirt as they got in line. Eve left on the Ray-Bans Miguel had picked out for her. Reagan wanted her hidden behind sunglasses so she'd be harder to identify for the time being.

People were definitely paying attention to them. A few were blatantly staring at Boone, others conducting not so subtle whispered conversations. Most of the gawking was concentrated on him, but a nonzero number were giving Eve curious looks, clearly wondering who she was. A bead of sweat trickled down her chest when she saw someone lift their phone to aim a camera in their direction.

"Is something wrong?" Boone whispered. He kept a pleasant expression on his face, but she could hear the implied frown in his tone. "You seem tense. Is it okay that I'm holding your hand?"

"It's fine." That wasn't the problem at all. But he didn't seem to believe her, because his fingers slackened on hers as if he was thinking of letting go. Eve squeezed his hand, holding on tight, and was gratified when he squeezed back. "I think I'm having stage fright," she whispered. "I can't remember how to act normal."

"Try to relax. You're doing great." His hand slipped out of hers and settled on the back of her neck, pulling her closer. As she leaned gratefully against him, strong fingers massaged her taut muscles, melting the tension away.

"Wow," she sighed happily. "Keep that up and I won't even be able to remember my own name."

"Acting is all about learning to be present in the moment." Boone's voice was a low, soothing murmur as he worked his magic on her neck and shoulders. "The key is paying attention to what's happening right now and letting go of the noise trying to distract you. If you keep your focus on what's in front of you, you'll forget to be worried about your own performance and react with authenticity."

Eve hummed in agreement. She was certainly present in *this* moment, incapable of focusing on anything but the blissful feeling of Boone's fingers rubbing her neck.

"Look at me," he commanded softly, and she lifted her gaze to his.

The lingering gnaw of dread in her stomach dissipated into a fluttery tightness as she stared into his eyes. He couldn't even see her properly through her sunglasses, but it felt like he was gazing directly into her soul.

"Giving all your attention to something else releases you from your own head and keeps you anchored in the moment. Concentrate on the feel of my fingers touching you and the sound of my voice. Focus on me and let everything else fall away."

Oh man. Was the point of this little exercise to make her swoon dead away? Cause if so, good job. She was seconds away from dissolving into a puddle on the floor.

"That's right, just like that." Boone's lips curved into a devastating smile. "There you are, gorgeous."

"Excuse me. The line's moving up," a polite and extremely ill-timed voice commented behind them.

Boone's smile flicked away. "Thanks, man. Sorry."

As they shuffled forward, Eve kept her focus on him like he'd instructed, relishing the excuse to brazenly stare at his perfect face. This was officially the greatest exercise ever. If this was acting, sign her up. She could do this all day.

"You're doing amazing," he whispered, bending close to her ear. "You're totally killing it right now."

A delicious shiver rippled through her as his warm breath tickled her neck, but for once Eve didn't try to hide it. She was living in the moment. Reacting authentically to sensations as she experienced them. Which was why, when she felt an impulse to reach up and run her fingers through Boone's beard, she went with it.

It was a pure delight for her fingertips, wiry-soft rather than scratchy like she'd imagined. And because she was so present and focused on him, she heard his breath catch and felt his stomach muscles contract.

He made a quiet noise in the back of his throat as her fingernails scraped lightly over his jaw. "That feels nice." His voice sounded deeper and rougher than it had a moment ago, and his eyes had gone dark, the pupils expanding like pools of spilled ink.

Damn, he was good at this. That did not look like the reaction of a man who was used to having women touch him all the time. He looked more like a starving man who'd had a cheeseburger dangled in front of him and was trying not to pounce and devour it whole. The guy deserved an Oscar.

The line moved up again, and Eve reluctantly dropped her hand from Boone's face to urge him forward. She could see the chalkboard menu now, and she read the list of drinks, debating whether she should get her usual cappuccino or something more adventurous.

Boone caught her fingers with his free hand. She turned to look at him, and he brought them to his lips, rubbing her knuckles against his beard. "You know what you want?"

You, she had the strongest urge to say.

Which would be highly inappropriate. No one would hear her say it except Boone. There was no call for that level of improv. Like her makeup, they only needed to look believable from a few feet away.

"I haven't decided," was what she said instead. "What about you?"

Beneath her fingers, his mouth twitched with a smile that seemed to imply they were sharing an inside joke. As if he knew what she'd been thinking and was thinking the exact same thing.

Obviously Eve had an overactive imagination. She might be getting a little too into character.

"Pretty sure you know my coffee order by heart," he said.

"Thought you might want to shake things up."

His shoulders lifted in a shrug. "I know what I like, and I like what I know."

By the time they made it to the front of the line, Eve had decided on the cappuccino. Boone paid for their order, was given a number, and they ventured out to the patio. A two-top with a clear view to the street had been reserved, and he steered Eve toward it.

"This is for us?" she asked.

He nodded as he pulled one of the chairs out for her. She was getting the full royal treatment. "Reagan's doing."

Now that they were outside and in the open again, Eve couldn't help thinking about the photographers lurking across the street. Shifting in her seat, she attempted to strike a casual yet flattering pose, then felt like an awkward jackass. What did she usually do with her hands? Ugh, now her nose had started to itch, but she was afraid to scratch it. Because of course that would be the photo that made all the gossip sites. *Boone Sheridan's New Lady Love Caught on Camera Picking Her Nose!*

"You're tensing up again," Boone said. "Stay with me, gorgeous."

"Sorry. It's hard not to think about them out there watching us and taking photos at what will undoubtedly be the worst possible moment."

"I know." He leaned forward and extended his arm across the table, palm up. "Give me your hand."

Eve laid her palm on his, and Boone's fingers wrapped around hers in a warm, reassuring grip. It helped, but didn't entirely banish her intrusive thoughts about unflattering angles and double chins and how much her stomach was pooching out because she was sitting down.

"Want to know what I thought the first time I laid eyes on you?"

Well, that had certainly succeeded in distracting Eve from everything else. "What?"

His mouth crooked in an evil smile. "I'll tell you if you tell me what you thought of me first."

"That's not fair. You're the one who brought it up."

He shrugged. "Guess you'll have to decide how bad you want to know."

"I seriously doubt you even noticed me the first time."

"Oh, I noticed you all right." A soft smile played on his lips as his thumb traced circles on her palm. "You were wearing bright purple lipstick and matching nail polish that day. Purple lips and purple nails to go with your purple Chucks."

Well, shit. He wasn't lying after all.

"I thought you looked scruffy," Eve said, and grinned when it got a laugh out of him.

"Thanks very much. Great for my ego as always."

"I liked it," she admitted, feeling her cheeks flush. "I thought you were even better looking in person. But also—"

She broke off, distracted by the approach of a waiter. But he was only delivering drinks to the table next to theirs.

Boone squeezed her hand. "But also what?"

She looked at him again, remembering how tense he'd seemed that first time she'd seen him, like a man who was bracing himself for something unpleasant. The way he'd glanced uneasily around him and avoided looking directly at anyone. "I thought you looked like you desperately wanted to be left alone."

His mouth flattened out as he stared down at their hands. "You weren't wrong about that."

"My turn," Eve said, rubbing her thumb over his.

His gaze lifted to hers. "I couldn't take my eyes off you."

"Come on." She shook her head in disbelief. "You're supposed to be honest, not feed me a line."

"It's not a line. It's the truth. Why do you think I came back every day?"

"Because you like coffee?"

Boone's sudden smile filled up her chest and warmed her whole body. "I can make coffee at home. There was only one place I had a chance to see you."

fifteen

BOONE WAS ALREADY AWAKE when Eve's alarm
went off at some ungodly hour on Monday morning. He'd
slept fitfully all night, too aware of her presence down the hall
and tormented by his own thoughts.

What he'd told her yesterday at the café was true. He
hadn't been able to take his eyes off her the first time he'd seen
her. But it wasn't the whole truth. The whole truth was too
much to admit.

He hadn't told Eve how she'd stood out to him like a shock
of color in a black-and-white photograph. Or the way her
smile had pierced the numb fog he'd been living in for months.
How he hadn't been able to stop thinking about her. How he'd
thought about her every night since.

Boone remembered every detail of their first encounter
with bizarre clarity. She'd done something to him that day,
something he still didn't understand.

It had started with the way she'd said *Hey* when he'd
approached the register. There'd been a hint of a smile in her
voice, a warmth like she was greeting an old friend, that had

instinctively made him look up even though he'd been trying to hide his face.

Looking into Eve's eyes for the first time had been like stepping outside on a dark morning and unexpectedly seeing a sunrise so spectacular you had to pause and appreciate it for a moment.

But then he'd watched her smile freeze in place and seen that telltale widening of her eyes. And disappointment had settled in his stomach like a lead fishing weight. Because she'd recognized him. Of course she had.

Most people who recognized him reacted in one of three ways: gushing at him, going painfully shy, or awkwardly trying to pretend they weren't staring while staring anyway. All three responses made Boone varying degrees of uncomfortable and generally spelled the end of any hope for normal human interaction. He'd girded himself for Eve's reaction, idly wondering which route she'd go.

But she hadn't done any of those things.

What she'd done instead was give him a small, kind smile. A smile that said she understood. As if he wasn't simply recognized, but *known*. It had caused a weird *ping* in his chest. Not painful, but startling, like someone had plucked a string under tension.

There'd been nothing shy or gushing or the least bit awkward about Eve as her bottomless brown eyes had gazed at him without blinking. *What can I do for you?* she'd asked, her voice slightly more subdued but still warm.

For some inexplicable reason, Eve had been living rent-free in his head ever since.

And now she was living *in his house*, of all the crazy things, sleeping down the hall from him. And they were supposed to be faking an intimacy Boone couldn't afford to admit how much he wanted.

He lay in bed listening to the floorboards creak as she

moved around her room. Followed by the sound of her shower running.

Which of course filled his head with images of Eve naked in said shower. Her skin wet and glistening, soap bubbles clinging to her full breasts, droplets of water dripping off her plump, round ass. Sweet Jesus, his morning wood was going to kill him.

He'd been messing with fire by asking Eve to play his fake girlfriend. Why the fuck had he gone and done that?

You know why.

As soon as he heard Eve's shower cut off, Boone forced himself out of bed and stumbled into his own bathroom. He got into the shower and turned on the cold water, the punishing, icy shock of it exactly what he needed and no more than he deserved.

He still felt ashamed of the way he'd let himself get carried away during their fake date yesterday. He should have been more careful than that, especially after Eve had admitted to being afraid to kiss him.

I'm not used to kissing that doesn't mean anything.

Boone wasn't sure why that had bothered him so much. Maybe because, now that she'd said it, he didn't like the thought of her getting used to it—and certainly not because of him.

Obviously, he was concerned she might read too much into it when they finally did kiss. He didn't want Eve to develop feelings for him and get hurt. That was a given.

But also, maybe he was worried *he* might not be able to kiss her without feeling anything. Maybe that was even the thing that worried him the most.

It was why he'd been trying to put more distance between them since. Initiating intimacy that wasn't strictly required was begging for trouble. He'd seen it happen on set enough times before, actors getting a little too comfortable with each other and blurring the line between the role and real life. He'd even done it himself a time or two.

He couldn't take that risk with Eve. She wasn't an actor. She was a real person with real feelings. Hell, she'd as much as admitted she had a crush on him—or used to have one, anyway. He had a responsibility to look out for her. Protect her. Not take advantage of her to satisfy his own reckless impulses. He shouldn't be doing anything to encourage feelings he wouldn't be able to follow through on.

Only somehow his good intentions had all gone up in smoke yesterday when he'd seen how apprehensive she was.

What was he supposed to do when the connection he'd been trying to keep to a minimum was the only thing that seemed to put her at ease? The more Boone had touched her, the more she'd seemed to relax and forget about the eyes and camera lenses on them. Eve had wanted physical comfort—needed it, even. How could he deny her that?

The problem, as always, was that he'd gone too far. He'd enjoyed having her close to him a little too much. So much that he'd forgotten for a moment they were only supposed to be pretending.

Especially when she'd run her fingers through his beard. It had hit him like an electric shock straight to the heart, waking up feelings he'd been trying hard to ignore. *Careful,* a voice inside his head had tried to warn him. *This is too risky.*

But Boone had been too present in the moment to listen to that cautious and oh so sensible voice. He'd tuned it out as extraneous noise and followed his instincts instead, letting his newly awakened heart be his guide.

That was why he'd said the things he'd said. Why he'd confessed what Eve had done to him the first time he'd laid eyes on her.

No more dropping truth bombs like that. He couldn't let her know how deep and tangled his feelings were for her. This arrangement would only work if he kept his feelings out of it and his hands as far away from Eve as possible.

By the time Boone finally made it downstairs, she'd already left for work, leaving the scent of her shampoo and perfume behind. Flowery and sweet, but not overbearing. Subtle enough to be enticing. It lingered in the house hours after she'd gone. He kept catching faint whiffs of it in unexpected places. Every time, it hit him straight in the gut.

Reagan called later that morning to let Boone know Hot Hollywood Nights had featured the photos from yesterday on the front page of the site with a headline touting a major scoop about a new mystery woman in Boone's life.

In the planted story accompanying the photos, an unnamed source reported they'd been seeing each other for several weeks and Boone was "absolutely head over heels" but trying to keep the relationship off the public radar to protect his new girlfriend from unwanted attention. "She doesn't work in Hollywood," the source was quoted as saying. "She's a preschool teacher. A regular person living a normal life, which is one of the things Boone loves about her."

Boone thought the whole thing sounded like transparently contrived bullshit, but it seemed to have done what it was meant to do. Most of his Twitter notifications were people posting the story and reacting to it—either negatively or positively—instead of hating on him for sleeping with their favorite football player's wife. So far, so good.

Maybe this whole stupid plan would actually work.

Assuming he didn't go losing his head.

"I guess I don't look so bad," Eve said when she saw the photos for the first time after she got home from work that evening.

Boone watched her from the chair opposite the couch (look at him, keeping his distance!), kicked back with his feet up on the coffee table. Eve's nose wrinkled as she swiped through the photos, as though she didn't like what she saw.

"A few other gossip sites have picked up the story," he said. "Reagan sounded pleased when she called today."

"That's good, I guess." Eve continued to frown at her phone as she sipped her wine.

"She wants us to stay off the radar for the rest of the week and avoid being seen together."

At that, she looked up at him. "Is that why you didn't come in for your usual coffee today?"

He nodded, ignoring the hollow ache in his chest. "It's probably not a good idea for me to keep showing up there anyway. Too much risk of someone seeing us together and ID'ing you as my mystery girlfriend. We *really* don't want people knowing where you work."

"Too bad," she said. "I missed seeing you today."

Boone had missed it too. His whole day had felt off-kilter. The hours had passed more slowly without his usual outing to break it up, and the house had felt extra empty without Eve in it. It had only taken a couple of days for him to get used to having her around the place.

He downed a mouthful of beer. "Reagan's planting another story in a different tabloid about how upset I am that our secret's out of the bag."

"How does that work exactly? Does she just call them up and say, 'Hi, I'm Boone Sheridan's publicist, and I'd like to feed you a story that may or may not be true, and oh by the way, you're not allowed to tell anyone it came from me?'"

"Depends on the outlet and the story. Sometimes it works exactly like that. Other times she'll have one of her assistants email an anonymous tip, or post it online somewhere under a fake profile."

"It really is like espionage."

"A little."

Eve looked back down at her phone as she tapped her thumb on the screen. "So now we do nothing and pretend to be hiding?"

"Until Saturday night. Reagan made us dinner reservations for our next appearance."

"Super," Eve said, not bothering to hide her grimace. "Can't wait."

He didn't like that she seemed to be dreading their next public appearance. When he'd dragged her into this whole thing, he hadn't considered that she might get stage fright. "It'll be fine. You did great yesterday."

Her lips pursed and pulled to the side. "Sure, except the part where I froze up—twice—and totally almost blew it because I was too nervous to act natural."

"No one noticed. You pulled it off like a champ."

"Only because you got me through it." Her eyes met his. "Thank you again for that. You knew exactly what to do."

Boone swallowed and looked away so she wouldn't see how guilty he felt.

"The fandom's talking about us," she said, blessedly changing the subject. "Mission accomplished there. Although a lot of the conversation is people arguing about whether it's a PR stunt."

"Hopefully we'll convince them soon."

"People are upset with you for abandoning Simone. Some of them think you're cheating on her with me."

He frowned. "Evie, don't read that crap. Reagan'll keep on top of it for us. You don't have to expose yourself to all the vitriol."

Eve looked up at him, her brow creased with what looked like a question in her eyes. It felt like she was trying to work herself up to asking him something.

"What?" he said warily.

Her lips parted, but before she could speak, his phone started buzzing loudly on the coffee table.

They both looked at it. Simone's name showed clearly on the screen.

"Her ears must have been burning," Eve said.

"Sorry," Boone muttered, grabbing it as he got to his feet. "I need to take this."

"Sure," she said. "Go ahead."

He retreated upstairs to his bedroom, closing the door as he took the call.

sixteen

BEING roommates with Boone wasn't as nerve-racking as Eve had feared. Mostly because she barely saw him.

She was scheduled for the opening shift at Antidote Monday through Friday that week, so she left at the crack of dawn every day and didn't get home until nearly seven. Even then, she didn't see much of him. He was either out somewhere, or down in his home gym, or up in his room with the door closed. Because Eve had been up since before sunrise, she went to bed by nine or ten. Most nights she was lucky if they ran into each other briefly in the kitchen or he called out a greeting on his way to or from his room.

After a few days, it was hard not to wonder if he was intentionally avoiding her. Was he that busy? Or did he regret inviting her to move in with him? She had no idea what his schedule was like or what he did with himself all day. Maybe he was just private and valued his alone time.

Whatever the reason, he didn't seem to have any interest in spending time with her, and Eve couldn't help feeling a little hurt by that. Last weekend she'd thought they were becoming friends. Now, not so much. Even though they were sleeping in the same house, they were like two strangers moving through their separate lives, hardly speaking at all.

It left Eve feeling pretty lonely in her new living situation. Having just lost her best friend and boyfriend in one fell swoop didn't help, even if she was well rid of both. So it was a welcome surprise when she got a text from Alice asking if she wanted to meet for lunch.

They arranged to meet the next day at a sandwich shop in Sherman Oaks, not far from the preschool where Eve worked.

"I hope you don't think it's weird that I invited you to lunch," Alice said after they'd placed their orders. She'd come from her office and was more dressed up than she'd been at the party in a floral blouse, cardigan, and work pants.

"No, not weird." Eve glanced down, checking her *Adventure Time* T-shirt for milk froth spatter. "Though I guess I was a little surprised."

Alice's smile grew slightly embarrassed. "I can't claim not to have an ulterior motive. Boone may have told Griffin you'd lost your apartment and moved in with him."

"I didn't exactly lose it," Eve said as she dipped her napkin in her water glass to wipe a milk stain off her shirt. "I still know where it is. I just can't stand the other person who lives there anymore."

"Boone wasn't very forthcoming about the circumstances."

"Shocker," Eve said wryly, earning a laugh from Alice.

"Yeah, that's Boone for you." Shaking her head, Alice reached for her iced tea. "So I figured I'd go directly to the source for the story."

Eve shifted uneasily in her chair. This was one of Boone's closest friends, and she didn't like lying to her. She also didn't want to cause any additional problems for him by saying the wrong thing. "I know it seems rash to take such a big step so fast. I don't blame you for being suspicious. You probably think I'm taking advantage of Boone."

"I wouldn't go that far." Alice's smile warmed. "I just figured, if you're going to be part of Boone's life, we should get to know each other better. Since the boys are best friends and all, we'll be seeing a lot more of each other."

"Well, *I'd* be suspicious if I had a rich friend who'd shacked up with a penniless barista he'd only known a few weeks. The whole thing seems pretty bananas to me, and I'm the one doing it."

"It's not all that crazy for Boone," Alice said with a shrug.

"Really?" Eve's eyebrows raised. "He makes a habit of sweeping minimum-wage service workers off their feet and inviting them to move in with him, does he?"

Alice huffed out a laugh. "No, not specifically. But he can be impulsive sometimes. He's got a kind heart and a tendency to make decisions based on his gut."

"Bet that gets him in trouble a lot."

"Not as much as you might think. He's got a pretty good gut." Alice's lips pressed together. "Usually."

Eve gathered there was a story there, and not a happy one. Although she was desperately curious to know what it was, she didn't feel entitled to pry. "Boone very generously offered to let me stay with him when I moved out of my apartment. He had to talk me into it. If I'd had anywhere else to go, I would have said no. Then again, if I'd had someplace else to go, I doubt he would have offered."

Alice smiled. "Like I said, he's got a kind heart."

An employee stopped by the table to drop off Eve's pork belly bánh mì and Alice's Thai mango salad.

As Alice stirred her salad around, she glanced up at Eve. "You don't have to tell me the details of what happened if you don't want to. I don't mean to be nosy."

"I don't mind," Eve said, picking a stray piece of cucumber off her plate.

Time had taken away enough of the sting that she thought

it might feel good to talk about it. So she told Alice about Vince and Becca, the sex tape, and her accidental encounter with Boone in the back hallway of the coffee shop.

Alice listened to the whole tawdry saga with a sympathetic ear, expressing shock and concern in the appropriate places. Seeing Alice's indignation—on behalf of someone she barely knew, no less—reassured Eve that she hadn't overreacted. Something she knew rationally, but it felt good to have it reinforced by an objective third party. Her brain's attempt at self-recrimination could officially go suck it.

"Now that I know the full story, I'm not the least bit surprised Boone invited you to move in," Alice said. "It sounds exactly like something he'd do under the circumstances."

Eve laughed uncomfortably. "I guess he felt sorry for me and decided to adopt me as his own personal charity case."

Alice considered her silently for a moment. "I don't think it's like that at all. In fact, I suspect Boone needed to be rescued as much as you did. The two of you just happened to find each other at exactly the right time."

Eve didn't know what to say to that.

Smiling to herself, Alice speared a piece of mango with her fork. "It's funny, because that's exactly what happened with me and Griffin. He swooped in and rescued me when I needed a job and a place to live." She popped the mango in her mouth and shook her head softly, glancing up at Eve as she swallowed. "But it turned out he needed me as much as I needed him. Apart, we were a couple of lost souls, but being together made us both stronger. I'll never stop being grateful we found each other."

A lump of emotion formed in Eve's throat. As much as she wished that could be true of her and Boone, it simply wasn't the case. Theirs wasn't a perfect love story like Alice and Griffin. They weren't any kind of love story at all. She and Boone were nothing more to each other than a temporary means to an end. But Eve couldn't explain that to Alice without breaking Boone's trust.

Even so, what Alice had said struck a chord. Especially when Eve thought about how solitary Boone was, how he often seemed to be holding something back, and the way he'd sometimes shut down and refuse to talk. Not to mention that he was deceiving all the people closest to him, including Alice and Griffin, by letting them believe he was in a real relationship. Why? What was he trying to protect himself from? Could he be as much of a lost soul as Eve?

"I'm honestly so relieved Boone's got you," Alice went on. "We were worried about him spending so much time alone, so it's good to know he hasn't been completely isolated. I was afraid he'd closed himself off too much, but it makes me feel better to know he's let you in."

A weight dropped through Eve's stomach. Boone hadn't let her in at all. Not really. Not the way Alice thought. "You said you thought he needed to be rescued. From what? Is there a reason you've been so worried about him?"

Alice gave Eve a long look as if she was weighing how much she should share. "Boone's been having a tough year," she said finally. "I assume you know about the stuff in the press right now."

"About Simone Alexander? I've seen some of it."

Alice nodded, falling silent again for a moment. Eve had the sense she was trying to tread carefully. "Boone's pretty private when it comes to things that are bothering him. He's not much into sharing—he's more of a 'bottle it all up inside until it eats away at him' kind of guy."

"I've noticed that." Eve was relieved to hear Alice confirm it. At least it wasn't something he only did with her.

"Has he told you he was supposed to be shooting a movie here in LA over his hiatus?"

Eve shook her head.

"It figures he wouldn't say anything." Alice frowned as she sipped her iced tea. "It was for one of the streaming services. He was excited about the project because it was a family movie, something his nephews would have been able to see him in. But also because it was potentially the start of a franchise that could have been a real boost for his career. It would have helped him break out into roles beyond *Abnormal Investigations*, which is something I know he's been wanting for a while." She paused, looking at Eve. "This is just between us, okay? It's not something he wants widely known."

"Of course," Eve promised. Even if she hadn't signed the NDA, she'd never spread Boone's private business around.

"After those photos were published of him leaving Simone's house, the scandal blew up much bigger than he was prepared for. Because her husband is such a high-profile NFL star, suddenly a lot of people who'd never heard of Boone before knew him as the TV actor who wrecked that famous football player's marriage." Alice scowled and shook her head. "Anyway, after that, the studio decided to replace Boone with someone less controversial—although the official story is that it was because of a scheduling conflict."

Now Eve understood why Boone had seemed so aimless all summer. The job he'd planned on having had fallen through, leaving him at loose ends. No wonder he'd seemed so bitter every time the subject came up.

"But that was just the icing on top of the cake," Alice continued, frowning as she pushed the remains of her salad around. "They've patched things up now, but Griffin and Boone had a falling-out at the end of last year."

"I thought I sensed some odd tension between them last weekend," Eve said carefully. "Even though it's obvious they're really close."

"They are. Or they were—Boone's been more distant since it happened. Not that he's ever been very big on opening up.

When I first met him, I thought he was this sweet, fun, easy-going guy—and he is, mostly. But he's also good at hiding when he's unhappy. He doesn't like to admit that something's wrong." Her lips pulled into a thin smile. "He and I have that in common."

It was hard to imagine Alice being unhappy when she seemed to have the perfect life. But no one's life was actually perfect, was it? Even people who lived in beautiful houses with their handsome movie star boyfriends.

Alice set her fork down and pushed the bowl away. "You ever have a friend who was in a relationship with someone you didn't approve of? And you're so convinced the person is bad news and your friend is going to get hurt that you decide you have to say something to them, because you can't just stand by and watch the train wreck unfold without trying to stop it?" Her eyes were troubled as they met Eve's. "Have you ever been in that situation?"

"In high school," Eve said. "I told my friend Imani that I thought her new boyfriend was hung up on someone else and just using her to make this other girl jealous."

"What happened?"

"Imani didn't speak to me for a month—until her boyfriend dumped her for the other girl."

Alice nodded. "That's sort of what happened with Griffin and Boone."

"Not because Griffin was dating you?" Eve couldn't believe it, given how much Boone seemed to like Alice. How could anyone think she was bad for Griffin?

"No, not because of me." Her lips pulled into a tight smile. "Although I suspect the fact Griffin was in his first serious relationship since Boone had known him might have been an exacerbating factor. But no, Boone was with someone who wasn't good for him. And Griffin told him so."

Simone Alexander. It had to be. Griffin must have warned Boone off dating his married costar.

"What happened?" Eve asked.

"Pretty much the same thing that happened with you and your friend. Boone got angry, and they didn't speak for a couple of months. Until the relationship fell apart, and Boone apologized to Griffin. But she'd already done a lot of damage by then." Alice's jaw clenched, her eyes harder than Eve had ever seen them. "That woman really did a number on him. She was—" Alice cut herself off and pressed her lips together. "Let's just say Boone wasn't in great shape for a while after they broke up. We've been concerned about him, but of course he won't talk about it. He just keeps insisting he's fine."

"I had no idea," Eve said. But it explained a lot of things. Like why he'd sounded so bitter when she'd asked him if he'd ever been in love.

"I figured." Alice shook her head. "It's not like Boone's going to tell you about any of it. But now you know why I was so happy to see him with you. I hope it means he's doing better."

"Why are you telling me all this? I'm not sure Boone would like it." Eve was certain he wouldn't, in fact.

"Probably not." Alice's gaze met Eve's, her expression serious. "But I wanted you to know so you could...I don't know, keep an eye on him, I guess? And maybe be a little gentle with him. Cut him some extra slack if he needs it."

Eve was at a loss for words. She barely knew Boone, and now Alice had trusted her with all this personal information and was asking her to look out for him like Eve was a permanent fixture in his life.

Alice's eyes widened as her expression grew anxious. "Oh god, I haven't scared you off, have I? Did I say too much? Are you planning your exit strategy now?"

"None of the above," Eve assured her. "It helps me make

sense of some things, actually." Everything Alice had confided made Eve feel an even stronger sense of empathy for him. He was hurting, and in a way that wasn't so different than her. That might explain why he'd been drawn to Eve. He hadn't just felt sorry for her when he'd seen her crying in the back hallway at Antidote—he'd been able to relate.

"Oh good." Alice let out a long exhale of relief. "Boone's a really, really great guy. I can tell you that with absolute certainty."

That, at least, was something Eve already knew about him.

EVE HAD A LOT TO THINK ABOUT AFTER HER CONVERSATION with Alice. She still hadn't decided what, if anything, she should do about this new information when she turned into Boone's gated driveway at the end of the day.

An unfamiliar luxury SUV was parked next to the house. As Eve pulled into the garage, she wondered if it belonged to Reagan or Kurt. She wasn't exactly thrilled by the prospect of dealing with either of them tonight.

As she came through the door between the garage and the hallway outside the gym, Boone called out to her from the rec room. "Eve? Is that you?"

"Yeah, it's me," she replied as she closed the door behind her.

"I want to introduce you to someone."

Curiosity propelled her down the hall. She stepped around the corner, into the rec room, and came to a dead stop.

Simone Alexander was seated on the sofa next to Boone.

seventeen

SIMONE ALEXANDER WAS HERE. Not in Vancouver. She was in Los Angeles. In Boone's *house*, of all goddamn places.

Eve couldn't believe it, considering how much trouble they were all going to in order to convince the world there was nothing going on between Boone and Simone. If the press caught wind of this, they'd have a freaking field day.

"C'mere," Boone said, waving Eve over. "Come meet Simone."

She was inhumanly beautiful and even smaller than she looked on TV. Her blonde hair was styled in perfect, glossy waves and her makeup flawless. Although it didn't quite hide how red her eyes were. She appeared to have been crying recently. And yet she still managed to offer Eve a picture-perfect smile.

"It's nice to meet you," Eve said, coming into the room and stopping a few feet away from them. Boone's expression was strained, and she sensed an odd undercurrent of tension in the air. It felt as if she'd walked into the middle of an argument or some other kind of heavy conversation. Not great. Not great at all.

"Boone's been telling me all about you." Simone turned the brightness of her smile up a few more watts, but it still didn't meet her eyes. "He said you're a fan."

"Did he?" Eve shot a look at Boone, not loving that he'd told Simone something he knew Eve found embarrassing.

He didn't appear to be listening, however, for all that he'd said he wanted to introduce them. Instead, he was staring down at his lap with his jaw set grimly.

"He told me you might come up to Vancouver to visit the set once we start shooting the new season." Simone's smile seemed to imply she was pleased by the prospect, but something about it felt brittle.

"I don't know," Eve replied, unable to interpret the mood in the room. "Maybe. I guess we'll see."

Before today, she'd idolized Simone. But right now she wasn't sure what to make of her. If Simone was the ex Alice had been talking about, if she'd hurt Boone that badly, Eve didn't want her anywhere near him. Not that Eve was entitled to have any say in the matter. She was just supposed to stand here and keep her mouth shut while he did whatever the hell it was he was doing with Simone right now.

"July and August are great months to visit," Simone said. Beside her, Boone continued to look distracted and sullen, leaving her to carry the conversation. "Lots of sunshine and not too much rain. October and November are pretty cold and dreary, which I'm sure you can tell from watching the show. Lots of scenes set in the rain with our breath fogging the air."

"I'll keep that in mind." Eve shifted her feet, feeling increasingly uncomfortable. She'd clearly interrupted *something* between them.

Simone glanced at Boone and her smile slipped. Reaching across the couch, she curled her fingers around his hand. He didn't look up, but his fingers flexed around hers before she drew her hand back and sat up again.

When Simone looked back at Eve, her expression was different—shakier and less resolutely cheerful, as if she'd given up trying to pretend everything was great. "I want you to know how much I appreciate everything you're doing for us, Eve."

"It's fine," Eve said, fixated on the word *us* and the way they'd held hands, all of which implied the two of them were some sort of team. "Don't worry about it."

Simone's mouth tightened. "I'm just so sorry it's necessary, and even more sorry it's going to bring unpleasant attention to you."

"I'm glad to help. Really." Eve was finding it difficult to reconcile the way Alice had described Boone's ex with the woman sitting next to him right now. The Simone in front of her seemed distressed and slightly fragile. Was she really the same person Alice had said was so bad for Boone?

"It means a lot to me." Simone looked at Boone again, and this time he raised his eyes to meet hers. "To both of us."

Again with the *us*. Did that mean the two of them were back together? Eve couldn't tell, but she was feeling some major third wheel vibes. Maybe that was why Simone was here, to try and get Boone back. Now that they had Eve providing cover for them, Simone figured it was safe to stake her claim again.

Whatever was going on, Eve didn't want to be in the middle of it. Hooking a thumb over her shoulder, she started edging backward. "I'm gonna head upstairs and let you two get back to…talking or whatever. Nice meeting you, Simone."

With a smile and a wave that hopefully didn't look as awkward as she felt, Eve turned and fled up the stairs.

"Nice meeting you too!" Simone called after her.

Up in her room, Eve shut the door and collapsed facedown on the bed with a muffled groan.

Welp, she'd met Simone Alexander. Talk about uncomfortable.

She wondered what Simone had been crying about. Whatever it was that had brought her here, it must have been pretty important to risk being spotted coming and going from Boone's house. Was it more trouble around her divorce? Or had she and Boone been fighting? About getting back together or something else entirely?

Eve doubted Boone would volunteer the answers to any of her questions. Not as closed off as he was with her. When it came down to it, she didn't know that much about him—because he didn't want her to know.

Up until now, Eve had been doing pretty okay with all of this. Getting used to her bizarre arrangement with Boone and even enjoying it. When they'd first started all this, she'd felt like the two of them were a team. It'd been easy not to think too much about Simone, both because she wasn't around and because Boone rarely talked about her.

But of course she'd been there all along, an invisible presence in Boone's life that Eve had underestimated.

She realized now she'd been deluding herself. Boone and Simone were the team. Eve was just a member of the support staff. An outsider granted limited access for a temporary period. It was something she needed to remember.

When Eve heard a car start ten minutes later, she went to the window and saw Simone's SUV drive away. It looked like she was by herself too. Huh. That was fast.

Figuring Boone might need some space after whatever had gone down between him and Simone, Eve stayed put in her room. Letting him have his privacy. Like a member of the staff should.

She was more than a little surprised when Boone knocked on her door a few minutes later.

"Come in," she said, sitting up on the bed.

He pushed open the door and leaned against the frame. "Hey."

"Hey."

His eyes stared past her at a random spot on the wall, his expression troubled. But he didn't make any move to say anything.

He hadn't come in here to lean and brood, had he? Not that Eve minded. She was happy to watch him do both, if that was what he wanted. But she assumed he must be here to *say* something. Something bad, based on his expression. Maybe he was going to ask her to move out.

"Is everything okay?" she asked after several more seconds of silence.

His jaw clenched and he looked down at the floor. Still not talking.

Okaaay.

"Want some mini peanut butter cups?" She leaned over to snag the container off her bedside table and held it out. "They're the good kind. From Trader Joe's."

He lifted his head, a spark of interest in his eyes. "Are they dark chocolate?"

"Of course," she said. "I'm not an animal."

He came over to the bed and fished one out. "Thanks."

"You paid for them." She scooted over to make room for him beside her. "Wanna sit?"

To her surprise, he took her up on it, leaning back against the headboard as he stretched his legs out on her bed. She set the container of peanut butter cups between them, and he helped himself to another.

After taking one for herself, Eve balled up the paper wrapper and flicked it toward the wastebasket in the corner of the room. It overshot the rim, bounced off the wall, and landed on the floor next to its fallen brethren.

Silently, Boone arched an eyebrow at the small collection of wrappers around the trash can.

Eve shrugged. "What can I say? I've got a sweet tooth and bad aim."

He placed both his balled-up wrappers in his palm and flicked them into the wastebasket, one after the other. Two perfect shots. Of course his aim was flawless, just like the rest of him.

"So," she said, giving him a side-eye. "I'm gonna assume this whole silent, broody thing you've got going on means everything's not okay."

He gave her a side-eye back. "It's nothing you need to worry about."

"Cool. Gotcha." She nodded and leaned back against the headboard, relieved she apparently wasn't being evicted at least. After another protracted moment of silence passed she said, "It's just I was thinking, since you came knocking on my door, there might be a reason. Like maybe you want to talk about it or something? Which, if you did, is totally fine, just so you know. I'm happy to listen if it would help."

All it got her was an expressionless stare.

"Or maybe not," she said, unwrapping another peanut butter cup with a shrug. "It's probably above my pay grade. I don't need to know the details of your personal life. It's none of my business what goes on between you and your ex-girl-friend—or current girlfriend—or whatever you two are." Eve shoved the peanut cup in her mouth to make herself stop talking.

Boone's face had developed an epic frown. "It's not like that."

She shrugged again. "Not my circus, not my monkeys."

"Don't do that."

"Do what?"

"Act like you don't care—or don't have a right to care. You don't have a fucking pay grade, Eve."

She shot a pointed look at him. "I would if you'd had your way."

"That's not—" He broke off, scowling, and scrubbed his hands over his face. "Fuck."

If it hadn't been her room, she would have left at that point to give him space. But he was sitting on *her* bed, and he was the one who'd sought her out—a decision she felt certain he must be regretting now. "I'm sorry," she said. "I'm trying to help and instead I'm making everything worse."

"No, you aren't!" he snapped, proving her point. Almost immediately, his face twisted with regret. "I'm sorry. I'm being a real asshole right now."

"It's okay. You're not."

"Which is it?" His mouth quirked wryly. "I'm not being an asshole? Or I'm being an asshole but it's okay?"

She rolled her eyes, unable to resist smiling, and shoved him with her shoulder. "The first one, you dork-ass loser."

He was full-on smiling at her now, and it was a beautiful sight. When he let his light shine out, it was like looking at a sunrise. "Am I allowed to give you a hug to say I'm sorry anyway?"

Eve nodded. "Always. You don't even have to ask."

"Good to know." His arms encircled her, and she leaned into him, soaking up the awesome feeling. "I'm sorry. I'm not used to having someone around who has to put up with my crappy moods."

"You're entitled to your privacy," she said. "I know I'm stepping on your toes by being here."

He let go of her and leaned back against the headboard again, leveling her with a frown. "Do you want to know why I knocked on your door just now?"

She bit the inside of her cheek as she nodded.

"Because I was feeling lousy and I wanted company. I wanted your company."

"Oh." Her grin unfurled as a warm, happy feeling bubbled up in her chest.

His mouth twitched—not quite a smile but definitely better than a frown. "We're friends, Evie. I never meant to make you feel like an employee."

"You didn't. I mostly did that to myself."

"Look, I know I'm not always the most forthcoming person in the world."

Her eyebrows arched. "You don't say?"

Once again, his mouth twitched. "There's a lot of stuff I find it hard to talk about. But that's about me and my shit. It's not because of you, okay?"

She inclined her head in acknowledgement, but otherwise said nothing.

He let out a mighty sigh. "If there's something you want to ask me, just go ahead and do it."

Eve considered him silently for a moment. He didn't exactly seem enthusiastic about it, but he had given her permission. And she figured she had a right to know. "Are you and Simone getting back together?"

"We've never been together. We're friends. That's all we've ever been."

"Really?"

He smiled faintly at her disbelief. "God's honest truth. We made a pact early on that we'd always have each other's backs. The two of us have been through a lot together the last ten years, and worked under some seriously unpleasant conditions. The tough times created a strong bond between us, but we're like old war buddies. There's love, but no attraction."

"But that photo of you coming out of her house—"

"Her marriage was falling apart and she needed a shoulder

to cry on. We'd been up all night talking. Nothing more. I'm pretty sure her husband is the one who tipped off the paps."

"Seriously? Holy shit."

"Yeah, well." The muscles in Boone's jaw bunched. "The guy's a real bag of dicks."

"Simone looked like she'd been crying today."

Boone looked away. Eve thought he'd shut down again until he said, "She's in town to meet with her divorce lawyer. The reason she came over was to ask me if I'd be willing to take a paternity test to prove her son isn't mine."

Whoa. Well, that certainly explained why Simone had looked so brittle. And why Boone was so upset.

"Shouldn't her husband be the one tested if there's any doubt about paternity?" Eve asked.

Boone's lips pinched. "They had fertility problems and used a sperm donor. But now I guess he's trying to claim their son's actually mine."

"Wow, that's a shitty thing to do to your kid."

"Yeah." His expression darkened, giving her a glimpse of all the anger he'd been keeping inside. "Father of the year, right?"

"Are you going to do it?"

"I told her I would."

Eve got out another peanut butter cup and held it out to him. "I'm sorry all this is happening to both of you. It's awful and unfair."

He gave her a weak smile as he accepted it. "So how was your day? I never even asked."

"It was all right." She leaned back and pulled her legs to her chest. "I went to lunch with Alice."

"Oh yeah? That's nice." He flicked his wrapper into the trash can. "I'm glad you two are becoming friends."

Yeah, well, he might not be so glad when he heard what they'd talked about. Namely him. Briefly, Eve considered keeping what Alice had told her to herself. But it felt dishonest to withhold it from him. Especially if it affected the way Eve treated him, which it already had by causing her to leap to the totally wrong conclusion about him and Simone.

"What's wrong?" Boone asked, picking up on her internal conflict. "You're frowning. Didn't you have a good time?"

"No, I did. It's just…" Eve took a breath. "Alice told me some things you might not have wanted her to. About you."

"What kind of things?" Already he looked tenser. It probably didn't help that Eve was tense as well, anticipating his reaction.

"She told me about the movie you were supposed to do over the summer that fell through."

He slouched down into the pillows with a grunt. "Yeah. That whole 'no such thing as bad publicity' adage is total bull-shit, as it turns out."

"She also mentioned you'd broken up with someone recently." Eve hesitated before adding, "Someone Griffin told you he didn't think was good for you, and that's what the two of you fell out over."

Boone's jaw popped loud enough that Eve could hear it. "She told you all that, huh?"

"She thinks the breakup's been difficult for you."

He stared up at the ceiling.

"Don't be mad at her. It sounds like she's been really worried about you. That's the only reason she told me that stuff. She wanted me to look out for you."

Silence.

"I assumed she was talking about Simone, but I guess not."

"It wasn't Simone. It was someone else." His voice was quiet and strained.

"Who was she?"

"Someone who lives in Vancouver. Her name's Gemma."

He flinched slightly as he said Gemma's name, which told Eve pretty much everything she needed to know. Whoever this Gemma person was, Eve hated her. So much she felt sick with it. She hated her for hurting Boone, for coming between him and Griffin, and for being the cause of the unhappy look on Boone's face right now.

"You're not over her."

"I'm over *her*," he snarled, his lip curling in disgust. "I'm not over all the fucked-up shit she did to me." He took a breath and blew it out slowly, trying to pull himself together. "Sometimes it feels like I never will be."

"You know, if you wanted to talk about it—"

"I don't." When he turned his face toward her, the misery in it made Eve's stomach clench. "I can't. I know you're trying to help, but—"

"It's okay," she broke in. "I understand."

He sagged with relief, giving her a grateful look before staring back up at the ceiling.

In the quiet that followed, Eve studied his profile. The hard set of his mouth and jaw, the furrow of his brow, the taut cords of his neck. She could see it so clearly now that she knew what was going on with him.

Boone wasn't happy. Not just at this particular moment, but in general. All the time.

That was what he'd been hiding from Eve and everyone else. He was still in pieces from whatever his ex had done to him, and he didn't want anyone to know it. That was why he'd lied to Griffin and Alice about his relationship with Eve. He knew they were worried about him, and he wanted them to think he was okay. But he wasn't.

A surge of protectiveness spurred Eve to reach for his hand. He let her twine their fingers together. When she squeezed his hand, he squeezed back.

"I get it now," she said. "Why you sometimes seem so

distant. It's because you're in pain and trying not to let it show."

He didn't say anything. But he didn't deny it either.

"I was afraid it was because of having me around."

His gaze cut toward her. "It's not. Please don't think that."

"I don't want you to feel you have to hide it from me or pretend everything's okay. Will you promise me something?"

He looked away and licked his lips. "Eve."

The quiet reproof in his voice stung, but she pushed on anyway. "Just hear me out. I want you to tell me when you're feeling sad. We don't have to talk about why if you're not up for it, but I want you to feel like you can always come to me and say, 'I'm feeling crummy today.'"

He turned a bemused expression on her. "What would you do if I did?"

"I don't know. Be extra nice to you?"

"You're always extra nice to me."

"Try to make you smile."

The corners of his mouth curved ever so slightly. "You always make me smile."

"I'll tell you how special you are. In case you need a reminder."

"You're the one who's special. I don't think you have any idea."

Eve felt her face flush but refused to be distracted. "I could give you a hug whenever you needed one. Anytime you're feeling down, you could ask me for a hug."

Boone rolled all the way onto his side to face her. "Evie," he said, his gaze somber and intent.

"Yeah?" Her voice wavered.

"Can I have a hug?" He opened his arms, making a space for her.

She snuggled into his chest and gave his rib cage a hard squeeze. With a breathy grunt, he rolled onto his back again, dragging her along with him and squeezing hard enough to crush the air out of her lungs in a surprised squeak.

"Sorry," he muttered, loosening his grip a little. "Didn't mean to hurt you."

"You didn't." She was impervious to pain with Boone's firm, warm body next to hers. The roof could fall on her and she wouldn't even notice.

He tucked one hand behind his head, but kept his other arm wrapped around her to hold her against him. That was fine with Eve. She was happy to stay exactly where she was forever if that was what he wanted. Shifting to arrange herself more comfortably, she laid her head on his chest and closed her eyes.

The bedroom windows were open, and an evening breeze wafted over them, carrying the scent of mock orange blossoms and sagebrush. It was so quiet up here in the hills. Like a slice of paradise.

Boone expelled a long breath, and she felt him relax beneath her. His hand smoothed down her arm before coming to a rest on her hip. "I know I haven't acted like it, but I'm glad you're here. You're the best thing that's happened to me in a long time. You make me feel..." He paused, and Eve held her breath. "Almost happy sometimes."

"Almost?" she whispered, her throat tight.

"Almost is better than I've felt for a long time."

"Oh." She swallowed around the big-ass lump in her throat, knowing how much it must have cost him to admit that.

"In case you haven't figured it out by now, Evie, I'm your number one fan."

eighteen

A RARE FEELING of peace stole over Boone as he held Eve in his arms. Breathing her in. Enjoying the closeness of her body.

They were cuddling *on her bed*, for chrissakes. He should let go of her and get up.

But he couldn't make himself do it. It felt too good. Too *right*. It'd been so long since he'd felt any real pleasure at all. He didn't want to give the feeling up. Not yet.

God, how he wanted to let his hands roam over her soft curves. But he was afraid to move and break the spell. So he simply held her. Soaking up the moment.

It was obvious Eve had no idea what she did to him, the way she pushed back the darkness that had been trying to drown him for months. One of her smiles could energize him for hours. The sound of her laugh damn near made him feel whole again.

That was why he'd sought her out tonight after Simone left. Eve's bright light had called to him like a beacon. Instead of longing for the solitude he usually sought refuge in, he'd longed for company. Not just anyone's company, but hers specifically.

Because he liked how he felt around Eve better than how he felt when he was by himself.

Maybe it was because she took him at face value. She didn't ask difficult questions or make assumptions because she felt like she knew him. She didn't push him to be something he couldn't be. She simply let him exist.

He felt more truly himself around her. He'd nearly forgotten what it was like, who he was before Gemma had ruined him.

Griffin had tried to warn him. He'd seen the red flags Boone had glossed over and told him exactly what he thought of Gemma and the way she treated him. Boone hadn't just ignored his advice, he'd gotten angry about it, said hurtful, shitty things to his best friend, and refused to speak to him for months.

That was exactly what Gemma had wanted, of course. Boone could see that now, with the clarity of hindsight. The way she'd sunk her fangs into him like a viper, breaking him down with her poison. All the small, razor-sharp insinuations she'd whispered in his ear when Griffin wasn't around. Implying that Griffin was jealous and resented her for stealing Boone's attention away. That Griffin thought he was better looking and more talented than Boone. That Griffin looked down on Boone and treated him like a faithful lap dog. That he only liked having Boone around to make himself feel more successful by comparison.

Insidious suggestions calculated to prey on Boone's buried insecurities and widen the fault lines she'd identified in his closest friendship. It had all been part of Gemma's design—to create a wedge between Boone and the people who cared about him most in order to drive him further into her arms. To tear him down, make him weaker, and ensure he was dependent only on her.

Boone would never be able to get back those months he'd

shut Griff out of his life, or take back any of the awful things he'd said to his friend. Griffin might have forgiven him for it, but Boone would never be able to forgive himself.

He sighed and pressed his face into Eve's hair, inhaling the tropical scent of her shampoo and the subtler scent of coffee that clung to her after she'd worked a shift. Boone still couldn't quite believe she hadn't badgered him to talk about his feelings or made him feel like a villain for being in a bad mood. Eve hadn't criticized him or accused him of being weak and over-sensitive. She hadn't told him what he should do to get over it or tried to fix him. She'd simply let him be. As if she understood exactly what he needed.

It was such an unfamiliar feeling, being known and accepted like that. Boone closed his eyes and basked in it, matching his own breaths to the soft rise and fall of Eve's chest.

After a while, her gentle twitches and soft snores told him she'd fallen asleep. Right there on top of him with her hand on his stomach and her fingers curling in his T-shirt.

He was sorely tempted to stay where he was and let himself drift off to sleep with her. But he couldn't do that. He didn't trust himself enough. His half-conscious, sleep-fogged brain might do something he couldn't take back.

Instead Boone waited until he was sure Eve was deep asleep. Then he carefully shifted her off him, covered her with a blanket, and crept back to his own room alone.

JUST LIKE HE HAD EVERY MORNING SINCE SHE'D MOVED IN, Boone woke up when Eve did. His hyperawareness of her dragged him out of sleep as soon as she started moving around in her room.

The last few days, he'd lain in bed pretending to sleep until he'd heard her car drive away. Like a complete fucking coward.

No more.

Boone was done hiding from her. Staying away from Eve wasn't doing anything to lessen his yearning. But more than that, it was hurting her. He'd seen it last night, and he couldn't bear it. She deserved better. No matter what it cost him, he needed her to be happy and safe.

He made it downstairs before her and started a pot of coffee brewing. It was barely past dawn, still mostly dark except for a watery yellow glow seeping through the June Gloom low in the eastern sky.

Eve came down a few minutes later, stopping short when she found him in the kitchen. "What are you doing up so early?"

"Thought I'd take an early run today," he said casually. "Coffee's nearly ready."

As she walked past him to get down a travel mug, Boone caught the scent of her freshly shampooed hair. It knocked the wind out of him a little, bringing on a powerful sense memory of the night before. Lying on Eve's bed with her scent perfuming every breath he took and her body tucked against his.

God, she'd felt so fucking good. The memory of her silky softness was seared onto the surface of his skin like a brand-new, tender tattoo. It'd been too long since he'd been held like that, since he'd allowed himself to get that close to anyone.

He'd been so numb these past few months, he hadn't realized how much he'd missed it. But Eve had ignited an awareness of what he'd been denying himself. It wasn't just sexual desire—although that was undeniably part of it. It was the feeling of physical closeness he'd been starved for, that intimate connection with another person. Now that his taste for it had been reawakened, his body craved it the same way it craved calories.

"Have I mentioned how much I love your guest room

shower?" Eve asked as she poured coffee into a stainless steel mug for herself and a ceramic one for him.

Boone smiled as he accepted the coffee she handed him. "You can thank my sister for that. She's the one who picked out the showerhead and pretty much everything else in the guest room."

"Your sister has excellent taste." Eve was wearing dark red lipstick this morning, and he couldn't take his eyes off her lips as she blew across the top of her coffee. "Seriously, I want to elope to Vegas with your shower. I'm gonna buy it some bling and lock that shit down."

"Do you have plans after work tonight?" he asked. "I was thinking I might make us dinner."

Eve's eyes widened beneath her dark lashes. "What, like cook? All by yourself?"

He laughed at her surprised reaction. "I was thinking about it. If you're interested."

"I'm definitely interested."

"Then I guess I'm cooking for us tonight."

Her smile was better than sunlight. "I can't wait."

BOONE WASN'T ANYWHERE NEAR AS GOOD A COOK AS GRIFFIN, but he knew the basics. Enough to follow directions. It had been a while since he'd felt like doing much cooking, but he thought it might be a nice way to thank Eve for putting up with his moody ass and show her she was appreciated.

After she left for work, Boone called his mom to get her pastitsio recipe. His mother was only too happy to give it to him after he said it was for his new girlfriend. He didn't love lying to his mom, but she wouldn't have understood if he'd told her the truth. She was so overjoyed to hear he was dating again that he only felt a little bad about it. And really, it was only a half-lie. He didn't need to lie about his feelings for Eve, which made it easy to answer most of his mom's eager questions about her truthfully.

The pastitsio was done and sitting in the oven when Eve got home from work that night. "Oh my god, it smells amazing in here," she said as she came into the kitchen. "Is that lasagna?"

Boone was putting the finishing touches on the salad. "It's pastitsio, a Greek baked pasta dish—kind of a cross between lasagna and baked ziti. Hope you're hungry because the recipe makes a ton."

"I'm starving." She went to the oven and peeked inside. "Whoa! Did you make this yourself? Like from scratch?"

"It's a family recipe my mom got from her yia-yia. Let's hope I did it justice."

It was a mild, pleasant night, so they ate on the terrace outside the dining room. The pastitsio hadn't turned out half bad. Still, Boone was nervous as he watched Eve take her first bite. He tensed in anticipation of her reaction, bracing himself for a stinging remark.

Whenever he'd tried to cook for Gemma, she'd always made it clear how inadequate his efforts were. Oh, she'd smile and tell him she liked it at first, but then she'd start in with the passive-aggressive comments, letting him know what she *really* thought.

She'd had a real knack for cutting him down to size. In the beginning, Boone had foolishly believed it was good for him. He'd mistaken her cruelty for support and believed her when she said she was only trying to help him improve. He used to tell people Gemma kept him grounded, that her honesty was a healthy counterbalance to the ass-kissing that came with celebrity. It had taken him an embarrassingly long time to understand how poisonous her remarks were and the extent to which she'd been systematically chipping away at his confidence, breaking him down one hurtful word at a time.

But Eve wasn't anything like Gemma. Boone had to keep reminding himself of that.

The way things had been with Gemma wasn't normal or healthy. It wasn't the way people were supposed to treat each other. It wasn't the way Eve treated him.

As he should have expected, Eve reacted to the pastitsio with unreserved delight, complimenting his efforts and refusing to accept his assertion that the noodles were too al dente and the béchamel sauce too dry. It was ridiculous how much pleasure it gave him to hear her praise his cooking. Almost as much pleasure as the moans she let out as she licked every speck off her fork. He watched, transfixed, his cock straining against the seam of his jeans, as she ate bite after bite of his food.

Only when she asked why he wasn't eating did Boone drag his gaze away from Eve and dig into his own plate, shifting in his chair to alleviate some of the pressure on his aching dick.

"It's so beautiful here," Eve said, gazing out at the yard and the twinkling Valley lights in the distance. "I really love your house. How long have you owned it?"

"Six years."

"It's sad you don't get to spend much time here."

He nodded as he wiped his mouth with his napkin. "Yeah, my condo in Vancouver is a lot smaller. It's a great location downtown near the waterfront, but coming back here always feels like going on vacation." As he sipped his wine, his gaze drifted around the yard below. "One of my sisters lived with me for the first few years after I bought the house, and she did a lot of the decorating. It was nice having someone here to take care of the place while I was away—she made it feel more like a home. These days I use a service to keep an eye on things while I'm gone, but it always feels sad and deserted when I first get back. Takes me a while to get used to being here again."

That had been especially true this summer. He'd already been in a bad headspace, and coming back to this big, desolate house with nothing to do with himself hadn't helped any. It wasn't until Eve had moved in that it had started to feel like a home again.

"How many siblings do you have?" she asked as she helped herself to more pastitsio.

"Two sisters, both younger. Carly—she's the one who lived with me—is a geologist. She's living in Texas now. My youngest sister, Shelby, is still in Fort Collins near our parents. She's a veterinarian and married with two little boys." Boone smiled as he watched Eve pluck a runaway macaroni noodle off the table and pop it in her mouth. "What about you?"

"Only child. My parents hate that I live so far away." Lines sprouted across her forehead as she speared more noodles onto her fork. "They keep trying to get me to move back home."

"You don't want to?"

She shook her head before glancing up at him. "You ever go to a new city for the first time and something about it feels...I don't know. It just sort of clicks? Like you're finally where you belong."

"Yes." He knew exactly what she meant. "That's how it felt the first time I came to LA."

"Me too." Eve's expression turned pensive again as she pushed her food around her plate. "Not that my life has gone all that great here. Maybe I'm kidding myself, and my parents are right that I should move back home."

Boone considered her in silence for a moment before he said, "Do you mind if I ask why you didn't finish college?"

The creases in her brow turned into full-fledged furrows as she downed a hasty drink of wine.

"You don't have to tell me if you don't want to. I'm not trying to be nosy."

"Sure you are." She flashed a teasing smile. "It's all right. I don't mind talking about it." Her nose wrinkled as she corrected herself. "Okay, I do mind a little, but I've learned it's something I need to be able to do."

He didn't say anything, not wishing to pressure her.

"I developed severe anxiety when I was in school." She said it with a shrug, almost but not quite meeting his eyes. "I guess it had always been there to some extent, but it didn't become an issue until I went off to college. Suddenly, I was all on my own in an unfamiliar setting, and everything started to feel overwhelming. Even simple things, like going to the dining hall or the library, became hugely intimidating. As the pressure piled up, it turned into this feeling that I didn't belong there. My brain kept telling me I wasn't smart enough, I wasn't good enough, and I wasn't cut out for college like everyone else seemed to be."

Boone hurt for her—both for the suffering she must have felt at the time and the strain he saw in her face now as she remembered it. "Evie…"

She shook her head, letting him know she wasn't done. "I struggled my way through the first two years thinking it would get better if I tried harder and applied myself more. If I could just be stronger and make myself knuckle down. But it doesn't work that way, and instead it spiraled into depression. I started missing even more classes, and my grades went completely off the rails. I got so far behind that I had to take incompletes for the semester and go home to get myself together. My parents sent me to a therapist who put me on medication."

The urge to reach for Eve to comfort her almost crushed him, but Boone resisted it, balling his hand into a fist on his thigh.

Her lips pinched together. "The therapy and medication helped a lot, but I hated being back home under my parents' thumb. And I still couldn't make myself catch up on my schoolwork, no matter how hard I tried. That was when I realized being in Los Angeles wasn't the problem. School was."

Shrugging stiffly, Eve reached for her wine. Boone stayed quiet, waiting for her to finish telling the story.

After a moment, she did. "My old roommate was looking for someone to share a lease, so I moved back here and got a job at Starbucks. It was only meant to be temporary until I could get more freelance graphic design work, but…here I still am, four years later, doing pretty much the exact same thing."

The fact Eve was so down on herself made Boone's heart ache. She had no idea how remarkable it was that she'd been brave enough to come back here and carve out a life for herself on her own.

"Has your anxiety gotten better?" he asked quietly. "Or is it still something you struggle with a lot?"

"It's always going to be there, but I've learned strategies to head it off before it gets too bad. It's mostly under control now without meds." Another faint shrug lifted one of her shoulders. "It's not like I'm going to have a breakdown on you or anything."

"I wasn't at all worried about that. I'm just glad you've found ways to manage it."

A tentative smile crooked her lips. "You want to hear something super duper embarrassing?"

"Always," he replied, smiling back.

"When my life started spiraling out of control, your show was what got me through it."

Boone's lips parted in surprise. "Really?"

Eve nodded, ducking her head as color tinged her cheeks. "It was an escape from my problems and my only real comfort. The more out of control everything else in my life became, the further down the fandom rabbit hole I went. For a while there, I was one of those super-obsessed fans who probably make you uncomfortable." She darted a skittish glance at him. "But that show was the only thing that made me feel happy during an awful time in my life."

"That's…wow." Uncomfortable was the last thing Eve's confession made Boone feel, but he'd never been good at expressing his emotions. He had to swallow around the lump thickening in his throat before he could speak, and the words that came out felt trite and inadequate. "I'm glad you had something that could give you that when you needed it, and I'm honored I could be part of it."

Eve laughed uncomfortably, still avoiding his eyes. "I'll bet you think I'm a total weirdo loser now, right?"

"I definitely don't." This time he couldn't stop himself from reaching across the table to cover her hand with his. "I think you're remarkable."

The way she wrinkled her nose in disbelief brought a smile to his face.

"You could stand to be better about taking compliments, but otherwise you're pretty much perfect."

As Eve's eyes went wide, Boone realized what he'd said.

Too much, he rebuked himself, withdrawing his hand. *Too real.*

After swallowing more wine, he cleared his throat. "Is that why you quit watching the show? Because you didn't need it anymore?"

The teasing smile that curved her lips socked him square in the chest. "No, I just got tired of waiting for the main characters to bang."

He laughed and raised his wineglass. "Touché."

"Don't worry. In case you're wondering when I'm going to go all Kathy Bates in *Misery* on you, there's reason to hope I won't be your problem for too much longer."

Boone froze. "What do you mean?"

"I think I might have found an apartment."

nineteen

"YOU'VE ALREADY STARTED LOOKING?"
Boone felt like the floor had dropped out from under him. He
hadn't realized Eve was in such a hurry to move out.

That hurt a little. More than a little, if he was being honest.
Though he supposed it shouldn't come as a surprise, given how
hard she'd fought against staying with him in the first place.
And he hadn't exactly made her feel welcome this week,
had he?

"Only online," she said. "I haven't been to look at it yet.
But it's close enough to my price range that I think I can swing
it, and it's not *that* much more of a commute."

Boone stared at her mutely as he grappled with the tremen-
dous sense of loss he felt at the prospect of Eve moving out. He
didn't want to think about why he cared so much.

"I've got an appointment to see it tomorrow morning," she
went on. "But even if I end up getting it, it's not available until
July first, so you're still stuck with me for a while longer."

"There's no hurry, Eve. You know that, right?"

"No, I know." She stroked her thumb around the rim of

her wineglass. "You're being very tolerant about having me here."

Tolerant. The wrongness of that word knifed through his chest. But he couldn't exactly tell her the truth—that she'd started to feel necessary to his existence.

He shoved his chair back and began stacking their dishes to clear the table.

Eve stood to help him. "The thing is, if I don't move fast, someone else will snap it up. And I haven't seen much else out there in my budget—nothing decent, anyway."

"Exactly how much farther away is this place?" he asked as they carried everything into the kitchen.

While he loaded the dirties into the dishwasher, she told him about the apartment, which was a studio all the way up in Sun Valley. The more she described it, the more he hated the sound of it. She didn't seem particularly enthused about it either, but it was the best thing she'd found so far.

"You shouldn't rush into anything," he told her.

"Sure, but you're leaving in a little over a month. I don't have much time to lollygag around if I expect to be out of here before you are."

Boone slammed the dishwasher shut and cleared his throat. "Yeah, about that...there's something I want to talk to you about."

The shift in his tone made Eve's brows draw together. "Is everything okay?"

"Everything's fine." Reflexively, he touched her arm and was heartened to see her worry ease. "I've just been thinking. If we release your name to the public like Reagan wants, I need you to do something for me."

Eve's eyes searched his, full of questions. "What's that?"

"I'm concerned about the attention you're going to get once you're linked with me. So I'd like you to stay here for the duration of our arrangement and maybe longer—at least until we're sure interest in you has died down."

He'd been thinking about it ever since Eve had agreed to let them out her by name. The idea of thrusting her into the public eye like that, then fucking off to Canada and leaving her to deal with the fallout all on her own, didn't sit well with him. He'd been holding off on raising the subject until she'd had a chance to get more comfortable here, but this apartment scheme she was hell-bent on rushing into changed things.

She frowned and shook her head. "I don't think that's—"

"Eve, please don't fight me on this," he cut in. "Some of the fan mail that gets sent to me is seriously unsettling. There are people out there who will perceive you as a threat to the fantasies they've constructed about me in their heads. I need to know you're safe. At least if you're living in this house, I can ensure you have decent security."

"It's sweet that you're so concerned, but I honestly don't think that's necessary. I'll be fine."

Of course she was resisting. God forbid she go along with something for her own good. She couldn't possibly just let him take care of her.

Boone hadn't wanted to play this card, but she left him no choice. He needed her to take this seriously and not assume he was being overprotective. "Did Alice tell you what happened to them? Why they bought that new house?"

"No."

"Their old house didn't have a fence or security gate. Griffin didn't think he needed it—until an overzealous fan figured out where he lived and broke in. The guy walked right into their backyard and jimmied one of the sliding glass doors open."

Eve's eyes went wide. "Please tell me they weren't home at the time."

"Thankfully, they weren't, and the break-in tripped the

alarm. When the security company showed up, they found the dude hiding in the bedroom closet clutching a knife he'd taken from the kitchen."

"Holy shit."

"Holy shit is right." Boone settled his hands on Eve's shoulders, seeking her full attention. "I won't be able to sleep at night if you're living in some apartment with zero security where any jealous fan with a mind to could show up at your door." A shiver ran down his back. Even just saying it out loud turned his skin cold. "Please, Evie. I'm not kidding about this. I need you to agree to it."

Her internal struggle played out on her face as he held his breath. Finally, she pursed her lips and nodded her assent. "If you're sure that's what you want, I'll do it."

A relieved breath gusted out of him. "Thank you. I'll feel a lot better knowing you're here when I'm gone."

Slipping out of his grasp, she turned away to tip her wineglass back. "I guess I can stop looking for an apartment now. I should probably be relieved—this will give me more time to save up some money."

"I'm sorry if I scared you. If you're having second thoughts—"

"I'm not." A soft, teasing smile lit her eyes when she turned around. "Stop trying to get out of our arrangement. You're stuck with me now, buddy. No take backsies."

"Glad to hear it." *So glad*. She had no idea.

"Speaking of our arrangement, what's the deal with tomorrow night? Has Reagan sent you the details yet?"

Boone nodded as he leaned against the counter behind him. "Miguel and his team will be here to meet you when you get home from work."

Eve's lips pulled to the side. "Swell."

"There's something else." Something he'd been putting off telling her.

Picking up on his tone, she gave him a wary look. "What?"

"Reagan wants us to move things to the next level."

"Meaning what exactly?"

"She wants photos of us kissing."

"Right." Eve's hair fell across her face as she looked down at her wineglass.

"Are you okay with that? Tell me the truth."

"Totally fine."

"Eve."

She looked up with a smile that didn't quite manage to hide the tightness around her eyes. "It's all good."

"I don't believe you."

"I promise. It's just—" Breaking off, she pinched her lips together.

"Evie, talk to me. I'm not doing this unless I know you're really okay with it. And right now I'm pretty convinced you're not."

"It's dumb." She grimaced as she shook her head. "I psyched myself out, is all. It happens sometimes with things I've never done before. I start to think too much about it, wondering what it will be like, and then it becomes a bigger deal in my head than it needs to be. It's like I give myself a mental block that can be hard to move past."

"You gave yourself the yips," he said, finally understanding.

Relief flooded her expression. "Exactly. It's not a rational fear. Really, I think a lot of what's making me nervous is the thought of people watching and taking pictures. Because what if I mess it up and everyone sees?"

"Mess it up how? How would you mess up a kiss?"

"I'm sure I could find a way. And then my kissing incompetence will be memorialized for all the world to see."

Boone rolled his lips together, trying not to smile. "I seriously doubt you're an incompetent kisser."

"You don't know that. Maybe I'll bite your tongue. Or accidentally stick my finger up your nose. There are a million embarrassing things I could do."

This time he did let himself laugh. "Now you're starting to give *me* the yips about it."

"See?" she said, smiling at him. "I told you it's not rational. But I'm not letting a little performance anxiety stop me. If Reagan wants a kiss, she's getting one, even if I have to hold you down outside that restaurant and lay it on you myself."

Boone studied her as he debated whether the thing he wanted to suggest was a good idea or a terrible one.

"There is something we could do that might help," he ventured. "We could rehearse it ahead of time."

"Rehearse…kissing?" Eve looked doubtful.

"That's how actors do it. On some sets they even bring in an intimacy coordinator to make sure everyone feels comfortable with the physical aspects of the scene."

"What an interesting job that must be."

"If it's the anticipation of a new experience and not knowing what to expect that's causing your block, rehearsing should help with that. Theoretically."

He watched her think about it, and the longer she did, the more he regretted the suggestion. Yeah, no, this was a terrible idea. They shouldn't do this.

"You know what, forget I said anything. We don't need to—"

"I want to do it," she said. "It's a good idea."

"Really?"

"I think you're right. It's the fear of the unknown that's gotten into my head. This will take care of that. Plus it'll give us a chance to work out the kinks without an audience."

Boone blinked, fighting to hold back a smile.

"I didn't mean *those* kinds of kinks!" Eve's face flushed

bright red. "Obviously. Oh my god." She buried her face in her hands.

"I know what you meant," he said, letting his smile loose.

She shook her head, smiling back at him. "Right, so we're rehearsing, yes? It's decided."

"Only if you're sure."

"I am."

"Okay."

Neither of them moved as they eyed each other across the six-foot chasm of space between them.

"Right now?" Eve asked.

"Whenever you're ready."

"Should I come over there, or——"

Boone pushed off the counter and took a step toward her. She immediately tried to step back, bumping into the island behind her.

He stopped with a sigh. "Eve."

"No! I'm sorry. That was—I don't even know what that was. But see? What if I'd done it in front of a photographer? It's a good thing we're rehearsing first."

"Maybe we should——"

"Don't give up on me." Her eyes implored him. "Please."

How could he possibly refuse her?

A different approach was clearly needed, however. "How about we start with something easier? A trust exercise."

Eve's nose wrinkled. "I'm not going to have to fall backward, am I?"

"No. Much easier than that. You're comfortable with hugs, yes? Let's start there."

"Oh." Her expression brightened. "I can do that, no problem."

This time Boone let her come to him. Without any hesitation whatsoever, Eve fit her body against his and wound her arms around his waist. It made him feel all sorts of things that he refused to let himself dwell on, because he was a professional actor, goddammit, and he was going to be professional about this even if it killed him.

He let himself hold her, but only loosely in case she got skittish again. (Also so he didn't accidentally tug her against his growing hard-on. *Ahem.*) Tentatively, he smoothed his hands over her back, scouting for signs of tension and finding none. "Better?"

"Much," she sighed against his chest.

Clearly she didn't mind being close to him. It was something about the prospect of kissing specifically that made her jumpy. He could work with that.

Professionally speaking, of course.

Bending his head, he spoke into her ear. "I'm not going to kiss you yet. I'll warn you before I do it, so you don't need to worry about it, okay?"

Eve nodded against him. "Okay."

Holding on to her shoulders, he shifted back enough to look into her eyes. Perfect kissing distance. But that wasn't on the menu right now. He'd meant what he said about that. "Remember what I told you before about being present in the moment to shut out the noise in your head?"

"So I should focus on you," she said, as intent and serious as he was.

"That's right. And remember, I'm not going to kiss you. Do you trust me?"

"Yes. Completely."

That also made him feel some sort of way, but he shoved those feelings aside, concentrating instead on what he was doing.

Gently, he squeezed her shoulders. "Are you okay with me touching you like this?"

She nodded without breaking eye contact.

Boone slid one of his hands down her arm. Goose bumps

formed beneath his fingertips as they glided over her skin. She shivered slightly, but otherwise seemed all right. When he reached her hand, he tangled their fingers together. "You're okay with holding hands, right?"

"Holding hands is fine."

He arched a teasing eyebrow. "Only fine?"

It inspired a smile. "Maybe better than fine." Eve's soft, delicate fingers slid through his, exploring the surface of his palm and the joints of his fingers. "You've got so many calluses."

"Sorry, my hands are probably rough."

"I don't mind."

"Good." Slowly, he skimmed his other hand over the top of her shoulder to the side of her neck and rubbed his thumb along the ridge of her collarbone. "Is this okay?"

Her throat bobbed as she swallowed. "Yes."

His fingertips followed the flush up her throat to trace the line of her jaw. "You'll stop me if anything makes you uncomfortable?"

"Promise."

He let his fingers drift higher to caress her cheek. Her eyelashes fluttered, but she didn't tense up or flinch like the last time. Feeling emboldened, he stroked his thumb along the edge of her lower lip. Her large brown eyes widened slightly, but stayed locked on his.

Cupping her cheek in his palm, he slid his fingers into her hair and bent his head. Her breath caught when his nose touched her cheek. "I'm not going to kiss you yet," he reminded her.

Her fingers squeezed his hand. "I know."

He rubbed his nose against her cheek before nuzzling her ear. She shivered again, and her hand clamped around his forearm.

"You want me to stop?" Boone asked, going still.

"No." She breathed it out like a sigh. "It tickles, that's all."

Drawing back, he gave her a smile. "You're doing really well."

Her eyes were hazy as she blinked at him. "I told you I trust you."

"Can I put my hands on your waist?" When she nodded, he settled his hands above her hips. He felt her rib cage expand as she breathed in.

"Is it all right if I touch you back?" she asked.

"You can do anything you want. I trust you too, Evie."

Her hands came to rest on his biceps, kneading gently before sliding up to his shoulders. Boone shifted closer as his fingers flexed on her hips. It required all his willpower not to pull her against him, but rubbing his erection on her definitely fell outside the bounds of this exercise.

Eve's hands explored his shoulders thoroughly before moving on to his neck. When her fingers slid into his beard, he had to bite down on his tongue to stifle a groan. Her eyes lifted to his, checking in, and he squeezed her waist to let her know it was okay to keep going.

She went back to running her fingers through his beard like she'd done at the café. He fought to keep his expression blank as waves of pleasure shivered through him. Without meaning to, Boone found himself shifting even closer, drawn to her like gravity.

Abandoning his beard, she slid her hands into his hair. This time there was no suppressing his groan when her fingernails scraped lightly over his scalp.

"Sorry," he muttered. "That's just—it feels really good."

Eve peered up at him from beneath her lashes, her dark eyes clear and luminous.

So fucking beautiful.

Just like the very first time he'd looked into her eyes, Boone felt something go *ping* in his chest.

The air seemed to shift as they gazed at one another, a new sort of energy humming between them. His stomach tightened with a reminder of how dangerous a game he was playing. This wasn't supposed to get this real.

Too late, a voice whispered in the back of his mind. He was helpless to stop it now.

His gaze dropped to her lips as he imagined how it would feel to kiss her. Like a dream, probably. One that was his for the asking.

"Eve." He breathed her name like a wish as he cupped her cheek, coaxing her head back. "I'm going to kiss you now, if that's all right."

He heard her take a shuddering breath before she nodded, granting permission.

A simple kiss. He could do this.

People kissed all the time without giving away their whole hearts. It didn't have to mean everything.

Boone leaned in, his fingers caressing the soft skin beside her ear as his other hand spread out over her lower back. At the last second, he hesitated when he felt her hand tighten in his hair.

With a huff of frustration, Eve gave his head a soft tug, letting him know she wanted him to keep going. Smiling, he closed the rest of the distance between them.

Warmth punched through him like sunlight as he brushed his lips over hers. They were so unbelievably silky and lush, he wanted to sink into them and never come back out.

He felt drugged, only barely in control of himself. The need to taste her was so urgent it made him dizzy, but he kept the kiss chaste, resisting the urge to part her lips with his. Some distant, practical part of him was clearheaded enough to remember he didn't have her permission for that. This was just supposed to be a stage kiss. Fake. Mere illusion.

Still, he lingered far longer than necessary, lavishing Eve's lips with slow, tender caresses, memorizing their shape and feel. He couldn't make himself let go of this moment, the sweet, heavenly press of her mouth, her body straining against his, her eager fingers twining in his hair.

Until he felt her lips part on a breathless gasp, and he came to his senses, realizing how long they'd been kissing. *Too long.*

Boone let go of her and backed away as he struggled to regain his bearings. Breathing heavily, Eve blinked up at him and licked her lips. The thought that her tongue was tasting him just about shattered his resolve.

It would be so easy to drop the pretense and make this thing with her real. If she told him it was what she wanted, he'd be helpless to resist. All it would take was a clear signal from her, and he'd walk right over there and pull her into his arms. It'd be the easiest thing in the world to lose himself in those plump, bright lips for real this time.

Clearing his throat, Boone edged back a little more. "How was that?" he asked and winced internally at the roughness of his voice. Eve had to see how affected he was. How could she not?

"Okay," she said. "That wasn't bad at all."

Ignoring the way his heart was pounding against his rib cage, he affected a teasing tone. "I'm bowled over by your effusive compliments."

An amused breath gusted out of her. "You know what I mean. I didn't freak out."

"I have to admit, I was a little worried about that finger up the nose thing. Not to yuck anyone's yum, but that's not one of my kinks."

When she laughed, Boone let out a quiet breath, relieved everything seemed to be normal between them.

Mostly normal.

The fact that his hands were shaking was certainly not normal. But that was nothing compared to the deep, unsettling stir of longing that had taken up residence in his chest and seemed to be growing stronger by the second.

Crossing his arms to hide the tremor in his treasonous appendages, he leaned back against the counter. "For the record, there was nothing incompetent about your technique. Five stars across the board."

"Thank you." Eve's eyes lowered shyly. "Your technique was every bit as impressive as promised. Much better than okay."

He wasn't going to feel a thrill of satisfaction at that. He wasn't. Boone cleared his throat. "How are you feeling about tomorrow now? Better? Worse? The same?"

"A lot better. I don't feel as nervous about kissing you anymore."

"Glad to hear it. Does that mean we're a go for kissing in front of the paparazzi?"

She gave him a confident nod. "Shouldn't be a problem."

For one of us, at least.

Because it was absolutely going to be a problem for Boone. Now that he'd gotten a taste of Eve, every cell in his body yearned for more.

A lot more.

twenty

PREPARE YOURSELF, Boone had warned Eve on the drive to the restaurant in Beverly Hills. *This is going to be different than last weekend.*

Boy, he wasn't kidding about that. Eve's stomach clenched as she saw flashbulbs go off in the parking lot ahead. Apparently someone exciting had gotten out of the black SUV in front of them. She couldn't tell who it was because the paparazzi were blocking her view. A cluster of them stood only a few yards from the valet stand, close enough to feel threatening.

This was the real deal. Boone had told her the paparazzi would be more visible and aggressive tonight, but she hadn't expected quite so much foofaraw. It was just a restaurant, for cripes' sake. Not even a very big one, and it was located next to a Fogo de Chão, of all things.

Maybe they could go there instead and have a peaceful dinner without drawing the notice of the paparazzi. Eve loved those Brazilian cheese ball thingies, and unlimited meat sounded right up Boone's alley.

He reached across the console and tangled their fingers together. "Just ignore them like we talked about."

Try not to look at them, he'd told her. *If they ask you questions, don't answer. Don't show any reaction at all, no matter what they say.*

"Don't worry. I won't be stopping to make conversation." Eve could hear the paps shouting at the couple who were walking toward the restaurant, but couldn't make out what they were saying over the music playing in Boone's car. She didn't recognize the people attracting so much attention. The man wore basketball shoes and a black vest over a white T-shirt that came down to his knees, while his date was dressed in a skintight fluorescent yellow top and matching knit beanie with olive drab camouflage leggings.

Eve looked down at her pink chiffon dress with a frown. She'd felt cute when she'd tried it on for Miguel at home, but now she worried it was too…something. Dressy. Boring. Uncool. *Bridesmaidy.*

"You look perfect," Boone said, reading her mind. "Don't worry about what other people are wearing."

She supposed the way Miguel had dressed her worked for the girl next door image Eve was supposed to be projecting. Not too flashy or fashion-forward. Even if the torturous heels he'd put her in cost more than she'd paid in rent last month, she looked like a regular person who'd dressed up for a date night. As did Boone, in his simple button-down and dark twill pants.

"Who are they?" Eve asked, still squinting at the mystery couple.

"No idea. Which usually means they're reality TV stars or social media influencers. People trying to get their photo taken for the publicity, same as us."

She could hear the scowl in his voice, and she turned to offer him a sympathetic smile, remembering that he hated this even more than she did. He didn't smile back, but he did bring her hand to his lips and brush a kiss over her knuckles, which drove all thoughts of the paparazzi out of Eve's head.

Ever since their kissing rehearsal, Boone had been notably more affectionate with her—a touch on her arm here, a hand on her back there, a kiss on the cheek when they'd said good night last night. He'd even kissed her forehead before they'd left the house for their date tonight.

Eve wasn't sure what to make of it. She tried to tell herself it was nothing more than casual, friendly affection. Probably he felt more comfortable around her now that he knew she wasn't going to jump out of her skin every time he touched her. It would be a mistake to read too much into it.

There was nothing casual about the way it made her feel, however. Every time Boone touched her, no matter how innocently, her heart beat faster and her stomach tried to leap out of her body.

And now he was kissing her hand, which didn't seem like the sort of thing people casually did with their friends. Not a brief, light kiss either. More like caressing her hand with his lips as he rubbed slowly back and forth over his beard. The same way he'd done on their coffee date last weekend. Except there was no one watching them right now, which made Eve think he was doing it because he wanted to. Because he *liked* it.

Did that mean he liked *her*?

The possibility sent a giddy rush of heat shooting through her already overstimulated body. She pressed her thighs together, hoping he wouldn't be able to see her flush in the dim light inside the car.

The car ahead of them finally moved up, and Boone dropped her hand to pull up to the valet stand. After that, everything happened fast. Eve's door was pulled open by a valet, and she stepped out of the car. At first, the paparazzi didn't pay any attention to her. Why would they? She was no one. It wasn't until they noticed Boone get out on the driver's side that they jumped into action.

Circling like hyenas, they pressed in closer. Eve turned her face away from the blinding flashes as Boone strode around the car and put a protective arm around her.

Just like he'd warned, the photographers shouted intrusive questions at him while he shepherded her toward the restaurant. "Who's your date? Is she your new girlfriend? Have you and Simone ended things? How long have you been having an affair with your costar? Is it true you're the father of Simone Alexander's son? How does it feel to steal the wife of an NFL MVP?"

It was horrible, the aggressive, confident way they surrounded them and shouted their rude accusations and lies. Fortunately, there were two security guards in polo shirts stationed outside the restaurant, and they stepped forward to clear a path and keep the paps from following them under the long awning that covered the walkway to the entrance.

The whole thing only lasted a few seconds, although it felt like much longer than that. It wasn't until Eve and Boone had made it into the restaurant with the door safely closed behind them that she let out the breath she'd been holding.

"You good?" he asked, searching her face.

"Fine," she said, forcing cheer into her voice. She felt surprisingly okay, in fact. Not that it had been particularly enjoyable, but she wasn't in danger of freaking out. Maybe she was getting better at this stuff.

Boone pulled her close and pressed a kiss to her temple, which more than made up for the minor inconvenience of a few annoying paparazzi.

Tragically, their clinch was cut short by the return of the hostess. As they were led to their table, Eve took her first real look around the sushi restaurant Reagan had picked for them. It wasn't what she'd expected. The interior was cozy and packed, the no-frills decor not all that different from the sushi bar by her old apartment.

She was relieved when they were seated at a table in the back, far away from the windows. There wasn't any privacy to be had in a place this small and crowded, but at least they were mostly safe from lookie-loos on the street outside. She'd just as soon not have her photo taken while cramming an entire piece of sushi into her mouth with chopsticks.

"Shit, I never asked if you like sushi," Boone said after they were seated.

"Lucky for you, I happen to love it." Eve tried not to be overawed by the prices on the menu. This place was nothing like the sushi bar by her apartment, after all.

"In that case, how adventurous are you feeling? Want to do the omakase and let the chef choose for us?"

She'd perused enough of the menu to be overwhelmed by all the choices, so she happily agreed. The seemingly never-ending parade of dishes that followed kept them occupied and entertained for the better part of the next hour. It wasn't until they'd made it to the trio of crème brûlées the waiter delivered for dessert that the conversation lapsed into a satiated silence.

As Eve sipped the last of her lychee martini, her gaze traveled idly around the restaurant. The other diners didn't appear to be paying much attention to Boone. She'd noticed one woman at a nearby table sneakily taking a photo with her phone earlier, but for the most part stares had been minimal.

"I do believe you're the most famous person here tonight," Eve observed.

He grunted. "That's the idea. Reagan wouldn't want us being overshadowed by Rihanna or George Clooney showing up."

"Too bad. It would have been cool to see Rihanna."

Boone's smile was halfhearted at best. At some point in the

last few minutes, his mood seemed to have shifted. He wasn't exactly selling the happy couple act.

"What's wrong?" Eve asked, leaning forward.

He shook his head as his gaze cut away.

"Boone." She reached across the table and wiggled her fingers, hoping he'd get the message.

At least he didn't leave her hanging. When his hand settled over hers, Eve interlaced their fingers and pressed their palms together.

"Talk to me. What's up? You seemed fine a minute ago."

"It's nothing," he muttered. "I just hate playing this game. All the pretense and bullshit. I'd never bring you to a place like this normally and make you walk through that fucking gauntlet outside."

She didn't point out that he never would have brought her anywhere with him, all things being normal. The pretense he hated so much was the only reason Eve was in Boone's life at all. While that might be a nice consolation for her, it wasn't so much for him.

"It must be awful, having to deal with being hounded and photographed like that all the time."

"I don't usually, that's the thing. Most of the time, when a celebrity gets photographed, it's because they want to be. Everyone knows which places the paps stake out, so it's not that difficult to avoid them."

"Unless someone tips them off and they stake out your house?" she said, thinking of the unfortunate photo that had set all of this off.

Boone grunted. "Yeah. They're always ready to chase up some dirt if they think there's a story in it for them. But it wouldn't be worth it for them to hang around Simone's house twenty-four seven on the off chance there was something to see."

"So you're telling me all those candid shots of celebrities

out walking their dogs or shopping—they're not really candid?"

"They're almost always pap walks that are arranged in advance because they've got something to promote."

"You're really blowing up all my delusions about Hollywood and celebrities, you know that?"

He gave her another one of those halfhearted smiles.

Eve couldn't blame him for being bitter. The whole situation was pretty seriously sucky for him and wildly unfair. He hadn't done anything wrong, but even she had jumped to the worst conclusion about him because of that one privacy-violating photo.

But as sympathetic as she was to his mood, it wouldn't make anything easier for Boone if someone around them noticed how down in the dumps he looked right now.

Leaning across the table, Eve crooked her finger, beckoning for him to meet her halfway. He gave her a puzzled look but leaned in toward her. She curled her hand around the back of his neck as she spoke quietly in his ear. "We're supposed to be in love, remember? If you don't dredge up a more convincing smile, people will think there's trouble in paradise."

The change in him was instantaneous. Like magic, he went from looking sullen and grumpy to looking like a man utterly besotted. *Actors. Damn.*

"You're right," he murmured, bringing her hand to his lips. "I'm sorry I needed the reminder. I'll do better."

"We're in this together, right? You look out for me and I look out for you."

This time his smile was so dazzling it left her breathless.

"You're really good at that," she said, allowing herself to look as awed as she felt. She was supposed to be a woman in love, after all. Gazing rapturously was part of the assignment.

"What?" Boone asked, rubbing his thumb over her knuckles in a way she found extremely distracting.

"Smiling."

His smile ticked wider, crinkling around his eyes. "You make it easy."

Well, that did it. It was difficult enough having all his handsomeness focused on her, but when he said things like that Eve went full-on mush-brain. It was impossible to know if he actually meant it, or if he was just getting into character. She tried to tell herself it was the latter, but her stupid, incautious heart wanted to believe otherwise.

"You ready to get this over with?" Boone asked, driving home that this was all merely for show.

Eve nodded and withdrew her hand from his. "Let me run to the restroom and make sure there's no seaweed in my teeth."

These shoes Miguel had forced on her were not her friends. The way her toes were cramped inside them was surely the reason she wobbled as she walked away from the table. It couldn't possibly have been anything else, like her knees feeling weak or her heart beating too fast.

In the bathroom, Eve did a mirror check to prep for facing the cameras again and popped a handful of the mints she'd brought in her purse for this exact moment. A giddy sense of anticipation fizzed in her stomach at the thought of kissing Boone again. Yes, they'd be doing it with a bunch of obnoxious strangers watching and taking photos and shouting rude questions at them, which were definite cons. But on the plus side, she'd have Boone's lips on her again. It more than balanced out in her opinion.

But not in his, she reminded herself. *Keep it professional, girl.*

He hated everything about this. Probably including kissing her. Not that he seemed repelled by it, but it must feel like work to him. What was it he'd said? He'd kissed dozens of women in front of cameras. Pretending to be dating Eve was just another role to him. One he'd had forced on him against his will.

She'd do well to remember that, lest she get tricked into

believing the illusion they were spinning. It'd be a mistake to buy into their own lie.

Boone had finished paying the check by the time Eve got back to the table. His hand rested against the small of her back as they made their way to the door. As soon as they stepped outside, the paps took notice. But they were relegated to the parking lot, unable to get too close to the restaurant. Boone handed his ticket to the valet, then set a hand on Eve's waist and pulled her aside, turning her back to the cameras pointed at them.

The paps were shouting for their attention, but Eve barely noticed. She only noticed the way Boone's hands held her hips, tugging her closer, and how he tilted his head to trace a path along her jaw with the tip of his nose.

"You still okay if I kiss you?" he whispered, his lips brushing her earlobe.

So okay. She'd never wanted anything more. The empty ache between her legs enthusiastically concurred. With a faint nod, she slipped her arms around Boone's waist, needing the support as much as she craved the closeness.

Drawing back, he cupped her face in both hands, his fingers stroking her cheeks with a touch so gentle it brought a lump to her throat. It hurt to think the way he was looking at her and touching her wasn't real. None of this meant anything to him, not the way it did to her. She felt a momentary pang of regret over that, knowing she'd pay a price for it later.

But then Boone's lips touched hers, and her stomach went into free fall. All other thoughts disappeared from her head, and every nerve in her body sparked to life, as if they were all connected directly to her mouth and therefore now to his.

The last time he'd kissed her it had been tentative and reserved. A stage kiss, nothing more. Not that it hadn't still blown Eve's mind, but their mouths had remained closed the whole time. She'd expected this one to be the same, but almost right away it felt completely different.

There was nothing tentative about the pressure of Boone's mouth on hers this time. Nothing reserved about the way he tilted her head, angling it just so. She felt his lips part on a husky exhale, coaxing hers open, and then their mouths were sliding together like interlocking parts falling into place. It felt like the most natural thing in the world when his tongue slid across her bottom lip. Of course hers sought to meet it.

She sighed into his mouth as he bent his head to deepen the kiss still further. It was everything Eve had imagined it could be, sweet and decadent and dreamy. Her toes curled in a way that had nothing to do with her torturous shoes, and she clutched at him as the ache between her legs intensified to a desperate throb.

Distantly, she was aware of the people watching and taking pictures, and that this wasn't the sort of kiss she'd ordinarily consider appropriate for a public place. But none of that mattered. There was nothing ordinary about this kiss.

Boone was the one who pulled back first with a surprised-sounding grunt. His hands slid down to her shoulders, and he took a hasty step back.

The loss of contact with his body hit Eve like a splash of cold water and was accompanied by a stunned awareness of the hardness in his pants she'd been more or less grinding against a moment ago.

He blinked slowly, his expression impossible to read. For a split second he looked like he was about to speak, but then his gaze flicked to something behind her. Without a word, he slipped his arm around her shoulders and turned her toward the valet stand where his car now sat waiting.

Eve winced at the blinding flashbulbs going off in front of them and the renewed shouts of the paparazzi they'd gifted with an eyeful of PDA. Putting himself between her and them, Boone led her to the car and helped her into her seat.

"You did good," he said, after he'd driven them out of the parking lot. "Reagan should be pleased."

"Great," was all Eve could rouse herself to murmur in response.

She was far too kiss-addled to make any sort of conversation. Boone didn't seem to be in the mood for talking either, and the rest of the drive home passed in silence.

twenty-one

BOONE WASN'T around when Eve got up the next morning. They'd both retreated to their rooms after they'd gotten home from the restaurant last night, but she'd been too busy replaying their kiss in her head to fall asleep. It had taken until nearly three a.m. for her to drop off. Thank goodness she'd requested the whole weekend off work.

When she finally crawled out of bed at a little past ten and ventured downstairs for coffee, she was greeted by a note from Boone explaining he was out running errands. That was fine. It wasn't like she wanted to talk to him. Avoidance was her preferred method of dealing with things she didn't know how to handle, and her confused feelings after last night's kiss definitely fell into that category.

A little alone time would help her get her head on straight and her emotions in check. She'd always known this would be hard. It was entirely predictable that she'd gotten carried away.

What wasn't so predictable was her sneaking suspicion that Boone had gotten carried away too.

Maybe he'd been method kissing. Present in the moment and all that jazz. It must happen to actors all the time, right?

And they shook it off like professionals instead of fixating like lovesick preteens. So that was what Eve would do. What she wasn't going to do was broach the subject with Boone. No way, no how. Best if they never spoke of it at all.

When he came home an hour later, Eve was in full sloth mode in the rec room, ensconced on the sofa in front of the TV with a box of Lucky Charms clutched to her chest.

"Morning!" Boone greeted her cheerfully when he walked in from the garage. "I brought donuts."

"Are you serious?" She lunged at the box he dropped onto the coffee table, her salivary glands kicking into overdrive when she saw the logo on it. He hadn't brought any old donuts from the nearest corner shop. These were fancy gourmet donuts from one of the trendiest donut shops in the city.

"I didn't know what you liked, so I got one of everything."

"Oh my god, I love you," Eve moaned around a mouthful of maple bacon donut that tasted like an orgasm in her mouth.

The silence that followed was deafening. When she dared a glance at Boone, there was a goofy grin on his face. He looked so pleased she couldn't even feel embarrassed about letting her mouth run away with her.

"What are we watching?" he asked as he plopped down on the sofa next to her.

"*10 Things I Hate About You.*"

"Classic." He selected a chocolate-covered donut and slumped back into the cushions.

They watched the movie together while they feasted on the donuts. At one point, Boone took Eve's coffee cup out of her hand and helped himself to a sip. It felt like an awfully intimate thing to do, but she supposed once you'd swapped spit with someone there wasn't any reason to be squeamish about sharing drinks.

When she couldn't eat any more donuts, Eve flopped down on her end of the couch and propped a cushion against the armrest to lay her head on. "My feet aren't bothering you, are they?"

"How would your feet be bothering me?"

"I don't know. Maybe you don't want them on your couch or next to your leg."

"You're fine," Boone said and laid his hand on her ankle. Like that was a perfectly natural place for his hand to be.

Maybe it was. Maybe it was the sort of thing he did with all his friends. Eve tried to ignore it and watch the movie, but that became impossible when he dragged her foot into his lap.

"You've got a blister."

"Those shoes last night did not agree with me." She rolled onto her back and tried to pull her gross, blistered foot back, but he was too intent on examining it to let go. "Don't look. It's disgusting."

Lips quirking, he arched an amused eyebrow at her. "Your feet are not disgusting. Believe me."

"Well thanks, but——" She broke off when he started massaging her foot. "Oh. You know, I don't really like to have my feet rubbed, so—*oh my god!*" She couldn't hold back her groan as he dug his thumbs into the arch of her foot. It was like he'd pushed a button she'd never known she had that turned her spine into a quivering puddle of pleasure. *What the fuck?*

Boone smirked as his strong fingers continued to work their magic. "Is that right? You moan like that when something feels bad, do you?"

"Not normally, no."

How was he so good at this? She'd never liked having her feet rubbed before—it was her least favorite part of getting a pedicure—but whatever sorcery Boone was doing with his hands was the best thing that had ever happened to her feet.

"You don't have to do this," she said when he switched to her other foot. Heavenly as it felt, she couldn't help her self-consciousness over the way he was getting up close and personal with her bare feet. And to think, she'd thought sharing a drink was intimate. Given the way her nipples were reacting and the situation ramping up between her thighs, Eve's feet were a previously unappreciated erogenous zone. This was probably why friends didn't rub each other's feet.

"Do you really not like it?" Boone's face was turned down, his attention on his work instead of the flush creeping up her chest.

Thank god for small miracles. "No, it feels amazing, but—"

"Then let me do it. I'm a full-service boyfriend. Foot rubs are part of the package."

It was like the man wanted to kill her.

None of this was making it any easier for Eve to keep her wayward feelings in check, so she made herself say, "You're not really my boyfriend though, are you?"

A slow, easy smile played on his lips. "I'm getting into my role. Happy to perform any other boyfriend services you want. All you have to do is say the word."

What? He was messing around, right? Teasing her. Surely that was it.

She shook her head, at a complete loss. "I don't know what to do when you say stuff like that."

Boone stiffened as if he'd been caught doing something wrong. All his playfulness from a minute ago dried up as he moved her feet off his lap. "I'm sorry. You're right. I shouldn't have—" Breaking off with a distressed expression, he leaned forward to rub his face.

Eve sat up, tucking her legs underneath her. "It's okay." She hadn't intended to make him feel bad. "Really. It's fine. It's just…"

His head swung toward her when she didn't finish. "What?"

"Confusing," she admitted, her mouth going dry. "Sometimes it almost seems like you're serious even though I'm pretty sure you're just joking around."

"What if I was serious?" His unsettlingly blue eyes simmered with a mix of emotions she couldn't interpret. Was this more teasing? Or something else entirely?

"See, this is exactly what I'm talking about," she said, gesturing at him in frustration. "One day you're saying and doing all these flirty things when there's no one around to see it, and the next you're shutting down and avoiding me. I can't tell what's real with you and what's not."

"Maybe I don't know either."

Eve stared at him. "What?"

He turned his face away, staring at the TV with unseeing eyes. For the longest time he didn't say anything. "That kiss last night," he muttered finally. "It was…"

She strained toward him as she waited to hear what he was going to say.

"Not part of the plan," he concluded, rubbing his temples like he had a headache.

"O-kay," she said slowly. Except it wasn't, because she still didn't understand anything. "What are you saying?"

Boone's eyes locked onto hers, and her stomach dropped at what she saw in them. He looked like he was in physical pain. "That wasn't how I was supposed to kiss you, Evie. That was me losing control."

"Oh," she said. And that was all. Because what exactly was she supposed to say? *I liked it. Please feel free to lose control again anytime you want.* She couldn't bring herself to do it. Not when he looked so miserable.

They stared at each other mutely. On the TV, Heath Ledger was serenading Julia Stiles, but it might as well have been white noise for all that they were paying attention to it.

Boone seemed to be waiting for Eve to say something else. When she didn't, he swallowed thickly and looked away. "Anyway, I apologize for the mixed signals. I swear I'm not doing it on purpose. I'm just…" He slumped back against the couch and dragged a hand over his face. "I don't know what the fuck I'm doing."

Things were getting way too heavy in here. Eve scooted closer, her stomach aching to put him at ease. "I didn't mind it. The kiss, I mean."

He swiveled his head to look at her, but said not a word.

"Don't beat yourself up over it," she continued nervously. "I mean, it's kind of a compliment, right? That I made you lose control. That's how I'm choosing to take it, anyway, so please don't burst my bubble."

A ghost of a smile flickered over his lips. "It's definitely a compliment."

"Maybe you have a crush on me," she teased.

He barked out a laugh. Actually *laughed*. Right in her face. As if she'd said something hilarious.

Jerking away, she turned and swung her legs to the floor as her face burned with humiliation.

It shouldn't have stung so much. She was the one who'd made it sound like a joke. Even so, she'd secretly hoped there might be a grain of truth in it. So much for that. Clearly it was the most preposterous thing he'd ever heard. That would teach her to get her hopes up.

"Hey," Boone said, reaching out for her. "I didn't mean—"

Eve shrugged his hand off as she propelled herself off the couch. Tears stung the back of her throat, and she didn't want him to see her cry. This was already humiliating enough.

"Fuck," he muttered, jumping up to follow her. "Evie, wait." He caught her by the arm and stepped in front of her.

She stared at his chest, her heart constricting painfully as she blinked back tears. "Let's pretend the last five minutes didn't happen, okay? I think that would be best."

"I shouldn't have laughed. I'm sorry."

Her shoulder twitched with a shrug. His apology only made her feel more pathetic. "You're allowed to feel what you feel. At least now I know."

"Evie, look at me." His hand smoothed up her arm when she didn't move. *"Please."*

It was the roughness of the last word that made her lift her head.

"You really have no idea, do you?" His eyes roved over her face. "You haven't got a clue. How can you not know what you do to me?"

"What?" she breathed as her heart pounded erratically in her chest. She kept telling herself not to hope, but hope kept bubbling up nonetheless, fizzing in her stomach like spilled champagne. She couldn't do anything to stop it from over-flowing as Boone shifted closer.

"I think about you…" Grim lines bracketed his mouth, and the rest of his words tumbled out in a headlong rush. "All the time. I can't stop. I think about touching you, the smell of your skin. I fall asleep with your face in my mind and wake up aching and hard with your name on my lips. I want you so fucking bad, I feel like I'm going out of my mind."

That was…*whoa*. A lot. Much more than she'd expected. "You do?"

He swallowed audibly. "Thought I was being real obvious about it."

"I just thought you were flirting."

"I was."

"Fake flirting. Not like you meant it. I thought it was an act. Like the rest of this."

"Wanting you doesn't require me to do any acting." Boone's eyes pinned her in place, the pale depths blazing with heat and frustration. He almost looked angry, as if he didn't want to want her.

"I think about you too," she confessed. "All the time. Every night."

He shut his eyes as if her words hurt him. "Don't."

"Boone." She lifted a hesitant hand to his cheek.

His eyes flew open at her touch, his jaw clenching. He grasped her hand and pulled it away from his face. "I want to. You have no idea how much. But we shouldn't."

"Says who?"

His chest rose and fell jerkily as they stared at each other, the tension arcing between them like a live wire.

Eve wanted him so much she could barely breathe. If he wanted her, there was no reason they couldn't have each other…

Involuntarily, her gaze dropped to his mouth as she remembered how it had felt to kiss him. "I liked it when you lost control last night. I think you should do it again."

"Eve." His voice was a growl of warning.

"I'm a big girl, Boone." Their mouths were only inches apart. So close she could almost taste him. God, how she wanted to taste him again. "You're not going to break me."

Before he could say anything, the sound of a car outside had them both turning to look out the window. A black Range Rover rolled up the curved driveway and came to a stop in front of the garage.

"Shit," Boone said, rubbing his forehead with a frustrated sigh. "I forgot they were coming."

twenty-two

APPARENTLY BOONE HAD MADE plans to work out with Griffin today, and Alice had tagged along. Under other circumstances, Eve would have been thrilled to see them, but today the timing really stank.

They were here now though. Nothing to do but make the most of it.

The boys had immediately disappeared to hit the gym, leaving Alice and Eve to entertain themselves.

Alice pulled a bag of limes out of the tote she'd brought. "I'm thinking we should whip up a pitcher of margaritas and hit the pool. What do you say?"

Eve sanctioned that plan wholeheartedly. Chilling out with some sunshine and tequila therapy was exactly what the doctor ordered right now. While she went upstairs to change into her swimsuit, Alice got to work on the margaritas.

It had been a while since Eve had worn a swimsuit. All she had was an old bikini she'd bought in high school. It was skimpier than she remembered. Also she was more generously proportioned these days, and the blue polka dot string bikini top barely managed to contain her boobs.

She frowned at her reflection in the mirror, choosing not to focus on the fact that there was nothing hiding her soft, rounded stomach. She was who she was, and there was no point pretending otherwise. Anyway, she was way more concerned about accidentally popping a tit.

"I love that suit," Alice said when Eve rejoined her in the rec room. She'd already finished juicing the limes and was measuring tequila and Cointreau into the pitcher.

"You don't think it's indecent?" Eve tugged at her top, attempting to cover more of her breasts. She envied Alice's sporty bikini that showed a lot less skin.

"Hell, no. I think you look smoking hot."

"You say that now, but when one of the girls pops out in front of your boyfriend you may feel different."

Alice snorted as she stirred the margaritas. "Will you run and grab us a couple of towels from the wardrobe in the bathroom?"

"Sure," Eve said, and headed down the hall.

The sound of a Disturbed song came from the open doorway of the gym, punctuated by clangs of metal hitting metal. After grabbing four striped beach towels from the bathroom, she dared a peek into the gym.

Boone lay on a weight bench pressing a loaded bar as Griffin spotted him. They'd both taken off their shirts, and while Griffin was certainly very muscular and attractive, Eve's attention was riveted by the sight of Boone's bulging arm and leg muscles. All that power and strength contained in such a perfect, graceful, hardened body. Her gaze lingered over the wispy dark hair on his chest before being drawn back to his striated thighs. God, those thighs were drool-worthy, vibrating under tension like that. And the way his hips were tilted as his back arched off the bench—it filled her head with all sorts of wicked, lustful thoughts.

Griffin glanced up and noticed her watching from the

doorway. He flashed a grin before turning his attention back to his spotting duties.

Blushing at having been caught in the act of leering, Eve hurried back to Alice, desperately in need of a margarita and a plunge in some very cold water.

THE GUYS DIDN'T JOIN THEM AT THE POOL UNTIL TWO HOURS later. After they finished in the gym, they'd gone for a run, waving as they jogged down the driveway.

By the time they got back, Eve was on her third margarita and feeling pretty darn relaxed as she reclined on a shady lounger. The heat had settled over them like a blanket, and Eve's eyes were half closed when she heard the guys come pounding up the driveway.

They were both still shirtless, their skin glowing in the sun and covered with a sheen of sweat. As they toed off their shoes beside the pool, she sat up for a better view of Boone in his low-slung running shorts.

"Hey, hot stuff, can I have your number?" Alice catcalled from the lounger beside Eve.

"Sorry, ma'am, I've got a girlfriend," Griffin said solemnly as he crawled on top of her.

"Mmmm, you're all sweaty." Alice threw her arms around his neck and pulled him down for a kiss.

Eve looked away from their PDA to find Boone watching her. No, not just watching. Staring. Ogling, even.

Belatedly remembering the precarious bikini she was wearing, she hastily checked to make sure nothing unseemly was showing. All the goods appeared to be covered—or as covered as they could get, anyway—which meant Boone was simply staring at *her*. At her body.

She wasn't used to showing off so much of it, but she

refused to act self-conscious in front of him, no matter how many actress-perfect bodies he'd probably seen. Pushing her sunglasses on top of her head, Eve met his stare with a challenging one of her own. "Yep, those are my boobs, all right."

He licked his lips as he continued to brazenly contemplate her chest. "Hard not to notice in that bikini."

"It's gotten a little small for me."

A smile tugged the corner of his mouth as his gaze traveled from her breasts to the swell of her hips. "Looks fantastic to me."

Now that they'd both admitted to their attraction, Boone's flirting had become more overt. His boldness made Eve bolder too.

She reached for the bottle of water she'd set on the ground and took a sip before offering it to him. "You look a little dazed. You're not feeling light-headed, are you?"

The smile lingered on his lips as his eyes met hers. "As a matter of fact, I am."

He came over and sat on the edge of her lounger. His hip bumped against her thigh, and she shifted to give him more room.

When his hand wrapped around the water bottle, her pulse jumped as his fingers slid over hers. He was close enough she could smell the sweat on his skin. The man must have some kind of magical-ass pheromones, because his sweat smelled so good she wanted to rub her face all over him.

As he tipped his head back to gulp down the water, she stared at his throat where the uneven line of his beard ended. Her gaze dropped lower, to his collarbone and the sparse dark hair below it. She suspected it would be much thicker if he was ever allowed to stop waxing it permanently. God, he even had a happy trail running down the middle of those delicious abs.

Before she got caught leering at his southern hemisphere, she lifted her eyes to study the tattoo on his chest, an intricate compass rose inked over his heart. They'd always hidden it with makeup on the show, but she'd seen fuzzy pictures of it on the internet before. Never in a million years would Eve have thought she'd be this close to it in person.

Boone scrubbed the back of his hand over his mouth and offered her back the water. "Thanks."

"You can keep it. You probably need it more than me." She tipped her chin at the tattoo. "That's beautiful work."

"I'm serious about getting you to design another one for me." The way his fingers stroked over his forearm where she'd drawn on him last weekend made her stomach flitter. He inclined his head to capture her eyes. "You doing all right? Having an okay time?"

"Yeah, I'm great," she murmured, caught in his gaze.

He blinked, his brow knitting slightly as they stared at each other for long enough that Eve's heart started to pound as tingles of heat pooled in her stomach. Breaking the spell, he glanced at the top of her head and smiled. "You're wearing my sunglasses."

"Alice said you wouldn't mind."

"Alice was right." He settled them back on Eve's face, and his smile stretched wider as he studied her. "They look great on you. You should keep them."

"I'm not going to do that. They're too nice." They were Dior. She couldn't even imagine how much they must have cost.

"Nothing's too nice for you."

Beside them, Alice let out a screech of protest as Griffin slung her over his shoulder and hauled her toward the pool. "Don't you dare!" she half squealed, half laughed as he tossed her into the deep end and jumped in after her.

"You been in the water yet?" Boone asked, turning back to Eve. There was a gleam in his eyes she didn't trust.

"Earlier," she said warily. "It was cold."

"I bet it'll feel good now." He slipped her sunglasses off, folded them up, and set them on the table.

"Boone—"

"What?" He licked his lower lip. "Do you not want me to?"

She opened her mouth. Then closed it again, because she couldn't honestly say she didn't.

"That's what I thought." Faster than she would have thought possible, he swept her off the lounger and into his arms.

Eve squeaked in surprise and clung to his neck. Struggling wasn't an option without risking a serious wardrobe malfunction. Not that she wanted to struggle. Being cradled against Boone's bare, sweaty chest was about the best thing ever.

"You can swim, right?"

"Yes, but there's a decent chance my top is going to fall off. Maybe we shouldn't."

"If it does, I promise not to look." The corners of his eyes crinkled. "Much."

When he stopped at the edge of the pool, she clutched him tighter, getting nervous now that he was holding her over the water. "I think I'm having second thoughts."

"We'll go in together, okay? On three." He waited for her nod before starting to count. "One…"

He jumped into the pool with her in his arms.

The water hit her back, shocking the air out of her lungs. Her arms and legs flailed as the water closed over her head, but then she felt Boone's warm hands grasp her waist and she twisted toward him to grab onto his shoulders. They sank to the bottom of the pool together and hung suspended in a moment of weightlessness before they both kicked their legs and rose to the surface.

"You said on three!" Eve sputtered, swiping her wet hair out of her face.

"It's more fun when it's a surprise." Boone grinned as he bobbed beside her. "But hey, your top stayed on."

She sent a splash of water at him, and he retaliated by grabbing her and shaking his head in her face like a shaggy dog. Letting out a laughing shriek of outrage, she launched herself onto his back and dunked him underwater.

When he popped up again, he pinned her arm against his collarbone so she couldn't dunk him again without going under with him. "That's enough of that. I'm too tired to fight you off."

"Fine. Truce." Eve let herself go slack in compliance with the cease-fire, but Boone kept a tight hold on her arm anyway.

"Told you the water would feel good."

The water was nothing compared to the way she was clinging to his back like a rhesus monkey. Their bodies were touching in so many places she couldn't even catalog them all, but something about being in the pool made it feel safer, as if the molecules of water between them meant the skin-to-skin contact didn't count.

Boone's pec flexed under her palm as he swam them out of the deep end. Reflexively, Eve's fingertips smoothed over his skin, sliding through the soft layer of chest hair. Just blatantly copping a feel.

He didn't appear to mind, since he kept holding her arm there even after he reached the middle of the pool where he could stand with his head above the water. Eve was not so tall, however. Since he hadn't let go of her, she had no choice, really, but to wrap her legs around his waist piggyback-style and hang there. Oh no. What a shame. This must be what it felt like to die and go to heaven.

"I'm getting a beer," Griffin announced as he climbed out of the pool. "Anyone else want anything?"

Boone wiped the water out of his eyes and slicked his hair back from his face. "I'll take one."

I'm good," Eve said when Griffin directed an inquiring look at her.

Alice had gotten out of the pool as well and was digging through a weatherproof storage chest. "Boone, where are all your good pool floats?"

"My nephews destroyed them last time they were here. Haven't gotten around to buying new ones." He hooked his free hand under Eve's leg, hiking it up higher on his hip. "Careful down there or you'll pull my shorts off," he murmured with a grin.

"What a shame that would be," she quipped. "But don't worry, I promise not to look…much."

His rumbling laugh vibrated through both their bodies, making Eve acutely conscious of the way her breasts were pressed against his back. Not to mention that the top of his ass was between her legs. She was trying not to actively grind on him, but it was becoming more challenging by the second.

When his fingers squeezed her thigh, all the air left her lungs. It was too easy to imagine that big, rough hand sliding higher and higher, his calluses dragging over her skin—

"I can feel your heart beating," he said.

Oh, Jesus. Someone please shoot her with a tranquilizer dart.

A pool noodle landed in the water in front of them. Then another one next to that. The skies were raining pool noodles.

"These will have to do," Alice said, and tossed two more pool noodles into the water before jumping in after them.

Finally, Boone released Eve's arm, and she swam toward the nearest pool noodle.

"Heads up," Griffin said, tossing a can of beer to Boone before sliding back into the water. He'd turned up the music and changed the soft, moody playlist Alice had put on earlier to guitar-heavy rock.

Eve rested her arms on her pool noodle and let herself float aimlessly on the surface of the water while Boone and Griffin talked. Alice was doing the same, but Griffin was holding on to her pool noodle to keep her from floating away. He was telling Boone about the prep he was doing for an animated musical he was about to start voice work for. Boone had all sorts of technical questions about the voice lessons he was taking and the songs he'd have to perform.

Most of it went over Eve's head, but it was nice seeing the two old friends so relaxed together and obviously enjoying each other's company. Something seemed to have changed between them since the party last weekend. The underlying tension she'd sensed then had been displaced by easy smiles and spontaneous laughter.

In fact, Boone seemed looser and more relaxed today than Eve had ever seen him before. She hadn't realized how hollow Boone's smiles had been before, but now that she was seeing the real deal the difference was like night and day.

He caught her watching him, and his gaze softened as a slow smile spread across his face. The way he was looking at her felt like he was trying to tell her something.

Whatever it was, it sent her stomach into free fall.

twenty-three

WHEN HER LAST margarita had worked its way to her bladder, Eve climbed out of the pool. "Back in a minute," she said, grabbing a towel before heading for the house. "Anyone need anything while I'm up?"

They all declined, and she made for the downstairs bathroom. It was a newer upgrade than the rest of the house, all slate gray tile and quartz countertops with bamboo accents. In addition to the shower, it had a wood-paneled sauna and a large whirlpool soaking tub. Not too shabby.

She finished her business and wrapped her towel around her waist before heading back out. As she emerged from the bathroom, Boone stepped into the hallway.

"Hey," he said, ambling toward her. He looked like he'd just come from a magazine shoot with his damp hair all disheveled, his skin glowing and dewy, and his wet running shorts functioning at maximum clingy. *Have mercy.*

Eve clutched the doorframe to steady herself as he stopped in front of her. "Hi."

He held up a bottle of sunscreen. "Noticed you were

looking a little pink. Thought you might need someone to put sunscreen on your back."

"Oh, really?" She twisted her head, trying to see if her shoulders were red.

"Here, look." His hand hooked her elbow, drawing her into the bathroom.

She peered over her shoulder at the mirror above the sink. "Doesn't look red to me."

Boone tossed the sunscreen on the counter and stepped in close. Grasping her waist with both hands, he backed her up against the edge of the sink.

Whoa. The breath rushed out of Eve's lungs at the sudden nearness of him and the feel of his hands on her bare skin. Heat radiated off him as he gazed down at her with an unnerving intensity.

When his fingers flexed on her hips, her back arched involuntarily, causing her stiff nipples to brush against his chest. He let out a harsh breath, his eyes darkening as his hands tightened on her waist.

Abruptly, he spun her around to face the mirror, and she grasped the edge of the counter as his chest pressed against her back. A breath gusted out of her at the feel of his sun-warmed skin, which seared her to the core everywhere it touched her.

Their eyes met in the mirror. Eve's heart gave a wild thump when Boone tugged at the towel around her hips, sending it to the floor at their feet. A sly smile played over his lips as he arched an eyebrow, challenging her to object.

She had no intention of doing any such thing. Her chin lifted as she stared back at him, meeting his dare with one of her own. *Keep going,* her eyes silently entreated. *Don't stop there.*

The tips of his fingers skimmed over the curve of her shoulder, and his gaze swept downward to her breasts. Her nipples weren't exactly being subtle right now. They were so painfully hard they were practically drilling holes through the thin fabric of her bikini.

His nostrils flared with another harsh inhale. "You're killing me with this fucking bikini, you know that?"

That hadn't been her intent, but she had zero regrets about the covetous, tormented expression it seemed to have put on his face. She watched him in the mirror as his fingers glided over her stomach, and her belly clenched when they drifted to the bottom edge of her bikini top.

"So gorgeous," he murmured under his breath. "I want to touch you so bad I can't think about anything else."

She wanted it just as bad. Her body responded of its own accord, leaning back into him until she felt the hard bulge of his cock press against the base of her spine. The helpless, needy sound he made intensified the ache between her legs, driving her to push against him even more.

"Fuck, Evie," he rasped as he dropped his face into her hair. "You make me weak. I don't think I can fight it anymore."

"Then don't." Her heart was beating so hard it felt like it was going to punch through her chest.

"Tell me you want it." His voice was low and rough as his lips ghosted over her ear.

"I want you to touch me." She was burning all over, her skin so tight she was about to explode. "Please, Boone. Don't make me beg."

His eyes squeezed shut for a second as a shudder shook his frame. He pressed a kiss to her temple, and his fingers tightened on her shoulder.

"You don't have to beg, gorgeous. You just have to ask." His eyes burned like a pair of blue flames as they found hers in the mirror again. Her thighs clenched in greedy anticipation when his other hand spread out over her stomach. "Show me where you want to feel me. Put my hands where you want them."

With shaking fingers, Eve grasped the hand on her shoulder and dragged it down to cover her breast. "Here."

A jagged breath gusted out of him as his fingers tightened on her needy flesh. He licked his lips, his expression rapt as he watched himself fondle her in the mirror.

Good god, that look on his face was too much. It blew her mind to think all that undisguised hunger was for her. She pressed into his hand, more turned on than she'd ever thought possible. But it wasn't enough. Not by a long shot. She needed his bare skin on hers without anything between them. Dizzy with lust, she hooked her finger under the edge of her bikini top and dragged it to the side.

Boone's breath caught as the fabric slipped over her puckered nipple, exposing it to him. "Jesus," he whispered, his eyes going glassy. "You're so fucking luscious."

He palmed her bare breast, gazing at it in the mirror before he rubbed his callused thumb around her nipple. Eve's head fell to the side with a moan, electric heat licking down her spine. His mouth dropped to the side of her neck, and he sucked at the tender skin as the hand on her stomach held her firmly against him.

"Boone," she breathed, squirming against his erection. "I need…"

"Tell me, gorgeous." His breath was choppy and hot on her neck as he pinched her nipple hard enough to make her moan again. "What else do you need?"

Too worked up to be coy, she covered his hand with hers and slid it from her stomach down between her legs.

Boone made an incoherent sound, and his head sagged weakly against hers. His fingers twitched over her bikini bottoms, the muscles in his arm trembling as if he was fighting to hold himself back.

Holding back wasn't going to work for her. Not one little bit. He'd driven her to the brink of delirium, and she needed relief. Eve pressed her hand against his, and they let out matching groans as she rubbed his fingers over her aching clit.

His eyes clashed with hers in the mirror. "You really want it, don't you?"

Fuck yes, she did. Her head jerked in a nod. "I need it."

With a grunt, he spun her around and hoisted her onto the countertop. His mouth crashed against hers, messy and frantic, as he stepped between her knees. She curled her fingers into his damp hair as their tongues slid together, his coarse beard dragging over the sensitive skin around her lips.

Boone's hands grabbed her ass to haul her against him, and she whimpered loudly when his thick hard-on prodded her swollen sex.

"Goddammit," he growled against her mouth. "How do you taste so fucking sweet?"

"Margaritas?" she guessed.

"No," he muttered between panting, exploratory kisses. "This taste is all you."

Eve tugged at his hair, angling his head so she could kiss him even deeper. There was no getting enough of him. She doubted she'd ever be able to.

Rough, hot palms slid around her hips to her thighs, pushing them farther apart as his mouth dropped down to suck at her neck. A tremor shook her body as he flirted with the fabric of her bikini bottoms, driving her to tilt her hips in invitation. When he pushed the fabric aside, her whole body jolted with pleasure as his fingers finally touched her.

"Boone." Her voice broke with a needy whimper.

He lifted his head, his heavy-lidded eyes seeking hers as he stroked her into a blissful frenzy. "You're beautiful, Evie." His lips brushed her temple. "So beautiful."

She couldn't believe how close she was to coming already. God. It wasn't going to take much to push her over the edge.

"Yo!" Griffin's voice echoed down the hallway to them. "Anybody else getting hungry?"

They both froze as their eyes locked together in twin expressions of frustration and dismay. Eve nearly wept when Boone slipped his hand out of her bikini bottoms. She'd been *so close*.

"Fuck," he whispered. His forehead rested heavily against hers as he called out a reply to Griffin. "Yeah, gimme a minute."

"I'm never buying a ticket to any of that cockblocker's movies ever again," Eve grumbled.

It inspired a grunt of amusement from Boone. He reached up to arrange her bikini top back over her breast. "You have to go out there first. I need some time to pull myself together."

Seriously? So unfair. But Eve couldn't exactly argue with the obvious hard-on tenting his shorts. The poor guy was just as worked up and frustrated as she was.

With a deep, annoyed sigh, she hopped off the counter and slipped out of the bathroom alone.

BOONE DEEPLY REGRETTED THE IMPULSE THAT HAD LED HIM TO invite Griffin and Alice over today. It had seemed like a good idea at the time. After the way he'd kissed Eve outside the restaurant last night, he'd wanted a distraction to keep him from losing his head again.

Yeah, that hadn't exactly worked out as planned. He'd been a fool to think anything short of a coma would keep his mind off Eve—even before he'd seen her in that fucking bikini.

Jesus.

His eyes had nearly popped out of his head, cartoon character style, when he'd first gotten a look at her in that thing.

The tiny bits of fabric straining over her lush curves and the sight of all that silky bare skin had left him dizzy and inconveniently hard. That skimpy bikini had been his undoing.

Unfortunately, Griff had raided Boone's fridge and announced he was making them all dinner when he found steaks and potatoes and enough makings for a salad. It'd all been delicious, of course—Griffin was a first-rate cook—but dinner was long over now and everyone was lingering over their wine.

Boone was in hell, his balls aching and his dick still semi-hard from his interrupted encounter with Eve in the bathroom. Honest to god, he was going to lose it if Griffin and Alice didn't go home soon. He loved them, he did, but he needed them to leave so he and Eve could finish what they'd started. If Griff so much as breathed the word dessert, Boone was going to snap and bodily throw him out of the house.

It didn't help Boone's mood that the conversation had somehow turned to the challenges of dating a celebrity, with Alice and Griffin offering Eve tips for surviving the spotlight.

"I'm not going to lie, it was hard to get used to at first," Alice told Eve. "It was almost a deal breaker for me."

Griffin grunted. "Yeah, as soon as she got her first taste of it she immediately dumped my ass."

Alice's expression grew tender as she shot him a smile. "Lucky for me, I came to my senses and realized he was worth the trouble."

"Lucky for *me*, because I was a fucking mess without you." Griffin leaned over and tugged her toward him for a kiss.

Boone felt a sharp pang of envy. Despite the challenges they'd faced, they made it look so easy. He doubted he'd ever be able to be that open with anyone.

When he looked away from them, he caught Eve watching him.

"Anyway, don't let the fame stuff scare you off." Alice

leaned forward to snag her wineglass off the table before settling back in her chair. "That part gets easier, I promise."

Eve reached for her own glass. "Isn't it hard to be apart for months at a time when Griffin's off somewhere shooting a movie? How do you do it?"

Alice shrugged as she smiled at Griffin again. "He loves acting and I love him. We want the best for each other, so we make it work."

"Damn right we do," Griffin said as he refilled his wineglass. "Being away from Alice definitely blows, but at least I know I'll get to go home to her at the end of it. It's still way better than not having her at all."

Boone gritted his teeth as he waved off Griffin's attempt to top up his glass. God have mercy, they were never leaving.

"You've been awfully quiet over there," Alice said, raising an eyebrow at Boone. "You okay?"

He forced a smile for her. "That workout we did is catching up to me, is all."

Odds were good Alice saw right through him, because five minutes later she was herding Griffin toward the door as they said their goodbyes.

For hours, Boone had been itching to get Eve alone again. But as soon as his wish was granted, he began to second-guess himself. What was his endgame here? How much did he think he'd be able to give her? Was he making a mistake by surrendering to this attraction between them?

The tightness in his chest told him the answer was yes. But maybe he was just nervous. He hadn't been with anyone since Gemma.

Apprehension settled over him like a snowdrift at the thought of her. He swallowed, trying to regain his equilibrium. Maybe he should nip this whole thing in the bud now, before it was too late. Before he did something he couldn't take back.

But then he walked into the kitchen where Eve was

finishing the cleaning up. She'd pulled a thin cotton cover-up on over her bathing suit before dinner. It was white and gauzy, practically transparent, and the thin fabric clung to the swell of her hips and the lush expanse of her thighs.

The sight of her steamrolled right over Boone's doubts. His dick twitched as he remembered how it had felt to hold her by those hips and slide his hands up those thighs. The sounds she'd made when he touched her. The way she'd looked at him with trust and desire.

It was too late for turning back. Letting go wasn't going to work. Eve had gotten under his skin and into his blood.

When she turned around at the sound of his approach, he saw echoes of her earlier desire in her eyes. That wasn't all he saw now though. There was nervousness as she twisted the dish towel in her hands. Uncertainty, just like he'd been feeling a moment ago. Some shyness too, in the way her eyes lowered after meeting his.

That was what did him in. The vulnerability. He didn't want to let her down. It would kill him to hurt her.

She must have seen the vestiges of doubt in his face because she took a sharp breath as if to brace herself for disappointment.

Boone moved toward her, swiftly enough to make her step back in surprise. She bumped up against the counter as he took her face in his hands and brushed his lips over hers in more of a nuzzle than a real kiss. "Evie."

The dish towel fell to the floor as she twined her hands around his neck with a sigh.

His thumbs stroked her cheeks as he kissed her slowly, gently, savoring the feel of her lips, mapping their surface until they parted for him with a soft gasp. He was lost to her. There was no pretending anymore. Boone gave himself up to it with a hum of pleasure as he sank into her plush sweetness.

Eve's hands slid over his neck as their mouths melded together. Every slide of her tongue seared through him, burning away his hesitation and doubts until he couldn't remember anymore why this might have been a bad idea.

Their kisses grew hungrier. Deeper. Less gentle and more frantic. Her mouth was addictive. She tasted so good he never wanted to stop.

He loved the way she kissed him. Like she couldn't get enough. Like she needed him as much as he needed her. Her hands were in his hair, his beard, stroking down his chest. Then slipping under the T-shirt he'd pulled on when he got out of the pool. He groaned when her fingernails raked through his chest hair.

The urge to rip those tiny, taunting bikini bottoms off and take her right here on the kitchen counter was so strong he couldn't see straight. God, how he wanted to spread those legs and thrust up into her without any preamble, fuck her hard and fast until she came apart on his dick. But if he was going to do this, he was going to do it right.

"Evie." He cradled her jaw, dragging his thumb along the rim of her kiss-swollen lips. "Tell me what you want."

She tipped her head up, her hands fisting in his T-shirt as her mouth moved to his ear. "Everything."

The word shivered through him with a mixture of excitement and unease.

Everything, everything, everything.

For one brief, panicked moment, he almost gave in to his doubts, almost remembered why this was so risky, why he'd been fighting it for so long.

But then he looked into Eve's melted chocolate eyes, so wide and trusting in her perfect, beautiful face. One clear, determined thought rose above all the others, blotting them out.

I can do that.

It would be easy to do it for her, to give her everything she wanted, because it was what he wanted too.

twenty-four

EVE WASN'T PREPARED for Boone to sweep her into his arms and carry her upstairs like a new bride. She was so dizzy and distracted from his kisses, she let out a shriek and clung to his neck for dear life when her feet unexpectedly left the floor.

"I'm not going to drop you," he said as he cradled her against his chest. "Retract your claws a little, kitten."

"Sorry." She tried to loosen her grip on his neck, but tensed up when he started to mount the stairs. This wasn't safe, was it? Shouldn't he have one hand free to hold the banister? "Maybe you shouldn't carry me up the stairs."

"You forget, I've done this before. Although it was a little easier when you were asleep and not doing your best to strangle me."

"I don't want you to hurt yourself." *Or me.*

"You're insulting me, Evie. Chill out."

She pressed her face into his neck and distracted herself by nosing the underside of his beard.

He grunted and squeezed her thigh. "That tickles."

"Good to know. I'm filing that information away for future reference."

Once they made it to the top of the stairs without calamity, Boone carried her down the hall to his bedroom. She'd never been in his room before. It smelled like a mix of his cologne and his soap and that delicious, unique scent of his skin.

He set her down on the edge of the bed. The lights were off, and he moved to the bedside table to turn on a lamp. It cast a soft yellow glow over half his face, leaving the other half in shadow.

When he reached behind his head to drag his T-shirt off, Eve got to her feet, unable to resist the lure of his beautiful torso. "Look at you," she murmured, caressing his stomach as she dipped her head to touch her lips to his chest. "You're like a work of art."

A shiver vibrated through him as she kissed her way across his pecs. His hands slid into her hair when she traced her tongue around one of his nipples, and he tipped her face up to capture her mouth with his.

His kisses were slow and searching. Just like his hands, which traced her curves as if he was memorizing them by touch. She reached up to stroke her fingers through his beard, and he reacted with a pleased hum.

Her body was coming alive at his touch, thrumming with need, her blood roaring through her veins. Distantly, over the pounding of her heart, she heard a whimper, and realized it had come from her.

When he grabbed the hem of her cover-up and yanked it up, she helped him slip it over her head. He tossed it onto the floor, then took a step back to look at her. Goose bumps rose on her skin everywhere his gaze traveled over her, as if it was a physical touch.

"Eve," he whispered, his tongue darting out to wet his upper lip.

The fervent gleam in his eyes incited her to reach behind her neck for the ties of her bikini top.

"Wait." His voice was rough, barely more than a croak. "I want to do it."

With a nod, she lowered her hands.

"I've been dying to do this all day." He moved in close again. As he untied the bow at the back of her neck, she shivered at the teasing graze of his fingertips.

The strings came loose and her top slithered down to her stomach, dangling by the remaining tie around her ribs.

Sighing as if he'd sighted paradise, Boone skimmed his fingers over her breasts. His worshipful focus made her feel like a goddess. No one had ever looked at her that way or made her feel so special.

His breath gusted over her chest as he reached behind her to loosen the other tie. Eve swayed a little, fighting the urge to press her bare breasts against him.

The bikini top fell to her feet, and she flicked it away with her toes. Boone's hands moved to the ties at her hips next, his breath growing more rapid. First one, then the other was worked loose. A swift yank sent her bottoms to the floor.

A smile hovered at the corner of his mouth as he brushed his lips over one of her nipples. Eve's whole body quivered at the delicious prickle of his beard.

"You like that?" he asked as he rubbed his coarse whiskers over her stiff peak.

She arched into him, her hands tangling in his hair. "Yes."

His tongue darted out to soothe the hypersensitive skin he'd abraded, then he sucked her nipple into his mouth. She moaned at the gentle bite of his teeth, the throb between her legs becoming unbearable.

"My turn." Her hands reached out blindly, fumbling for the waistband of his running shorts. "Let me see you."

Boone helped her out by shoving them down to the floor.

When he straightened, his cock bobbed against his lower stomach, thick and curved. All Eve could do was stare for a second, utterly transfixed, until an urgent need to touch him broke her trance. But when she reached for him, he caught her arms with a hoarse grunt and walked her back toward the bed. Her calves hit the edge of the mattress, and she sank down on it, unable to tear her eyes away from him.

Yanking open the bedside table, he rummaged around and came up with a strip of condoms. Impatiently, Eve scooted back on the bed as he tore one of them open. She needed to feel him pushing inside her, filling her up with his hot, throbbing cock. She needed it so badly.

Her belly fluttered as she watched him roll on the condom. When he was done, he crawled onto the bed and braced himself above her, his biceps flexing as he lowered his mouth to hers. She smoothed her hands over his shoulders as his bare chest pushed against her breasts, skin sliding over skin, their tongues dueling and plundering between panting breaths.

His hips settled heavily between her legs, the mass of his body pressing down on her like the best weighted blanket in the world. Eve moaned as his cock throbbed between them, sliding through her slippery folds, the friction exquisite but not what she ached for.

"Boone…" She canted her hips with a pleading whimper. "Get in me. I want you so much."

His head sagged forward and he drew in a shuddering breath. She bit her lip as the thick, wide crown of his cock nudged against her opening. He slipped halfway inside, and she felt herself stretching, that wonderful pressure as her body slowly gave way to him. God, it felt so *good*, the way her whole body pulsated around him.

She wriggled her hips to help him along, and Boone grunted as he eased a little deeper. Another small push of his hips and Eve was gasping, drunk with the feel of him opening her up.

Beautiful didn't begin to cover the sight of him straining above her, a sheen of sweat on his brow, his jaw locked tight in concentration, his muscles flexing and contracting. All of it for her. *With* her. It felt like a miracle, not because of who he was, but because of what he'd come to mean to her.

Whatever happened after this, she knew she'd never be the same.

"Evie," he whispered, kissing her jaw. "Baby."

Her inner walls parted for him, and he slid the rest of the way home with a groan, filling her completely and hitting a spot so deep it made her breath catch and her vision blur. She could feel every throb of his cock, every breath he took, every beat of his heart against her breast.

"I knew you'd feel perfect." Boone's nose nudged her cheek as he kissed the corner of her mouth. "It's so much better than I ever… God, Evie."

She turned her head to catch his lips with clumsy kisses that turned clumsier when he started to move. Every stroke of his cock lit her up inside. She clutched at his shoulders, her thighs trembling as she rolled her hips to meet him, finding the perfect pace together.

The world narrowed until it was only *him* and *her*. The two of them together. Everything else faded to insignificance.

Boone's pale eyes gazed into hers, shining in the lamplight as he surged deep inside her. She couldn't look away from those eyes. They claimed her. Owned her. It was all too much, a connection that was like nothing Eve had ever experienced. They'd barely even started, and she was already so close to coming undone.

"More," she gasped between thrusts. "Harder."

He grasped the back of her thigh to hold her open as he obeyed her command. Her fingernails dug into his skin, gripping him like a lifeline as he drove into her, touching a place that was so exactly *right*, the rhythmic pulse inside her building and building, finally reaching a crescendo.

A wave of pure relief rolled over her. Her orgasm started slow and grew in intensity, breaking her apart and tearing mindless cries from her throat.

Boone buried his face against her neck. "Evie," he murmured. "Baby." He chanted the words over and over as his thrusts grew harder and more frantic. Until finally his whole body tensed with a shuddering groan and he slumped against her.

They lay there limply, chests heaving together, utterly wrecked. After a moment, Boone's lips found her cheek, and Eve turned her head to look at him, drinking in every detail as she traced a finger along his bristly jaw.

"Evie." With a touch so tender it made her throat burn, he brushed a lock of hair off her forehead. "That was…" A line formed between his brows, emotion clouding his clear blue eyes.

"I know," she whispered, feeling as lost as he looked.

It wasn't supposed to feel like this. Especially not the first time.

A thought bloomed somewhere deep in the back of her mind, a voice whispering something she both wanted and didn't want to believe.

This is what it feels like when you're in love.

twenty-five

BOONE WOKE WITH A START, numb with cold, his skin drenched with sweat. Darkness everywhere he looked. A weight was crushing his chest, which felt as hollow as an empty eggshell. Any second now, he'd crack wide-open and fracture into a million pieces too small to put back together.

He had to get away. Get out from under this thing on his chest weighing him down. Trapping him. Breaking him. Slicing him open and stripping him to the bone.

He sucked in a gasping, painful breath as his eyes adjusted to the dark. He was in his bed. A warm arm lay across his chest. A soft body against his. Eve, beside him, fast asleep, breathing soft and slow.

He closed his eyes and fought to push away the panic with his memories of last night. The way Eve had felt in his arms, how she'd clung to him as they'd come together. The hours they'd spent satisfying and taking pleasure in each other. The feeling of peace that had stolen over him as he'd drifted off to sleep with her body pressed against his.

Even as he tried to hold tight to that peace, shadows swarmed around the edges of his memories, casting everything into doubt. That kind of happiness couldn't last. It never did. It was a mirage. A delusion. When the fantasy ended, it would leave only ruin behind.

He should have known he wasn't ready for this. He couldn't trust his emotions enough to protect himself like he needed to. He'd let himself believe Eve was saving him, but that was the same mistake he'd made last time. It was happening all over again.

Distantly, the rational part of his brain protested that it wasn't the same. Eve wasn't anything like Gemma. She could never be.

But rational thoughts didn't matter when he was suffocating, his chest too tight to breathe and his limbs ice-cold. The only way to make it stop was to get as far away from Eve as he could. Far enough that she couldn't reach him.

Only when nobody could reach him would he be safe.

EVE'S ALARM JARRED HER AWAKE. WEIRD, SINCE SHE WAS IN Boone's bed, surrounded by his heavenly scent, and she could have sworn she'd accidentally left her phone charging in the kitchen last night.

She reached out and found Boone's side of the bed empty and cold. That was disappointing.

When she sat up to shut off her phone, she found a text from him.

Went for a run.

A sense of unease settled in the pit of her stomach as she stared at the words. She tried to rationalize it away. Maybe he was one of those people who couldn't sleep with someone else in the bed. He'd probably just had insomnia. She hoped.

Nice of him to bring her phone upstairs for her though. Otherwise she would have overslept and been late for her shift.

She fired off a quick text to thank him before getting ready for work.

Boone still wasn't back by the time she left. He hadn't responded to her text either. Eve texted him again on her way out of the house.

Missed you this morning. See you tonight!

She'd spent an absurdly long time going back and forth on that exclamation point. Briefly, she'd considered a question mark instead, but that had felt too much like she needed reassurance. (She did though. She really did.) A period had seemed too much like a command. Like she was making a threat. In the end she'd settled on the false cheer of an exclamation point, although as soon as she hit send she immediately wished she'd gone with a smiley face emoji instead.

After all her punctuation anxiety, Boone didn't reply to that text either. As the day wore on, a sense of dread seeped into Eve's bones. It grew heavier with every hour that went by without a word from him.

By the time she got home that night, her stomach was twisted up in knots with the certainty something was wrong. So when she walked into the kitchen and found him sitting at the counter, she felt a surge of relief. He was here and safe. Thank god for that.

Then she registered the way his shoulders were hunched, and the flat, distant look on his face as he stared straight ahead. Not at her, even though she'd just walked in, but at some empty space in front of him. He'd made no move to greet her or even acknowledge her presence.

Something was wrong, and Eve was afraid she knew what it was. It was so obvious. He'd slept with her, then gone radio silent, and now he couldn't even look at her. When someone did that, it always meant the same thing.

A stinging lump clogged her throat. Swallowing around it, she forced herself to take a breath. Maybe it wasn't that.

Maybe something else had happened that had nothing to do with her. What if he'd gotten bad news? What if something terrible had happened?

"Boone?" She moved closer, setting her purse down. "Are you okay? What's going on?"

When he finally looked at her, the emptiness in his expression froze her in her place. His jaw clenched before he spoke. "We need to talk."

It was such a fucking cliché she nearly laughed out loud. The bastard child of a laugh and a sob bubbled up her esophagus, and she clamped her jaw shut so it wouldn't escape.

"Fine," she said when she was sure her voice wouldn't break. "Say it, then."

"Last night was a mistake. One that can't happen again."

She wanted to cry, but her pride wouldn't let her. She couldn't stop him from casting her aside, but she refused to let him see how much he'd hurt her. She'd stand here with her chin up as she listened to whatever he had to say, and she'd smile and she'd nod and she'd pretend he hadn't just kicked her feet out from under her.

"Okay." She considered it a minor victory that her voice only shook a little.

"I can't be in a relationship. I told you that up front." He sounded almost accusatory.

"You did," she agreed. Her bad for thinking he'd changed his mind.

Boone's shoulders slumped suddenly, and he scrubbed a hand over his face. "I'm sorry. It was selfish of me to let things go so far. I never should have let it happen. You and I—" His jaw bunched like the words tasted bad in his mouth. "It's just not a good idea under the circumstances."

"Right. Do you want me to move out?" Her voice was curt and matter-of-fact. This was happening whether she liked it or not.

He visibly flinched at the suggestion. "No, Eve. That's the last thing I want. That's why we can't do this. I don't want it to jeopardize our arrangement."

"Arrangement," she echoed numbly. Was that all she was to him? An arrangement?

"Friendship," he corrected with a wince. "I'm not just talking about the deal we made, okay? I could give a fuck about that. I don't want to lose your friendship, Evie. You're too important to me."

Not important enough for him to want to be with her. He'd made her think she was special, but she wasn't anything of the sort. He'd probably looked at all the girls he'd hooked up with like that. He'd probably told all of them their friendship was important to him.

It hurt to realize that was all last night had been to him. A hookup. A one-off fling. A scratching of a temporary itch. Now that he'd gotten her out of his system, he wasn't interested in anything more. She'd been naïve to think it might be otherwise. It wasn't as if he'd made her any promises, after all.

Boone's face fell at her expression. "It's too late, isn't it? I've already ruined everything."

His seemingly genuine anguish thawed her anger a little. It wasn't fair to put this all on him when she shared a healthy portion of the blame. Hadn't he explicitly told her up front that he didn't want a girlfriend?

More than that, Eve knew he was still a wreck over his last one. That alone should have been enough to stop her from jumping into bed with him. It wasn't like she didn't know better than to let herself be the rebound lay.

Boone had tried to keep his hands off her. He'd told her it wasn't a good idea, and she'd responded by basically throwing herself at him. Daring him to go against his better instincts.

It served her right, really. She'd set herself up for this heartbreak. From the very beginning Eve had known she was headed for a world of hurt, but that hadn't slowed her down any. She'd wanted him too much to be sensible. This was what you got when you let yourself be led by lust.

"It's not too late," she said with a sigh. "If you don't want to be with me, that's fine. I can get over it."

Her words didn't seem to give him any comfort. If anything, he looked even more unhappy. "It's not about what I want. I wouldn't be able to give you what you need. I'd only end up hurting you even more."

She couldn't listen to this. Her head and her heart both ached too much. "We don't need to talk about it anymore. You made your feelings known, and I've heard you loud and clear."

He flinched again. "Evie, I—"

"If you're serious about wanting to move past this, you're going to have to give me some space." She wasn't entirely convinced moving past it was possible, but she was willing to try.

There wasn't any other option, unless she wanted to renege on their deal and find somewhere else to live. That was most likely what she'd end up doing, but it wasn't a decision she was going to make in the heat of the moment. She'd take some time to calm down first, see how she felt after a couple of days. Then she'd figure out what to do.

Remorse etched Boone's expression, as though he could read her thoughts. "I know I hurt you, but please don't shut me out completely."

She didn't have any choice. It was the only way to protect herself. "You told me what you need, and now I'm telling you what I need. I've always given you space when you wanted it. You owe me the same courtesy now."

He looked away and nodded. "You're right."

Eve picked up her purse, clutching it to her stomach as she turned to go. Her limbs felt numb and heavy. As soon as she got to her room, she was going to get in the shower and have a good, long cry where Boone wouldn't be able to hear her.

"I'm sorry," he said behind her.

"I know," she replied without looking back, so he wouldn't be able to see her heart breaking. "Me too."

twenty-six

BOONE WAS as good as his word and avoided Eve like the plague. He stayed in his bedroom with the door closed every morning when she left for work, and every evening from the time she got home until she went to bed.

She wouldn't have known he was home at all if she hadn't seen both his cars in the garage. The changing state of the dirty dishes and the occasional sounds of him moving around in his room served as the only proof of life.

She should have been relieved he was leaving her alone like she'd asked, but instead it felt like more rejection. Some part of her had secretly hoped he'd fight for her. A petty and passive-aggressive part, granted. But it was what it was. She wanted him, even now, and the evidence of how much he didn't want her back hurt even more.

It took Eve a couple of days to accept Boone wasn't changing his mind. He'd meant what he'd said. She didn't know how much longer they could go on ignoring each other like this. Eventually one of them would have to break.

The weekend was approaching, and with it allegedly their next pap walk. She couldn't bear to think about it, frankly. The thought of playing girlfriend with Boone was too painful to contemplate.

Eventually he'd have to raise the subject, wouldn't he? Or maybe not. Maybe he'd changed his mind about keeping up their charade.

She'd already started looking for an apartment. It seemed like the smart thing to do. Not that she'd gotten very far. All she'd managed so far were some halfhearted internet searches. It was hard to motivate herself to do much of anything with Boone's rejection still a raw, painful wound.

She intended to spend her lunch hour on Wednesday making a more concerted effort. Since she had the following morning off, she should really spend it driving around to visit apartment prospects. But her best intentions were thwarted by a monster headache. Concentration was a no-go, and staring at her phone only seemed to make her head throb even more.

It got worse as the afternoon wore on. Her skin felt too tight, and her joints ached like she was a hundred years old. She was so spacey her supervisor at the preschool noticed. Eve's confession of a headache, combined with her flushed appearance, got her marched to the school nurse. A thermometer shoved in her ear revealed a temperature of a hundred and one. Eve was given two Tylenol and sent home with instructions not to come back until she'd been fever-free for twenty-four hours.

As bad luck would have it, Boone was in the kitchen when she got home. He looked up from whatever food he was making, clearly thrown by her surprise appearance in the middle of the afternoon.

It was the first time they'd been face-to-face since he'd rejected her. Two days had done nothing to dull the pain. Nor had it dulled Eve's attraction to him. He was as heart-stoppingly handsome as ever, which only made seeing him now hurt even worse.

There was a long, awful pause as he stared at her like some stranger who'd suddenly wandered in off the street. "You're not usually home this early."

No shit, she thought irritably. She forced her feet to start moving again, gritting her teeth as she moved around him to get to the fridge. "I've got a fever, so they sent me home."

"Are you okay?"

Irrationally, his concern irritated her even more.

"It's just a fever," she muttered as she helped herself to one of his Gatorades without bothering to ask permission. "I'm fine."

When she shut the fridge he was right there, right in front of her. His blue eyes stopped her in her tracks. Creases formed around them as he searched her face.

A shiver racked her body, and his frown deepened.

"Can I do anything?" The softness of his voice caused her throat to thicken.

"No." Her reply came out sounding too harsh. She winced, giving him a tight smile as she held up her drink. "This is all I need."

His lips flattened. "I'm here if you change your mind. Just let me know if you need something."

She couldn't bear the wounded sadness in his eyes. Swallowing thickly, she stepped around him and walked out of the kitchen without another word. He didn't stop her, and that was yet another disappointment. Yes, she was being unfair, and no, she didn't give a damn.

Up in her room, Eve crawled into bed and pulled the quilt up under her chin. Between being sick and seeing Boone, she felt like complete and utter shit.

IT WAS DARK OUTSIDE WHEN EVE WOKE UP. SHE WAS SWEATING and freezing at the same time, every muscle in her body throbbing. Her head hurt so bad she wanted to curl up in a ball and die.

Staggering to her feet, she shuffled downstairs for the painkillers Boone kept in the kitchen. The rest of the house was dark and quiet. According to the microwave, it was coming up on midnight.

She popped two ibuprofen and chased them with an entire glass of water. The cold liquid raised goose bumps on her arms and caused her to convulse with a violent shiver.

Eve jerked open the fridge, hugging her chest as she stared inside. Her lip curled as she surveyed the contents. She hadn't eaten anything since lunch, but her stomach lurched unpleasantly at the faint, lingering smell of whatever Boone had cooked earlier.

In fact, that glass of water she'd chugged wasn't sitting all that great. Maybe she should have some crackers or something. She wandered to the pantry and scanned the shelves. It was hard to focus with her vision swimming. She rubbed her eyes, groaning as the throb in her head increased.

On second thought, maybe she should just go back to bed…

As she started to head upstairs, a sudden wave of nausea twisted through her stomach.

Oh god, no. Please don't let this be happening.

No sooner had she finished the thought than she was seized by another, even more urgent and agonizing surge of nausea.

This. Was Happening.

Gagging as she fought to hold back her rising gorge, Eve sprinted for the hall bathroom. She slammed the door shut behind her as she dove for the toilet, barely managing to get the lid open before she was sick.

Boone heard Eve come out of her room at eleven forty-five. It was the first sound she'd made in over six hours. Before that he'd been lying in bed fretting and debating if he should knock on her door to check on her.

She'd looked awful when she'd come home earlier. Still beautiful enough to temporarily rob him of oxygen, but definitely not well. He was still haunted by the dark circles hollowing her eyes and the unhealthy flares of red on her cheeks and chest against the sickly pallor of her complexion.

The way she'd stiffened at the sight of him had driven a stake through his heart. His first panicked thought was that she'd been crying and her unhealthy appearance was because of him. He hadn't laid eyes on her in two days. For all he knew, she'd been like this since their conversation Monday evening.

It had almost been a relief to find out she was sick. Except it hadn't been a relief at all because Eve was *sick*.

That had inspired a different kind of panic. Boone's chest had constricted with the need to pull her shivering body into his arms and press his hand to her fevered forehead the way his mom used to do when he was sick. To carry Eve upstairs and tuck her into bed while stroking her hair and murmuring words of comfort in her ear. To bring her water and lemonade and trays with soup and ice cream and whatever else she needed to make her feel better. To stay by her side watching over her until he knew she was all right.

But Eve had rejected his offer of help and recoiled from him when he'd approached her. That had been another stake in his heart. All his own fault, of course. He'd done this to them. Broken their friendship when he'd repaid Eve's affection by hurting her.

So he'd let her go and left her alone like she wanted. Like he'd been doing for days. And he'd talked himself out of checking on her, because he suspected his presence would make her feel worse instead of better.

He breathed a little easier now as he listened to her shuffling steps along the hallway and down the stairs. After that there was silence again. Boone continued to wage an internal battle with himself. What he wanted to do was get up and see how she was doing, but she'd made it crystal clear she didn't want his help. Still, he couldn't help worrying she might need something. What if she'd gotten sicker? Or wanted something they didn't have in the house?

The thought that Eve might decide to drive herself to the store was what finally made up his mind. He was going down there, dammit. Just to make sure she was okay and didn't need anything.

When he ventured downstairs, he found the kitchen light on but Eve was nowhere in sight. He was about to make his way down to the rec room when the sound of retching had him turning toward the bathroom by the stairs. His stomach clenched in sympathy at the desolate moan that followed.

"Evie?" he called through the closed door.

"Don't come in here!" she shouted hoarsely.

The toilet flushed, followed by the sound of the sink faucet running.

"Can I bring you anything?" he asked when the water shut off.

"No. I'm fine." This obvious lie was immediately followed by another bout of vomiting.

He waited until it ended before he spoke again. "You're not fine. You're sick. Let me help."

"Please go away," she pleaded.

Boone closed his eyes and pressed his forehead against the doorframe. "I know you're mad at me, but I'm not leaving you alone like this."

"Please." She sounded miserable, her voice a feeble croak.

"It's embarrassing. I don't want you listening to me puke my guts up."

"You don't have anything to be embarrassed about. You're sick."

Before she could answer, Eve started vomiting again. This time it went on and on, the sounds of her suffering almost too much for Boone to bear. He waited it out, clenching both sides of the doorframe so hard he was shocked he hadn't left finger dents in it.

"Evie?" he said when it finally eased up.

There was no answer except the toilet flushing. Over the sound of the tank refilling, he heard her sob.

That did it. He couldn't stand on the other side of this fucking door doing nothing at all. "I'm coming in, Evie."

When she didn't object, he tried the doorknob. It was unlocked, thank god. He was more than frantic enough to kick it in if he had to.

Eve was huddled on the tile floor next to the toilet, shivering as she hugged her knees. Her skin was as ashen as the stucco wall, her eyes glassy and surrounded by circles as dark as bruises.

"Baby." He dropped to his knees and carefully pulled her into his arms. She was sticky with sweat and blazing hot to the touch.

Rather than protest, she sagged against him with a pained whimper.

He stroked her damp hair as his mind raced to think of ways to help her. It'd been an age since he'd had a stomach bug or been around anyone else suffering from this sort of illness. Holding a drunk buddy's head after a night of drinking wasn't the same thing as taking care of someone with a fever.

"When's the last time you took your temperature?"

Another shiver racked her frame. "At school. This afternoon."

Boone didn't even know if he had a thermometer in the house. *Fuck.* "What about painkillers to bring down the fever? Have you taken any?"

"Tried," she croaked. "Threw them up."

"Okay." He smoothed his hand up and down her back. There wasn't much point in giving her medicine or fluids until her body had finished purging itself.

"Cold," she whispered, curling into him. "I'm so cold."

"I know, baby." He held her tighter, rubbing his hands over her bare arms.

"I'm not mad at you," she mumbled, clutching at his T-shirt as she burrowed into his chest. "I wasn't mad. I was just sad."

God. That was…so much worse.

"I thought…" Her chest hitched as she drew in a breath. Abruptly, she pushed out of his arms with a moan and lurched toward the toilet.

Boone gathered her hair back for her. When the retching stopped, he flushed the toilet and wiped her face with a damp hand towel.

"You don't have to do that," she moaned pitifully. "I'm sorry I'm so gross. I'm sorry for being so much trouble."

"Stop apologizing." Propping her against the wall, he placed the wet towel on the back of her neck and laid one of her hands over it to keep it there. "Stay here."

Her fingers clamped onto his arm. "Don't leave me."

His heart dropped to his stomach, and he bent to kiss her forehead. Her skin felt alarmingly hot against his lips. "I'll only be gone a minute. I promise."

He sprinted through the house, gathering things to make her more comfortable until she was well enough to leave the bathroom. When he got back, Eve's eyes were closed and her head tipped back against the wall. Tossing two cushions onto the floor, he knelt and wrapped a fleece blanket around her. Her eyes blinked open as he tucked it around her shoulders.

"How's that?" he asked. "Any better?"

She nodded, pulling it tighter around her. "Not as warm as you though."

Suppressing the urge to smile, he sat cross-legged on one of the cushions and shifted her onto his lap. She snuggled into him with a sigh, and he rearranged the blanket around her.

"You want to try drinking some water?"

She shuddered and made an unhappy noise in the back of her throat.

"Okay," he said, smoothing her hair back from her face. "You let me know if you change your mind or think of anything else you need."

He held her until the next bout of retching started. Once again, he held her hair back and helped her clean up after it passed. The cycle repeated like that for the next hour. Each time around, Eve seemed to get a few minutes longer to rest between purges, but she also got noticeably weaker the longer it went on. By the end, Boone was supporting her head and rubbing her back to comfort her while she sobbed between dry heaves.

When the paroxysms subsided, she curled up on the hard tile with a whimper, resting her head in his lap. It tore at his heart to see her in such misery and know there was no way for him to make it stop or take her pain away.

Eventually, Eve's stomach settled enough to let her fall asleep. He stroked his fingers over her forehead and along her hairline as he watched the slow rise and fall of her chest. Once he felt certain the worst had passed, he scooped her up off the floor.

She lay limp in his arms, moaning softly in her sleep as he carried her upstairs. After laying her in his bed, he pulled the sheet up over her. Then he got in bed next to her, sitting up with his back against the headboard so he could watch over her.

He didn't even consider trying to get some sleep.

As long as Eve was sick, he wouldn't be able to rest.

EVE DREAMED SHE WAS IN BOONE'S ARMS. IT HAD TO BE A dream because he was holding her and telling her everything was going to be okay. After that she dreamed she was back in his bed. She could smell him all around her, familiar and soothing.

But she couldn't get comfortable. She was too cold. Freezing to death. Shivers shook her body. Her teeth chattered. Everything hurt so much. Her head throbbed, her throat burned, her stomach and every muscle and joint in her whole body ached. It felt like all her insides had been hollowed out and she was the battered shell left behind.

She whimpered and reached out for Boone, equally relieved and surprised to find him next to her.

His hand touched her face. "Shhh. You're okay."

She plastered herself against him, clinging for dear life. He was the only thing that felt solid and good amid all the agony.

"I'm here. I've got you." Something warm and soft settled over her. A hand rubbed circles between her shoulder blades until she drifted back into the peaceful relief of darkness.

EVE WOKE IN HELL. THE SURFACE OF HER SKIN WAS ROASTING. Her chest was a big ball of flame burning her from the inside out. She kicked her legs, clawing her way out from under the blankets suffocating her.

"Ow!" Boone said. He was in the bed next to her.

Eve was in his room. In his bed. With him.

Hazy memories floated back to her. Cold tile. The taste of bile. Boone holding her hair back as she vomited. Huddling in his lap next to the downstairs toilet. Lying on the bathroom floor, trapped in an endless misery of nausea and throwing up until it felt like her stomach had turned itself inside out and she was shaking herself apart with every muscle-rending heave.

Boone came around to her side of the bed and sat on the edge of the mattress, peering down at her. The concerned furrows traversing his brow told her she looked as awful as she felt.

"Think you can sit up?" It was still dark outside the windows. The only light came from the bathroom, spilling in around the door he'd left cracked.

Eve nodded weakly and let him help her up to a sitting position. Her mouth tasted like acid. The room spun, and she slumped against the headboard in exhaustion, waiting for it to stop.

"Drink this." Boone held something under her nose.

It smelled like fruit punch. The same Gatorade that had come back up last night when the barfing started. She made a face and turned her head away, praying to god she didn't start puking again.

"You need to drink," he said. "We have to replenish your fluids."

"Water." The word tore its way out of her raw throat.

He put a glass of water in her hand and helped guide it to her mouth.

It soothed her throat and washed away some of the vile taste in her mouth, but she pushed the glass away as soon as the water hit her stomach. Not a great feeling. She swallowed thickly, trying not to gag at the ripple of nausea.

The glass in her hand was replaced by one of those big plastic souvenir cups. "Here. In case you need to throw up."

Eve clutched the cup, breathing in and out slowly, and managed not to puke. A minor miracle.

"Doing okay?"

Boone was being so caring and patient it made her tear up with emotion. A cool palm pressed against her forehead. She leaned into it and closed her eyes with a sigh.

"You're burning up. I need you to take some pills, okay? Can you do that for me, Evie?"

Obediently, she swallowed the pills he put in her hand. They hurt her throat going down, but she hardly gagged at all.

He smoothed her sweaty hair back from her face. "Think you can drink the rest of that water?"

It took her a while, but she managed it. She slumped against the headboard, and he helped her lie back down.

"Covers or no covers?"

"No covers."

Boone leaned over her to adjust her pillow, then smoothed her hair back some more.

"Nice," she mumbled, blinking up at him. "You're being so nice to me."

An unhappy look came over his face.

Eve reached up to touch his cheek, intending to smooth his frown away, but got distracted petting his beard. Her eyes fell closed as she trailed her fingers along his jaw, combing through the whiskers she loved so much.

He made a sound in his throat. "Evie…"

She could feel the tension trembling through his body, but she couldn't make herself stop touching him. As long as she was sick, she could get away with it. He'd tolerate her neediness out of pity. But once she was well again, things would go back the way they were.

Despair punched through her chest. It would wreck her to lose him all over again. Another bullet to her foolish, weak heart.

A tear slipped out of the corner of her eye and slid across her cheek. "I wish you liked me the way I like you." The fever had burned up all her defenses. She couldn't hold the words in any more than she could hold back her tears.

The mattress shifted, and Boone's lips touched her face, kissing the tear away. "Evie," he whispered against her fever-heated skin. "Baby."

He'd whispered the exact same thing to her in this same bed on the night they'd spent together. It hurt to remember it now, and she failed to stifle the sob that choked out of her.

Boone's fingers threaded through her hair. "Shh. We'll talk about it when you're not sick."

"Don't leave." Her voice was trembling and pathetic. No wonder he didn't want her.

His body curled around hers, holding her tight. "I'm right here."

That wasn't the same thing. It didn't mean she wouldn't have to let him go again.

But it was enough to make her feel a little better. Enough that she could fall back asleep in the comfort of his arms.

twenty-seven

THINGS GOT hazy again for a while after that. Sometimes Eve was alone in the bed, tossing and turning as her body burned itself up. Other times Boone was there pressing a cool washcloth to her forehead or urging her to drink various fluids. Taking care of her. He'd acquired ginger ale and lemon-lime Gatorade somehow, and she drank those more willingly than the despised fruit punch. At one point he put a thermometer in her mouth and seemed unhappy about what it told him.

Time no longer had any meaning. It could have been hours or days passing for all Eve knew. She fought hard against waking up. The pain was too much when she was awake. She'd drink whatever Boone told her to drink and flop back against the pillow, seeking the relief of unconsciousness.

When her fever spiked she woke whimpering. Boone was there with her, his cool hands on her face, talking to her in the dark. She couldn't seem to hold on to the words he was saying, but the soft, gentle sound of his voice soothed her back to sleep.

The next time she woke, Eve was soaking wet. Her T-shirt was drenched with sweat and so were the sheets. The bed was empty, which was just as well since she was a disgusting, soggy, stinky mess.

Sunlight poured in between the slats of the closed shutters. One of the balcony doors was ajar, and she saw Boone leaning on the railing outside with his phone against his ear.

He spoke in a low voice she could only just make out. "I don't know. She's been sleeping quietly the last hour, and I didn't want to wake her. But her skin feels cooler, I think." He sounded anxious. There was a long pause before he spoke again. "You don't think I need to take her to urgent care?"

While the person on the other end talked, he began pacing back and forth.

"Okay. I'll do that." Boone shoved his hand through his hair and tugged on the ends. "Yeah, I know. I will. Thanks again for all your help. …Okay, I will. Love you, Mom. Bye."

He came back into the bedroom and stopped when he saw Eve was awake.

"Shit, did I wake you? Sorry."

She shook her head, wincing at the way the movement made her head and neck ache, though it wasn't anywhere near as bad as before. Thank the baby Jesus. She yawned and rubbed her eyes. "What time is it?"

"A little after nine." Boone perched on the edge of the bed and set his palm to her forehead. "Feels like your fever might be down finally."

"Is it Thursday?"

"That's right. I called the coffee shop when it opened to let them know you were sick, but they said you weren't scheduled to work today."

"Thank you for doing that."

He jiggled a thermometer in front of her face. "Open up."

"Thank you for taking care of me." Her words came out garbled around the thermometer.

His index finger touched the underside of her chin. "Don't talk."

He looked exhausted. Shadows darkened the skin around his bloodshot eyes, and deep worry lines etched his face.

When the thermometer beeped, he slipped it out of her mouth. "Only one hundred. That's a big improvement."

"Was that your mom you were talking to on the phone?"

He nodded as he put the thermometer away. "She's a nurse. I called her for advice last night when your fever got up to a hundred and four." His gaze settled on Eve once more with a frown. "You scared the hell out of me."

"I'm sorry. Did you get any sleep at all last night?"

"A little. I'm fine."

"Liar. You've got bags under your eyes."

A smile flickered over his lips. "Always with the compliments."

"Someone's got to keep you humble."

He winced and looked away. "You want to try eating something? Maybe some dry toast or a banana?"

The thought of it made her clutch her stomach. "No, not yet. Please don't make me."

"Fine, but I need you to sit up and drink something. Mom's orders."

She let him help her to a sitting position, and he handed her a bottle of yellow Gatorade. It felt okay in her stomach, so she gulped a bunch down. Turned out she was thirsty. "I need to pee."

"That's a good sign. You want help to the bathroom?"

She shook her head and swung her legs over the edge of the bed. "You've sacrificed yourself enough already. I'll manage."

Boone hovered close by as she pushed herself to her feet. When she got a head rush from standing upright for the first time in hours, he gripped her arm to steady her. "Take it slow. You're probably a little weak."

A little was an understatement. It was an effort just to hold her head up, and her legs were like wet noodles beneath her, protesting the idea they should support her weight *and* remember how to walk. She was like a toddler taking her first wobbly steps.

"How about I walk you there, just for my own peace of mind?"

Being escorted to the toilet was a fun new humiliation, but Eve resigned herself to it. She might not feel like boiling death anymore, but she was still a long way from operating at one hundred percent. After all the vomiting, crying, and delirium Boone had already witnessed, her pride was a dot in the rearview mirror at this point anyway.

As soon as they made it into his bathroom, she let go of Boone and leaned on the counter for support. "I can take it from here."

"You sure?" He was hesitant to leave her on her own.

Waving him off, she shuffled along the counter to the toilet door. Eve gave him a thumbs-up. "I'm good. You can go."

"I'm leaving the outer door open," he said as he backed out. "Call if you need anything."

After she'd managed to accomplish the journey to the toilet and back to the sink, she discovered that Boone had set a brand-new toothbrush out for her. Bless him.

The face staring back at Eve in the mirror looked like a member of the undead. She smelled like one too. Her T-shirt and pajama pants were damp and stank of sweat. Same went for her hair. She cast a longing look at Boone's shower, but wasn't confident she could stand up long enough to wash her hair on her own.

In fact, maybe she'd sit down right here on the floor for a minute while she thought about it…

She felt like she'd been hit by a truck. Not that she'd ever been hit by a truck before, but she imagined it must feel something like this.

There was a tentative knock on the door. "Evie? You okay in there?"

"Yeah. Fine."

"Can I bring you anything?"

She considered asking for clean clothes, but what was the point without a shower? "Nope."

"Is it okay if I come in?"

"Sure." *Why not?* He'd already seen her at her worst.

Boone stood over her with his hands on his hips. "Hey, buddy. Whatcha doing down there?"

She plucked at her sweaty T-shirt. "I wanted to get out of these gross clothes and take a shower, but I got tired after I brushed my teeth and needed to sit down."

"Yeah, I'm thinking that might be a challenge right now." His lips pulled to one side as he contemplated her. "How about I run you a bath instead?"

"A bath sounds amazing." She could have cried with relief at the thought of it.

He leaned over the giant spa tub and started the water running. "You want bubbles?"

"Yes, please."

After squirting some bath gel in the water, he disappeared into the adjoining walk-in closet and came back out with a T-shirt and a pair of knit boxer shorts. "You can change into these after—unless you'd rather I get something else from your room for you?"

The thought of Boone pawing through her period underwear was enough to put her off that idea. "No, these are great. Thank you."

He set them on the counter closest to the tub, then went to get her a clean towel and washcloth. The scent of sage and seawater wafted through the bathroom as the tub filled. It smelled like nuzzling into the crook of Boone's neck.

"All right, let's get you into the tub." Offering Eve his hand, he hauled her off the floor.

She only got a minor head rush when she stood up this time. Small victories. But she could feel his anxious eyes on her as she shuffled to the tub.

"The sides are pretty high," he said. "It's a little awkward getting in."

He wasn't kidding. It was daunting in her unsteady state.

"I'll manage," she assured him as she stared at it, attempting to work out how she was going to do that.

"Yeah, but see, here's the thing: if you crack your head open in my bathroom, I'll take it up the ass on my home-owner's insurance. I think you need to let me help you get in."

Eve shook her head, crossing her arms over her chest at the thought of stripping in front of Boone—not to mention letting his hands guide her naked body into the tub. *Nope. Definitely not happening.*

The look he gave her somehow managed to be reproachful and regretful at the same time. "It's not like I haven't seen you naked before."

"This is different." For one thing, she was disgusting. No one should have to see her naked like this. For another, the last time he'd seen her naked it was because he'd wanted to. Now? Not so much. He'd made that clear. She wasn't foisting her nudity on him when she knew it was unwelcome.

"I'll keep my eyes closed if it makes you feel better."

Eve thought about it. She really wanted to get in that tub and didn't have the energy to fight him on it. "Fine," she agreed reluctantly.

As promised, Boone's eyes stayed shut as she wrestled out of her clothes, grabbed onto his arm, and ungracefully clambered into the tub—all without any death-inviting incidents. Hooray.

The water felt wondrous as she slid into its warm embrace, and she sank under the bubbles with an orgasmic sigh.

"You good?" His voice sounded slightly taut.

"Amazing. It's the best thing I've ever felt in my life."

His lips quirked in wry amusement. "I'll try not to take that personally."

Eve was in no way prepared for him to start making jokey references to their unfortunate night of passion already. As she felt her cheeks flush, she sent a splash of bathwater at him in retaliation.

"Hey," he protested as he wiped his damp arm.

"Your eyes are open!"

"Sorry," he muttered, covering them with his hands.

"It's fine. You can relax. I'm under the bubbles anyway."

Cautiously, Boone lowered his hands. A muscle ticked in his jaw, his gaze growing heavy and slightly hazy as it flicked over her. The foam frothed on the surface of the water and sloshed against her skin, a few meager bubbles the only thing shielding her body from his eyes.

"You don't have to stay," she told him. "I'm fine."

"If you want me to leave you on your own, you have to sing."

"Sing?"

"That's what I make my nephews do when I leave them alone in the tub, so I know they haven't drowned."

Eve snorted. "I'm not a child. And I'm not singing."

"Then I guess I have to stay and keep an eye on you."

"Do what you want." She was beyond caring anymore. With another happy sigh, she sank lower under the water and propped her feet on the rim of the tub.

Boone sat behind her head on the edge of the tile platform surrounding the tub. "Feel better?"

"A million times better. Amazing what a bath will do for you."

He made a vague hum of agreement.

Eve asked for the washcloth and he dutifully passed it over. She tried to ignore his presence behind her and enjoy getting clean, but it was hard to fully relax with him lurking back there. "If you insist on sticking around, you could make yourself useful and wash my hair."

"Okay." He said it with no hesitation.

She'd been kidding, but far be it from her to turn down the offer if he was serious. And he seemed to be serious.

After he'd retrieved his shampoo from the shower, Boone reached for the handheld sprayer on the tub and sat behind her again. His fingers touched her shoulder, giving it a gentle nudge. "Lean forward."

Gripping the edge of the tub, she hauled herself upright while he adjusted the temperature of the water. Thank god there were so many bubbles, because her nipples were just barely underwater when she was sitting upright.

He laid his hand on top of her head, tipping it back. Her eyes fell closed as soothing warm water washed over her hair. Once it was thoroughly wet, he squirted shampoo into his hand. When he started massaging it into her hair, she let out an embarrassing moan.

"Feel good?" he asked, sounding amused.

"Oh, wow, yes." It was all she could do not to moan continually as he ran his fingertips over her scalp, exerting exactly the right amount of pressure. "I take back what I said. *This* is the best thing I've ever felt."

He breathed out a laugh. "Nice to know I'm good at something."

"*Very* good. Exceptional, even."

Boone grunted as he rubbed the base of her skull, then slid his soapy fingers down the back of her neck. She whimpered with pleasure as he dug into the sore muscles, working over them slowly and carefully. Next he moved on to her stiff shoulders, his fingers slipping over her wet skin as he massaged all the tension away. By the time he was done, Eve felt like a rag doll, and he had to help support her head so he could rinse the soap out of her hair.

"You want conditioner?"

She shook her head. He'd spoiled her most of the way into a coma. "After that, all I can think about is getting back into bed."

He made an odd sort of noise and got to his feet, gallantly looking away as he held out a towel. Once she'd wrapped it around herself, he helped her climb out of the tub.

"I'll let you get dressed on your own," he said. "Unless you need help."

She assured him she could manage, and he looked relieved as he slipped out of the bathroom.

The bath had left Eve as weak as a newborn kitten, and it took her a while to get herself dried off and dressed. The plain navy T-shirt he'd set out for her was faded with age and amazingly soft. She'd worried his boxer shorts might be too tight on her hips, but they turned out to be nice and stretchy.

When she came out of the bathroom, Boone was putting clean sheets on the bed. He paused long enough to hand her a banana. "Eat this."

She sank down on the sofa in front of the fireplace and managed to eat the whole thing by the time he'd finished making up the bed. He made her take two more ibuprofen and drink a whole glass of water before he let her crawl under the covers.

"You're the best." She flopped back on the bed with an exhausted sigh. "Seriously. I don't know what I'd do without you."

"I'll leave you to get some sleep now." He turned to go.

"You don't have to."

He paused halfway to the door but didn't turn around.

When he didn't say anything, Eve lost some of her nerve and started to backtrack. "I mean, it's fine if you want to go—if you have stuff to do or whatever. I just thought you might be tired since you were up all night. You could stay and take a nap if you wanted. Or not." She stretched her arm out toward the empty space beside her. "It's a king bed. There's plenty of room."

"It won't bother you now that you're feeling better?" He still had his back to her so she couldn't see his face.

"I'm not feeling that much better." She let out a yawn for illustrative purposes. "I'll probably fall right to sleep. Anyway, it's not like we haven't slept in the same bed before."

She wasn't sure that was the right thing to say. Maybe she'd made him more uncomfortable by bringing up That Night. She couldn't tell. All this had been a lot easier when she was delirious with fever. It seemed ridiculous that she was lying in his bed, wearing his clothes—his *underwear*, even—after he'd *washed her hair*, and things were this awkward between them.

Eve held her breath, waiting to see what he'd do. It felt like there was a lot more at stake than whether or not he wanted to take a nap. It felt like the entire future of their friendship hung on this one choice. If Boone walked out now, it would mean they'd never be able to get back what they had, and everything between them would always feel awkward and awful.

"All right." He turned around, his expression uncertain, but maybe—she thought, she *hoped*—also a bit pleased. "I guess I am pretty wiped."

She patted the mattress again, trying not to smile too much and scare him away. "Take a load off, pal, and get comfortable."

He slid between the sheets, leaving a good foot and a half of space between them. Neither of them spoke as they lay side by side staring at the ceiling. Despite her physical tiredness, Eve's mind wouldn't quiet enough to let her sleep. Not with Boone so near yet still so far away.

A flush crept over her chest as she remembered the way she'd clung to him last night. How he'd held her and soothed her to sleep. What would he do if she scooted across that vast distance between them and curled up against him now that she was more lucid? Would he welcome her into his arms still? Or would he stiffen and shift away? She was afraid to find out.

Cautiously, she cast a sidelong look at him. His eyes were open, staring up at nothing. Not asleep, then, any more than she was.

Turning onto her side to face him, Eve tucked her hands under her pillow. "Thank you," she said quietly. "For taking such good care of me."

His face seemed to pinch, but otherwise he didn't move. "I wish you'd stop thanking me."

"Why?"

He didn't answer. Just kept staring at the ceiling as if he hadn't heard her.

"Boone," she whispered into the heavy silence. When he still didn't acknowledge her, she reached across the gulf and slid her hand into his.

She braced herself for him to shake her off, knowing it would crush her soul if he did.

He didn't crush her soul. Instead his fingers curled around hers. And they kept holding on tight. As if he needed the contact as much as she did.

It gave her hope and more courage. Enough to broach the subject hanging over them like a dark cloud. "Maybe we should talk about the thing we've been avoiding talking about."

"Okay." The word gusted out of him on a quiet sigh as he continued to stare at the ceiling.

"I think I owe you an apology."

"What?" It got him to look at her finally, his brow furrowing in confusion. "Evie, no."

"I should have listened to you better. You told me you weren't ready for a relationship because you were still hurting over your last one. I knew that, and I didn't think enough about what it meant. When you said we shouldn't act on our attraction, I didn't listen. I knew you were conflicted, and I didn't care."

"Evie," he said quietly. Just that. His eyes were sad as they searched hers—so sad, she felt a fresh wave of remorse for not understanding better what he'd needed.

She swallowed around the stinging in her throat and clung to his hand, wishing things could be different than they were. "I wanted you so much that I didn't think about what it would do to you. What it would do to us."

"I wanted you just as much. I could have held back, but I didn't. I made my own choice, knowing what I was doing. I thought I could handle it. I wanted to believe it so badly I convinced myself it was true."

"It sounds to me like we're both equally to blame for what happened. I think that means we can call it a wash and stop beating ourselves up."

The misery in his expression didn't magically go away like she'd hoped. "I hate that it's created all this distance between us."

"I hate it too. This week really sucked, even before I got sick."

"You've done so much for me, Evie. You have no idea how much. I can't stand that I hurt you."

She nodded solemnly and squeezed his hand. "I can tell you're feeling really sad and crummy right now. You remember what that means, don't you? You're allowed to ask for a hug if you want one."

His frown didn't change, and once again she worried she'd

said the wrong thing. Maybe when he'd said he hated the distance between them he hadn't meant that he wanted it to stop. Maybe he'd only meant he hated that it was necessary and would continue to be necessary from now on.

"Evie," he said after an interminable, nerve-racking moment. "Can I have a hug?" Only then did he allow the beginnings of a smile to show.

She more or less flung herself across the bed at him, and his arms enveloped her, crushing her against his chest. She was back in her happy place, the best place on earth.

"I missed you," she snuffled, blaming her urge to cry on her lingering low-grade fever.

His face pressed into the top of her head. "I missed you too. I don't want to lose you."

God, she was so relieved to hear him say that. "Then you don't have to. We can get past this. We'll figure it out. I don't have to be your girlfriend. I can just be your friend if that's what you need."

She felt him draw in an unsteady breath. Boone's arms tightened around her for a second, squeezing almost hard enough to hurt before he loosened them again.

"Okay," he said as his hand smoothed over her still-damp hair. The raw relief Eve heard in that one softly spoken word made her eyes tear up even more.

This was all she needed. It would be enough just to have this much of Boone. They could go back to the way things were before and take it slow. Maybe in time he'd feel able to offer her more. Or maybe he wouldn't, but she didn't need to think about that yet.

"I don't deserve you," he said in a rough, quiet voice.

"Of course you do." Eve lifted her head to direct a frown at him. "Why would you say that? It's not true at all. Tell me you don't really think that."

"I don't really think that," he responded as requested.

It didn't sound like he meant it. It sounded like he was only saying it to appease her.

She was troubled that he felt that way. She wanted to ask him why, what on earth had ever made him think something like that? Didn't he know how special and amazing he was? Not only had he offered her a place to live when she'd needed it, he'd worn himself out nursing her back to health last night. And what had she ever done for him? Enjoyed kissing him too much, taken advantage of him, and then made him feel bad for it. Some friend she'd been.

"You deserve everything," she insisted. "There's nothing in this world that's too good for you." When he blinked and looked away, she snuggled against his chest again, holding him tight. "One day you're going to believe me. I'll make sure of it."

His arm wrapped around her, but he didn't say a word.

They lay quietly like that for a long time. Long enough that Eve's exhaustion started to catch up to her again. She was on the verge of falling asleep when Boone finally spoke.

"My ex-girlfriend Gemma, she's a psychotherapist."

Eve held still, afraid to breathe or move or do anything that might make him clam up again.

"She used to brag about how well she understood people," he went on, his voice quiet and eerily vacant. "How weak and predictable humans were. How easily manipulated. She said we were all victims of our inability to understand and control our own emotions."

Apprehension pooled in the pit of Eve's stomach. She didn't know exactly where he was headed with this, but she felt certain it would be bad.

"Gemma was really smart. Smarter than almost anyone I'd ever met. A lot smarter than me, for sure." He sounded like he was reading aloud from a textbook instead of dredging up a painful memory. "I liked that about her. I liked a lot of things about her. We were together for nearly a year, and I was crazy in love with her."

"Boone," Eve whispered, unable to stay silent while he was ripping open a half-healed wound.

His hand stroked down her back. "It's okay. I can tell you."

She rested her chin on his chest so she could look at him. "You don't have to."

"I know," he said, his expression softening as he gazed at her. "That's why I can."

Eve laid her head down again and twisted her fingers in his shirt.

After a long breath, Boone said, "I fell for Gemma harder and faster than I'd ever fallen for anyone. I was so in love with her that it blinded me to who she was."

"Who was she?" Eve whispered.

"A manipulator. Someone who was using me." The way he said it was so flat and matter-of-fact it made her chest constrict.

"Using you for what?"

"To make herself feel more important, I guess. Or maybe she just got off on it. I don't know." He fell quiet for a beat before continuing. "Griffin saw through her the first time they met. He tried to warn me, but I was too far under her spell by then. I got angry at him for attacking the woman I loved, and Gemma used that anger to drive the wedge deeper. She got me to believe a lot of stupid shit."

Tension vibrated through Boone's body as he tipped his head back into the pillow. "God, it's so embarrassing to look back on it now and realize how easily I bought into her bull-shit. I wanted to believe it—that was how she got me. She figured out all my weaknesses and preyed on them to fuck with my head, filling it with her poisonous lies. I've always struggled with imposter syndrome, so it didn't take much for her to convince me I didn't deserve anything I had."

So many things about him were falling into place. Eve

understood now where that *I don't deserve you* had come from—directly from his ex-girlfriend. The more Eve learned about her, the more murdery she felt.

A sigh rumbled through Boone's chest. "She broke me down so I'd feel lucky that she wanted me, grateful that a woman like her was willing to put up with my sorry ass. She had me convinced all my worst fears about myself were true."

Some of what he was saying made Eve think of Becca. And how oblivious Eve had been to the kind of person her supposed best friend was.

She propped her chin on Boone's chest again. "That's what Becca was doing to me."

His eyes found hers. "I know."

"Is that why you helped me? Because you saw yourself in me?"

"I helped you because I liked you. I was a goner for you long before I found out about all that. But it did make me extra sympathetic to what you were going through."

"So what happened with you and Gemma?" Eve asked. "What made you break up?"

"It was Griffin, actually. The things he'd said stuck with me, even though I initially rejected them. I started to see through some of Gemma's gaslighting and push back on it. The more I did, the worse she got, and the harder it became to excuse. One night we had this really bad fight at my place, and she totally lost it. Started screaming all this hateful stuff and breaking shit. The last straw was when she threw a mug of steaming hot tea at my head."

"She *what?*" Eve's whole body vibrated with outrage.

His mouth tightened. "I'm pretty sure she was going for my face on purpose, because she wanted to ruin my acting career."

"What the fuck?" She'd progressed from vaguely murderous feelings to actively plotting Gemma's slow and painful demise. Possibly something involving fire ants, but she wasn't sure if they had them in Canada.

"Lucky for me, she had crap aim."

"I hate her," Eve said. "I'm not sure I've ever hated anyone this much before."

Boone's lips twitched as he pushed his fingers through her hair. "Now you know how I feel about Becca."

"It's not the same thing at all. Becca was a selfish, back-stabbing hagfish, but the things Gemma did to you, it's—" Eve blinked away angry tears. "I don't even know what to say."

"Hey, shh. It's okay." Boone cupped her face, stroking his thumb across her cheek. "It's over and done with now."

"It's not though. She might have missed you with that mug, but she still left scars behind. No wonder you can't bring your-self to talk about her or—" *Or love me*, Eve had been about to say and only barely bit back the words before they slipped out.

"You're right. I'm still trying to put myself back together after…" His lips pressed into a grimace. "Because of what she did—what I *let* her do to me—I can't trust my own instincts anymore. They failed me completely with her, and I'm terrified of making another mistake. I can't—" He broke off with a stricken expression.

Eve hurt for Boone so much it was hard to breathe. She couldn't blame him for being gun-shy after everything he'd experienced. It was all so unfair. Gemma might be long gone, but she was still actively hurting him.

"Eve." The way he said her name sounded like both a plea and apology.

"I understand." She curled around him, laying her cheek on his stomach so he wouldn't see the grief on her face. There was no doubting anymore that she was in love with him. But it didn't matter. It wasn't enough. She held him tight, seeking to comfort herself as much as him. "I'm glad you told me."

Boone's hand settled on the back of her head. "Me too."

She closed her eyes against the throbbing pressure behind her face. Was it due to her lingering fever or because the person she loved wasn't able to love her back? Who was to say?

They both fell quiet again, but it was a peaceful sort of quiet. Easier than the tense silences Boone sometimes retreated into that Eve understood much better now.

A gentle breeze stirred through the room from the balcony door. As Boone's fingers gently toyed with her hair, her exhaustion returned with a vengeance. It had been an emotionally draining conversation after a physically draining night—for both of them.

But it had been good too. A purging of secrets and a sharing of pain. There was still plenty of sorrow, but it wasn't the same as the sharper hurt and confusion she'd felt before. Understanding had brought détente.

It was enough. It would have to be enough.

twenty-eight

THINGS WENT BACK TO NORMAL. A new kind of normal.

Eve's fever was gone by the afternoon, and she slept in her own room that night, missing the feel of Boone's body beside her.

He continued to be sweetly solicitous, plying her with food like a Mexican grandmother as her appetite slowly returned. There was no further snuggling, however, and no more tender caresses. Now that she was on the road to recovery, they were back to simply being roommates. Pals. Buddies. Just good friends.

Boone didn't entirely avoid physical contact though. A light touch on the arm to get her attention, a hand on her forehead to check for the return of fever, a brush of fingers on her back as he edged past in the kitchen—all these things seemed to be fair game in their new normal. He even gave Eve a good-night hug when she went to bed, and she managed not to cling too much and make it weird.

On Friday, she roused herself at dawn for work as usual. Boone got up to make her breakfast and fretted over her wan appearance. He tried to get her to stay home and take another day to recover, but Eve didn't want to leave her coworkers shorthanded.

"I look worse than I feel," she assured him in a barefaced lie. "I'll be fine."

He sent her off to work with yet another hug. They were rocking this "just friends" thing like a couple of pros. Maybe one day she'd even manage to stop having so many hot, smutty, distinctly unfriendlike feelings about him.

After putting in shifts at two different jobs, Eve was almost too exhausted to move by the time she got home in the evening. She collapsed on the couch and let Boone wait on her hand and foot, as he seemed determined to do.

"You're really going to need to stop fussing over me at some point," she told him when he handed her a mug of soup and draped a throw blanket over her legs. "But I don't have the energy to fight you on it right now."

"Be quiet and eat your soup," he said. "If you finish all of it, I'll bring you some ice cream."

When she started to doze off in front of the TV, he nudged her awake and sent her up to bed with another one of those friend-hugs. At least he hadn't carried her.

Except she kind of wished he had.

She'd requested all her weekends off until Boone was due to go back to Vancouver, so she slept in Saturday morning and woke up feeling almost back to normal. Their next scheduled pap walk wasn't until brunch tomorrow, so Eve spent the day on the couch in the rec room watching TV.

While Boone was out running some errands, she pulled up an old episode of *Abnormal Investigations*. The fact that it happened to be the one where Boone's character runs around in his underwear (after being exposed to a libido-enhancing alien plant and stripping down for a decontamination shower) was purely coincidental and had nothing to do with any feelings of attraction or sexual frustration Eve might or might not have been dealing with.

After it ended, she skipped ahead to the next season and found the episode where Boone's character wears a very small, very *tight* bathing suit. Not that she'd picked it because of that. She was watching it for the plot. Obviously. Not because she was a shameless, horny pervert with the hots for her roommate.

When she heard the rumble of the garage door opening, Eve fumbled around on the couch for the remote. She'd had it just a few minutes ago. Where the frick was it? It'd be awkward as hell if Boone walked in and caught her watching him on TV.

Her search grew increasingly frantic as she heard the door to the garage open and footsteps approaching in the hallway. A split second before he walked into the rec room, Eve finally located the stupid remote and smashed the pause button.

"Hi!" she greeted him cheerfully. "How were your errands?"

"Successful. That's about all I can say for them." He carried a case of protein shakes behind the bar.

"You got your hair cut." It wasn't a dramatic change, but it had been trimmed and neatened up, as had his beard.

"It was getting a little too shaggy. Didn't want people mistaking me for Bigfoot."

"I'm glad you didn't shave the beard. I know you'll have to when shooting starts again, but I like it on you."

"I'm glad I kept it, then." His smile froze as his attention caught on the TV screen, which was freeze-framed on a shot of him chasing a suspected werewolf through a dark Vancouver forest. "What are you watching?"

"Nothing," Eve mumbled, feeling her face go hot.

He raised his eyebrows. "I thought you said you quit watching the show."

She shrugged, playing it cool. Totally chill. *Nothing to see here.* "Feeling nostalgic, I guess."

Boone's gaze lingered on her for a too-long moment. "Well, don't let me stop you," he said as he headed upstairs.

As soon as he was out of sight, she grabbed the remote and found something else to watch.

Ten minutes later, Boone came back downstairs with a big bowl of popcorn.

"What the hell's this?" he said as he flopped down onto the couch next to her. "I thought you were watching my show."

"I got tired of it," Eve said with a shrug.

He gave her a mock-aggrieved look. "Wow. Rude."

"It's nothing personal." She leaned in for some popcorn, but he pulled the bowl out of her reach.

"Sorry, my popcorn's not for fair-weather fans." He gestured at the TV in disdain. "I can't believe this. Did you seriously forsake me for a goddamn Chuck Hammer movie? Why don't you just stick a knife through my chest?"

Eve's lips twitched as she fought a smile. "This is a great movie."

"Are you trying to give me an inferiority complex? Gimme that remote." Shoving the popcorn bowl into her lap, Boone leaned forward to snag the remote off the table.

Eve crammed a handful of popcorn in her mouth as he navigated back to *Abnormal Investigations* and restarted the episode she'd paused. "Do you really want to watch this?" she asked, propping her bare feet on the table.

"Why not? I haven't watched any of these old episodes in years. It might be fun to take a little trip down memory lane." As he reached into her lap to grab some popcorn, his ridiculously hard triceps pressed against her arm. She offered to pass the bowl back to him, but he shook his head.

"You don't get self-conscious watching yourself?" She tried

not to think about how close they were sitting. Friends sat close to each other sometimes. It was fine.

"Oh no, I totally do. Are you kidding?" He scooted even closer as he reached into her lap for more popcorn. "Look at this ridiculousness. Can you believe I do this for a living? I'm just running around Stanley Park waving a sword at some poor guy in a fur suit and rubber mask. Bananas."

"It's a good show."

"But not as great as a Chuck Hammer movie, right?" The sulky side-eye Boone shot her didn't quite hide the smile hovering around his mouth. "Maybe I should switch back to that." He pointed the remote at the TV and paused the episode.

"Hey, don't do that." Eve attempted to take it from him, but he shoved it behind his back, playing keep-away.

Well, shit. She'd have to basically tackle him in order to get it, and that didn't feel safe for either of them. And yet, his raised eyebrows and smug smile looked for all the world like he was daring her to do it.

Was he? *Should she?* She wanted to, god knew she did, but she didn't think it was a good idea.

"Don't be a baby," she grumbled, refusing to take the bait. "If you want to watch the episode, let's watch the episode."

"I thought you were tired of it?"

She shook her head as she set the popcorn bowl on the table. "I only turned it off so I wouldn't make you self-conscious."

"Is that right?" He pinned her with a disbelieving look. "That's the only reason? You sure about that?"

"Okay fine. Maybe I was a little embarrassed you caught me watching it."

"Why would you be embarrassed about that?"

"No reason. Can I have the remote, please?"

"No. Not until you tell me the truth. Why were you embarrassed?"

"Boone," she huffed impatiently.

"Eve," he replied, attempting to stare her down. After a second, he broke into a diabolical grin. "I'll bet I know why. Let's see what other episodes you've been watching, shall we?"

She made a grab for the remote when he pulled it out from behind his back. "Let's not."

"Ah ah ah." He wrapped a steely arm around her, trapping her against him as he flipped through the episode lists for the previous seasons. "Didn't anyone ever tell you grabbing is rude?"

Eve didn't make any attempt to get away because she liked being so close to him, even if they were only goofing around. Just regular friend stuff. Perfectly innocent wrestling on the couch.

There was no reason her pulse should be racing like this just because Boone's forearm lay across her stomach. She definitely, *definitely* had no business thinking that she'd only have to turn her head a little and her mouth would practically be touching his.

"I knew it!" he shouted, cackling when he found the last episode she'd been watching. "The sex pollen episode!"

Well, crap. This was easily the most embarrassing thing that had happened to her in at least twenty-four hours. The fact that she was so completely turned on right now didn't do anything to lessen her embarrassment. And his husky laugh next to her ear wasn't making her less turned on. Eve couldn't even tell whether the heat flooding her face was a flush of shame or sheer horniness.

God help her, this was getting out of hand. She tried to squirm away, but it only made him hold her tighter and somehow his arm ended up wedged beneath her breasts.

Boone's laugh petered out as he seemed to become aware

of where his arm was. Surely now he'd let her go.

But he didn't.

"Eve," he murmured against the shell of her ear, sending a surge of unnerving heat licking down her spine. "Why were you only watching episodes where I take off my clothes?"

She squeezed her eyes shut as her heart thudded wildly against her ribs. Did he really expect her to admit she'd been perving on him? And then what?

They couldn't do this. No matter how much she wanted it. This was not harmless friend behavior.

Drawing in a deep breath, Eve forced out the words she didn't want to say. "Let me go."

He released her without hesitation. She scooted away from him, pulling her legs up onto the couch as they stared at each other across the space she'd put between them.

Boone's brows pulled together as his eyes swept over her face. "Tell me what you're thinking."

She shook her head. "I can't."

"Why not?"

"Because we can't do this. *You* can't."

His jaw clenched as an emotion she couldn't decipher passed over his face. "I was wrong."

"It's okay," she said quickly, not wanting this one little incident—barely anything at all, really—to ruin their friendship. "It's not a big deal. We can just forget—"

"I meant I was wrong before."

Eve blinked at him, not understanding. "When?"

"I was kidding myself to think I could ignore the way I feel about you. This just being friends thing isn't working for me."

"Oh." Her shoulders slumped as disappointment surged through her with a flush of itchy heat.

"No, that's not—" He shook his head with a grimace. "What I mean is that just being friends isn't enough. I want more than that."

twenty-nine

EVE'S HEART dropped out of her chest. Boone wanted to be more than friends? That was…amazing.

And confusing.

"But I thought you said we were a bad idea. You're not ready for a relationship, remember?"

"I only said that because I panicked." His eyes lowered as he squeezed the back of his neck. "After we spent the night together, I woke up in a cold sweat, unable to breathe because I was so terrified the same thing that happened with Gemma was happening again."

Eve stared at him in horror. He couldn't really think that about her, could he? "Boone, I would *never*—"

"I know." He reached across the couch to capture her hand. "It didn't have anything to do with you. I wasn't prepared for how strong my feelings for you were. It felt like I was losing myself again, and I couldn't handle it."

"I would never let you get lost," she said. "I promise to always help you find your way."

"I know." His thumb stroked the back of her hand as he shifted closer. "You're my North Star."

Eve's throat thickened. There was so much trust and tenderness in Boone's eyes, but it only made her more hesitant, given what he'd said and what she'd just promised him.

His fingers clutched hers. "I want to give this another chance. I just—" He inhaled a sharp breath. "I need you. I'm done denying it."

What was she supposed to do here? Listen to what he'd said before, or what he was saying now? Wasn't that the whole problem, that he changed his mind from one minute to the next, and—

Boone's hand slipped around the nape of her neck, and his lips pressed against hers.

God, his lips.

She'd missed them so freaking much. Not kissing him back wasn't a possibility. She melted into him, lust and longing bubbling up in her veins as his tongue slipped easily into her mouth.

The next thing Eve knew, he'd hauled her into his lap and she was straddling his thighs as they continued to devour each other's mouths.

Oh, god. Oh wow. The way that hard bulge behind the fly of his jeans pressed between her legs made her see stars. Him too, judging from the little grunts and groans he was making.

"Boone," she gasped as his tongue lashed the side of her neck. This wasn't right. She'd made him a promise. "Maybe we—" She broke off with a shudder when his teeth nipped the skin above her collarbone. "Maybe this isn't a good idea."

"But it feels so good." His warm, rough hands slid under her T-shirt and stroked up her back. "I'm tired of fighting it. Aren't you?"

Yes! So tired!

But there was a reason it was bad. If she could just remember what it was. Hard to do with Boone's hips rocking beneath her. They both moaned as his erection rubbed against her sex. The man was so not playing fair.

When she felt him unclasp her bra, she struggled for a breath. "We should talk about this."

"Sure, okay." He palmed one of her breasts. "Let's talk."

"What you're doing right now is not something people who are just friends do."

"You're right. Neither is this." His other hand slid inside the leg of her loose terry shorts, diving into her underwear to stroke between her legs.

She whimpered helplessly. Damn him, using his sexual superpowers against her. "Boone, please."

His finger stilled, teasing at her entrance. "Please what? Please stop? Or please keep making you feel good."

It took every ounce of willpower Eve had to make herself say, "Please stop."

His brows lowered as he withdrew both his hands and laid them flat on the tops of her thighs—which was still awfully distracting but at least they weren't moving anymore.

"Okay," he said quietly. "We can talk."

Eve closed her eyes as her body and emotions waged an epic battle with her head. The temptation to say *fuck it* and throw herself at him was nearly too strong to resist.

She counted to three and opened her eyes, focusing on Boone's Ramones T-shirt instead of his face. "I don't want to make another mistake with you."

"It's not a mistake."

"You told me yourself you can't trust your instincts. You think you want this, but—"

"I *do* want this. I'm certain about that."

"Right now, sure. When you're all horny and listening to your dick. But what happens after it gets what it wants? I can't do casual with you. I'm sorry, but I just can't."

Hurt flashed across his face. "Jesus Christ, this isn't about my dick, Eve. There's nothing casual about my feelings for you."

She believed him. It was obvious he meant it. But that didn't mean he'd be able to go all in. "We've been here before. When it starts to feel like too much for you, you'll get scared and bolt again."

"I'm not going to bolt."

"I'm sure that's what you thought the last time too. Right before you got scared and bolted." She said it gently, not trying to hurt him, but she could tell it had anyway.

Boone fell silent, his jaw shifting grimly.

"It's okay," she said, hating how the light in his eyes had dimmed. "I understand—really, I do. It's not your fault. But I can't keep letting you get my hopes up, only to have them crushed again. It hurts too much when you pull away."

They shouldn't be having this conversation while sitting like this. Eve twisted to clamber off his lap, but his hands dragged her back. Strong arms wrapped around her, drawing her against his chest.

A lump clogged her throat as she breathed in the scent of him. "Boone…"

"Shh." His hand cupped the back of her head. "Give me a second, okay?"

She squeezed her eyes shut and relaxed against him, cherishing the warmth and solidness of him while she still could.

His nose nuzzled into her hair. "I love how you always smell like coffee. Even after you wash your hair I can detect faint traces of it."

"I can't even smell it anymore. I'm desensitized to it at this point."

"It always reminds me of the first time I saw you."

She sniffled, and his hand slid down to squeeze the back of her neck.

His voice was rough when he spoke again. "You don't even know it, but you changed my life that day."

"How did I do that?" she asked.

"I'd been sleepwalking since the breakup. I'd bottled every-thing up for so long, I'd made myself numb. I couldn't feel anything—just like you with the smell of coffee."

His hand was massaging her neck, turning her into a human jellyfish. Even though what he was saying broke her heart, the most she could manage to do was clutch his T-shirt in her fist.

"When I saw you that day, you were like a light shining out of the fog. I can't explain it, but it was the first time in months I'd actually *felt* something. It was like you woke me up and pointed me toward the way out of the darkness."

Eve's eyes misted as his words washed over her.

He huffed a soft laugh into her hair. "And you never had any idea. I had such a crush on you, I used to dream about you at night. That probably sounds creepy, doesn't it?"

Not even a little. Hard to believe, yes. But definitely not creepy. "Did you forget I used to write smutty fanfiction about you? So no, it doesn't sound creepy to me."

Boone's fingers threaded through her hair. "I went to that coffee shop every single day to see you, but I never let myself talk to you."

"Why not?"

"I was fighting it. You know when you've been asleep for too long, and even though you know you're ready to get up, you stay under the covers trying to fall back asleep? That was me. I didn't talk to you because then I'd have to do something about the feelings I was having. I'd have to decide if I was going to act on them or not."

"And then I went and crashed into you that morning and ruined everything."

Another husky laugh huffed out of him. "Yeah, you

forced my hand. Hard to avoid a decision that literally throws itself into your chest." His arm tightened around her protectively. "When I saw you crying, I couldn't just walk away. It must have seemed odd—here I was, this total stranger, taking such a sudden interest in you out of the blue."

"A *famous* total stranger who I had a massive crush on, no less."

"I'm guessing that's the only reason you were willing to have anything to do with me. Otherwise you probably would have decided I was a creeper and run for your life."

"You're probably right," she said, laughing under her breath.

The hand on her neck grew still. "Do you regret that you didn't run for your life when you had the chance?"

Eve lifted her head to look him in the eye so he'd know she meant it. "Never."

He let out a long, deep breath and cradled her jaw in his palm. "I promise I'm not going to push you away again. I learned my lesson the last time. It made me realize how much better I am with you."

Swallowing hard, she slid her hands around his neck, stroking her fingertips over the soft, freshly shaved skin until she found his pulse flickering at the edge of his beard. It was racing as fast as hers.

"I shouldn't have been afraid." Boone pressed a soft kiss to her forehead. "I should have known you were exactly what I needed." His lips moved to caress her temple. "I know it now, Evie." His lips ghosted over hers in the gentlest of kisses. "I'm ready to let myself fall."

Her whole body sagged with relief when his mouth opened to hers. She gave herself up to him, falling into his luscious, greedy kiss as her whole body throbbed with need.

"We're not a mistake," Boone murmured, peppering her

lips with tiny, delicate kisses. "I'll prove it to you. We can take it slow if you want."

She hummed in response, chasing his mouth as her hands slid under his shirt, their lips gliding together in a sensual slow dance

"I'll be the best fucking boyfriend you've ever had." His fingers stroked over her thigh, and she shifted restlessly in his lap. He groaned and caught her lower lip in his teeth. "God, you feel…"

"You too," she panted, angling her head to take his searching tongue deeper. Every touch, every stroke, every caress seared through her in a cascade of sensation that left her dizzy and trembling.

His hips rocked beneath her, the friction on her aching sex amping up her lust-driven frenzy. "Is there something you need?" he teased as he bent his head to suck at her throat.

"You," she moaned, grinding against him. "I want you. I want to feel you."

"I'm right here." The tip of his finger slipped into her underwear again, shoving it roughly aside to stroke her needy, aching pussy.

Eve's head fell back as her entire body tightened with a surge of molten pleasure. His fingers were magic, lighting her up with sensation.

"That's it." His eyes watched her hungrily as he rubbed the callused pad of his thumb over her clit.

She made a pitiful noise in her throat, shaking with need as he played her with expert precision. Somehow he knew exactly how to drive her to the edge and keep her dangling there until she wanted to weep. "Boone…"

"It's okay," he murmured and slid a finger inside her. "Tell me this doesn't feel right."

Her fingernails dug into his chest as she rolled her hips,

pushing against his hand. The tension inside her was perfect and unbearable at the same time.

"Fuck, baby." He cradled the back of her skull as she rode his hand. "You're so gorgeous. I can't get over it."

His finger curled inside her, hitting just the right spot. When his thumb nudged her clit, that was that. Stars splashed across Eve's vision as her whole body pulsed around his finger, and he leaned in to kiss the cry from her lips.

She slumped against him, dazed and panting. As she came back down to earth, his magic fingers on her neck did that heavenly massaging thing some more. Like she wasn't relaxed enough already. Her body was so boneless she was in danger of trickling onto the floor.

"Feel better now?" Boone asked.

She answered with a contented hum and nuzzled his chest. "Boyfriend, huh?"

"If you'll have me."

"I don't know," she said, pushing herself upright as she pretended to think about it. "You're only my dream come true. Why would I want a boyfriend like that?"

The corner of his mouth crooked. "In the interest of full disclosure and consumer protection blah blah blah, you should be aware you're getting a gently used model in need of some TLC."

Eve trailed a finger over his stomach, smiling at the way the taut muscles contracted. "How much TLC are we talking about? I've already got two jobs, after all. I'm a busy girl."

"Just your standard girlfriend stuff. Regular hugs. Frequent kisses. Cuddling and touching on an as-needed basis."

"Touching, you say?" Her fingers traveled over the front of his pants, and he stifled a groan. Poor guy. His hard-on was definitely in need of some attention. "What sort of touching exactly?"

"That would be entirely at your discretion. I meant it when I said we could go slow."

Her eyebrows lifted. "You call what you just did to me slow?"

He took her hand off his pants and lifted it to his lips. "It can be if we stop there. That'll be your call."

"What about sleeping arrangements?"

"My preference is you in my bed, always. But we don't have to do anything more than sleep." He grinned as he kissed her knuckles. "And cuddle, obviously."

The thought of sleeping with Boone every night made her hopelessly giddy. She wasn't sure how she felt about taking things slow, however. On the one hand, she could see how it might be sensible. She appreciated that he was leaving the ball in her court—not to mention, delayed gratification could be a lot of fun. But on the other hand, she was pretty eager to get his cock inside her again. Would she even be able to wait? *Outlook not so good.*

There was just one more thing Eve needed to know before she went all in with her heart. She hated to ask about it, because she was fairly sure it would kill the nice mood they had going on right now. But putting off the conversation wasn't an option. Not for her. And not with the clock ticking away the minutes Boone had left in LA.

"What happens when you go back to Vancouver?"

The smile slid from his face as deep furrows sprouted across his brow.

Yep, she'd definitely ruined the mood. Her stomach clenched as she waited to hear what he'd say. Had he even thought it through?

Boone gathered her against him in a crushing hug. "We'll make it work somehow. I'm not saying it'll be easy, but you don't have to worry about me abandoning you, okay?"

Her eyes burned with an overload of emotion as she nodded against his chest. "Okay."

The thought of it was scary as fuck. Nine months out of every year was a long-ass time to be away from someone. Was it even possible to build a lasting relationship on such a meager foundation?

They were about to find out.

thirty

THE NEXT MORNING, Eve woke to the exquisite sensation of Boone's head between her thighs.

"You're still here," she mumbled drowsily, her body lax and tingling with a low hum of pleasure.

"Glad you noticed." He smiled up at her with lips that were shiny and wet from kissing her sex. God, what an incredible sight first thing in the morning.

She pushed her fingers through his sleep-rumpled hair, half convinced she was still asleep. Any second now she'd wake up and discover the last two weeks had all been a dream. "I mean you didn't freak out this time."

His hand found hers on the mattress. As he threaded their fingers together, he pressed a kiss to the inside of her thigh. "Told you I wouldn't."

"Waking up like this is way better than waking up alone, that's for sure."

"What can I say? I woke up hungry this morning." His blue eyes gleamed bright as he dragged his tongue through her sensitive folds.

Holy wow, that beard of his took oral to the next level. All men should have beards. It ought to be a rule. When Boone shoved his face into her pussy, she nearly rocketed off the bed from the bristly friction. His fingers dug into her thighs, holding her still as he licked and sucked with an enthusiasm that had been sorely lacking in her past sexual partners. The man was seriously gifted. Fourteen out of ten. All the gold stars. No notes.

Eve's eyes fell shut as she succumbed to the incredible sensation. The pressure built and built, narrowing her world to this perfect moment. Everything else ceased to exist. It was just her and Boone and—

The harsh sound of the front gate buzzer blared through the house.

"Nooo," she whined when Boone took his awesome mouth away. She'd been *so close* too. Curses!

"Shit," he muttered, nuzzling her thigh. "Sorry, gorgeous. I thought we had enough time." He pushed himself up and crawled across the bed to grab his phone from the nightstand.

Ugh. Right. It was Sunday. Her styling team was here to prep her for their pap walk at the Farmers Market this morning.

Boone buzzed them in the gate and bent over to give her a soft but far too swift kiss. "I'd better go let them in."

She grabbed his head and pulled him back down for another, slower kiss. "You might want to wash your face before you open the door, loverboy."

"Good tip," he said with a grin and rubbed his beard all over her cheek.

Laughing, Eve pushed him away. "I've got to take a quick shower so I don't smell like sex."

A smirk tugged at his lips as he gazed at her from the bathroom doorway. "We're finishing this later. As soon as we get back today, I'm picking up where I left off."

"These new photos of you two are hot as hell. Damn!" The excitement in Reagan's voice made it sound even more distorted through the speakerphone. "That's some serious chemistry. Whatever you're doing, keep it up."

Boone shot a smirk at Eve, and she buried her face against his shoulder to smother her snicker. Sexual frustration made for good candid photos, apparently. Or maybe it was that they were both so happy now that they were together.

They hadn't been able to keep their hands off each other as they'd strolled around the Farmers Market yesterday, trailed by a few mostly unobtrusive paparazzi. Eve had been so focused on Boone, she'd practically forgotten the photographers were there.

The Hot Hollywood Nights post this morning had featured a big, bold headline that read simply, *Simone Who?* and described Boone's unnamed girlfriend as "the love of his life." The accompanying slideshow featured multiple photos of them stealing some not-so-chaste kisses on their cuddly stroll through the market stalls. Boone's hands were clearly visible grabbing Eve's ass in several shots, and there were a couple where you could even see tongue. Amazing what those long-range lenses could pick up.

"It's going better than I'd hoped," Reagan continued. "We've definitely gotten people talking about you two. I'll be honest, I was a little worried when those pap shots surfaced of Simone arriving at LAX last week, but I think it turned out to be a good thing for us in the end. It primed the pump for us to drop these super-hot pics of you and shut down any speculation that Boone and Simone are still an item."

Eve felt him stiffen on the couch beside her, and she reached up to run her fingers through his beard. One of the many things she'd been pleased to discover was how much he liked it when she played with his whiskers. It worked like a magic button to distract and relax him.

As predicted, as soon as she sank her fingers into his beard, his muscles unclenched and he made a soft, growly noise in the back of his throat.

Worked like a charm, every time.

Reagan's voice interrupted their canoodling, all brisk efficiency. "Moving on to other agenda items. I've got everything set for your brunch on Saturday. And you're on the guest list for the *Prepare for War* premiere next week. Boone, I want some chummy shots of you and your best pal Griffin Beach, do you hear me? Swallow that annoying pride of yours for one night and bask in the reflected glow of your BFF's stratospheric popularity. Eve, make sure he's hearing me."

She poked a finger into Boone's side under his rib cage. "Are you hearing her?"

"Ow," he hissed as he trapped her finger in his fist. "Yes, I'm hearing her."

Reagan made a *humph* sound. "That means you're going to do it, right? You're going to shamelessly trade on your friend's success like the professional, publicity-minded celebrity you are."

"Sure, fine, whatever," Boone grumbled, rolling his eyes. "I'll do it."

Eve rewarded him by pressing a kiss to his lovely, pouty lips.

"That's what I like to hear," Reagan said. "Speaking of red carpet appearances, Eve's name is on the VIP guest list that's going to the entertainment press and wire services, which means she'll be identified as your plus-one. I'd like to out her on social media before that to capitalize on the reveal and get people hyped to see you two together at the premiere."

Once again, Eve felt Boone tense up. She laid her hand on his thigh. "That's fine," she said before he could object. "I'm ready whenever you are."

"We'll do it in an Instagram post later this week. Once that happens, it'll be time to stop being coy and amp up the cute factor on your social media. Which means I need you to send me a selection of cozy, couple-y photos that show us your pretty faces. I want to see you two cuddling, having fun, and relaxing together at home. Relatable, intimate, private moments, you know what I'm saying? We want to make everyone envious of how deliriously happy and madly in love y'all are. Got it?"

"Got it," Eve said, looking forward to the assignment. She could already think of a few photos she'd like to take of Boone that his fans were going to go wild over. "Will do."

"Loving that positive attitude, girl. See if you can get some of it to rub off on your boyfriend."

Smiling at him, Eve stroked her hand up his thigh and inside the leg of his athletic shorts. Her smile grew wider as his expression heated. "I'm working on it. Don't worry."

"Are we done?" Boone asked in a strained voice when her fingers brushed against his swiftly hardening cock.

"One last thing," Reagan said, and he dropped his head back on the couch with a stifled groan. "Boone, I'm setting up a modest media blitz for you before you head back to Van City in three weeks. I'll send you the schedule, but so far I've got you booked for Michael Rosenbaum's podcast, Spencer Devlin's satellite radio show, a *Rolling Stone* video interview, and print interviews with *EW* and *Glamour*. Ostensibly, you're promoting the upcoming season of the show, but I want you talking about your relationship with Eve at every opportunity."

"Great, whatever you want," Boone said distractedly as he covered Eve's hand and pressed it against his thick, heavy hard-on.

"You can expect to get questions about your relationship with Simone, and it's time for you to address them head-on to get your side of the story out there. Are you willing to do that?"

His jaw clenched tight, and Eve rubbed her knuckles over his erection ruthlessly enough to make him gasp. "Yeah, okay. I'll do it," he forced out as his whole body vibrated with tension.

"Wow, I expected you to put up more of a fight," Reagan said. "Your girlfriend really must be rubbing off on you."

Boone bit down on his lip while Eve clapped her free hand over her mouth to muffle her giggle. He lurched forward to grab the phone off the coffee table, speaking brusquely. "If that's everything, we've got to run. Thanks, Reagan."

As soon as he cut off the call, Eve lost it and doubled over with laughter.

He shot a dry look at her over his shoulder. "Enjoyed that, did you?"

"You have to admit, phone calls with your publicist are way more fun with me around."

With a grunt, Boone lunged and grabbed her wrists, pinning her beneath him on the couch. Muscled arms held her hands captive on either side of her head as he gazed down at her with a smile tugging his lips to one side. "You're trouble, you know that?"

Wriggling under the sublime weight of his rock-hard body, Eve pressed one of her thighs between his legs until he groaned and covered her mouth with his. The kiss quickly turned rough and messy, melting her bones in a surge of liquid heat.

"How much time before you have to leave?" he asked as he devoured her neck.

Dammit. She'd gotten so distracted, she'd forgotten she'd only come home for lunch and needed to be at the preschool soon. A glance at the clock on the wall caused her to let out a dejected sigh. "Ten minutes."

In an impressive display of strength and agility, Boone flipped them over so he was on his back with Eve on top of him. "Guess we'll have to make the next ten minutes count."

Sitting back on her haunches, she hooked her fingers under the waistband of his workout shorts. Ever so helpful, he lifted his hips so she could yank them down his thighs.

The sight of the beautiful man stretched out beneath her was too much for her fragile human heart to take. To think he was hers to touch as much as she liked. What an absolute miracle.

"Guess we will." Taking his stiff cock in her hand, Eve bent and swirled the tip of her tongue teasingly over the swollen head. A smile curved her lips at the shuddering gasp it drew out of him. "Whatever can we do in under ten minutes, do you think?"

For some reason Talking Heads's "This Must Be the Place" had been stuck in Boone's head all week. He hummed it under his breath as he stood at the sink hand-washing their wineglasses from dinner. As he visualized the fingering for each note, his hands itched to play them. It was the first time in over a year he'd felt the urge to get his guitar out.

"Take your shirt off," Eve said, coming into the kitchen behind him.

In one smooth motion, he yanked his T-shirt off and tossed it onto the counter before reaching for the dish sponge.

"Wow, you didn't even hesitate or ask why."

"I've got no problem being your eye candy, gorgeous." He tossed a grin over his shoulder.

Eve's attention was on her phone as she aimed it at him like she was taking a picture. "Turn around. I only want your back."

"Okay, well, now I'm starting to feel a little objectified." Not that it stopped him from doing as she asked and shamelessly flexing his back muscles.

"Oh, shut up. You love it."

He didn't try to deny it. Eve could objectify him all she wanted. He was a sucker for her attention. "If this is for your spank bank, I'm happy to take my pants off too."

She snorted. "It's for Instagram, you dork."

"Shit, really?" he said, twisting around again.

Reagan had revealed Eve's identity on Instagram the night before with a black-and-white selfie Boone had taken of the two of them cuddling in bed. The post had gone up in the middle of the night, captioned only with three red hearts followed by Eve's handle.

Last he'd looked, it had three hundred thousand likes and two thousand comments. Eve's account had gained several thousand followers since then, and her older posts had been getting all kinds of drive-by comments and likes.

Boone had made the mistake of looking at a few of them, then gotten ragey and deleted Instagram from his phone. So far, Eve was taking it way more in stride than he was. She'd skimmed through a few of the comments after work, said *fans will be fans,* and tossed her phone aside with a bored shrug.

"You messed up my shot, dang it." Lips pursing, she gave him an impatient hand wave. "Come on, show me those back muscles, hot stuff."

"You're not seriously taking a cheesecake shot of me doing dishes, are you?"

"Heck yeah, I am. Your fans are going to eat this up."

"No one wants a photo of me doing dishes, Eve."

"Au contraire, mon frère. There is literally nothing sexier than a hot man who does housework—except maybe a hot man with a baby. Trust me, this photo's gonna go viral. Get ready to be an internet hero."

"This is ridiculous," he said, even as he turned back to the sink so she could get her shot.

Boone wasn't accustomed to giving the public such an intimate look into his home life. Eve had needed to talk him into the cuddling-in-bed selfie he'd taken. But with her encouragement, he was slowly getting more comfortable with it. If anyone had insight into what his fans wanted, he figured it was her. He trusted her judgment—but more than that, he trusted her to look out for him. And wasn't that something? The fact that he'd recovered his ability to trust felt like a major miracle.

"I'm a freaking genius, is what I am," Eve boasted as he resumed washing glasses. "Reagan's going to kiss me on the mouth for this shot. All right, I'm done. You can stop flexing now, Schwarzenegger."

Moving to his side, she stroked her fingers over the back of his neck and rose on her toes to kiss his cheek. He turned his head to catch her lips before she could pull away.

"I'm going up," she murmured with a smile.

"I'll be right behind you as soon as I finish here."

"Don't keep me waiting too long, pretty boy." She smacked his ass cheek, startling a laugh out of him.

After she'd gone upstairs, Boone went back to humming Talking Heads while he dried the wineglasses and put them away. He was still humming as he locked up the house, turned out the downstairs lights, and followed Eve up to bed.

She was in the shower when he got to his room. The scent of her shampoo, which now resided next to his on the shelf in his shower stall, wafted into the bedroom on a cloud of steam.

After setting his phone on the nightstand to charge, Boone wandered over to the guitars hanging on the wall. He used to love playing and singing—not that he had any illusions of making a second career out of it. He was good enough not to embarrass himself, but that was as much as he could say for his musical talent. It had been a hobby, nothing more. A way for him to unwind and work off stress, or something fun to do when he was hanging out with his friends.

Back when he used to enjoy hanging out with friends regularly. When he still played guitar. Before Gemma.

He'd played a Black Keys song for her once because they were her favorite band, and she'd complimented him in that patronizing tone she used when she was pretending to be supportive. Which would have been fine. She wasn't required to like his singing.

But later, she'd made some offhand comment about actors who wanted to be rock stars and how clichéd and pathetic it was. A few days after that, they'd been at a party hosted by one of her colleagues, and Boone had listened to Gemma tell a group of her smart doctor friends how, in addition to being on "his little TV show," her actor boyfriend fancied himself a musician. "Isn't it adorable?" she'd said to everyone. "He sings *and* plays the guitar." Then she'd laughed in a way that made it clear she didn't find it adorable at all.

He hadn't picked up a guitar since. She'd stolen the joy out of it by making him feel like the butt of a joke.

That was their whole relationship in a nutshell. Gemma tearing him down and systematically sucking all the joy from his life. He never should have given her that kind of power. He should have recognized what she was doing and left her that very night. But instead of believing in his own worth, he'd handed her the keys to his self-esteem.

As he stared at the guitars, Boone's fingers twitched with a desire to hold one of them in his hands. It felt like a huge step forward that he had the urge to play again. Like he was putting himself back together finally. Plugging some of the holes Gemma had made. Taking back the joy she'd stolen from him.

He lifted his favorite acoustic Gibson off its hanger and carried it over to the bed. Perching on the edge of the mattress, he settled the instrument across his lap, enjoying the familiar feel of the wooden neck in his hand. His fingers moved over the strings experimentally, and he winced at the jarring twang.

Taking his time, getting used to handling the instrument again, he plucked at the strings as he adjusted the tuning pegs. When he was satisfied, he strummed the strings again, smiling as the warm sound hummed through him.

Now that the guitar was in tune, he began to pick his way through the beginning of "This Must Be the Place," the song that had been haunting him for days. His muscle memory was rusty, but the more he played, the more his fingers remembered what to do. Before long, his stumbling notes turned into a recognizable melody, and he began to murmur the lyrics under his breath.

When the shower cut off, his fingers fumbled on the strings, and he clamped his hand over the frets. He'd gotten so immersed in the music, he'd forgotten Eve was in the bathroom.

He held himself still as his stomach clenched with apprehension. After a tense, protracted interval, Eve's hair dryer started up, and he exhaled again. Swallowing down the anxiety trying to clog his throat, he went back to playing.

A few minutes later, when the hair dryer shut off, he pushed through his uneasiness and made himself keep playing. This moment was a test, both for him and for Eve. A trust fall. The fear that one of them might fail sent a cold trickle of doubt down his back, but he refused to let it get the better of him. He wanted to play for her—to share something he loved with the woman he loved.

Nothing but silence came from the bathroom, even though Boone knew she must have heard him by now. It felt like an eternity before Eve came out and padded toward him quietly. He could see her in his peripheral vision, wearing one of his T-shirts she'd taken to sleeping in, her legs bare from mid-thigh down.

As she drew near, he stopped playing and swallowed thickly. He glanced up at her, not trusting himself to speak.

The smile on her face was like the sunrise breaking over the horizon after a long, dark night. "That's beautiful," she whispered. "I feel like I know that song."

"It's an old Talking Heads song." He reached up to rub the back of his neck. "The Lumineers did a cover of it a few years back."

"Right. I know it now." Her eyes were bright in the soft lamplight, glowing with admiration. "I've seen videos of you performing at cons. You have a great voice."

His impulse was to deflect with a joke, but he resisted the temptation. "Thank you."

It'd been forever since he'd volunteered to play at a fan convention. He used to love it, goofing around onstage and getting the crowd to sing along. It'd been a way to share a piece of himself with the fans without sacrificing his privacy.

Eve sat on the bed beside him and pulled her legs up underneath her. "Would you sing for me?"

The way she was looking at him, all that hopeful, eager anticipation he saw in her face…it snapped the last threads of tension running through him, allowing him to let go of it with a liberating breath.

"All right," he said, feeling his mouth pull into a smile. "If you want."

She made a happy sound and scooted back against the headboard.

He started over at the beginning of the song. This time he sang the lyrics with his full chest, pouring his heart into the words. It was a love song, but really it was about finding peace. No wonder it'd been stuck in his head all week.

When he finished the song, a heavy quiet followed the last shimmering notes. He lifted his head, and his gaze connected with Eve's. The way she'd looked at him before was nothing compared to how she was looking at him now.

Her eyes were shining, emotion written across her face. "That was so…"

Heat swarmed up Boone's throat as he leaned toward her, eager to hear the next word.

"Incredible," she whispered.

A dopey grin spread across his face.

"And hot," Eve added, scooting to his side "So incredibly hot."

As she pressed her lips to his, an exhilarating surge of…*something* came over him. An energy that licked over his skin, waking up every one of his nerve endings.

It felt an awful lot like joy. Imagine that.

thirty-one

BOONE HAD ALWAYS HATED red carpet events. It was one thing to have people dressing him up and fussing over him in order to shoot a scene—that was his job, and as long as he had a job to focus on he didn't mind the rest of it.

But there was nothing for him to *do* at a movie premiere except strut down a rented rug attempting to look cool as he posed for photos. There was a reason he'd become an actor instead of a model—he felt like a first-class fool doing shit like that. Photo shoots were just as bad, but at least they generally happened on a closed set where there weren't so many eyes on him. There weren't hundreds of cameras and a penned-off crowd of people watching and recording his every movement and expression.

At Griffin's premiere today, however, Boone had an important job to focus on. It was Eve's first big public event, and he could tell she was terrified. Even though she kept insisting she was fine. She was trying to be brave for his sake, which only made him more determined to make this as painless an experience for her as he could.

He popped up from the couch as soon as he saw her

making her careful way down the stairs with her stylist's assistance. And then he got a look at her, and his brain hung up an "Out for Lunch" sign. *Holy fucking shit.*

The slit cut up one side of her black knee-length dress stopped just shy of heaven, showing off most of one sumptuous thigh. Boone's dick was already straining to give it a standing ovation when he noticed the top half of the dress. Thin straps exposed the sleek expanse of Eve's shoulders, and a deep-V neckline plunged down between her breasts all the way to the top of her stomach. As if that wasn't enough, the thin, silky fabric lovingly clung to every one of her curves, showing off the contours of her luscious shape.

All he could think was *mine.*

And also *thank god.*

Reagan let out an appreciative whistle while Boone struggled to recover the power of speech. He opened his mouth to say something, but then the neckline of Eve's dress shifted, exposing more of her breast, and he choked on the drool puddling in his mouth.

Everyone stared at him as he coughed into the crook of his arm, feeling his face go bright red.

Eve stepped off the last stair and gave him a concerned look. "Are you all right?"

He nodded, waving away the water bottle Reagan offered to him. "Wow," he managed, his voice no more than a croak. "Look at you."

Uncertainty creased Eve's expression as she glanced down at herself. "Do I look okay?"

"Are you kidding? You're stunning. I was so overcome by the sight of you, I almost died on the spot."

Her shoulders lowered as she relaxed fractionally. "There's so much tape holding this dress in place, I don't know how I'll ever get it off."

"I will definitely help you solve that problem later." Boone licked his lips, imagining himself unwrapping her like a Christmas present. The end of this evening couldn't come too soon.

Miguel drifted toward Boone with a knowing smile. "Don't worry," he murmured, "that tape pulls right off painlessly." As the styling team bustled down the stairs with all the beauty implements they'd brought, Miguel called out a cheerful "Good luck," kissed Eve on the cheek, and followed them out the door.

"You ready to do this?" Boone asked, unable to stop gaping at Eve. He yearned to kiss her but knew better than to mess up her lipstick before they reached the red carpet.

She lifted her chin with a nod. "As ready as I'll ever be."

"Then let's get this show on the road," Reagan said, striding toward the door.

"You're gonna knock 'em all dead," Boone told Eve as he took her hand.

Her lips quirked to the side. "Oh goody, a mass casualty event. How fun."

He laughed and brought the back of her hand to his lips. That was safe enough to kiss, at least. "Keep that sense of humor tonight, and you'll do just fine."

As red carpets went, a movie premiere was a slightly more sedate affair than an awards show. Fewer celebrities meant fewer fans and press. There was still plenty of hullabaloo, especially for a big summer blockbuster like this, but it wasn't out of hand the way something like the People's Choice Awards could be.

Still, as Boone helped Eve out of the hired car, he saw her nerves kick in at her first taste of the noise and commotion. Event staffers in headsets scurried through the throng of talent, security staff and PR teams, directing the well-organized chaos of the new arrivals. Shouting from the photography pen combined with screaming from the stands where the fans and autograph hunters had been corralled, producing an unholy racket.

Drawing Eve to his side with a protective hand on her hip, Boone bent his head to speak in her ear. "Still doing okay?"

She answered with a distracted nod as she glanced down at her chest. "I've never showed this much boob to so many people at once before."

"You have exceptional boobs." His lips quirked as he indulged in an earnest study of them. "You should show them off all the time."

Color tinted Eve's cheeks despite the dry look she gave him. "My grandparents are going to see these photos, you know."

"Honestly, you look like a work of art. Extremely tasteful."

"Sure, until a nip bursts free of the tape."

"If it does, I promise to throw myself on it like a land mine." He squeezed her hip to emphasize his enthusiasm for the assignment.

"How self-sacrificing of you." A smile flickered over her glossy, crimson lips. God, how he wanted to devour them. Not being able to kiss her properly was torture.

"Rest assured, my eyes will be on your breasts all night so I'll be the first to notice if anything starts to slip."

"My hero." Eve reached up to brush her fingers over his freshly trimmed beard. As always, it filled his chest with a warm, liquid glow of pleasure that made him want to purr and expose his belly like a housecat.

"Have I mentioned how much I appreciate you doing this?" he said seriously, gazing at her in ardent admiration.

Her smile twitched wider. "Only about a million times."

"I feel bad you had to take off work."

"Don't sweat it. My boss was surprisingly chill about it

once I told her what it was for. I guess everyone likes a Cinderella story."

"Am I the Cinderella or are you?"

"I am, you doofus." She poked him in the chest. "You're the Prince Charming."

"I don't know. Pretty big shoes to fill."

Eve's expression softened as she stroked his jaw again. "You're doing amazing so far."

"You're the one who's amazing, Evie. I'd still be wandering around lost and miserable if I hadn't found you." The truth of that humbled him.

"Lucky you did, then. For both of us."

"All right, lovebirds." Reagan appeared in front of them, pursing her lips. "Save that cute for the red carpet. It's almost go time."

"Don't worry," Boone told her with a wink, slipping into the persona he used for public appearances. "I've got boundless reserves of cute."

A staffer in a headset gestured to Reagan, who herded Boone and Eve toward the start of the red carpet. "You're up. Don't forget to smile and show everyone how happy you are to be here together."

This last was meant for Eve, who'd gone a bit deer-in-the-headlights as they moved toward the blinding lights and camera flashes aimed at the step and repeat backdrop.

"You've got this," Boone murmured in her ear as he stroked her back.

As planned, he stepped forward first, while Eve hung back with Reagan. Trying not to wince at the flashes and shouting voices vying for his attention, he smiled and affected a series of poses for the cameras. After a minute of solo photos, he let his gaze slide over to Eve standing nervously at the edge of the step and repeat, and he felt his smile soften into something warmer and more genuine as their eyes met.

At Reagan's prompt, Eve started toward him and he strode over to meet her halfway. An excited ripple went through the crowd when Boone slipped his hand into hers. Eve clutched it in a panicky grip as people began shouting her name, yelling questions and appeals for her to look their way.

"Thirty more seconds and then you're done," Boone said, stroking his thumb over hers while he gazed out at the cameras.

She squeezed his fingers appreciatively, smiling for the photographers. Thanks to Reagan's crash course in red carpet posing, Eve looked like a pro. Boone doubted anyone but him could tell how terrified she was behind her serene expression.

He turned to slip his arm around Eve and spoke into her ear. "You look so fucking hot right now. When we get home I want you to sit on my face and pedal my ears."

As intended, it surprised a laugh out of her. Her smile broke loose in all its natural beauty, her dark eyes sparkling as she gazed up at him. A surge of affection flooded Boone's chest, and he leaned in to place a tender, lingering kiss next to the corner of her mouth.

The strobing flashes kicked into overdrive as the press eagerly captured the moment. Once they'd had time to snap their fill, Boone took Eve's hand again, tucked it into the crook of his elbow, and led her away from the step and repeat.

"The worst part's over," he said as they moved down the carpet.

"Not for you." She shot him a sympathetic look and squeezed his arm.

True, because now it was time for Boone to face the press line on his own. Reagan had spent half the afternoon coaching him on his sound bites for the one-minute interviews she'd lined up with various media outlets here today.

Before he could respond to Eve, Chuck Hammer's hulking

shape loomed in front of them. "Eve! Fancy meeting you here!"

"Chuck! Hi!" Eve's smile was so bright you could probably see it from the Bay Area.

"You look exquisite as always," the shameless flirt said as if he'd seen her more than once before today. "That dress takes my breath away."

Boone bristled as Chuck leaned in to kiss Eve's cheek. Not that he actually believed for a second he needed to worry about Chuck, but…well…maybe Boone was a little sensitive about the starstruck look Eve got when she was around the muscle-bound action hero.

"Good to see you, Chuck," Boone said, perhaps a little more loudly than necessary.

Chuck pulled away from Eve and clapped a heavy hand on Boone's shoulder. "Hey there, little buddy! How's it going?"

"Peachy." Boone's cheeks were aching with the effort of maintaining his smile.

A deafening roar went up from the crowd as Griffin made his first appearance on the red carpet.

"Sounds like the man of the hour's arrived," Chuck commented, glancing behind them. "Look at him, hamming it up. Kid's a natural."

Boone grunted in agreement, although he knew Griffin hated this shit as much as he did.

Chuck beamed his smile on Eve again, hooking a thumb at Boone. "You're still sticking with this guy, huh? He treating you right?"

"Like a queen," Eve said as she gazed up at Boone adoringly.

Okay, *that* was much better.

Boone endeavored to be less of a cranky, jealous dickhead while they chatted with Chuck for the next few minutes until his publicist pulled him away for an interview.

As soon as he was gone, a wrinkle formed between Eve's brows as she peered at Boone. "You okay?"

"I'm great," he said and leaned in to kiss her cheek.

"You seemed a little weird there." Her eyes narrowed. "You weren't jealous of Chuck, were you?"

He held up his index finger and thumb, a half inch apart. "Maybe a little."

She shook her head. "I thought you were just joking around about that. You *really* have no reason to be."

"I know that. It's not rational, but I can't say I love seeing him flirt with you."

"He's not my type," she said, stroking her hand down his chest. "*You* are."

Boone's smile pulled wide as his heart turned over. "That's what I like to hear." Reagan reappeared to hustle him off to his first interview, but before he let her drag him away he leaned in to nuzzle Eve's cheek. "Thanks for putting up with me."

"I'm your number one fan, remember?"

The lovestruck smile it put on Boone's face stayed with him all the way through his first three interviews.

"Nice boobs, girl!"

Eve grinned as she stepped forward to greet Alice with a hug. "These old things? I got them from my mom."

"That's a great dress," Alice said, stepping back. "You look fantastic. Well done!"

"Thanks, back at you."

Alice waved off the compliment. "I had nothing to do with it. It's all the stylist's magic."

"Same here," Eve said. "I just let them do whatever they want and hope for the best."

Kimberleigh Cress passed by and reached out to touch

Alice's elbow, flashing a quick smile at both of them as her team hovered around her impatiently. "I'll see you two at the party later, right?"

"Definitely," Alice replied, waving as Kimberleigh was hustled away to do interviews. Turning back to Eve, Alice said, "So, how's your first red carpet experience going so far? Are you having fun? Or completely freaking out?"

"A little of both," Eve admitted. She had to keep reminding herself she was living out a fantasy by being here casually hobnobbing with celebrities—even if it was abjectly terrifying.

"Lucky you," Alice said. "I was solidly in the completely freaking out camp my first time."

"You seem pretty relaxed right now."

Alice shrugged. "Do enough of these things and they become tedious instead of intimidating."

"Can't wait for that."

"You'll get there." Alice elbowed Eve and pointed toward the press line. "Watch this."

Craning her neck, Eve spotted Griffin sneaking up behind Boone, who was in the middle of a video interview. Griffin popped up behind his shoulder to surprise him, and the two men exchanged an exuberant on-camera hug. They finished out the rest of the interview together with Griffin's arm draped around Boone's shoulders. Off to the side, Reagan looked as pleased as Eve had ever seen her.

"Griffin looks like he's enjoying himself," Eve remarked.

"It's all an act," Alice said, popping open her clutch. "He hates it as much as Boone, believe me. His stomach was so upset earlier, I had to run out and buy him some Pepto." She smirked at Eve as she pulled out a compact. "Feel free to tell him I told you that."

"I guess pretending to enjoy these kinds of events is a required skill in their line of work."

"It's such a weird job they have, isn't it?" Alice frowned at her reflection as she moved the mirror around her head. "How's the back of my hair look? The bobby pins aren't coming loose, are they?"

"No, you're good," Eve assured her.

Alice glanced over at the press line again as she slipped her compact back into her clutch. "Boone seems to be bearing up well. Whatever you're doing, keep it up."

"I didn't do anything."

"Yeah, sure." Alice held out a mint. "These will help calm your stomach if you're having nerves."

"Thanks," Eve said, gratefully popping it in her mouth.

Alice took a mint for herself before tucking the tin back into her clutch. "I've never seen Boone like this before."

"Like what?"

"Happy."

"He's just putting on an act for the press."

"I'm not talking about that—trust me, I've seen his happy-go-lucky act plenty. I'm talking about that light in his eyes. That's something completely new. I noticed it last weekend when we were all together." Alice elbowed Eve again. "You can't tell me that's not because of you.

"Oh, I don't know…"

"I do. It's obvious that man is head over heels for you."

Eve's heart stuttered to hear Alice say it. "You think so?"

"I can tell by the way he looks at you."

"How does he look at me?"

"Like you're his favorite thing to look at."

Was that true? Eve wanted to believe it. Her heart told her Alice was right.

But Eve's head still had a few questions. Particularly about what would happen after Boone went back to Vancouver the week after next. Now that things were going better for him, maybe he wouldn't need her so much. Maybe he'd forget about her once he was busy with work again. Out of sight, out of mind.

Sure, he'd said otherwise, but how could he know how he'd feel once he got back to his old routine? He hadn't even told Eve he loved her. How strong could his feelings for her be? Strong enough to keep him invested in a long-distance relationship for most of the next year?

If she let herself think about it too much, everything she had with Boone felt terrifyingly precarious.

Just as she was starting to feel shaky, he turned and looked her way. The second their eyes met, a wave of warmth swept over her, pushing her doubts into the background. What they had was working right now. That scary future lurking around the corner? Eve wasn't going to let it ruin the time they had left.

thirty-two

BOONE'S last two weeks in LA passed entirely too quickly for his liking. Between Griffin's premiere, Eve's two jobs, and the interviews Reagan had him doing, it felt like he barely had any free time with Eve.

As his return to Vancouver loomed ever nearer, they'd both avoided discussing it. He sensed Eve was dreading it as much as he was and preferred not to waste what was left of their time together dwelling on such an unpleasant subject.

Except Boone had been dwelling on it, almost nonstop. Their impending separation was never far from his mind, especially as he gave interview after interview talking about Eve and how important she'd become to him.

In too many of those interviews, he was asked what his return to Vancouver would mean for their relationship. He always gave the same answer, that long-distance relationships were difficult, but they'd find a way to make it work. The more he repeated the words, the more hollow they began to feel in his mouth. The truth that haunted him more and more with every passing day was that he didn't know if they would be able to make it work long distance.

As the clock ran down on the borrowed time they'd been living on, it felt like a crater was growing in Boone's chest. When he'd opened his eyes this morning to the realization that there were only two days left before he flew back to Vancouver, the hole had felt so large he could hardly breathe.

That was why he was still in bed right now even though Eve was downstairs. She had the morning off today, but he'd slept in after a late night finishing the last of the interviews Reagan had arranged.

He should get up now and go find Eve. This would be their last few hours alone together before everything changed. His assistant was flying in this afternoon to help him pack. Things would only get busier after Priya got here, and it would be harder to find time to have the conversation he wanted to have with Eve.

If he waited much longer, it would be too late.

It was something he'd been turning over in his head for several days, nurturing it from a faint spark of an idea to a full-blown plan. But he'd yet to bring it up to Eve. He wasn't sure why. Fear, most likely. For one thing, he suspected it might be a totally batshit thing to even suggest.

Then again, batshit pretty much defined the entire progression of their relationship so far, and she hadn't seemed to mind too much.

The real sticking point was the fact that if he proposed his idea and Eve said no...well, he wasn't sure what he'd do then. He didn't know if they'd be able to move past it after he'd put her on the spot like that.

But if he didn't do *something*, he was afraid he might end up losing Eve anyway.

His chest crater grew a little wider, pushing up against his heart.

With a sigh, Boone threw the covers back and got out of bed.

When he finally wandered downstairs, Eve was in the sunroom doing yoga along with a video on her laptop. A smile pulled at his lips as he watched her go through a sun salutation.

With the golden morning sunlight streaming in the windows behind her, she looked like an angel. When she lowered into a forward fold and stepped back into downward-facing dog, he couldn't tear his gaze from the sight of her perfect ass and plush thighs squeezed into a pair of pink leggings that left very little to the imagination. Not that he needed to use his imagination. He'd committed every inch of her body to memory.

Letting his footfalls on the wood floor announce his presence, he approached the sunroom as Eve shifted into warrior II.

"You're up," she said, smiling at him over her shoulder.

"If I'd known you were down here doing this, I would've gotten up sooner so I could watch."

The smile lingered on her lips as she turned to gaze out over her fingertips. "You could always join me."

"Maybe I will."

When she twisted into revolved triangle pose, Boone saw her hips and shoulders roll in, causing her balance to wobble.

"Here." He moved behind her and held out his hands, seeking permission to do a manual adjustment. "Do you mind?"

"No, go ahead. I could use all the help I can get."

Placing the outside of his thigh against her shoulder for support, he laid a hand on her hip to square it up. Then he grasped her top shoulder and gently rolled it back. "Feel that? How much more open your chest is?"

"Yeah." She was smiling. "It's a lot easier with you holding me in the position."

"The point of guiding touch is to help you learn to embody the pose on your own." He cupped the back of her head to tuck her chin in slightly. "Good. Now breathe into your rib cage. It's harder to breathe in a twist, so you want to work on conscious breathing to release tension and lengthen the muscles around the rib cage."

Once he was sure she had it, he let go of her and cautiously stepped back to let her balance on her own.

"How do I look?" she asked.

"Beautiful," he said as he reached up to rub his chest. He couldn't shake the feeling that if he let himself blink, she'd be gone. "Remember how it feels."

Eve came to standing and shot him a grin as she tapped the laptop to pause the video. "If you ever get tired of acting, you could always teach yoga instead."

He grunted, pulling off his T-shirt as he walked over to his yoga mat. "I'll keep it in mind."

She started the video over from the beginning, and they moved through the poses together. It was a simple beginner flow that wasn't challenging for him, but he found it centering nonetheless. It made him wish they'd started doing this together sooner. They could have been doing it all along. Now there was no telling when they'd have the chance again.

There were so many things he wished he had time to do with her. But time was slipping through their fingers.

"That's it, I'm done," Eve said, collapsing out of a plank. She rolled onto her back with an exhausted groan. "I give up."

While she rested in corpse pose, Boone moved through a few advanced positions on his own.

"Fuck me," she said when he went into crow pose. "Why didn't I know you're a freaking yoga superman?"

"Yoga Superman sounds like the most useless superhero ever." Slowly, Boone raised his legs toward the ceiling and straightened his arms into a handstand. Was he trying to impress her? Hell yes, he was.

"Hope you don't mind that I'm just lying here objectifying you."

"Whatever keeps your practice centered."

"Oh, I'm very centered. I'm so centered I'm leaving a pool of drool on the floor."

Laughter bubbled in his chest, causing him to lose his balance.

"That was very impressive." Eve sat up as he came to rest in lotus and shook out his wrists. "How long did it take you to be able to do that?"

"A few months of daily practice."

"A few months! Jeez. I could practice for a million years and still not be able to pull that off."

"Sure you could. You can do just about anything when you have the time and resources to devote to it."

Now would be the perfect time to ask her to come to Vancouver with him. But all he could do was stare at her flushed cheeks, afraid to speak the words aloud.

She leaned over to run her fingers through his beard. "I'm going to miss this when you shave it."

Ask her. Just fucking say it.

She smiled as she drew back. "Can I watch you do that handstand thing again?"

"If you want," he said, unable to refuse her anything.

It took him longer to find his balance this time, knowing Eve was watching and admiring his every move. When he finally straightened his legs and arms, she hummed in appreciation.

"I can hear you drooling over there," he teased, trying not to smile and lose his center.

"I'll bet you can."

Belatedly, something occurred to him. "Are you taking a video?"

"Maybe," she admitted. "This is way too hot to keep to myself. You don't mind, do you?"

"Knock yourself out." It didn't bother him in the least.

Eve had been right about the dishwashing photo. It had been a huge hit, just as she'd predicted, getting almost as many likes as their relationship announcement. And unlike his dishwashing skills, Boone was proud of his body and his yoga practice. He'd worked hard at both and didn't mind showing off the results to his fans, even if it was a flagrant ploy for likes. He was coming around to the idea that it wasn't necessarily the worst, sharing more of himself to win over the public.

Slowly, with more control this time, Boone lowered himself back to the ground. After pushing himself upright, he crawled over to kiss Eve.

"I like that you're all bendy and strong," she said, sucking at his lower lip like candy. "Like, *really* like it."

"Can I see the video?" he asked when she pulled away.

Nodding, she picked up her phone. He scooted closer to rest his chin on her shoulder as she played it for him. He had to admit, he looked pretty fucking impressive. And he liked how Eve watched the screen, completely fixated, as if she couldn't tear her eyes from it.

"Reagan's gonna go flipping nuts for this," she said when the video ended. "Oh hey, that reminds me. She called me this morning."

Boone raised a distrustful eyebrow as he leaned his back against the wall. "You sound weirdly happy about that."

"I happen to like Reagan." Eve shoved her shoulder against his with a huffed laugh. "And you can relax—she wasn't calling about you. Her wife's opening a restaurant and—"

"Reagan's married?" he interrupted. He wasn't sure why that should be such a surprise to him. Maybe because she'd always seemed so single-minded, as if she lived and breathed

PR twenty-four seven. It had never occurred to him she might have a family or any sort of personal life outside work.

"Seriously?" Eve gaped at him. "How can you not know that? She's *your* publicist."

He shrugged and stretched his legs out. "We only ever talk business."

She made a *humph* of disapproval. "You know, maybe if you weren't always in such a hurry to get off the phone with her, you'd like her too."

"Maybe," he admitted.

"Anyway…" Eve smiled as she gave him an affectionate shoulder bump. "Reagan's wife Nikki is opening a restaurant, and she's looking for someone to design the branding and menus. And guess what? Reagan suggested me! I've got a meeting with Nikki next week!"

"That's…wow." Boone swallowed, his mouth suddenly dry. "That's great. I'm excited for you."

"I don't have the job yet, but at least it's a shot at some real work."

"Yeah." He reached up to rub his chest, which had started to ache anew. "That's great," he said again.

Fortunately, Eve was so excited about her news, she didn't seem to notice his odd reaction. "I'll have to go over my portfolio and make sure it's up to date. It's been a while since I've shown it to anyone."

"Can I see it?" Boone asked, wondering why he'd never asked before.

Her face lit up at his interest. "Sure, if you want. It's all online—here." She dragged her laptop over and settled against the wall beside him before pulling up the website.

She was good. Better than good. Her work was incredible. He'd known it would be, but he was still overwhelmed with pride.

"This is really impressive, Eve." A lump formed in his

throat as she clicked through image after image. Logos, invitations, social media graphics, presentation templates, and screenshots of websites she'd designed. And then there were the illustrations, each of which was beautiful enough to frame and hang on the wall. He was going to do just that, he decided, when he got to Vancouver. He'd fill his condo with her art so it'd be all around him.

She smiled shyly at the screen. "I'm pretty okay, right?"

The uncertainty in her voice tore at his heart. "You're amazing. You should be doing this full-time."

She was so talented. It wasn't right that she wasn't using all that skill to do something she obviously loved.

Boone sucked in a breath. He could do this. He *could*. "There's something I've been wanting to talk to you about."

"Sounds serious." Her tone was light and teasing, but the smile slid from her lips when she saw his face. She set the laptop aside and turned toward him with a frown of concern. "What is it?"

He reached for her hand, squeezing it to put her at ease and to give himself courage. "I want you to come with me to Vancouver."

She stared at him, her face frozen in surprise. "What?"

"I can't stand the thought of living without you for months at a time. I want to wake up with you every morning and come home to you at the end of every day. I don't want to be apart. I want you with me."

She gave him a sad, regretful look. "I can't just pick up and leave. I have a job—two of them."

"You could quit. Why not? You can't tell me either of those jobs are what you want to be doing."

"That's not the point." Her chin lifted with that stubborn pride of hers. "I need to be able to support myself."

"You're not paying rent anymore, Evie. You already agreed to keep living here, so you don't need to work two jobs anymore. You don't even need to work one job. If you wanted, you could quit and come to Vancouver with me."

Her lips pressed together. "Boone."

"Just hear me out." Eagerness forced his words to spill out in a rush. "You told me it was hard to build up a graphic design business with all the hours you work. Why keep doing it when you could be doing work you love instead? Don't you see? This is the perfect opportunity. You can focus on your graphic design full-time. And you don't have to be in LA for that. You can do it from Vancouver. With me, Evie. You could be with me."

"You're leaving in two days! I can't believe—" Her jaw bunched as she bit back whatever she'd been about to say. "I've got a meeting next week *in LA*."

"Obviously, you'd need to stay for that." He'd never stand in the way of her success. She had to know that. But she could have everything she wanted *and* they could be together. How could she not see it? "But you could come up after. Imagine it —you'll be in control of your own schedule, so you can fly back and forth as much as you need to. My condo has an office I never use—we'll make it your office and you can fix it up however you like."

"Boone."

The sharpness of her voice stopped him cold. He snapped his mouth shut as a sense of foreboding settled in his stomach.

At some point during their exchange Eve had slipped her hand out of his. Whatever she saw in his face now made her reach for it again, her expression softening with regret. "I can't just up and move to Canada."

He squeezed her fingers between his. "You can do what- ever you want. That's what I'm saying. You have the time and resources now to do anything you set your mind to. What happens next is up to you."

She flinched as if he'd sucker punched her. When she

spoke, her voice was barely more than a whisper. "You make it sound so easy."

"Maybe it won't be easy," he admitted. "But it doesn't have to be easy to be worth it."

She was torn. He knew it. He could see the flicker of a *yes* in her eyes.

"We don't have to be apart, Eve. Not if you come to Vancouver. Everything's better when we're together. You know it is."

He thought he might have convinced her. He really wanted to believe it.

But then she looked away, and his hopes came crashing down. "I'm not coming with you. I'm sorry, but I can't."

thirty-three

EVE WINCED as her answer landed like a dropped glass
hitting a hard floor.

"You don't mean that." Boone's voice was stony, but she
could sense the hurt beneath it.

When she forced herself to look at him, the disappointment
in his eyes skewered clear through her chest. At some point in
the last month his pain had become her pain, and right now he
was bleeding internally.

"You don't want to," he said. "That's what you're saying."

"Of course I want to."

He pushed himself to his feet and paced away from her,
dragging a hand through his hair. "If you did, you would. It's
that simple."

Not fair. Not fucking fair at all.

"It's not simple for me," she shot back, surging off the floor.
"You can't spring something like this on me with no warning
and expect me to make a huge, life-changing decision on the
spur of the moment."

He didn't respond. Or move. He stood still as a statue with
his back to her. As he stared down at his feet, the sunlight

burnished the skin stretched over his taut muscles with an ethereal glow. Despite his clenched fists, she could tell by the droop of his shoulders and the rhythm of his breathing that he wasn't angry. He was upset.

"Boone?" Her voice broke a little on his name.

His rib cage shook with a deep, unsteady breath before he finally turned around. The flatness of his expression wasn't enough to hide his pain from her. "If it's because you don't trust me—"

"It's not," she rushed to assure him. "I trust you. Too much, maybe."

"What does that mean?"

She moved toward him, but stopped when she saw him tense. "I can't let myself become dependent on someone else—not even you. And I know, I'm not exactly standing on my own two feet right now, considering I already agreed to live here and sponge off you. But following you to another city would be like a whole other level of hanger-on. It's too much."

He exhaled a bitter laugh. "You're not sponging off me, Eve. You act like our relationship is one-sided, but it's not. I could sign over the deed to this house, and it still wouldn't be enough to pay you back for all the support and comfort and peace you've given me. All I'm asking is for you to let me give some of the same back to you."

She could tell he really believed that, and it made her love him even more. But this wasn't just about her pride or independence or fear of change—although it was a little bit about all those things.

It was also about him not trusting his own instincts or being able to control his emotions, and how she'd promised never to let him get lost. This scheme of his was pretty much the epitome of letting your emotions lead you to lose your head.

What was it he'd said? That he'd realized how much better he was with her. She wanted to help him get better, but maybe the way to do that was not to let him get too dependent on her. He needed to know he could be okay on his own and not use her as an emotional crutch.

She shook her head. "It's not that I don't want to say yes."

"Then say yes." His voice crumbled as his eyes pleaded with her.

God, he was breaking her heart. Or she was breaking his. They were breaking each other's hearts. But they hadn't even been together long enough to say *I love you*, for god's sake. It was insane enough that they were living together. Running off to Canada was out of the question.

She pressed the heels of her hands to her eyelids and took a slow breath. When she spoke, her voice was quiet but firm. "It's better if I say no. At least for now. I think it's best if you go without me."

"Well, then." His lips pinched as he clenched his jaw. "That's that. I'm leaving and you're staying here."

There was nothing she could say to that. Nothing at all. He'd summed up the situation perfectly.

Panic hit as the painful truth sank in, squeezing Eve's lungs and burning the back of her throat. It wasn't as if she hadn't known it was coming. Boone's time in LA had always had a countdown timer hanging over it. But it hadn't felt real until now.

As her eyes filled with tears, her chest hitched audibly, the sound cutting through the grim silence.

Boone's head jerked up. The next thing she knew, he'd closed the distance between them to tug her against him.

Eve's whole body sagged, weak with relief, as she buried her face in his chest. His smooth, warm skin surrounded her as he held her tight. "I'm sorry." The words bubbled out of her chest with a sob. "I don't want—"

He tilted her head up and kissed her, hard, like he was trying to draw her soul into his body. She clung to him frantically as a fist of fear clogged her throat. What if this was a goodbye kiss? The thought tore her heart in two.

"I don't want to lose you," she pleaded, gripping his hair. "Please don't let go of me."

"I won't." A wrinkle formed between his brows. "As long as you still want me—"

"I do." She rose up and kissed him again, putting all her need into it to show him how much she meant it. When she moaned into his mouth, he squeezed her ass and hauled her against him. By the time they finally separated, they were both breathing hard.

"I want you with me," Boone said, brushing gentle fingers over her cheek. "But it's your choice."

Eve sniffled. "I'm trying to do the grown-up thing here and not uproot my entire life because a cute boy I just met a month ago asked me to."

"I guess that's fair." The ghost of a smile quirked his lips. "Cute, huh?"

"The cutest." She nuzzled into his neck and smoothed her hand over his chest. Beneath the muscle, she could feel his heart beating, fast but steady.

He rubbed her back. "I shouldn't have asked."

"No." Her fingers stroked the soft skin beneath his beard. "I'm so happy you did. It's nice to be wanted."

"You don't sound happy."

"Because I hate that I hurt your feelings."

"I'll get over it," he said gruffly.

"It also drove home that this is really happening," she admitted. "You're leaving."

He pulled her closer. "I'm sorry."

"Don't be sorry. I know you have to. Just like I have to stay."

They stood there like that for a long time, swaying slightly.

Wrapped up in each other. Holding on to the feeling while they still could.

Reluctantly, Eve said, "I need to go shower and get ready for work pretty soon."

By the time she got home tonight, Boone's assistant would be here. This was the last chance they'd have to be alone together for weeks or possibly months.

"Okay," Boone said, making no move to let go of her.

"I don't suppose you'd want to come up and shower with me?"

By way of an answer, he hoisted her off the floor and carried her toward the stairs.

Eve wrapped her arms and legs around him, determined to hold on as tight as she could for as much time as they had left.

EVERYTHING WAS FINE. *THEY* WERE FINE. THEY WOULD BE FINE. Eve repeated this mantra to herself repeatedly.

Boone's assistant, Priya, was an efficient, no-nonsense Indian woman in her forties who swooped in and took charge of everything, including Boone. Eve enjoyed watching her chastise him and boss him around. But also, she noticed how well Priya took care of him by keeping him organized and making sure he'd have everything he needed in Vancouver.

(Everything except Eve, of course. Even Priya couldn't do anything about that.)

Priya made sure Eve had important things too, like the phone numbers for the security company, the service that took care of the house when Boone was away, and the nearest friendly neighbors, in case anything went wrong. And Priya made sure Eve had her number too, so if Eve ever needed to get in touch with Boone when he was on set, Priya could track him down.

Eve felt better knowing Boone would have someone looking after him and keeping him out of trouble. Not better enough to keep her from worrying. But nothing would keep her from worrying about him.

Things felt different between them after their argument Friday morning. On the surface, everything seemed fine. But she couldn't help feeling it had changed things in ways she couldn't put her finger on and wouldn't have time to unravel before he left. She just had to hope it hadn't done too much lasting damage.

They'd made love again that night and the next, slowly and quietly, conscious that they were no longer alone in the house. But it felt like they were trying to savor those last stolen moments and make them last as long as they could.

Eve had pushed her face into the crook of Boone's neck to muffle sobs that were half pleasure, half grief, and tried to tell herself everything would be okay. He'd be all right without her, and she'd be all right without him.

It wasn't like they were breaking up. He'd still be there for her if she needed him, even if it was only on the other end of a phone line.

With all the upheaval of last-minute preparations, they didn't manage to talk much. Even at night, alone in their room, they clung to each other without saying much.

Maybe they'd said everything there was to say. No point in dwelling on the painful inevitable or rehashing conversations they'd already put to bed.

Time seemed to fly by, as it always did when you wished it would slow down. Before Eve knew it, it was Sunday morning, and she was standing next to the hired car that would take Boone away. Priya sat inside the car with the driver, politely not watching as Eve and Boone said goodbye.

"Don't cry," Boone said, kissing a tear off her cheek. "My heart can't take it."

"Deal with it," Eve said. "I already miss you."

"I already miss you too."

Another tear squeezed its way down her cheek. "You're not going to forget me when you're busy being a big TV star, are you?"

"Hey." He held her tighter, pressing his face into her hair. "Forget my number one fan? Never."

She clutched his waist. Saying goodbye fucking sucked. "We're going to be okay, right? Tell me again we're going to be okay."

"Of course we are." It was a noble effort, but his voice lacked the conviction she'd been looking for.

She didn't want to do this. It hurt too much. She could still change her mind and go with him. Stop fighting it and lose herself in him. But the thought made Eve's mouth go dry and her stomach recoil. She couldn't do it. This was how it had to be.

"I have to go," Boone said.

Their mouths met in a fumbling, tentative, despondent kiss. It wasn't how she wanted to remember their last kiss, but her lips and her heart were too numb for anything else.

"I have to go," he said again, resting his forehead against hers.

"I know."

He tore himself away from her and walked to the waiting car. The door closed behind him. And then he was gone.

———

EVE WENT ON WITH HER LIFE LIKE NORMAL. IT WAS surprisingly easy, except the part where her heart felt bruised and she was so restless and out of sorts she couldn't concentrate or sleep. Missing Boone became a constant preoccupation, like a toothache that throbbed in time with her pulse.

It was fine though. *They* were fine. They would be fine.

They texted frequently and talked on the phone almost every day. Boone sounded tired and a little distracted, but that was to be expected as he adjusted to the demanding schedule that came with being back at work.

On the bright side, Eve's meeting with Reagan's wife, Nikki, had gone great. So well that Eve had already sent over a contract and started playing around with some preliminary concepts. So that was exciting.

Okay, maybe Eve was finding it harder to make herself get up when her alarm went off in the morning, and she'd begun to resent going to work more than ever. When she was dealing with cranky, entitled customers or whiny, snot-nosed preschoolers, it was hard not to think about the fact that she didn't have to be there.

If she'd said yes to Boone, she'd be in Canada right now. Getting to work on her graphic design business full-time from the office in Boone's condo, looking out at a spectacular view of Vancouver Harbor and the North Shore mountains. He'd sent her a photo of it so she could see exactly what she was missing out on. Which definitely didn't make her feel worse. Not at all.

She still believed she'd made the right decision for both of them. It was her only consolation.

When Boone's episode of Spencer Devlin's satellite radio talk show aired, Eve signed up for a free trial account so she could download it. Most of the interviews Boone had done before he left wouldn't come out for a while, so it was the first time she'd heard him talk about her publicly, other than a couple of quick sound bites from Griffin's premiere.

The sound of Boone's voice shot straight to the pit of her stomach, even though they'd talked on the phone just the day before. He sounded different over the radio show's recording equipment. Clearer. Closer. More real.

He didn't talk like her Boone though. He talked like the Boone Sheridan she remembered from before she knew who he really was. Before he was hers. This charming, carefree, laid-back celebrity talking to Spencer Devlin with Boone's voice was practically a stranger to her.

Until Spencer brought up the rumors about Boone and Simone. He just straight out asked him if they'd ever had an affair, and Eve found herself cringing and pressing her fists to her mouth. Tiny cracks began to form in Boone's carefree persona as he talked at length about his deep and abiding friendship with Simone, and how everyone had jumped to the completely wrong conclusion over the infamous photo of him leaving her house.

Then they moved on to the subject of Eve, and the cracks in Boone's public persona grew so wide they pretty much fell away altogether. When he said, "She's my soul mate," he didn't sound the least bit carefree anymore. He sounded like someone who cared intensely. He sounded exactly like the Boone that Eve knew and loved. "She's changed my life," he said, which was the same thing he'd said to her once. "I never used to buy into the idea of fate, but I really believe the universe threw her into my path for a reason."

He just went on and on like that, saying all these incredible things. And the more he talked, the more Eve's eyes filled with tears.

Especially when Spencer asked about Boone's return to Vancouver. "Will you take her with you when production starts? Or will she stay here in Los Angeles?"

There was a long, fraught pause. In the quiet, the mic picked up the unsteady breath Boone took before answering. "I don't know yet," he said, and Eve suddenly remembered he'd gone to the studio to record this interview the day before that awful conversation when he'd asked her to follow him to Vancouver. "Nothing would make me happier than to have her there, but she's got her own life here, you know? It's not fair to expect her to give it all up for me. I want what's best for her, even if that means we can't be together as much as I'd like. But I don't know, man. I've got my fingers crossed. I guess we'll see if it works out."

The tears were streaming in rivers down Eve's face by that point. She tried to hold them back, but the eager hope she heard in Boone's voice was more than she could take. She'd crushed all that hope right out of him. Just crushed it right into dust and watched it die in his eyes. She could still see it now, as if it was happening all over again.

And for what? Why had she done it? Because she didn't trust him to know his own mind? The idea was so obviously ridiculous. This Boone on the radio didn't sound like a man who was in over his head. He sounded like a man who knew exactly what he wanted.

And what he wanted was *her*.

thirty-four

BOONE WAS HAVING A SHITTY DAY. Actually, more like a shitty week. In fact, it was shaping up to be a shitty month.

The scripts for this season were even more ridiculous than the last. He'd hoped the new blood in the writers room would breathe some life into the show, but so far it was just more of the same clichéd, uninspired crap they'd been churning out for the last few years. He was so fucking sick of it. Was this really what he'd left Eve behind for?

That was the real crux of the problem. Not the crappy scripts, but the fact that he wasn't where he wanted to be —with Eve.

Implausibly, he'd finally found someone who made him feel truly, heart-explodingly happy, someone he was absolutely certain he wanted to spend every minute of the rest of his life with, and he wasn't with her.

It made him cranky as fuck.

But otherwise, he had to admit he was doing okay. A hell of a lot better than he'd been doing at the end of last season. Yes, he found it difficult to sleep without Eve beside him, which wasn't doing his mood any favors. And every time he saw something that made him think about her, it hit him like a punch in the diaphragm. And since pretty much everything made him think about her, because she was always on his mind, he walked around all the time with his abdomen feeling like a punching bag.

But he wasn't broken. He wasn't even brokenhearted. He just missed Eve so much sometimes it was hard to breathe. But he was still breathing anyway. Still memorizing his lines and going to set and hitting his marks like always.

Every day when he woke up, Boone drew another slash on his kitchen calendar, marking off the days since he'd last seen Eve. All the days he'd made it through, days that stood between him and the next time they'd be together.

She'd said she might be able to fly up in another month. She was going to try and get enough time off for a four-day weekend if she could work it out with both of her jobs.

Boone refused to get his hopes up. Obviously, he wanted to see her. But if he got his hopes up and it turned out she had to postpone, it would only make things harder. And things were hard enough as it was.

The lack of sleep was killing him today. His brain was only functioning at half capacity and kept tripping up on the nonsense incantations he had to recite in this afternoon's scene. In desperation, he texted Priya on a break between setups to ask if she'd run out and get him one of those mocha energy smoothies from the juice bar he liked.

She texted back that she was out running errands and wouldn't be able to do it until later. *Great. Fine. Whatever.* Guess he could make do without. He had no clue what errands she was running, but she usually knew better than he did what needed to be done.

"Wow, you're extra grouchy-pants today," Simone

commented when she caught him scowling at his phone. "What crawled up your asshole?"

"Nothing," Boone muttered. "Just haven't been sleeping well."

"Poor baby." Her smile was half teasing and half sympathetic. "Pining for your girlfriend still?"

"I'm not pining," he said, even though that was *exactly* what he was doing. "I just miss her, okay?"

"I know," Simone said more gently, giving him a consoling pat on the back. "I think it's really sweet."

"It doesn't feel sweet. Believe me."

"It's not improving your personality much either, Grumpy Bear. But don't worry, it'll get easier."

"Will it?" he asked miserably. "When?"

"Usually when you least expect it." The second assistant director called them back to places, and Simone hooked her arm through Boone's. "Come on, Romeo. Back to our demon exorcism."

TWO HOURS LATER, AFTER HE'D FINISHED EXORCISING AN ancient Sumerian demon who'd possessed an Irish wolfhound, Boone trudged back to his trailer covered in dog hair and slobber. There was still no sign of Priya, so that was fucking great. He was sure whatever she was off doing was very important and he'd thank her for it later, but right now he really wished she was here to get him a smoothie.

He mounted the stairs, yanking open his trailer door, and froze at the sight of someone curled up on his couch asleep.

He blinked. Rubbed his eyes. Blinked some more.

It couldn't be, could it?

Kneeling next to the sleeping figure, he reached out a hand

to brush her glossy black hair off her face. "Evie?" he breathed, unable to believe it. "Baby."

Her eyes fluttered open, and she broke into a heart-stopping smile. "Hi."

"Am I dreaming?" he asked in wonder.

"I'm the one who was asleep."

"Yeah, but I'm pretty sure I'm hallucinating right now."

Eve's arms went around his neck, pulling him down for a kiss. His entire body sighed with relief as her soft lips parted against his. She tasted like pure happiness, warm and so, so real. Pure fucking bliss.

She hummed against his mouth, then bit his lower lip hard enough to make him growl. "See? Not hallucinating."

Boone scooped her off the couch and sank down against the cushions, cradling her in his lap. "I can't believe it," he said as she snuggled against his chest. "You're really here."

"I'm really here." She lifted her head, nose wrinkling. "Why do you smell like a wet dog?"

"You don't want to know," he said with a laugh. "Tell me how you got here."

"I flew. Duh."

"How did you get here inside my trailer? How did you even get on the set?"

"I asked Priya to arrange it. She booked my flight, picked me up at the airport, and brought me here to wait for you."

"That's what her mysterious errands were." To think he'd been pouting over a smoothie while his amazing assistant had been arranging the best surprise ever. There was definitely another raise in her near future.

"She's dropping my luggage off at your condo now. I hope you have plenty of space, because I brought lots of luggage."

"You know you can have all the space you want, gorgeous."

"I was thinking I might stay for a couple of weeks, if that's okay."

He grinned with giddy excitement. "Are you serious?"

"Yeah." Eve bit her lip. "I may have, um, quit both my jobs."

He blinked. "You did? When? Why didn't you tell me?"

Grinning, she answered all of his rapid-fire questions in order. "Yes. Two weeks ago. I wanted to surprise you."

"Mission accomplished on that last one."

Uncertainty dimmed her smile. "You're not upset I showed up unannounced, are you? Priya promised me you'd like it."

"Are you kidding?" He cupped Eve's face and covered it with kisses. "I'm so fucking overjoyed to see you, I wouldn't care if you'd fallen out of the sky and landed on my head. Though I kind of wish I'd known to straighten up my place for you, but—*fuck*, all that matters is that you're here, Evie." He sucked in a breath as emotion clogged his throat. "I hated being away from you. God, baby, I've missed you so damn much."

"I've missed you too."

"Enough to quit your jobs, apparently." He couldn't believe it. She'd actually gone and done it—and then kept it secret so she could show up here to surprise him.

"I didn't just do it because I missed you, although that was definitely a motivating factor. I kept thinking about everything you said and realized I'd made a mistake. I should have said yes when you asked me to come with you. I'm sorry I didn't."

"It's okay. It was a big thing to ask. I didn't think about it enough from your perspective."

"I don't know if you've noticed this about me, but I can be resistant to change."

"No! You? Never." He shook his head. "And here I am, one nonstop agent of chaos in your life."

"In the best possible way. I have a hard time making decisions, and I can sometimes freak out a little when they're sprung on me with no warning."

He hauled her against him and buried his face in her silky hair. "I should have raised the idea sooner, so we could talk it through and you'd have more time to think about it."

"Boone, there's something I forgot to tell you before you left."

"What's that?"

"I love you," Eve said, her voice muffled against his chest. "I never should have let you leave without telling you that."

Boone's heart flipped over and tried to jump out of his throat. He lifted his head, seeking her eyes. The truth of her words shined in the dark depths, but uncertainty lay behind her tremulous smile. The fact that she wasn't sure how he felt was a grievous wrong in need of rectifying.

"Baby." His hand curled around the nape of her neck as he rested his forehead against hers. "I love you too, you know."

A deep, shuddering breath whooshed out of her. "Oh thank god."

"You didn't really doubt it, did you?"

"Well...I mean, I may have—"

His mouth captured hers in an exuberant, adoring, joyous kiss that felt like the first unrestrained breath he'd ever taken. He lapped her up as she melted against his tongue, sweet as honey.

"I need you, Boone," she said between kisses. "You were right. Everything's better when we're together."

"I love you," he whispered, kissing her eyes, her temple, her cheek. "I love you so much."

"I was just wandering until I found you." Her hands cradled his face. "You're my home. Wherever you are is where I want to be."

"You're my heart, Evie. You're my everything." A tear fell down her cheek and he kissed it away. "Don't cry, baby. I can't take it."

"Deal with it," she said, laughing through her tears. Her

fingers stroked over his jaw, mapping it like unexplored terrain. "I can't get over your face. It feels so strange that it's smooth."

"Do you love me even without my beard?"

Her lips pursed as she cocked her head to the side, pretending to think about it. "Well…"

"Wow," he said, laughing. "Really?"

"Of course I love you without your beard, you absolute walnut. You could go completely bald, and I'd love you just as much."

"That does it. I'm keeping you forever."

"Sounds perfect to me," she said, resting her head on his shoulder.

Happiness bubbled up in him as his heart swelled with love for this woman who had added so much color and comfort to his world. Now that he had Eve at his side, it felt like his life was finally beginning.

Grinning giddily, he pressed his lips to her forehead. "You and me together. There's nothing more perfect than that."

epilogue

EVE LOOKED up from her laptop when she heard the front door open. It was close to two in the morning, but she was still awake, waiting for Boone to get home. Now that she was a freelancer, she could set her own hours and match them to his irregular shooting schedule. Most of her design work was done at the desktop computer set up in the condo's home office, but tonight she was catching up on some business development from the comfort of their bed.

"Hey," she said when Boone came into the bedroom after shucking his shoes and jacket by the door.

Smiling through the exhaustion on his face, he padded toward her in his socks. "You're still up. I thought for sure you'd be asleep by now."

"Nope." As he bent down for a kiss, Eve tilted her face up to meet his lips with a hum of pleasure. He tasted like coffee and the mint gum he chewed to stay alert during late nights on set, but underneath that he tasted like comfort. Her hands slid around his neck to massage the tight muscles at the base of his skull.

Groaning with a mix of weariness and pleasure, he sat on

the edge of the bed beside her. "You didn't have to wait up for me."

"I know," she said, drawing another groan from him by scratching her fingernails over his scalp the way he liked so much. "You look tired."

"I am. Long day." His head drooped forward onto her shoulder. As he nuzzled into her neck, she smelled fresh soap and shampoo, which meant he'd showered in his trailer before coming home.

"Bad day?"

Lifting his head, he mustered another weak smile as he reached up to unbutton his flannel shirt. "Just long. We had a lot of pages to get through to make up for last week's delays. Felt like we'd never finish."

"Here, let me." Eve pushed his fumbling fingers out of the way and took charge of his buttons for him. When she was done, she helped him slide the long-sleeved shirt off, exposing the rose tattoo on the inside of his forearm that he'd had done shortly after she'd joined him in Vancouver.

Boone shucked off his T-shirt, socks, and jeans next, all of which he tossed onto the chair in the corner. Down to only a pair of boxer briefs, he crawled into his side of the bed with a bone-deep sigh. Nestling up against Eve's hip, he hugged her leg like a kid hugging a teddy bear. "I'm so tired I can't move."

Her fingers brushed through his hair, which was free of product and downy-soft. "If you let go of my leg, we can go to sleep."

He shook his head against her hip and squeezed her leg tighter. "My body's beat, but my brain's still wired. Too much coffee."

"Would a bedtime story help?"

"Yes, please."

She opened her laptop again and pulled up Archive of Our

Own in her browser. "Let's see, where did we leave off last time?"

A grin spread over Boone's face as he stretched out on his back and tucked his hands behind his head. "Jules and Deke had escaped the Yeti and broken into an empty cabin to shelter from the snowstorm."

"Right. Okay." Eve found the appropriate chapter and began to read aloud.

A few months ago, she'd finally let Boone look at her old fanart notebooks in an attempt to cheer him up after a particularly rough day on set. He'd been so delighted, he'd begged her to let him read her old fanfic as well. Since she hadn't expired of embarrassment from showing him her old drawings of him —in fact, she'd rather enjoyed his enthusiasm—she'd eventually relented and shown him her AO3 page.

Somehow, he'd even convinced her to read aloud to him. Ever since, he'd been requesting it regularly, and they'd slowly been working their way through all her stories.

At first, Eve had found it painful to read her own writing out loud—especially to the man who'd inspired her explicitly erotic fantasies. But over time she'd shed her inhibitions and become comfortable with it. Perhaps some of the unselfconsciousness Boone had cultivated for his acting was rubbing off on her. Or maybe it was simply the level of trust and openness in their relationship that made sharing her fantasies with Boone feel like the most natural thing in the world.

After a few minutes, he shifted onto his side and reached for Eve's hand. As Deke and Jules attempted to hide their romantic feelings while the snowstorm raged outside their secluded cabin, Boone toyed with the engagement ring on Eve's finger.

Just before Christmas, he'd surprised her with both the marriage proposal and the stunning, ethically sourced two-carat square diamond ring from a boutique jeweler in Gastown.

Eve had said yes with no hesitation whatsoever.

Some people—like her parents—might think six months wasn't long enough to know someone before committing the rest of your life to them. But Eve already knew everything she needed to know. She and Boone were best friends, soul mates, and life partners who'd committed their hearts to each other months before. Marriage was just a formality by that point—not to mention a convenience, since it would allow Eve to stay in Canada with Boone for as long as he had a work permit.

Their engagement hadn't been announced to the public yet, but it was just a matter of time before some enterprising fan or paparazzo snapped a photo of the rock on Eve's left hand and the news got out. She and Boone were still talking about the wedding—where and when it would be and how big. He was in talks to star in a rom-com opposite Poppy Montgomery over his next summer hiatus, which could mean a big wedding would have to wait. If that was the case, it might be that they'd have a small, quickie wedding sooner rather than later and do a big shindig in Los Angeles at a later date when all their friends and family could be there.

Eve wasn't overly fussed about it. Either way, she and Boone were together, which was all that mattered to her.

"I have a question," he piped up, interrupting as Jules was treating Deke's wounds from the Yeti fight. "Exactly how slow burn is this story? Are we getting to the comfort part of the hurt/comfort anytime soon?"

"She's comforting him right now."

"Yeah, yeah, but how much longer do I have to wait for them to bang?"

Boone's eagerness for smut over plot never failed to amuse her, but Eve tried to suppress her smile and adopt a disapproving tone. "If I told you, that would be a spoiler."

Sitting up with a *humph,* he commandeered the laptop. "Maybe we could just scroll down to the sexytimes…"

"But you miss all the character development and rising sexual tension that way."

"And I'm sure it's all great, babe, but I'm good and tense already. I want to get to the fucking." He scratched his bare chest as he squinted at the words on the screen.

Resting her head on his shoulder, Eve slipped her arm around his waist and spread her fingers over his taut, hairless stomach. As much as she'd liked the hairier Boone she'd first fallen in love with, there was truly something to be said for the silky-smoothness of his waxed chest and the deliciously rough scrape of five o'clock shadow on his clean-shaven jaw. Plus, she could see his dimples without his beard.

"Here we go." The glow of the laptop bathed his face in blue light as he grinned at the screen. "They're in the bed huddling for warmth and…bingo! *Jules feels him tremble when her hand brushes the rigid jut of his erection. Confronted by the incontrovertible evidence of his desire, she's unable to hold herself back…*"

Settling against the headboard, Boone continued reading the scene out loud. Eve loved it when he did that. Hearing him slip into Deke's good-old-boy twang as he read her fantasies back to her never failed to blow her mind. But her favorite part was what inevitably came after, which Eve might have tried to hasten along by stroking her fingers over Boone's lower abs.

He only made it through a few more paragraphs before he cast the laptop aside with an impatient growl and pushed Eve onto her back. Eager hands worked her pajamas off in between greedy, aching kisses. As soon as he'd removed her underwear, his cock notched against her welcoming entrance. His blue eyes locked onto hers, steady as a calm sea, as he pushed into her. When he thrust all the way home, they both sighed with relief at the feeling of completeness.

"Evie," he murmured as he rocked into her, giving her

everything she needed and more. "I love you, baby. I fucking love you so much."

She clutched him to her, luxuriating in the weight and strength of his body as it moved in perfect sync with hers. Waves of incandescent pleasure washed over her, building and building until they shattered her into a million shining pieces and put her back together again, lighter and brighter and even more whole. Boone followed her, coming with a shuddering groan as he buried his face in her neck.

"I love you," Eve whispered, hugging him close as his fragmented breaths spilled over her skin. Her magnificent, generous, loving, perfect man. It was impossible to imagine her life without him.

"Love you too." Rolling onto his side, Boone gathered her to his chest, pressing tiny, tender kisses to her brow.

As she snuggled into the arms she knew would always be there to catch her, Eve closed her eyes with a sigh of contentment. Who'd have thought she'd ever be this lucky?

The best part was that it wasn't a fantasy. This was real life. *Her* life. Which was infinitely better than any fantasy she could have dreamed up on her own.

about the author

SUSANNAH NIX is a RITA® Award-winning and *USA Today* bestselling author of rom-coms and contemporary romances who lives in Texas with her husband. On the rare occasions she's not writing, she can be found reading, knitting, lifting weights, drinking wine, or obsessively watching *Ted Lasso* on repeat to stave off existential angst.

To learn more about Susannah Nix, visit:

susannahnix.com

Or follow her on social media:

facebook.com/SusannahNix

twitter.com/Susannah_Nix

instagram.com/susannahnixauthor

bookbub.com/profile/susannah-nix

goodreads.com/susannah_nix

www.ingramcontent.com/pod-product-compliance
Lightning Source LLC
Chambersburg PA
CBHW061044190726
48286CB00006B/1595